WEST
of
EDEN

BANTAM BOOKS BY HARRY HARRISON

Homeworld

The Stainless Steel Rat for President

The Stainless Steel Rat Wants You

Starworld

Wheelworld

WEST
of
EDEN

Harry Harrison

ILLUSTRATIONS BY
Bill Sanderson

BANTAM BOOKS
TORONTO · NEW YORK · LONDON · SYDNEY · AUCKLAND

WEST OF EDEN

A Bantam Book / August 1984

Library of Congress Cataloging in Publication Data

Harrison, Harry.
West of Eden.

I. Title.
PS3558.A667W4   1984   813'.54   84-6306
ISBN 0-553-05065-6

Published simultaneously in the United States and Canada

Bantam Books are published by Bantam Books, Inc. Its trademark, consisting of
the words "Bantam Books" and the portrayal of a rooster, is Registered in the
United States Patent and Trademark Office and in other countries. Marca
Registrada. Bantam Books, Inc., 666 Fifth Avenue, New York, New York
10103.

PRINTED IN THE UNITED STATES OF AMERICA

FG   0   9   8   7   6   5   4   3   2   1

for
T. A. Shippey and
Jack Cohen
without whose aid this book
would never have been written

particular thanks as well to
John R. Pierce and Leon E. Stover

CONTENTS

8   And the LORD God planted a garden
eastward in Eden;
and there he put the man
whom he had formed.

16   And Cain went out from the presence
of the LORD, and dwelt
in the land of Nod,
on the east of Eden.

GENESIS

The great reptiles were the most successful life forms ever to populate this world. For 140 million years they ruled the Earth, filled the sky, swarmed in the seas. At this time the mammals, the ancestors of mankind, were only tiny, shrew-like animals that were preyed upon by the larger, faster, more intelligent saurians.

Then, 65 million years ago, this all changed. A meteor six miles in diameter struck the Earth and caused disastrous atmospheric upheavals. Within a brief span of time over seventy-five percent of all the species then existent were wiped out. The age of the dinosaurs was over; the evolution of the mammals that they had suppressed for 100 million years began.

But what if that meteor had not fallen?

What would our world be like today?

PROLOGUE: KERRICK

I have read the pages that follow here and I honestly believe them to be a true history of our world.

Not that belief was easy to come by. It might be said that my view of the world was a very restricted one. I was born in a small encampment made up of three families. During the warm seasons we stayed on the shore of a great lake rich with fish. My first memories are of that lake, looking across its still water at the high mountains beyond, seeing their peaks grow white with the first snows of winter. When the snow whitened our tents, and the grass around as well, that would be the time when the hunters went to the mountains. I was in a hurry to grow up, eager to hunt the deer, and the greatdeer, at their side.

That simple world of simple pleasures is gone forever. Everything has changed—and not for the better. At times I wake at night and wish that what happened had never happened. But these are foolish thoughts and the world is as it is, changed now in every way. What I thought was the entirety of existence has proved only to be a tiny corner of reality. My lake and my mountains are only the smallest part of a great continent that stretches between two immense oceans. I knew of the western ocean because our hunters had fished there.

I also knew about the others and learned to hate them long before I ever saw them. As our flesh is warm, so is theirs cold. We have hair upon our heads and a hunter will grow a proud beard, while the animals that we hunt have warm flesh and fur or hair, but this is not true of Yilané. They are cold and smooth and scaled, have claws and teeth to rend and tear, are large and terrible, to be feared. And hated. I knew that they lived in the warm waters of the ocean to the south and on the warm lands to the south. They could not abide the cold so did not trouble us.

All that has changed and changed so terribly that nothing will ever be the same again. It is my unhappy knowledge that our world is only a tiny part of the Yilané world. We live in the north of a great continent that is joined to a great southern continent. And on all of this land, from ocean to ocean, there swarm only Yilané.

And there is even worse. Across the western ocean there are even larger continents—and there there are no hunters at all. None. But Yilané, only Yilané. The entire world is theirs except for our small part.

Now I will tell you the worst thing about the Yilané. They hate us just as we hate them. This would not matter if they were only great, insensate beasts. We would stay in the cold north and avoid them in this manner.

But there are those who may be as intelligent as hunters, as fierce as hunters. And their number cannot be counted but it is enough to say that they fill all of the lands of this great globe.

What follows here is not a nice thing to tell, but it happened and it must be told.

This is the story of our world and of all of the creatures that live in it and what happened when a band of hunters ventured south along the coast and what they found there. And what happened when the Yilané discovered that the world was not theirs alone, as they had always believed.

BOOK ONE

Isizzô fa klabra massik, den sa
rinyur meth alpi.

---

*Spit in the teeth of winter, for he
always dies in the spring.*

CHAPTER ONE

Amahast was already awake when the first light of approaching dawn began to spread across the ocean. Above him only the brightest stars were still visible. He knew them for what they were; the tharms of the dead hunters who climbed into the sky each night. But now even these last ones, the best trackers, the finest hunters, even they were fleeing before the rising sun. It was a fierce sun here this far south, burningly different from the northern sun that they were used to, the one that rose weakly into a pale sky above the snow-filled forests and the mountains. This could have been another sun altogether. Yet now, just before sunrise, it was almost cool here close to the water, comfortable. It would not last. With daylight the heat would come again. Amahast scratched at the insect bites on his arm and waited for dawn.

The outline of their wooden boat emerged slowly from the darkness. It had been pulled up onto the sand, well beyond the dried weed and shells that marked the reach of the highest tide. Close by it he could just make out the dark forms of the sleeping members of his sammad, the four who had come with him on this voyage. Unasked, the bitter memory returned that one of them, Diken, was dying; soon they would be only three.

One of the men was climbing to his feet, slowly and painfully, leaning heavily on his spear. That would be old Ogatyr; he had the stiffness and ache in his arms and legs that comes with age, from the dampness of the ground and the cold grip of winter. Amahast rose as well, his spear also in his hand. The two men came together as they walked towards the water holes.

"The day will be hot, kurro," Ogatyr said.

"All of the days here are hot, old one. A child could read that fortune. The sun will cook the pain from your bones."

They walked slowly and warily towards the black wall of the forest. The tall grass rustled in the dawn breeze; the first waking birds called in the trees above. Some forest animal had eaten the heads off the low palm trees here, then dug beside them in the soft ground to find water. The hunters had deepened the holes the evening before and now they were brimming with clear water.

"Drink your fill," Amahast ordered, turning to face the forest. Behind him Ogatyr wheezed as he dropped to the ground, then slurped greedily.

It was possible that some of the creatures of the night might still emerge from the darkness of the trees so Amahast stood on guard, spear pointed and ready, sniffing the moist air rich with the odor of decaying vegetation, yet sweetened by the faint perfume of night-blooming flowers. When the older man had finished he stood watch while Amahast drank. Burying his face deep in the cool water, rising up gasping to splash handfuls over his bare body, washing away some of the grime and sweat of the previous day.

"Where we stop tonight, that will be our last camp. The morning after we must turn back, retrace our course," Ogatyr said, calling over his shoulder while his eyes remained fixed on the bushes and trees before him.

"So you have told me. But I do not believe that a few days more will make any difference."

"It is time to return. I have knotted each sunset onto my cord. The days are shorter, I have ways of knowing that. Each sunset comes more quickly, each day the sun weakens and cannot climb as high into the sky. And the wind is beginning to change, even you must have noticed that. All summer it has blown from the southeast. No longer. Do you remember last year, the storm that almost sank the boat and blew down a forest of trees? The storm came at this time. We must return. I can remember these things, knot them in my cord."

"I know you can, old one." Amahast ran his fingers through

the wet strands of his uncut hair. It reached below his shoulders, while his full blond beard rested damply on his chest. "But you also know that our boat is not full."

"There is much dried meat . . ."

"Not enough. We need more than that to last the winter. The hunting has not been good. That is why we have journeyed farther south than we ever have before. We need the meat."

"One single day, then we must return. No more than that. The path to the mountains is long and the way hard."

Amahast did not speak in answer. He respected Ogatyr for all the things that the old man knew, his knowledge of the correct way to make tools and find magic plants. The oldster knew the rituals needed to prepare for the hunt, as well as the chants that could ward off the spirits of the dead. He had all of the knowledge of his lifetime and of the lifetimes before him, the things that he had been told and that he remembered, that he could recite from the rising of the sun in the morning to the setting at night and still not be done. But there were new things that the old one did not know about, and these were what troubled Amahast, that demanded new answers.

It was the winters that were the cause of it, the fierce winters that would not end. Twice now there had been the promise of spring as the days had grown longer, the sun brighter—but spring had never come. The deep snows had not melted, the ice on the streams stayed frozen. Then there had been hunger. The deer and the greatdeer had moved south, away from their accustomed valleys and mountain meadows that now stayed tight-locked in winter's unyielding grip. He had led the people of his sammad as they had followed the animals, they had to do that or starve, down from the mountains to the broad plains beyond. Yet the hunting had not been good, for the herds had been thinned out by the terrible winter. Nor was their sammad the only one that had troubles. Other sammads had been hunting there as well, not only ones that his people were joined to by marriage, but sammads they had never seen before. Men who spoke Marbak strangely, or not at all, and pointed their spears in anger. Yet all of the sammads were Tanu, and Tanu never fought Tanu. Never before had they done this. But now they did and there was Tanu blood on the sharp stone points of the spears. This troubled Amahast as much as did the endless winter. A spear for hunting, a knife for skinning, a fire for cooking. This was the way it had always been. Tanu did not kill

Tanu. Rather than commit this crime himself he had taken his sammad away from the hills, marching each day towards the morning sun, not stopping until they had reached the salt waters of the great sea. He knew that the way north was closed, for the ice there came to the ocean's edge and only the Paramutan, the skin-boat people, could live in those frozen lands. The way south was open but there, in the forests and jungles where the snow never came, were the murgu. And where they were was death.

So only the wave-filled sea remained. His sammad had long known the art of making wooden boats for summer fishing, but never before had they ventured out of sight of land or away from their camp upon the beach. This summer they must. The dried squid would not last the winter. If the hunting were as bad as that of the winter before then none of them would be alive in the spring. South, then, it must be south, and that was the way they had gone. Hunting along the shore and on the islands off the coast, in fear always of the murgu.

The others were awake now. The sun was above the horizon and the first shrieks of the animals were sounding from the depths of the jungle. It was time to put to sea.

Amahast nodded solemnly when Kerrick brought him the skin bag of ekkotaz, then dipped out a handful of the thick mass of crushed acorns and dried berries. He reached out with his other hand and ruffled the thick mat of hair on his son's head. His firstborn. Soon to be a man and take a man's name. But still a boy, although he was growing strong and tall. His skin, normally pale, was tanned golden now since, like all of them on this voyage, he wore only a deerskin tied at his waist. About his neck, hung from a leather thong, there was a smaller version of the skymetal knife that Amahast also wore. A knife that was not as sharp as stone but was treasured for its rarity. These two knives, the large and small, were the only skymetal the sammad possessed. Kerrick smiled up at his father. Eight years old and this was his first hunt with the men. It was the most important thing that had ever happened to him.

"Did you drink your fill?" Amahast asked. Kerrick nodded. He knew there would be no more water until nightfall. This was one of the important things that a hunter had to learn. When he had been with the women—and the children—he had drunk water whenever he had felt thirsty, or if he had been hungry he had nibbled at the berries or eaten the fresh roots as they dug them up. No more. He went with the hunters now, did what they did, went without food and drink from before sunrise until after dark. He gripped his small spear proudly and tried not to start with fright when something crashed heavily in the jungle behind him.

"Push out the boat," Amahast ordered.

The men needed no urging; the sounds of the murgu were growing louder, more threatening. There was little enough to load into the boat, just their spears, bows and quivers of arrows, deerskins, and bags of ekkotaz. They pushed the boat into the water and big Hastila and Ogatyr held it steady while the boy climbed in carefully holding a large shell that contained glowing embers from the fire.

Behind them on the beach Diken struggled to rise, to join the others, but he was not strong enough today. His skin paled with the effort and great drops of perspiration stood out on his face. Amahast came and knelt beside him, took up a corner of the deerskin that he was lying on and wiped the wounded man's face.

"Rest easy. We'll put you into the boat."

"Not today, not if I cannot climb aboard myself." Diken's voice was hoarse, he gasped with the effort of speech. "It will be easier if I wait here for your return. It will be easier on my hand."

His left hand was now very bad. Two fingers had been bitten, torn away, when a large jungle creature had blundered into their camp one night, a half-seen form that they had wounded with spears and driven back into the darkness. At first Diken's wound had not looked too serious, hunters had lived with worse, and they had done all the things for him that could be done. They had washed the wound in sea water until it bled freely, then Ogatyr had bound it up with a poultice made from the benseel moss that had been gathered in the high mountain bogs. But this time it had not been enough. The flesh had grown red, then black, and finally the blackness had spread up Diken's arm; its smell was terrible. He would die soon. Amahast looked up from the swollen arm to the green wall of the jungle beyond.

"When the beasts come my tharm will not be here to be consumed by them," Diken said, seeing the direction of Amahast's gaze. His right hand was clenched into a fist; he opened and closed it briefly to disclose the flake of stone concealed there. The kind of sharp chip that was used to butcher and skin an animal. Sharp enough to open a man's vein.

Amahast rose slowly and rubbed the sand from his bare knees.

"I will look for you in the sky," he said, his expressionless voice so low that only the dying man could hear it.

"You were always my brother," Diken said. When Amahast left he turned his face away and closed his eyes so he would not see the others leave and perhaps give some sign to him.

The boat was already in the water when Amahast reached it, bobbing slightly in the gentle swell. It was a good, solid craft that had been made from the hollowed-out trunk of a large cedar tree. Kerrick was in the bow, blowing on the small fire that rested on the rocks there. It crackled and flamed up as he added more bits of wood to it. The men had already slipped their oars between the thole pins, ready to depart. Amahast pulled himself in over the side and fitted his steering oar into place. He saw the men's eyes move from him to the hunter who remained behind upon the beach, but nothing was said. As was proper. A hunter did not show pain—or show pity. Each man has the right to choose when he will release his tharm to rise up to erman, the night sky, to be welcomed by Ermanpadar, the sky-father who ruled there. There the tharm of the hunter would join the other tharms among the stars. Each hunter had this right and no other could speak about it or bar his way. Even Kerrick knew that and was as silent as the others. "Pull," Amahast ordered. "To the island."

The low, grass-covered island lay close offshore and sheltered the beach here from the strength of the ocean waves. Further to the south it rose higher, above the salt spray of the sea, and there the trees began. With grass and shelter there was the promise of good hunting. Unless the murgu were here as well.

"Look, in the water!" Kerrick called out, pointing down at the sea. An immense school of hardalt was passing beneath them, tentacles trailing, their seemingly numberless, boneless bodies protected by their shells. Hastila seized up his spear by the butt end and poised it over the water. He was a big man, taller even than Amahast, yet very quick for all of that. He waited a moment—then plunged the spear down into the sea, deep down until his arm was in the water, then heaved upward.

His point had struck true, into the soft body behind the shell, and the hardalt was pulled from the water and dumped into the bottom of the boat where it lay, tentacles writhing feebly, black dye oozing from its punctured sac. They all laughed at that. He was truly named, Hastila, spear-in-hand. A spear that did not miss.

"Good eating," Hastila said, putting his foot on the shell and pulling his spear free of the body.

Kerrick was excited. How easy it looked. A single quick thrust—and there was a great hardalt, enough food to feed them all for a day. He took his own spear by the butt, just as Hastila had done. It was only half the length of the hunter's spear but the point was just as sharp. The hardalt were still there, thicker than ever, one of them roiling the surface just below the bow.

Kerrick thrust down, hard. Feeling the point sink into flesh. Seizing the haft with both hands and pulling up. The wooden shaft shook and tore at his hands but he held on grimly, tugging with all of his strength.

There was a great thrashing of foam in the water as the wet-shining head rose up beside the boat. His spear tore free of the thing's flesh and Kerrick fell backwards as the jaws opened, rows of teeth before him, a screeching roar so close the stinking breath of the creature washed over him. Sharp claws scratched at the boat, tore pieces from the wood.

Then Hastila was there, his spear plunging between those terrible jaws, once, twice. The marag screamed louder and a gush of blood spattered the boy. Then the jaws closed and, for an instant, Kerrick looked into that round unblinking eye poised before his face.

A moment later it was gone, sinking beneath the surface in a flurry of bloody foam.

"Pull for the island," Amahast ordered. "There will be more of these beasts, bigger ones, following after the hardalt. Is the boy hurt?"

Ogatyr splashed a handful of water on Kerrick's face and rubbed it clean. "Just frightened," he said looking at the drawn face.

"He is lucky," Amahast said grimly. "Luck comes only once. He will never thrust a spear into darkness again."

Never! Kerrick thought, almost shouting the word aloud, looking at the torn wood where the thing's claws had raked deep. He had heard about the murgu, seen their claws on a necklace, even touched a smooth and multicolored pouch made from the skin of one of them. But the stories had never really frightened him; tall as the sky, teeth like spears, eyes like stones, claws like knives. But he was frightened now. He turned to face the shore, sure that there were tears in his eyes and not wanting the others to see them, biting his lips as they slowly approached the land. The boat was suddenly a thin shell above a sea of monsters and he desperately wanted to be on solid ground again. He almost cried aloud when the prow grated against the sand. While the others pulled the boat out of the water he washed away all traces of the marag's blood.

Amahast made a low hissing sound between his teeth, a hunter's signal, and they all froze, silent and motionless. He lay in the grass above them, peering over the rise. He motioned them flat with his hand, then signaled them forward to join him. Kerrick did as the others did, not rising above the grass, but carefully parting the blades with his fingers so he could look between them.

Deer. A herd of the small creatures was grazing just an arrow-shot away. Plump with the rich grass of the island, moving slowly, long ears twitching at the flies that buzzed about them. Kerrick sniffed through widened nostrils and could smell the sweetness of their hides.

"Go silently along the shore," Amahast said. "The wind is blowing from them towards us, they will not smell us. We will get close." He led the way, crouching as he ran, and the others followed, Kerrick bringing up the rear.

They notched their arrows while still bent low behind the bank, drew their bows, then stood and let fly together.

The flight of arrows struck true; two of the creatures were down and a third wounded. The small buck was able to stagger some distance with the arrow in its body. Amahast ran swiftly after it and closed on the creature. It turned at bay, its tiny span of horns lowered menacingly, and he laughed and jumped towards it, seized the horns in his hands and twisted. The creature snorted and swayed, then bleated as it fell. Amahast arched its neck back as Kerrick ran up.

"Use your spear, your first kill. In the throat—to one side, stab deep and twist."

Kerrick did as he was bid and the buck bellowed in agony as the red blood burst out, drenching Kerrick's hands and arms. Blood to be proud of. He pushed the spear deeper into the wound until the creature shuddered and died.

"A good kill," Amahast said proudly. The way that he spoke made Kerrick hope that the marag in the boat would not be talked about again.

The hunters laughed with pleasure as they opened and gutted

the carcasses. Amahast pointed south towards the higher part of the island. "Take them to the trees where we can hang them to drain."

"Will we hunt again?" Hastila asked. Amahast shook his head.

"Not if we are to return tomorrow. It will take the day and the night to butcher and smoke what we have here."

"And to eat," Ogatyr said, smacking his lips loudly. "Eat our fill. The more we put into our stomachs the less we will have to carry on our backs!"

Though it was cooler under the trees they were soon crawling with biting flies. They could only beat at them and plead with Amahast for the smoke to keep them at bay.

"Skin the carcasses," he ordered, then kicked a fallen log with his toe: it fell to pieces. "Too damp. The wood here under the trees is too wet to burn. Ogatyr, bring the fire from the boat and feed it with dry grass until we return. I will take the boy and get some driftwood from the beach."

He left his bow and arrows behind, but took up his spear and started off through the grove towards the ocean side of the island. Kerrick did the same and hurried after him.

The beach was wide, the fine sand almost as white as snow. Offshore the waves broke into a rumble of bubbling froth that surged far up the beach towards them. At the water's edge were bits of wood and broken sponges, endless varicolored shells, violet snails, great green lengths of seaweed with tiny crabs clinging to them. The few small pieces of driftwood here were too tiny to bother with, so they walked on to the headland that pushed a rocky peninsula out into the sea. When they had climbed the easy slope they could look out between the trees to see that the headland curved out and around to make a sheltered bay. On the sand at the far side dark forms, they might be seals, basked in the sun.

At the same moment they became aware that someone was standing under a nearby tree, also looking out over the bay. Another hunter perhaps. Amahast had opened his mouth to call out when the figure stepped forward into the sunlight.

The words froze in his throat; every muscle in his body locked hard.

No hunter, no man, not this. Man-shaped but repellently different in every way.

The creature was hairless and naked, with a colored crest that ran across the top of its head and down its spine. It was bright in the sunlight, obscenely marked with a skin that was scaled and multicolored.

A marag. Smaller than the giants in the jungle, but a marag nevertheless. Like all of its kind it was motionless at rest, as though carved from stone. Then it turned its head to one side, a series of small jerking motions, until they could see its round and expressionless eye, the massive out-thrust jaw. They stood, as motionless as murgu themselves, gripping their spears tightly, unseen, for the creature had not turned far enough to notice their silent forms among the trees.

Amahast waited until its gaze went back to the ocean before he moved. Gliding forward without a sound, raising his spear. He had reached the edge of the trees before the beast heard him or sensed his approach. It snapped its head about, stared directly into his face.

The hunter plunged the stone head of his spear into one lidless eye, through the eye and deep into the brain behind.

It shuddered once, a spasm that shook its entire body, then fell heavily. Dead before it hit the ground. Amahast had the spear pulled free even before that, had spun about and raked his gaze across the slope and the beach beyond. There were no more of the creatures nearby.

Kerrick joined his father, standing beside him in silence as they looked down upon the corpse.

It was a crude and disgusting parody of human form. Red blood was still seeping from the socket of the destroyed eye, while the other stared blankly up at them, its pupil a black, vertical slit. There was no nose; just flapped openings where a nose should have been. Its massive jaw had dropped open in the agony of sudden death to reveal white rows of sharp and pointed teeth.

"What is it?" Kerrick asked, almost choking on the words.

"I don't know. A marag of some kind. A small one, I have never seen its like before."

"It stood, it walked, like it was human, Tanu. A marag, father, but it has hands like ours."

"Not like ours. Count. One, two, three fingers and a thumb. No, it has only two fingers—and two thumbs."

Amahast's lips were drawn back from his teeth as he stared down at the thing. Its legs were short and bowed, the feet flat, the toes claw-tipped. It had a stumpy tail. Now it lay curled in death, one arm beneath its body. Amahast dug at it with his toe, turned it over. More mystery, for clutched in its hand he could now see what appeared to be a length of knobbed black wood.

"Father—the beach!" Kerrick called out.

They sought shelter under the trees and watched from conceal- ment as the creatures emerged from the sea just below the spot where they stood.

There were three of the murgu. Two of them very much like the one that had been killed. The third was bigger, fat and slow- moving. It lay half in and half out of the water, lolling on its back, eyes closed and limbs motionless. The other two pushed at it, rolling it further up on the sand. The large creature bubbled through its breathing flaps, then scratched its stomach with the claws on one foot, slowly and lazily. One of the smaller murgu thrashed its paws about in the air and made a sharp clacking sound.

Anger rose up in Amahast's throat, choking him so that he gasped aloud. Hatred almost blinded him as, with no conscious volition, he hurled himself down the slope with his spear thrust out before him.

He was upon the creatures in a moment, stabbing at the nearest one. But it had moved aside as it turned and the stone point only tore through its side, glancing off its ribs. The beast's mouth gaped and it hissed loudly as it tried to flee. Amahast's next blow struck true.

Amahast pulled the spear free, and turned to see the other one splashing into the water, escaping.

It threw its arms wide and fell as the small spear hurtled through the air and caught it in the back.

"A good throw," Amahast said, making sure the thing was dead before wrenching the spear free and handing it back to Kerrick.

Only the large marag remained. Its eyes were closed and it seemed oblivious to what was happening around it.

Amahast's spear plunged deep into its side and it emitted an almost human groan. The creature was larded with fat and he had to stab again and again before it was still. When he was done Amahast leaned on his spear, panting heavily, looking with disgust at the slaughtered creatures, hatred still possessing him.

"Things like these, they must be destroyed. The murgu are not like us, see their skin, scales. None of them has fur, they fear the cold, they are poison to eat. When we find them we must destroy them." He snarled out the words and Kerrick could only nod agreement, feeling the same deep and unthinking repulsion.

"Go, get the others," Amahast said. "Quickly. See, there, on the other side of the bay, there are more of these. We must kill them all."

A movement caught his eye and he drew back his spear thinking the creature not yet dead. It was moving its tail.

No! The tail itself was not moving, but something was writhing obscenely beneath the skin at its base. There was a slit there, an opening of some kind. A pouch in the base of the beast's thick tail. With the point of his spear Amahast tore it open, then struggled against the desire to retch at the sight of the pallid creatures that tumbled out onto the sand.

Wrinkled, blind, tiny imitations of the adults. Their young, they must be. Roaring with anger he trampled them underfoot.

"Destroyed, all of them, destroyed." He mumbled the words over and over and Kerrick fled away among the trees.

Enge hantèhei,
agatè embokèka lirubushei kakshèsei,
hèawahei; hevai`ihei,
kaksheintè, enpelei asahen enge.

========

*To leave father's love and enter the
embrace of the sea is the first pain of
life—the first joy is the comrades who
join you there.*

CHAPTER TWO

The enteesenat cut through the waves with rhythmic motions of their great, paddle-like flippers. One of them raised its head from the ocean, water streaming from its dark hide, rising it higher and higher on its long neck, turning and looking backward. Only when it caught sight of the great form low in the water behind them did it drop beneath the surface once again.

There was a school of squid ahead—the other enteesenat was clicking with loud excitement. Now the massive lengths of their tails thrashed and they tore through the water, gigantic and unstoppable, their mouths gaping wide. Into the midst of the school.

Spurting out jets of water the squid fled in all directions. Most would escape behind the clouds of black dye they expelled, but many of them were snapped up by the plate-ridged jaws, caught and swallowed whole. This continued until the sea was empty again, the survivors scattered and distant. Sated, the great creatures turned about and paddled slowly back the way they had come.

Ahead of them an even larger form moved through the ocean, water surging across its back and bubbling about the great dorsal fin of the uruketo. As they neared it the enteesenat dived and turned to match its steady motion through the sea, swimming beside it close to the length of its armored beak. It must have seen them, one eye moved slowly, following their course, the blackness of the pupil framed by its bony ring. Recognition slowly penetrated the creature's dim brain and the beak began to open, then gaped wide.

One after another they swam to the wide open mouth and pushed their heads into the cave-like opening. Once in position they regurgitated the recently caught squid. Only when their stomachs were empty did they pull back and spin about with a sideways movement of their flippers. Behind them the jaws closed as slowly as they had opened and the massive bulk of the uruketo moved steadily on its way.

Although most of the creature's massive body was below the surface, the uruketo's dorsal fin projected above its back, rising up above the waves. The flattened top was dried and leathery, spotted with white excrement where sea birds had perched, scarred as well where they had torn the tough hide with their sharp bills. One of these birds was dropping down towards the top of the fin now, hanging from its great white wings, webbed feet extended. It squawked suddenly, flapping as it moved off, startled by the long gash that had appeared in the top of the fin. This gap widened, then extended the length of the entire fin, a great opening in the living flesh that widened further still and emitted a puff of stale air.

The opening gaped, wider and wider, until there was more than enough room for the Yilanè to emerge. It was the second officer, in charge of this watch. She breathed deeply of the fresh sea air as she clambered onto the wide ledge of bone located inside and near the top of the fin, her head and shoulders projecting, looking about in a careful circle. Satisfied that all was well she clambered back below, past the crewmember on steering duty who was peering forward through the transparent disc before her. The officer looked over her shoulder at the glowing needle of the compass, saw it move from the coursemark. The crewmember reached out next to the compass and seized the nodule of the nerve ending between the thumbs of her left hand, squeezing it hard. A shudder passed through the vessel as the half-sentient creature responded. The officer nodded and continued her climb down into the long cavern of the interior, her pupils expanding swiftly in the half-lit darkness.

Fluorescent patches were the only illumination here in the living-walled chamber that extended almost the full length of the uruketo's spine. To the rear, in almost complete darkness, lay the prisoners with their ankles shackled together. Cases of supplies and pods of water separated them from the crew and passengers in the front. The officer made her way forward to the commander to give her report. Erafnaiš looked up from the glowing chart that she held and signed agreement. Satisfied, she rolled the chart and returned it to its niche, then moved off to climb the fin herself. She shuffled when she walked, a childhood injury to her back which was still scarred and wrinkled from the same wound. Only her great ability had enabled her to rise to this high rank with such a disfiguring handicap. When she emerged on top of the fin she also breathed deep of the fresh air as she looked about her.

Behind them the coast of Maninlè was slipping out of sight. There was land barely visible on the horizon ahead, a chain of low islands stretching northwards. Satisfied, she bent over and spoke, expressing herself in the most formal way. When issuing orders she would be more direct, almost brusque. But not now. She was polite and impersonal, the accepted form of address to be used by one of lower rank to one of higher. Yet she was in command of this living vessel—so the one she spoke to must indeed be of exalted position.

"For your pleasure, there are things to be seen, Vaintè."

Having spoken she moved to the rear, leaving the vantage point in the front clear. Vaintè clambered carefully up the ribbed interior of the fin and emerged onto the inner ledge, followed closely by two others. They stood respectfully to one side as she stepped forward. Vaintè held to the edge, opening and closing her nostrils as she smelled the sharp salt air. Erafnaiš looked at her with admiration, for she was indeed beautiful. Even if one did not know that she had been placed in charge of the new city, her status would have been clear in every motion of her body. Though unaware of the admiring gaze Vaintè still stood proudly, head high and jaw jutted forward, her pupils closed to narrow vertical slits in the full glare of the sun. Strong hands gripped hard while wide-spread feet balanced her; a slow ripple moved the bright orange of her handsome crest. Born to rule, it could be read in the very attitude of her body.

"Tell me what that is ahead," Vaintè said abruptly.

"A chain of islands, Highest. Their name is their being. Alakasaksehent, the succession of golden, tumbled stones. Their sands and the water about them are warm all the year round. The islands extend in a line until they reach the mainland. It is there, on the shore, that the new city is growing."

"Alpèasak. The beautiful beaches," Vaintè said, speaking to herself so that the others could not see or hear her words. "Is this my destiny?" She turned to face the commander. "When will we be there?"

"This afternoon, Highest. Certainly before dark. There is a warm current in the ocean here that carries us swiftly in that direction. The squid are plentiful so the enteesenat and the uruketo feed well. Too well sometimes. Those are some of the problems of commanding on a long voyage. We must watch them carefully or they go slowly and our arrival . . ."

"Silence. I wish to be alone with my efenselè."

"A pleasure to me." Erafnaiŝ spoke the words, backing away at the same time, vanishing below the instant she had finished.

Vaintè turned to the silent watchers with warmth in her every movement. "We are here. The struggle to reach this new world, Gendasi, is at an end. Now the greater struggle to build the new city shall begin."

"We help, do as you bid," Etdeerg said. Strong and solid as a rock, ready with all her strength to aid. "Command us—even unto death." In another this might have sounded pretentious; not with Etdeerg. There was sincerity in every firm motion of her body.

"I will not ask that," Vaintè said. "But I will ask you to serve at my side, my first aide in everything."

"It will be my honor."

Then Vaintè turned to Ikemend who drew herself up, ready for orders. "Yours is the most responsible position of all. Our future is between your thumbs. You will take charge of the hanalè and the males."

Ikemend signed ready acceptance, pleasure—and firmness of endeavor. Vaintè felt the warmth of their companionship and support, then her mood changed to one of grimness. "I thank you both," she said. "Now leave me. I will have Enge here. Alone."

Vaintè held tight to the leathery flesh as the uruketo rode up and over a large wave. Green water surged across its back and broke against the black tower of the fin. Salt spray flew, some splashing Vaintè's face. Transparent nictitating membranes slipped across her eyes, then slowly withdrew. She was not aware of the sting of the salt water for her thoughts were far ahead of this great beast that carried them across the sea from Inegban∗. Ahead lay Alpèasak, the golden beaches of her future—or the black rocks that she would crash upon. It would be one or the other, nothing in between. In her ambition she had climbed high after leaving the oceans of her youth, leaving behind many in her efenburu, surpassing and climbing beyond efenburu many years her senior. If one wished to reach the peak one had to climb the mountain. And make enemies along the way. But Vaintè knew, as few others did, that making allies was equally important. She made it a point to remember all of the others in her efenburu, even those of lowly station, saw them when she could. Of equal, or greater importance, she had the ability to inspire respect, even admiration, among those of the younger efenburu. They were her eyes and her ears in the city, her secret strength. Without their aid she would never have been able to embark upon this voyage, her greatest gamble. Her future—or her failure. The directorship of Alpèasak, the new city, was a great step, an appointment that moved her past many others. The danger was that she might fail, for this city, the furthest ever from Entoban∗, already had troubles. If there were delays in establishing the new city she was the one who would be brought low, so low she would never rise again. Like Deeste whom she was coming out to remove as Eistaa of the new city. Deeste had made mistakes, the work was going too slowly under her leadership. Vaintè was replacing her— and taking on all of the unsolved problems. If she failed—she too would be replaced in turn. It was a danger, but also a risk worth taking. For if it were the success they all hoped it would be, why then her star would be in the ascendancy and none could stop her.

Someone clambered up from below and stood beside her. A familiar presence yet a bittersweet one. Vaintè felt now the comradeship of one of her own efenburu, the greatest bond that existed. Yet it was tempered by the dark future that lay ahead. Vaintè had to make her efenselè understand what would happen to her once they were ashore. Now. For this would be the last chance that they would have to talk in private before they landed. There were too many listening ears and watching eyes below to permit her to speak her mind before this. But she would speak now, end this foolishness once and for all.

"We have made our landfall. That is Gendasi ahead. The commander has promised me that we will be in Alpèasak this afternoon." Vaintè was watching out of the corner of her eye but Enge did not speak, merely signaled agreement with a motion of one thumb. The gesture was not insulting—nor was it revealing of any emotion. This was not going well, but Vaintè would not permit it to anger her or stop her from doing what must be done. She turned about and stood face to face with her efenselè.

"To leave father's love and enter the embrace of the sea is the first pain of life," Vaintè said.

"The first joy is the comrades who join you there," Enge added, finishing the familiar phrase. "I abase myself, Vaintè, because you remind me of how my selfishness has hurt you . . ."

"I want no abasement or apologies—or even explanations of your extraordinary behavior. I find it inexplicable that you and your followers are not decently dead. I shall not discuss that. And I am not thinking of myself. You, just you, that is my concern. Nor do I concern myself with those misled creatures below. If they are intelligent enough to sacrifice their freedom for indecent philosophies, why then they are bright enough to make good workers. The city can use them. It can use you too—but not as a prisoner."

"I did not ask to be unshackled."

"You did not have to. I ordered that. I was shamed to be in the presence of one of my efenburu who was chained like a common criminal."

"It was never my desire to shame you or our efenburu." Enge was no longer apologetic. "I acted according to my beliefs. Beliefs so strong that they have changed my life completely—as they could change yours, efenselè. But it is pleasing to hear that you feel shame, for shame is part of self-awareness which is the essence of belief."

"Stop. I feel shame only for our efenburu that you have demeaned. Myself, I feel only anger, nothing more. We are alone now, none can hear what I say. I am undone if you speak of it, but I know you won't cause me injury. Hear me. Rejoin the others. You will be bound with them when you are brought ashore. But not for long. As soon as this vessel leaves I'll have you away from them, free, working with me. This Alpèasak will be my destiny and I need your help. Extend it. You know what terrible things are happening, the cold winds blow more strongly from the north. Two cities are dead—and there is no doubt that Inegban* will be next. It is the foresight of our city's leaders that before that happens a new and greater city will be grown on this distant shore. When Inegban* dies Alpeàsak will be waiting. I have fought hard for the privilege of being Eistaa of the new city. I will shape its growth and ready it for the day when our people come. I will need help to do that. Friends around me who will work hard and rise with me. I ask you to join with me, Enge, aid me in this great work. You are my efenselè. We entered the sea together, grew together, emerged together as comrades in the same efenburu. This is a bond that is not easily broken. Join with me, rise with me, stay at my right hand. You cannot refuse. Do you agree?"

Enge had her head lowered, her wrists crossed to show that she was bound, lifting her joined hands before her face before she raised her eyes.

"I cannot. I am bound to my companions, the Daughters of Life, with a bond even stronger than that of my efenburu. They follow where I have led . . ."

"You have led them into wilderness and exile—and certain death."

"I hope not. I have only spoke what is right. I have spoken of the truth revealed by Ugunenapsa, that gave her eternal life. To her, to me, to us all. It is you and the other Yilanè who are too blind to see. Only one thing can restore sight to you and to them. Awareness of the knowledge of death that will give you the knowledge of life."

Vaintè was beside herself with anger, unable for the moment to speak, raising her hands to Enge like an infant so she could see the inflamed red of her palms, pushing them before her face in the most insulting of gestures. Growing more angry still when Enge was unmoved, ignoring her rage and speaking to her with tenderness.

"It need not be, Vaintè. You can join us, discover that which is larger than personal desires, greater than allegiance to efenburu . . ."

"Greater than allegiance to your city?"

"Perhaps—because it transcends everything."

"There is no word for that which you are speaking. It is a betrayal of everything we live by and I feel only a great repulsion. Yilanè live as Yilanè, since the egg of time. Then into this order, like a parasite boring into living flesh, your despicable Farneksei appeared preaching this rebellious nonsense. Great patience was shown to her, yet she persisted and was warned, and persisted still—until there was no recourse but to expel her from her city. And she did not die, the first of the living-dead. Were it not for Olpèsaag the salvationer, she might be living and preaching dissension still."

"Ugunenapsa was her name because through her this great truth was revealed. Olpèsaag was the destroyer who destroyed her flesh but not her revelation."

"A name is what you are given, and she was Farneksei, inquirer-past-prudence, and she died for that crime. That is where it will end, this childish belief of yours, dirty thoughts that belong down among the corals and the kelp." She took a deep and shuddering breath, fighting hard to get her temper under control. "Don't you understand what I am offering you? One last chance. Life instead of death. Join with me and you will climb high. If this unsavory belief is important to you keep it, but speak to me not of it, or to any other Yilanè, keep it beneath your cloak where none can see. You will do it."

"I cannot. The truth is there and must be spoken aloud . . ."

Roaring with rage, Vaintè seized Enge by the neck, her thumbs twisting cruelly at her crest, pushing her down and grinding her face into the unyielding surface of the fin.

"There is the truth!" she shouted, pulling Enge's face about so she would understand every word clearly. "The birdshit that I grind your stupid moon-face into, that is reality and the truth. Out there is the truth of the new city at the edge of the wild jungle, hard work and filth and none of the comforts you have known. That is your fate, and certain death, I promise you if you do not abandon your superior attitude, your weak mewling . . ."

Vaintè spun about when she heard the tiny choking sound, to see the commander climbing up to join them, now trying to draw back out of sight.

"Get up here," Vaintè shouted, hurling Enge down onto the ledge. "What does this interference, this spying mean?"

"I did not mean . . . there was no intent, Highest, I will leave." Erafnaìs spoke simply, without subtlety or embellishment, so great was her embarrassment.

"What brought you here then?"

"The beaches. I just wanted to point out the white beaches, the birth beaches. Just around the point of land you see ahead."

Vaintè was happy for the excuse to turn away from this distasteful scene. Distasteful to her because she had lost her temper. Something she rarely did because she knew that it placed weapons in others' hands. This commander now, she would bear tales, nothing good could come of it. It was Enge's fault, ungrateful and stupid Enge. She would be her own destiny now, get exactly the fate she deserved. Vaintè clutched hard to the edge as her anger faded, her breathing slowed, looking at the green shore so close to hand. Aware of Enge climbing to her feet, eager as they all were to see the beach.

"We will get as close as we can," Erafnais said, "close inshore."

Our future, Vainte thought, the first glorious topping of the males, the first eggs laid, the first births, the first efenburu growing in the sea. Her anger was gone now and she almost smiled at the thought of the fat and torpid males lolling stupidly in the sun, the young happily secure in their tail pouches. The first births, a memorable moment for this new city.

Under the guidance of the crew the uruketo was being urged even closer inshore, almost among the breaking waves. The shore moved by, the beaches came into view. The beautiful beaches.

Enge and the commander were struck dumb by what they saw. It was Vainte who cried aloud, a sound of terrible tortured pain.

It was drawn from deep inside her by the sight of the torn and dismembered corpses that littered the smooth sand.

CHAPTER THREE

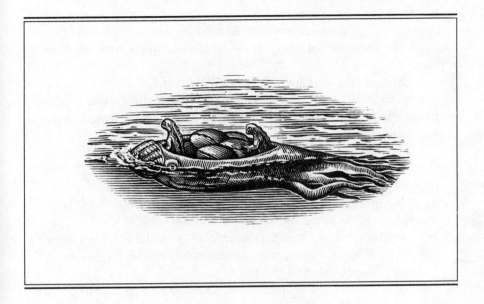

Vaintè's cry of pain ended abruptly. When she spoke next all complexity was gone from her words, all subtlety and form. Just the bare bones of meaning were left, a graceless and harsh urgency.

"Commander. You will lead ten of your strongest crewmembers ashore at once. Armed with hèsotsan. You will have the uruketo stand by here." She pulled herself up and over the edge of the fin then stopped, pointing to Enge. "You will come with me."

Vaintè kicked her toeclaws into the uruketo's hide, her fingers found creases in the skin as she climbed down to its back and dived into the transparent sea. Enge was just behind her.

They surged up out of the surf beside the slaughtered corpse of a male. Flies were thick about the gaping wounds, covering the flesh and congealed blood. Enge swayed at the sight, as though moved by an invisible wind, winding her thumbs and fingers together, all unknowing, in infantile patterns of pain.

Not so Vaintè. Rock-hard and firm she stood, expressionless, with only her eyes moving over the scene of slaughter before her.

"I want to find the creatures that did this," she said, her words betraying no emotion, stepping forward and bending low over the body. "They killed but did not eat. They are clawed or tusked or horned—look at those slashes. Do you see? And not only the males, but their attendants are dead too, killed the same way. Where are the guards?" She turned about to face the commander who was just emerging from the sea with the armed crewmembers, waving them forwards.

"Spread out in a line, keep your weapons ready, sweep the beach. Find the guards who should have been here—and follow those tracks and see where they lead. Go." She watched them move out, turning about only when Enge called to her.

"Vaintè, I cannot understand what kind of creature made these wounds. They are all single cuts or punctures, as though the creature had only a single horn or claw."

"Nenitesk have a single horn on the end of their noses, large and rough, while huruksast also have a single horn."

"Gigantic, slow, stupid creatures, they could not have done this. You yourself warned me of the dangers of the jungles here. Unknown beasts, fast and deadly."

"Where were the guards? They knew the dangers, why were they not doing their duty?"

"They were," Erafnaìs said, walking slowly back down the beach. "All dead. Killed the same way."

"Impossible! Their weapons?"

"Unused. Fully loaded. This creature, these creatures, so deadly . . ."

One of the crewmembers was calling out to them from far down the beach, her body movements unclear at this distance, the sound of her voice muffled. She ran towards them, clearly greatly agitated. She would stop, attempt to speak for an instant, then run closer until finally her meaning was finally understood.

"I have found a trail . . . come now . . . there is blood."

There was uncontrolled terror in her voice that added grim weight to what she had said. Vaintè led the others as they moved quickly to join her.

"I followed the trail, Highest," the crewmember said, pointing into the trees. "There was more than one of the creatures, five I think, a number of tracks. All of them end at the water's edge. They are gone. But there is something else, something you must see!"

"What?"

"A killing place of much blood and bones. But something . . . else. You must see for yourself."

They could hear the angry buzzing of the flies even before they reached the spot. There were indeed signs of great slaughter here, but something more important. Their guide pointed at the ground in silence.

Pieces of charred wood and ashes lay in a heap. From the center a gray curl of smoke lifted up.

"Fire?" Vaintè said aloud, as puzzled by its presence here as the others. She had seen it before and did not like it. "Stay back, you fool," she ordered as the commander reached down towards the smoking ashes. "That is fire. It is very hot and it hurts."

"I did not know," Erafnaìs apologized. "I have heard of it but I have never seen it."

"There is something else," the crewmember said. "On the shore there is mud. It has been baked hard by the sun. There are footprints on it, very clear. I tore one free, it is there."

Vaintè strode over and looked down at the cracked disc of mud, bending over and poking at the indentations in the hard surface.

"These creatures are small, very small, smaller than we are. These pads are soft with no marks of claws. *Tso!* Look there—count!"

She straightened up and spun about to face the others, extending one hand with fingers outspread, angry color rippling across her palm.

"Five toes, that's what they have, not four. Who knows what kind of beasts have five toes?" Silence was her only answer. "There are too many mysteries here. I don't like it. How many guards were there?"

"Three," Erafnaìs said. "One at each end of the beach, the third near the center . . ."

She broke off as one of the crewmembers came crashing through the undergrowth behind them. "There is a small boat," she called out. "Landing on the beach."

When Vaintè came out from under the trees she saw that the boat was rocking in the surf, laden with containers of some kind. One of the occupants was holding on to the boat so the creature would not stray: the other two were on the beach staring at the corpses. They turned about as Vaintè approached and she saw the twisted wire necklace that one of them wore about her neck. Vaintè stared at it.

"You are the esekasak, she who defends the birth beaches—
why were you not here defending your charges?"

The esekasak's nostrils widened with rage. "Who are you to
talk to me like that—"

"I am Vaintè who is now Eistaa of this city. Now answer my
question, low one, for I lose patience."

The esekasak touched her lips in supplication, stumbling backward a step as she did. "Excuse me, Highest, I didn't know. The
shock, these deaths . . ."

"Are your responsibility. Where were you?"

"The city, getting food and the new guard."

"How long have you been away?"

"Just two days, Highest, as always."

"As *always!*" Vaintè could feel herself swelling with rage that
added harsh emphasis to her words. "I understand none of
this. Why do you leave your beach to go to the city by sea?
Where is the Wall of Thorns, the defenses?"

"Not yet grown, Highest, unsafe. The river is being widened and deepened and has not been cleared of the dangerous
beasts yet. It was decided for safety's sake to site the birth
beach on the ocean, temporarily of course."

"Safety's sake!" Vaintè could no longer control her rage
as she pointed at the corpses, shouting. "They are dead—all of
them. Your responsibility. Would that you were dead with them.
For this, the greatest of crimes, I demand the greatest of penalties.
You are ejected from this city, from the society of speakers, to
rejoin the speechless. You will not live long, but every moment
until you die you will remember that it was your charge, your
responsibility, your mistake that brought on this sentence." Vaintè
stepped forward and hooked her thumbs around the metal emblem
of high office and pulled hard, tearing it free. The broken ends
cutting the esekasak's neck. She hurled it into the surf as she
chanted the litany of depersonalization.

"I strip you of your charge. All of those present here strip you
of your rank for your failure of responsibility. Every citizen of
Inegban*, the city that is our home, every Yilanè alive joins us in
stripping you of your citizenship. Now I take away your name and
no one living will speak it aloud again but will speak instead of
Lekmelik, darkness of evil. I return you to the nameless and
speechless. Go."

Vaintè pointed to the ocean, frightening in her wrath. The

depersonalized esekasak fell to her knees, stretched full length in the sand at Vaintè's feet. Her words were barely understandable. "Not that, no, I beg. Not to blame, it was Deeste who ordered it, forced us. There should have been no births, she didn't enforce sexual discipline, I cannot be blamed for that, there should have been no births. What has happened is not my fault . . ."

Her voice rumbled in her throat, then died away; the movement of her limbs slowed and stopped.

"Turn the creature over," Vaintè ordered.

Erafnaiš signaled two of her crew members who hauled at the limp body until it flopped on its back. Lekmelik's eyes were open and staring, her breathing already slowed. She would be dead soon. Justice had been done. Vaintè nodded approval, then dismissed the creature from her thoughts completely; there was too much to do.

"Erafnaiš, you will stay here and see that the bodies are disposed of," she ordered. "Then bring the uruketo to the city. I will go now in this boat. I want to see this Eistaa Deeste who I was sent here to replace."

As Vaintè stepped aboard the boat the guard there signaled humbly for permission to speak. She spoke slowly, with some effort. "It will not be possible for you to see Deeste. Deeste is dead. For many days now. It was the fever, she was one of the last to die."

"Then my arrival has been delayed too long already." Vaintè seated herself as the guard spoke commandingly into the boat's ear. The creature's flesh pulsed as it started forward, moved by the jet of water it expelled.

"Tell me about the city," Vaintè said. "But first, your name." She spoke quietly, warmly. This guard was not to blame for the killings, she had not been on duty. Now Vaintè must think of the city, find the allies she would need if the work were to be done correctly.

"I am Inlènat," she said, no longer as fearful as she had been. "It will be a good city, we all want it that way. We work hard, though there are many difficulties and problems."

"Was Deeste one of the problems?"

Inlènat turned her hands away to hide the color of her emotions. "It is not for me to say. I have only been a citizen for a very short time."

"If you are in the city you are of the city. You may speak to me because I am Vaintè and I am Eistaa. Your loyalty is to me. Take your time and think of the significance of that. It is from me that authority flows. It is to me that all problems will be brought. It is from me that all decisions will radiate. So now you know your responsibilities. You will speak and answer my questions truthfully."

"I will answer as you command, Eistaa," Inlènat said with assurance, already settling herself into the new order of things.

Bit by bit, by careful and patient questioning, Vaintè began to build a picture of events in the city. The guard was of too low a station to have knowledge of what had happened in the higher reaches of command—but she was well aware of the results. They were not pleasing.

Deeste had not been popular, that was obvious. She had apparently surrounded herself with a group of cronies who did little or no work. There was every chance that these were the ones who had forgotten their responsibilities, had not taken the other roads of satisfaction when egg-time came, who had instead used the males despite the fact the birth beach was not ready. If this were true, and the truth could be found out easily enough, there would be no waste of a public trial. The criminals would be put to work outside the city, that was all, would work until they fell or were killed or were eaten by the wild creatures. They deserved little else.

The news wasn't all bad though. The first fields had been cleared, while the city itself was over half grown and going according to plan. Since the fever had been countered there had been no medical problems other than normal injuries caused by the heavy work. By the time the boat had entered the river Vaintè had a clear picture of what must be done. She would check on Inlènat's stories of course, that was natural, but her instincts told her that what the simple creature had told her held the essence of the city's problems. Some of her tales would be just gossip, but the body of her facts would surely stand.

The sun was setting behind a bank of clouds as the boat pulled in between the water roots of the city, where they stretched out into the harbor. Vaintè automatically pulled one of the cloaks around her as she felt the chill. The cloak was well-fed and warm. It also concealed her identity—and there was nothing wrong with that. Had it not been for the slaughter on the beach she would have insisted on a formal welcome when the uruketo had arrived. That would be unseemly to do now. She would make her way quietly into Alpèasak, so that when the news of the killing reached the city she would be there to guide them. The deaths would not be forgotten, but they would be remembered as the end of the bad period, the beginning of the good. She made solemn promise to herself that everything would be very, very different from now on.

CHAPTER FOUR

V aintè's arrival did not go unnoticed. As the boat drew up at the dock she saw that someone was standing there, tight-wrapped in a cloak and obviously waiting for her arrival. "Who is that?" Vaintè asked. Inlènat followed her gaze.

"I have heard her called Vanalpè. Her rank is the highest. She has never spoken to me."

Vaintè knew her, at least knew her reports. Business-like and formal with never a word about personalities or difficulties. She was the esekaksopa, literally she-who-changed-the-shape-of-things, for she was one of the very few who knew the art of breeding plants and beasts into new and useful forms. Now she was the one with responsibility for the design and actual growth of the city. While Vaintè was Eistaa, the leader of the new city and its inhabitants, Vanalpè had the ultimate responsibility for the physical shape of the city itself. Vaintè tried not let the sudden tension show: this first meeting was of vital importance for it could shape their entire relationship. And upon that relationship depended the fate and the future of Alpèasak itself.

"I am Vaintè," she said as she stepped out onto the raw wood of the dock.

"I greet you and I welcome you to Alpèasak. One of the fargi saw the uruketo and the approach of this boat and reported to me. It was my greatest wish that it be you. My name is Vanalpè, one who serves," she said formally, making the sign of submission to a superior. She did it in the old-fashioned way, the full double-hand motion, not in the usual and more modern shortened way. After that she stood square-legged and solid, waiting for orders. Vaintè warmed to her at once and on impulse seized her hand in a gesture of friendship.

"I have read your reports. You have worked hard for Alpèasak. Did the fargi tell you anything else . . . did she speak of the beach?"

"No, just of your arrival. What of the beach?"

Vaintè opened her mouth to speak—and realized that she could not. Since that single scream of pain she had kept her feelings under perfect control. But she felt that now, if she spoke of the slaughter of the males and the young, that her anger and horror would push through. That would not be politic nor help the image of cold efficiency that she always maintained in public.

"Inlènat," she ordered. "Tell Vanalpè what we found on the beach."

Vaintè paced down the length of the dock and back, not listening to the voices, planning the order of all the things that she must do. When the voices fell still she looked up and found them both waiting for her to speak.

"Now you understand," she said.

"Monstrous. The creatures who did this must be found and destroyed."

"Do you know what they possibly can be?"

"No, but I know one who does. Stallan, who works with me."

"She is named huntress by design?"

"She is truly named. She alone has ventured into the jungle and forests that surround the city. She knows what is to be found there. Knowing this I have made modifications of the city design that I must give you details . . ."

"Later. Though I am now Eistaa the less pressing duties can wait until something is done about the killings. The city goes well—there are no immediate problems?"

"None that cannot wait. It goes as it should. The fever has been stopped. A few died."

"Deeste died. Will she be missed?"

Vanalpè was silent, eyes lowered in thought. When she did

speak it was obvious that she had considered her responsibilities and weighed her words carefully. "There has been bad-feeling in this city and many say that Deeste was responsible for that. I agree with that opinion. Very few will miss her."

"Those few . . .?"

"Personal associates. You will quickly discover who they are."

"I understand. Now send for Stallan and order her to attend me. While we wait show me your city."

Vanalpè led the way between the high roots, then pushed aside a hanging curtain that shivered at her touch. It was warmer inside and they dropped their cloaks onto the pile beside the door. The cloaks extruded slow tentacles that probed the wall until they smelled the sweetness of the saptree and attached themselves to it.

They passed through the temporary structures close to the waterfront, translucent sheets fastened to skeletal, fast-growing trees. "This technique is new," Vanalpè explained. "This is the first city to be founded in a very long time. Since the last founding the days were used wisely and great improvements have been made in design." She was animated now, smiling as she slapped her hand against the brittle sheets. "I developed these myself. A modified insect pupa greatly enlarged. As long as the pupae are well fed in the larval stage they will produce large numbers of these sheets. They are peeled off and joined together while they are still soft. They harden with exposure. Nor is this resource wasted. See, we come to the city tree now."

She pointed to the network of heavy roots that now formed the walls, where they wrapped and engulfed the translucent sheets. "The sheets are pure carbohydrate. They are absorbed by the tree and form a valuable energy input."

"Excellent." Vaintè stopped under a light that huddled next to a heater which had spread its membranous wings. She looked about in unfeigned admiration. "I cannot tell you how pleased I am. I have read all of your reports, I knew what you were accomplishing here, but seeing the solidity of the growth itself is a different matter. It is impressive impressive impressive." She indicated a repetition and enlargement of the last word. "My first report to Entoban∗ will say just that."

Vanalpè turned her head away in silence, not daring to speak. All of the work of her lifetime had been in city design and Alpèasak was the culmination of those labors. The new Eistaa's unchecked enthusiasm was overpowering. Long moments passed before she was able to speak, pointing to the heater. "This is so new you won't have seen it in the reports." She stroked the heater which withdrew its fangs from the saptree for a moment, turned sightless eyes towards her and squeaked thinly. "I have been breeding these experimentally for years. I can truthfully report now that the experiments were successful. They are longer-lived and need no nourishment other than the sugars of the saptree. And feel the body temperature, it is certainly higher than any other."

"I can only admire."

Proudly, Vanalpè led the way again, between the curtains of entangled roots. She bent as she went through an opening, holding the roots up so Vaintè could enter, then pointed at the thick trunk that formed the rear wall. She laughed and held out her hand, palm upwards. "It lay there on my hand, that small, it seemed impossible to believe the days and days of labor needed to prepare the mutated gene chains that went into it. And no one was absolutely sure until it grew that our work had been successful. I had this area cleared of brush and trees, insect life as well, then I fertilized and watered the ground myself, pushed a hole into it with my thumb—then planted the seed. I slept beside it that night, I couldn't leave. And next day there was the tiniest green shoot. I can't describe how I felt. And now—it is this."

With great pride and happiness Vanalpè slapped the thick bark of the great tree that rose there. Vaintè went and stood beside her, touching the wood herself and feeling the same joy. Her tree, her city.

"This is where I will stay. Tell everyone that this is my place."

"This is your place. Walls will be planted to ring the place of the Eistaa. I will now go and wait for Stallan, then bring her here."

When she had gone Vaintè sat in silence until a passing fargi looked her way, then sent her for meat. But when the fargi returned she was not alone.

"I am called Hèksei," the newcomer said in the most formal manner. "Word has spread of your arrival, great Vaintè, and I have hurried to greet you and welcome you to your city."

"What is your work in this city, Hèksei?" Vaintè asked, just as formally.

"I attempt to be of aid, to help others, to be loyal to the city . . ."

"You were a close friend of the now-dead Eistaa, Deeste?"

It was more of a statement than a question and the barb struck home. "I don't know what you have heard. Some people are jealous of others, carry tales—"

Her words cut off as Vanalpè returned, followed by another who wore a sling across one shoulder from which there was suspended a hèsotsan. Vaintè glanced at it, then looked away, saying nothing although its presence here was forbidden by law.

"This is Stallan of whom I spoke," Vanalpè said, her eyes slipping over Hèksei as though she did not exist.

Stallan made the sign of formal salutation, then stepped backwards towards the door.

"I am in error," she said hoarsely, and Vaintè noticed for the first time the long scar that puckered her throat. "Unthinkingly, I wore my weapon. Not until I was aware of you looking at it did I realize that I should have left it behind."

"Wait," Vaintè said. "You wear it always?"

"Always. I am out of the city as much as I am in. This is a new city and there are dangers."

"Then wear it still, Stallan, if you have need of it. Has Vanalpè told you about the beach?" Stallan signaled yes in grim silence. "Do you know what the creature could be?"

"Yes—and no."

Vaintè ignored Hèksei's gesture of disbelief and contempt. "Explain yourself," she said.

"There are swamps and jungles in this new world, great forests and hills. To the west there is a large lake and beyond that the ocean again. To the north endless forests. And animals. Some very much like the ones we know in Entoban*. Some are very different. The difference is greater to the north. There I have found more and more ustuzou. I have killed some. They can be dangerous. Many of the fargi I took with me were injured, some died."

"Dangerous!" This time Hèksei laughed out loud. "A mouse under the floor dangerous? We must send for an elinou to take care of your danger."

Stallan turned slowly to face Hèksei. "You always laugh when I speak of this matter about which you know nothing. The time has come to stop that laughing." There was a coldness in her voice that allowed no answer. They stood in silence as she went out the entrance, to return a moment later with a large, wrapped bundle.

"There are ustuzou in this land, fur-bearing creatures that are larger than the mice beneath the floor that you laugh at. Because that is the only kind of ustuzou we knew of before coming to this new shore we still think that all ustuzou must be tiny vermin. The time has now come to abandon ourselves of this idea. Things are different here. There is this nameless beast, for instance."

She snapped the bundle open and spread it across the floor. It was the skin of an animal, a fur-animal, and it reached from wall to wall. There was only shocked silence as Stallan took up one of its limbs and pointed to the foot on its end, to the claws there, each one as long as her hand.

"I answered yes and no to your question, Eistaa, and this is why. There are five claws here. Many of the larger and most dangerous fur-creatures have five toes. I believe that the killers on the beach were ustuzou of some kind, of a species never encountered before."

"I think you are right," Vaintè said, kicking a corner of the thick fur aside and trying not to shudder at its soft and loathsome . touch. "Do you think you can find these beasts?"

"I will track them. North. The only way they could have gone."

"Find them. Quickly. Report to me. Then we will destroy them. You will leave at dawn?"

"With your permission—I will leave now."

Vaintè permitted herself an expression of slight incredulity, enough to be enquiring yet not derisive or insulting. "It will be dark soon. Can you travel at night?" she asked. "How can a thing like that be possible?"

"I can only do it near the city where the coastline is most regular. There are large cloaks and I have a boat that is nocturnal. It will follow the shoreline so that by dawn we will be well on our way."

"You are indeed a hunter. But I do not wish you to venture out alone, to face these dangers by yourself. You will need aid. Hèksei here has told me that she helps others. She will go with you, help you."

"It will be a strenuous voyage, Eistaa," Stallan said, her voice flat and expressionless.

"I am sure she will profit from the experience," Vaintè said, turning away, ignoring Hèksei's unhappiness and frantic signals for attention. "May your voyage be a successful one."

Naudinza istak ar owot at kwalaro, at
etcharro—ach i marinanni terpar.

———————

*The hunter's path is always the hardest
and longest. But it ends in the stars.*

CHAPTER FIVE

ightning flickered, low on the horizon, briefly lighting the banks of dark clouds. Long moments passed before it was followed by the distant, deep rumble of thunder. The storm was retreating, moving out to sea, taking the streaming rain and the torrential wind with it. But the high seas still broke heavily on the beach, running far up the sands and into the salt grass beyond, almost as far as the beached boat. Just beyond the boat was a small copse where a temporary shelter of skins had been lashed to oars between the trees. Smoke drifted from beneath it and hung low under the branches. Old Ogatyr leaned out from the shelter and blinked at the first rays of afternoon sunlight that pierced the receding clouds. Then he sniffed the air.

"The storm is over," he announced. "We can go on."

"Not in those seas," Amahast said, poking at the fire until it flared up. The chunks of venison smoked in the heat and dripped sizzling meat juices into the flame. "The boat would be swamped and you know it. Perhaps in the morning."

"We are late, very late—"

"There is nothing we can do about it, old one. Ermanpadar sends his storms without worrying too much whether it suits us or not."

He turned from the fire to the remaining deer. The hunt had been a good one with herds of deer roaming the grassy scrublands of the coast. When this last beast was butchered and smoked the boat would be full. He spread the deer's front legs and hacked at its skin with the sharp flake of stone—but it was no longer sharp. Amahast threw it aside and called out to Ogatyr.

"This is what you can do, old one, you can make me a new blade."

Grunting with the effort, Ogatyr pushed himself to his feet. The continual dampness made his bones ache. He walked stiffly to the boat and rooted about inside it, then returned with a stone in each hand.

"Now, boy, you will learn something," he said, squatting down slowly onto his haunches. He held out the stones towards Kerrick. "Look. What do you see?"

"Two stones."

"Of course. But what of these stones? What can you tell me about them?" He turned them over and over in his hands so the boy could examine them closely. Kerrick poked at them and shrugged.

"I see only stones."

"That is because you are young and you have never been taught. You will never learn this from the women, for this is a man's skill only. To be a hunter you must have a spear. A spear must have a point. Therefore you must learn to know one stone from another, to see the spearpoint or the blade where it hides inside the stone, learn to open the stone and find that which is hidden inside. Now your lesson begins." He gave the rounded, water-worn rock to Kerrick. "This is the hammerstone. See how smooth it is? Feel its weight. It is a stone that will break other stones. It will open this one which is named a bladestone."

Kerrick turned the pebble over and over in his hands, staring at it with fierce concentration, noting its rough surface and shining angles. Ogatyr sat patiently until he was done, then took it back.

"There is no spearhead trapped in here," he said. "It is the wrong size, the wrong shape. But there are blades here, one here, see it? Feel it? I now release it."

Ogatyr carefully placed the bladestone on the ground and struck it with the hammerstone. A sharp chip cracked off the side.

"There is the blade," he said. "Sharp, but not sharp enough. Now watch closely and see what I do."

He took a bit of deer antler from his bag, then placed the chip of stone on his thigh and pressed the edge carefully with the tip of the antler. Each time he did this a tiny chip was flaked off. When he had worked the length of it, the blade was sharp and true. He handed it to Amahast who had patiently watched the entire operation. Amahast bounced it in his palm and nodded with appreciation. With practiced skill he slashed an opening in the deer's hide and cut it from neck to groin.

"No one in our sammad can make the stone yield up its blades as this one can," Amahast said. "Let him teach you, my son, for a hunter without a blade is no hunter at all."

Kerrick seized the stones eagerly and cracked them together. Nothing happened. He tried again, with as little success. Only when Ogatyr took hold of his hands and put them in the right position did he succeed in breaking free a ragged chip. But he was quite proud of this first effort and labored to shape it with the bit of deer horn until his fingers were sore.

Big Hastila had been gloomily watching his efforts. Now he crawled out from under the shelter, yawning and stretching, sniffing the air as Ogatyr had done, then plodded up the embankment behind them. The storm was gone, the wind growing gusty as it died down, the sun just beginning to break through. Only the white-topped waves stretching to the horizon still bore witness to the past day's fury. On the landward side the embankment fell away again down to a grassy marsh. He saw dark forms picking their way through it; he slowly crouched and moved back to the shelter.

"More deer out there. The hunting is good in this place."

"The boat is full," Amahast said, slicing away a bit of smoking meat. "Any more and she will sink."

"My bones ache from lying here all day," Hastila grumbled, seizing up his spear. "The other thing the boy must learn is how to reach the game in order to kill it with a sharp new point. Come, Kerrick, take up your spear and follow me. If we cannot kill the deer we can at least stalk them. I will show you how to move upwind and crawl close to even the wariest prey."

Kerrick had his spear in his hand, but looked to his father before he followed the big hunter. Amahast nodded as he chewed the tough meat. "Hastila can show you much. Go with him and learn."

Kerrick laughed happily as he ran after Hastila, then slowed to walk at his side.

"You are too noisy," Hastila said. "All the creatures of the forest have good ears and can hear you coming long before they see you . . ."

Hastila stopped and held up his hand in a gesture of silence. Then he cupped his hand to his ear and pointed to a hollow in the dunes ahead. Kerrick listened carefully but could hear only the distant rumble of the surf. It slackened for a moment and the other sound was clear, a tiny crackling from the other side of the dune. Hastila raised his spear and moved forward silently. Kerrick could feel his heart beat loudly as he followed the big hunter, moving as quietly as he could; the crackling was louder now.

As they came to the base of the dune they smelled the sweet and sickening smell of rotting flesh. The remains of the butchered deer carcasses had been dumped here, well away from their camp. The crackling sound was much louder now, as well as the buzzing of countless flies. Hastila signaled Kerrick to wait while he moved up the slope and peered carefully over. He drew back and turned to Kerrick, his face twisted with disgust, and waved the boy up to join him. When they were both below the crest he raised his spear into throwing position and Kerrick did the same. What was there? What creature were they stalking? Filled with a mixture of fear and curiosity Kerrick crouched—then jumped forward just behind the hunter.

Hastila shouted loudly and three creatures looked up from their grisly work, stood motionless for an instant at his sudden appearance. The hunter's arm snapped down, his spear flew straight, struck the nearest one between the forelegs. It fell and thrashed, screeching loudly. The others fled, hissing with fear, long legs pumping, necks and tails outstretched.

Kerrick had not moved, still stood with his spear held high, rigid with fear. Murgu. The one that was dying, clawing at the spear with sharp-clawed toes, was too much like the marag he had speared in the sea. Mouth open. Sharp teeth. Something from a nightmare.

Hastila had not looked at the boy, did not notice his open fear. He was too obsessed with his own hatred. Murgu. How he loathed them. This carrion eater, blood and bits of decay still on its head and neck, snapped feebly at him as he came up. He kicked it aside, stood on its neck while he pulled his spear free. It was scaled and green-spotted, pale gray as a corpse, as long as a man although its head was no bigger than his hand. He plunged the spear home again and it trembled and died. He waved the clouds of flies from his face as he climbed back out of the pit. Kerrick had lowered his spear and fought to control his trembling. Hastila saw this and put his hand on the boy's shoulder.

"Do not be afraid of them. For all their size they are cowards, carrion eaters, filth. Hate them—but do not fear them. Remember always what they are. When Ermanpadar made the Tanu from the mud of the river, he made the deer and the other animals as well for the Tanu to hunt. He put them down in the grass beside the mountains where there is clean snow and fresh water. But then he looked and saw all the emptiness to the south. But by then he was tired and far distant from the river so he did not return to it but instead dug deep into the green slime of the swamp. With this he made the murgu and they are green to this day and fit only for killing so they can decay back into the swamp from which they were born."

While he spoke Hastila plunged his spear into the sand and twisted it to remove all the stains of the marag's blood. When this was done he was quieter; most of Kerrick's fear had ebbed away. The marag was dead, the others gone. Soon they would leave this shore and return to the sammad.

"Now I will show you how to stalk your prey," Hastila said. "Those murgu were eating or they would have heard you—you sounded like a mastodon going up the slope."

"I was quiet!" Kerrick said defensively. "I know how to walk. I stalked a squirrel once, right up so close that I was only a spear length away—"

"The squirrel is the stupidest animal, the longtooth is the smartest. The deer is not smart, but he can hear the best of all. Now I will stand here in the sand and you will go up the bank and into the deep grass. Then stalk me. In silence—for I have the ears of the deer."

Kerrick ran happily up the slope and through the wet grass— then dropped and crawled away from the camp. He went on this way, as silently as he could, then turned towards the ocean again to work his way up behind the hunter. It was hot, wet work—and to little avail, for when he finally reached the top of the ridge again Hastila was already there waiting for him.

"You must look carefully each time before you put your foot down," the hunter said. "Then roll it forward and do not stamp. Part the grass and do not force your way through it. Now we try again."

There was little beach here and Hastila went down to the water's edge and splashed his spear into the sea to wash away any remaining trace of the marag's blood. Kerrick once more pushed his way up the slope, stopping for breath on the top. "This time you won't hear me," he called out, shaking his spear in defiance at the big man.

Hastila waved back and leaned forward on his spear.

Something dark surged out of the surf behind him. Kerrick called out a horrified warning and Hastila spun about, spear ready. There was a snapping sound, like the breaking of a stout branch. The hunter dropped his spear and clutched at his midriff and fell face first into the water. Wet arms pulled him under and he vanished among the foam-flecked waves.

Kerrick screamed as he ran back to the encampment, met the others running towards him. He choked out what he had seen as he led them back along the beach, to the spot where the terrifying event had taken place.

The sands were empty, the ocean as well. Amahast bent and picked the hunter's long spear out of the surf, then looked out to sea again.

"You could not see what it looked like?"

"Just the thing's legs, the arms," he said through his chattering teeth. "They reached up out of the sea."

"Their color?"

"I couldn't see. Wet, green perhaps. Could they have been green, father?"

"They could have been anything," Amahast said grimly. "There are murgu of all kinds here. We will stay together now, one will be awake always while the others sleep. As soon as we can we return to the sammad. There is only death in these southern waters."

Alaktenkèalaktèkan
olkeset esetakolesnta* tsuntesnalak
tsuntensilak satasat.

========

*What happens now, and next to
now, is of no importance as long
as tomorrow's-tomorrow is the
same as yesterday's-yesterday.*

CHAPTER SIX

The storm had passed and the rain had stopped; the ground was steaming now in the heat of the fierce sunlight. Vaintè stood in the shade of the dead tree and looked on as the workers carefully planted the seedlings in neat rows. Vanalpè herself had marked the rows in the ground that the others were to follow. She came up to Vaintè now, moving slowly with her mouth gaping wide in the heat, to stand at her side in the shade.

"Are the seedlings dangerous to handle?" Vaintè asked. Vanalpè, still breathing heavily, signaled a negative.

"Only when the thorns begin to grow, and that is only after eighty days. Some of the animals will still graze them then, but not after the thorns begin to exude the toxins. The taste is bitter to the ruminants, deadly to anything smaller."

"Is this one of your new modifications?" Vaintè asked, moving out into the sun.

"Yes. It was developed in Inegban* so we could bring the seed with us. We are so familiar with the thorn hedges around the city fields, always far higher than our heads, that we might forget that they have not been there since the egg of time. They were planted once, were small before they grew large and spread. Now the young branches grow over the old to make an impenetrable barrier. But a new hedge in a new city asks for a new answer." She was speaking easier now with her mouth no longer gaping. Cool enough to move until part of her body was in the sun. "This new hedge I have developed is fast growing, short lived—and toxic. But before it dies we will have seeded the usual thorn hedge to grow and eventually take its place."

"And the trees?" Vaintè asked, looking in the direction of the leafless dead trees that stood gauntly about the new field.

"They are already being destroyed—see where the limbs have fallen from that large one. They are riddled with wood-consuming beetles, most voracious. When the supply of wood is gone the beetles will enter a larval stage. Then we can gather the coarctate pupae which preserve themselves in hardened cuticula. They can be stored until needed again."

Vaintè had moved back into the shade and she noticed that most of the workers had done the same. The afternoon was hot and comfortable, but not a time for getting any work done.

"When these seedlings have been planted send the workers back to the city," Vaintè said.

Enge was working alongside the others; Vaintè waited until she caught her eye, then signaled her over. Enge expressed gratitude before she spoke.

"You have taken the shackles off your prisoners. We are most thankful."

"Don't be. The reason that I had them shackled on the uruketo was so they could not attempt to seize the craft and escape."

"You don't understand the Daughters of Life, do you? Violence is not our way . . ."

"I'm pleased to hear that," Vaintè said dryly. "My way is to take no chances. Now that the uruketo has gone there are only forests and jungle to escape to should anyone not be satisfied with her lot. Not only that, your companions will work better unshackled."

"Yet we are still prisoners."

"No," Vaintè said firmly, "you are not. You are free citizens of Alpèasak with all the rights and duties of other citizens. Do not confuse what happened with what will happen. The council of Inegban* deemed you unworthy of citizenship in that city and sent you here. To make new lives in a new city. I hope you will not repeat the same mistakes here that you did there."

"Is that a threat, Vaintè? Does the Eistaa of Alpèasak think that we are different from other citizens here—that we will be treated differently?"

"It is not a threat, but a warning, my efensalè. Learn by what happened. Believe what you will among yourselves—but keep your secrets to yourselves. You are forbidden to talk of these matters to others. The rest of us do not wish to know."

"You can be that sure?" Enge asked sternly. "You are that wise?"

"Wise enough to know that you are trouble-makers," Vaintè snapped. "Sure enough of that fact to take the precaution that you shall be watched closely. You'll not make the trouble here that you did in Inegban∗. I shall not be as patient as the council there."

Enge's body scarcely moved while she spoke, her words neutral and unoffensive. "We make no trouble, intend no trouble. We just believe . . ."

"Fine. Just as long as you do your believing in dark places where others cannot hear. I will brook no subversion in *my* city."

Vaintè knew that she was beginning to lose her temper, as she always did when faced with the rock-like immobility of Enge's strange beliefs. She therefore welcomed the sight of the fargi hurrying towards her with a message. Though the youngster did not speak very well her memory was good.

"The city . . . comes one . . . name of Stallan. Things of importance to be said . . . presence requested."

Vaintè waved her off, then turned her back rudely on Enge and made her way into the city. Stallan was there, awaiting her arrival, success obvious in every attitude of her hard body.

"You have done that which I asked you to do?" Vaintè said.

"I have, Eistaa. I followed the killer-beasts until I came upon them. Then I shot and killed one myself and have returned with the body. It is close by. I left the worthless one Hèksei to look after it. There are strange things about this ustuzou that I find disturbing."

"Strange? What? You must tell me."

"I must show you so that you will understand."

Stallan led the way in silence to that part of the city closest to the river. Hèksei waited here, standing watch over a tightly wrapped bundle. Her skin was filthy and scratched and she began to wail in protest as soon as they appeared. Before the first words had been spoken Stallan struck her on the head and hurled her to the ground.

"Worse than useless," Stallan hissed. "Lazy, noisy on the

hunt, filled with fear. Slowed me down and almost got us both killed. I want nothing more to do with her."

"Nor does Alpèasak," Vaintè said in quick judgement. "Leave us. Leave the city. Join the ambenin."

Hèksei started to protest, but Stallan kicked her cruelly in the mouth. Hèksei fled, her screeches of agony rebounding from the aerial roots and leaves overhead. Vaintè put the worthless creature instantly from her mind and pointed at the bundle.

"Is this the killer animal?"

"It is."

Stallan pulled at the covering and Hastila's corpse rolled out onto the damp earth.

At the sight of it Vaintè spoke wordlessly of horror and amazement. Controlling her feeling of revulsion she stepped forward slowly, then prodded it with her foot.

"There were four of the creatures," Stallan said. "All smaller than this one. I found them and I followed them. They did not walk on the shore but were in the ocean. Nor did they have a boat. Instead they sat on a tree in the water and pushed it forward with bits of wood. I watched them kill other fur animals, just as they must have killed the males and their guards on the beach. They do not use teeth or claws or horns because they are hornless as you can see, while their teeth and claws are small and weak. Instead they do their killing with a thing like a sharp tooth fixed to a length of wood."

"They do many tricks, these fur animals. They have brains."

"All creatures have brains, even a primitive hèsotsan like this," Stallan tapped the weapon hanging from her shoulder. "But this hèsotsan is not dangerous by itself if handled correctly. These things are. Now, if you would, look closely at the beast. They have much fur here, as you can see, on the top of their bodies about the head. But this other fur, lower down, does not belong to the creature but is bound about it. It bears a pouch, and in the pouch I found this. What appears to be a shaped piece of stone with a sharp edge. See, this bound-about skin comes away and the creature has its own fur beneath."

"It is a male!" Vaintè shouted. "A male fur-creature with a dim and bestial brain that now is bold enough to threaten *us*, the Yilanè. Is that what you are trying to tell me? That these ugly beasts are a danger to us?"

"I believe so, Vaintè. But you are Eistaa and you are the one who decides what thing is what thing. I have merely told you what I have seen, shown you what I have found."

Vaintè held the hard sharpness of the stone between her thumbs, stared down at the corpse for a long time before she spoke again.

"I believe that it is possible that even a ustuzou might grow to have a low kind of intelligence and cunning. Our boats understand a few instructions. All animals have brains of some kind. Enteesenat can be trained to search out food in the sea. In this savage part of the world so far from our own, who can possibly say what strange things have happened since the egg of time? Now we are beginning to find out. There are no Yilanè here to order and control things. It is therefore possible, and hard to deny since the evidence is here before our eyes, that a species of disgusting mammal has attained some form of perverted intelligence. Enough to find bits of stone and learn to kill with them. Yes, it is possible. But they should have remained in their jungle, killing and eating each other. They mistakenly ventured forth. Vermin like these, male vermin, and they have killed our males. So understand now what we must do. We must seek them out and slaughter them all. We have no choice if our city is to live on these beaches. Can we do that?"

"We must do that. But we must go in strength, taking everyone who can be spared from the city. All of them armed with hèsotsan."

"But you said there were only four of the beasts? And only three of them remain alive now . . ."

Realization came to Vaintè as it had come to Stallan when she had found the small group moving north. "Could there be others? More of these?"

"There must be. These few must have voyaged away from the main pack for some reason. Now they return to it. I am sure of that. We must move in force and find them all."

"And kill them all. Of course. I will issue the orders so we can leave at once."

"That would not be wise since the day is long advanced and there will be many of us. If we leave at dawn, take only the best fed and fastest boats, we will easily catch them because they move slowly. Follow them and find the others."

"And butcher them as they butchered the males. It is a good plan. Have this creature taken to the ambesed and spread out for all to see. We will want supplies, fresh water, enough to last a few days at least so we won't have to stop."

Fargi were sent hurrying to all parts of the city, spreading the word, ordering the citizens to gather in the ambesed until it was crowded as it had never been before. An angry murmur rose from the mass of Yilanè as they pushed each other for a chance to see the body. Vaintè herself was entering the ambesed when her eye was caught by Ikemend signaling for attention; she stopped instantly.

"A few words, please, Eistaa."

"There is no trouble with your charges?" Vaintè asked in sudden fear. Ikemend, her efenselè, had been appointed to the vital position of guarding and sheltering the males. After the briefest session of questioning the previous guardian had revealed that it was her lack of control that had resulted in all the deaths on the beach. She had sickened and died when Vaintè had stripped her of her name.

"All is well. But the males have heard about the dead ustuzou and want to see it. Should they be permitted?"

"Of course—they are not children. Let them think about their responsibilities. But not until the ambesed is clear. We don't want any hysterical scenes."

Ikemend was not the only one seeking her attention. Enge blocked her way, nor would she move when ordered aside.

"I have heard what you plan to do, follow and kill the fur-beasts."

"What you have heard is correct. I am going to make the public announcement now."

"Before you do that—there is something that I must tell you. I cannot support you. None of the Daughters of Life can. It goes contrary to everything that we believe in. We cannot be a part of this killing. Base animals are as they are because they lack the knowledge of death. To destroy them because of this is not possible. We kill when we must eat. All other killing is forbidden. Therefore you understand that we cannot . . ."

"Silence! You will do as I order. Anything else will be treason."

Enge answered her rage with cold reason. "What you call treason we call the gift of life. We have no recourse."

"I do. I can have you all killed at once."

"You can. Then you will be the murderess and the guilty one as well."

"I have no guilt—just anger. And hatred and loathing that an efenselè of mine could betray her race in this manner. I won't kill you because I need your bodies for hard work. Your people will be chained together until we return. You will be chained with them. You have no more special privileges. I disown you as a efenselè. You will work with them and die with them. Disowned and loathed for your treachery. That is your fate."

Alitha thurlastar, hannas audim senstar,
sammad deinarmal na mer ensi edo.

———————

*The deer is killed, a man may die, a
woman grows old—only the sammad endures.*

CHAPTER SEVEN

Kerrick was in his usual position in the prow of the boat, tending the fire. But this was a boy's work and he had wanted to row with the others. Amahast had permitted him to try but he was too small, the great oar too clumsy for him to handle. He leaned forward now, squinting his eyes to see through the fog, but nothing was visible. Unseen seabirds cried out with the voices of wailing children, invisible in the mist. Only the crash of breaking waves off to the left gave them any guide. Normally they would have waited until the fog had lifted, but not this day. The memory of Hastila being pulled forever beneath the sea was with all of them. They moved as fast as they could: they wanted this voyage over and finished with. Kerrick sniffed the air, raised his head and sniffed again.

"Father," he called out. "Smoke—I can smell smoke!"

"There is smoke on us and on the meat," Amahast said, yet he paddled a little faster at the thought. Could the sammad be that close?

"No, this is not old smoke. This is fresh—on the wind from ahead. And listen to the waves. Are they not different?"

They were indeed. With the reek of the skins and the meat there may have been some doubt about the smoke. But not the waves. Their sound was growing fainter, falling behind them. Many of the tents of the sammad had been pitched on the banks of a great river, where it ran into the sea. The waves might very well be going up this estuary now, dying away in the flow of fresh water there.

"Pull towards shore!" Amahast ordered, leaning hard into his own oar.

The sky was growing lighter now: the mist was lifting. Above the screams of the gulls they heard a woman calling out and they shouted in answer.

Once the sun began burning through the fog it began to lift faster and faster. It still lay close to the surface of the water, but beyond it was the shore and the waiting tents, smoking fires, piles of debris—all of the familiar bustle of their encampment. The boat was seen now and a great shout went up and people rushed from the tents to the water's edge. Everyone was crying out with happiness and there were echoing trumpetings from the meadow where the mastodons were grazing. They were home.

Men and women both were splashing into the water, calling out—but their shouts of welcome died away as they counted the places in the boat. Five had left on the hunting expedition. Just three had returned. As the boat grated against the sandy bottom it was seized and pulled up onto the beach. Nothing was said but the woman of Hastila, suddenly screamed with horror as she realized he was missing, as did the woman of Diken and his children.

"Both dead," were Amahast's first words, lest they have false hopes that the others were following behind. "Diken and Hastila. They are among the stars. Are there many away from the encampment?"

"Alkos and Kassis have gone up the river, to get fish," Aleth said. "They are the only ones not close by."

"Go after them," Amahast ordered. "Bring them back at once. Strike the tents, load the beasts. We leave today for the mountains."

There were shouts and cries of protest at this because they were not prepared for this sudden departure. While on the move they would break camp every morning: they did this easily because just the essentials were unpacked. This was not true now. The summer encampment sprawled along both sides of the small river, while in the tents all their baskets, furs, everything were spread about in confusion.

Ogatyr shouted at them, his voice rising over the women's wails of distress. "Do as Amahast says or you will die in the snows. The season is late, the path long."

Amahast said nothing more. This reason was as good as any. Perhaps even better than the real reason, for which he could give no evidence. Despite this lack he was sure that he was being watched. He, a hunter, knew when he was being hunted in turn. For all of this day, and the day before, he had felt eyes upon him. He had seen nothing, the sea had always been empty when he looked. Yet something was out there, he knew it. He could not forget that Hastilà had been pulled beneath the ocean and had not returned. Now Amahast wanted them to leave, this day, pack the travois and lash them behind the mastodons and turn their faces away from the sea and what lay beneath it. Not until they were back among the familiar mountains would he feel safe.

Although he worked them until they ran with sweat, it still took the entire day to break camp. He shouted at the women and beat the youths when they slowed down. It was no easy thing to leave a summer camp. Scattered goods had to be brought together and packed, the tentacles of hardalt from the drying racks loaded into baskets as well. Nor were there enough baskets for all the hardalt and there was wailing and complaining when he ordered that some of the catch be left behind. There was not even time to mourn the dead; that would come later. Now they must leave.

The sun was dropping behind the hills before they were ready. They would have to travel by night, but they had done that before. The skies were clear, the new moon just a crescent of light, the tharms of warriors were bright above and would guide them on their way. There was much trumpeting and waving of trunks as the mastodons, long unharnessed, bellowed their protests. Yet they permitted the boys to climb up to their backs, and watched with rolling eyes as the great poles were lashed into place. Two to each beast, trailing behind on both sides, making a frame to which the crosspieces were tied, then the tents and stores were loaded on top.

Kerrick sat on the neck of the great bull, Karu, tired as they all were, but still pleased that the sammad was leaving. He wanted to be away from the ocean as soon as it was possible. He was afraid of the sea and of the creatures in it. Out of the entire sammad he was the only one who had seen the arms rise from the sea to pull Hastila down. Dark arms in the ocean, dark forms in the sea.

He looked out at the sea and his screams, over and over again, cut through the voices, silencing them, drawing every eye to the ocean where he pointed and screamed and pointed again.

Out of the evening darkness even darker forms were emerging. Low, black boats that had no oars yet moved more swiftly than any Tanu boat, rushing forward in a line as straight as a breaking wave. Nor did they stop until they were in the surf and rasping on the shore. From them came the murgu, clearly seen despite the failing light.

Ogatyr was close to the water when they landed, could see them clearly. He knew them for what they were.

"The ones we killed, on the beach . . ."

The nearest marag raised the length of stick and squeezed with both hands. It made a loud crack and pain struck Ogatyr's chest and he fell.

Other sticks were cracking now and above the sound were the human cries of pain and terror.

"They flee!" Vaintè shouted, waving the attackers forward. "After them. None shall escape."

She had been the first ashore, had fired the first hèsotsan, had killed the first ustuzou. Now she wanted to kill more.

It was not a battle but a massacre. The Yilanè butchered all the living creatures indiscriminately: men, women, children, animals. Their casualties were few. The hunters had no time to find their bows. They had their spears, but while a thrown spear could wound or kill, most of the hunters held their spears as they rushed in and were shot down before they could use them.

All that the Tanu could do was flee—followed by the killers from the sea. Frightened women and children ran past Karu and the mastodon raised his head high, trumpeting in fear as well. Kerrick seized handfuls of the beast's thick hair so he wouldn't be hurled off, then climbed down the wooden shaft to the ground, running to grab up his spear. A strong hand seized his shoulder and spun him about.

"Run!" his father ordered. "Escape to the hills!"

Amahast turned about swiftly as the first of the murgu came around the bulk of the mastodon, jumping over the wooden pole. Before it could aim its weapon Amahast pierced it through with his spear, wrenched it free.

Vaintè saw the murdered fargi fall and was shaken by the need for vengeance. The blood-dripping point was swinging towards her—but she did not flinch away. She stood her ground, raising the hèsotsan, squeezing off quick explosions, dropping the ustuzou before it could reach her. She had not noticed the small one, didn't know it was there until pain lanced through her leg. Roaring with agony she struck the creature down with the butt end of the hèsotsan.

The wound was bloody and painful—but not serious, she could see that now. Her rage died away as she examined it, then turned her attention to the battle raging around her.

It was almost over. Few if any of the ustuzou remained alive. They lay in tumbled heaps among the baskets, limp corpses on the skins and poles. The attackers from the sea were now meeting up with the others who had moved up the river to attack from behind, an encircling movement they had used in their youth to catch their prey in the sea. It had worked as well on land.

"Stop the killing at once," Vaintè ordered, calling out to those nearest her. "Tell the others. Stop now. I want some survivors. I want to know more about these fur beasts."

They were just animals who used sharp bits of stones, she could see that now. They had a crude social organization, rough stone artifacts, and even made use of the larger animals that were now being killed as they fled in panic. All of this indicated that if there was one group this size—why then there might very well be others. If that were so then she needed to find out everything she could about the creatures.

At her feet the small one she had struck down stirred and whimpered. She called out to Stallan who was near by.

"Hunter—tie this one so it cannot escape. Throw it into a boat."

There were more darts in the container suspended from the harness she wore. The ones she had expended in the battle must be replaced. The hèsotsan had been well-fed and should be able to fire for some time yet. She prodded it with her finger until the loading orifice dilated, then pushed the darts into their correct positions inside.

The first stars were appearing now, the last red of the sky fading behind the hills. She needed a cloak from the boat. She signaled a fargi to bring one to her and was wrapping herself in its warm embrace when the survivors were brought before her.

"This is all?" she asked.

"Our warriors were hard to control," Stallan said. "Once you start killing these creatures it is hard to stop."

"Full well I know that myself. The adult ones—all dead?"

"All dead. This small one I found hiding and brought it out." She held the thing by its long hair, shaking it back and forth so it wailed with pain. "This very young one I found inside another's coverings." She held out the infant, a few-months-old baby that she had pulled from its wrappings, that had been held tight in its mother's dead arms.

Vaintè looked at the tiny hairless thing with disgust as Stallan held it towards her. The hunter was used to touching and handling all kinds of repulsive creatures; the thought of doing it herself sickened her. Yet she was Vaintè, Eistaa, and she could do anything any other citizen could do. She reached out slowly and took the wriggling thing in both hands. It was warm, warmer than a cloak, almost hot. Her disgust ebbed for a moment as she felt the pleasant heat. When she turned it over and over it opened a red and toothless mouth and wailed. A jet of hot excrement from it ran down Vaintè's arm. The instant pleasure of the heat was replaced by a wave of disgust.

It was too much, too revolting. She hurled the creature, as hard as she could, against a nearby boulder. It became silent as she went quicly to the water to scrub herself clean, calling back to Stallan.

"It is enough. Tell the others to return to the boats after they have made sure that none live."

"It will be done, Highest. All dead. The end of them."

Is it? Vaintè thought as she plunged her arms into the water. Is it the end? Instead of elation at the victory she found herself sinking into a dark depression.

The end—or just the beginning?

CHAPTER EIGHT

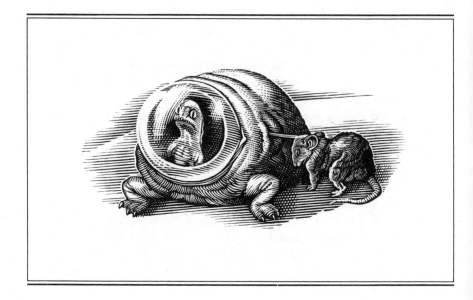

E nge moved close to the wall and leaned against it so she could feel the warmth of the heater. Though the sun had risen, the city still held some of the chill of the night. Around her the varied animals and plants of Alpèasak stirred to life, but this was so normal that she took no heed. Beneath her feet was the latticework of the floor that rested on the thick layers of dried leaves below. Within the leaves there was the rustle of large beetles and the other insects that cleared away debris, even the movements, had she listened, of a scurrying mouse. All around her there were stirrings as the ebb of life accelerated with the coming of day. High above, the sun was already shining on the leaves of the great tree, as well as on the many other plants that made up this living city. Water vapor was now being drawn from the stomata of these leaves, to be replaced by water that moved slowly upwards through the vessels of the trees, vines, creepers, water brought into the living system by the millions of root hairs beneath the ground. At Enge's side, unheeded, the tendril of her discarded cloak twitched as it sucked at the saptree.

To Enge all of this was as natural as the air she breathed, the richness of the intertwined and interdependent life forms that existed on all sides of her. Occasionally she thought about it and all of its moral implications. But not today, not after what she had heard. Boasting of murdering another species! How she longed to talk to these innocent braggarts, to explain to them about the meaning of life, to force them to understand the terrible crime that they had committed. Life was the balance of death, as sea was the balance of sky. If one killed life—why, one was killing oneself.

Her attention was drawn as one of the fargi pulled at her manacled hands, confused by her status and unsure how to address her. The young fargi knew that Enge was one of the highest—yet her wrists were bound like one of the lowest. Lacking the words she could only touch Enge to draw her attention.

"The Eistaa wants you to come now," the fargi said.

Vaintè was sitting in her place of power when Enge entered, the seat formed by the living bark of the city tree. There were memory creatures on the table beside her and one of them had the tendril above its withered eyes pressed into a fold of the ugunkshaa, the memory-speaker. The ugunkshaa spoke quietly while at the same time its organic molecule lens flickered with motion, a black and white picture of the Yilanè who had originally spoken to the memory-creature. Vaintè silenced the ugunkshaa when Enge entered and picked up the stone spearpoint that was lying next to it.

"Approach," she ordered, and Enge did so. Vaintè clasped the stone blade in her hand and raised it; Enge did not quail or pull away. Vaintè seized her by the arm.

"You have no fear," Vaintè said. "Even though you can see how sharp this scrap of stone is, as good as any of our string-knives."

She sawed through the bindings and Enge's hands were free. Enge rubbed gently at her skin where it had been irritated by the bonds. "You are freeing us all?" she asked.

"Do not be too greedy. Just you—since I have need of your knowledge."

"I will not aid you in murder."

"There is no need to. The killing is over." *For the time being,* she thought to herself, knowing better than to mention it aloud. If she did speak, whatever she said would reveal her thoughts completely. Not only was she unable to tell a lie but the very concept of a lie was completely alien to her. It was impossible to tell a lie when every movement of one's body revealed a meaning. The only way for a Yilanè to keep her thoughts secret was not to speak of them. Vaintè was most adept at this form of concealment. She practiced it now since she needed Enge's help. "We have come to the time for learning. Did you not study the use of language at one time?"

"You know that I did, with Yilespei. I was her first student."

"You were. Her first and best. Before the rot ate into your brain. You did all sorts of foolish things as I remember, watching the way that children communicate with each other, sometimes doing it yourself to draw their attention. I understand that you even eavesdropped on the males. That puzzles me. Why those stupid creatures of all things? What could one possibly learn from them?"

"They have a way of talking among themselves when we are not about, a way of saying things in a different manner . . ."

"I'm not talking about that. I mean why study such things? Of what importance can it be how others speak?"

"Of greatest importance. We are language, language is us. When we lack it we are mutes and no better than animals. It was thoughts and studies like these that led me to the great Ugunenapsa and her teachings."

"You would have been far better off to have continued with your language studies and kept yourself out of trouble. Those of us who will become Yilanè must learn to speak as we grow up—that is a fact or you and I would not be here. But can a young one be *taught* to speak? It seems like a stupid and repellent idea. Can it be done?"

"It can," Enge said. "I have done it myself. It is not easy, most young ones don't want to listen, but it can be done. I used the training techniques the boatmasters use."

"But boats are almost as stupid as cloaks. All they ever learn to understand are just a few commands."

"The technique is the same."

"Good." Vaintè looked shrewdly out of the corner of her eyes and chose her words carefully. "Then you could teach an animal to understand and to speak?"

"No, not to speak. To understand, yes, a few simple commands if the brain is big enough. But speaking requires vocal apparatus and areas of the brain that animals do not possess."

"But I have heard animals talking."

"Not talking, repeating sound patterns they have learned. Birds can do this."

"No, I mean talking. Communicating with each other."

"Impossible."

"I am talking about fur animals. Filthy ustuzou."

Enge began to understand the point that Vaintè was making and she signed her understanding. "Of course. If these creatures have some degree of intelligence—the fact that they use crude artifacts suggests that—why then, they might very well talk to each other. What an extraordinary thought. You have heard them talk?"

"I have. And so can you if you wish. We have two of them here." She waved over a passing fargi. "Find the hunter Stallan. Bring her to me at once."

"How are the animals faring?" Vaintè asked when Stallan appeared.

"I have had them washed, then I examined their injuries. Bruises, no more. I have also had the filth-ridden fur removed from their heads. The larger one is female, the smaller one a male. They drink water, but will eat nothing I have provided so far. But you must be careful if you get close to them."

"I have no intention of doing that," Vaintè said, shivering with disgust. "It is Enge here who will approach them." Stallan turned to her.

"You must face them at all times. Never turn your back on a wild animal. The small one bites, and they have claws, so I have manacled them for safety."

"I will do as you say."

"One other thing," Stallan said, taking a small sack from her harness and opening it. "When I cleaned the beasts I found this hung about the male's neck." She placed a small object on the table beside Vaintè.

It was a blade of some kind, made of metal. There was an opening pierced at one end, while simple patterns had been scratched upon it. Vaintè poked at it with a tentative thumb.

"It has been thoroughly cleaned," Stallan said. Vaintè picked it up and examined it closely.

"The patterns are unfamiliar, as is the metal," she said, not liking what she saw. "Where did the animals find this? Who made the design? And the metal, where did they get that from? Do not try to tell me that they have the science to grow metal." She tested the edge against her skin. "Not sharp at all. What can it possibly mean?"

There were no answers to these disturbing questions—nor had she expected any. She handed the bit of metal to Enge.

"Another mystery for you to solve when you learn to speak to the creatures." Enge examined it and handed it back.

"When may I see them?" she asked.

"Now," Vaintè said. She signaled Stallan. "Take us to them."

Stallan led the way through the corridors of the city, to a high, dark passage. Signaling for continuing silence, she swung open a hatch set into the wall. Vaintè and Enge looked through into the chamber beyond. They could see that it was sealed by a single heavy door. There were no other openings and the only illumination was the feeble light that filtered down through a tough transparent sheet high above.

Two repellent little creatures lay on the floor below. Tiny versions of the mutilated corpse that Enge had been forced to look at in the ambesed. Their skulls were bare and scratched where their fur had been removed. With the fur gone, and deprived of the stinking bits of skin that they had been bound about with, it could be seen that they were completely covered with repulsive, single-colored and waxy skin. The larger one, the female, was lying flat and making a repetitive wailing noise. The male squatted beside the female and emitted varied grunting sounds. This went on for a long time, until the wailing stopped. Then the female made other sounds as well. Vaintè signaled Stallan to close the hatch and leave.

"It might be a kind of talking," Enge said, excited despite herself. "But they move very little when they make the sounds, which is very confusing. It will take much study. The whole concept is a novel one, a different language, the language of ustuzou, a different type of creature from any of those we have ever studied. It is a tremendous and exciting idea."

"Indeed. So exciting that I command you to learn their way of speaking so you can converse with them."

Enge made a sign of submission. "You cannot command me to think, Eistaa. Even your great power does not extend into another's skull. I will study the talk of the animals because I wish to."

"I do not care about your reasons—as long as you obey my commands."

"Why do you wish to understand them?" Enge asked.

Vaintè chose her expressions carefully so as not to reveal all of her motives. "Like you, I am challenged by the thought that an animal might speak. Don't you believe that I am capable of intellectual pursuits?"

"Forgive the negative thought, Vaintè. You were always first in our efenburu. You led then because you understood when we didn't. When do I begin?"

"Now. This instant. How will you go about it?"

"I have no idea for it has never been done before. Let me return to the hatch and listen to the sounds. While I do this I will make a plan."

Vaintè left silently, immensely pleased with what she had accomplished. It had been imperative to get Enge's cooperation, for if she had refused it would have meant messages back to Inegban*, to then suffer the long wait while someone was located and sent out to investigate the talking beasts. If they really were talking and not just making noises. Vaintè needed that information at once since there might be more of the creatures about that could be a menace. She needed information for the safety of the city.

First she must learn all she could about these fur-animals, find out where they lived and how they lived. How they bred. That would be the first step.

The second would be to kill them. All of them. Exterminate them completely from the face of the earth. For even with their low cunning and crude stone artifacts they were still just miserable animals. Deadly animals who had slaughtered the males and the young without mercy. That would be their ruin.

Enge watched from the darkness, studying the creatures, deep in thought. Had she had a single clue to Vaintè's real motives she would, of course, have refused to cooperate. Even if she had stopped to think for a moment she might have realized Vaintè's concealed intentions. She had not done this because her thoughts were entirely on this fascinating linguistic problem.

She stood observing in silence for almost half a day, listening and watching and trying to understand. In the end she understood nothing of what she had heard, but she did have the glimmerings of a plan where she should begin. She silently closed the hatch and went in search of Stallan.

"I'll stay with you," the huntress said as she unbarred the door. "They can be dangerous."

"Just for a short time. As soon as they quiet down I will need to be alone with them. But then you will stand by outside. If there is any need I will call for you."

An uncontrollable shiver rippled Enge's crest as Stallan opened the door and she stepped through. The coarse smell of the beasts struck her. It was too much like entering an animal's lair. But intelligence overcame physical revulsion and she stood firm as the door closed behind her.

Kennep at halikaro, kennep at hargoro,
ensi naudin ar san eret skarpa tharm
senstar et sano lawali.

========

*A boy can be fleet of foot and strong of
arm—but he is a hunter only when there is
a beast's tharm upon his spearpoint.*

CHAPTER NINE

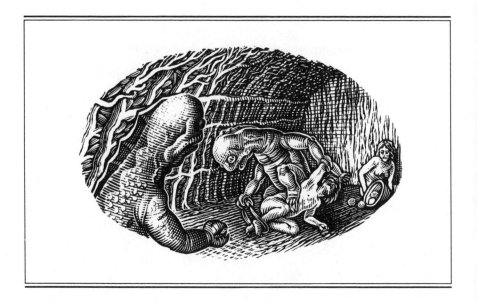

"They killed my mother, then my brother, right beside me," Ysel said. She had stopped the shrieking and crying now, but tears still filled her eyes and trickled down her cheeks. She wiped them away with the back of her hand, then went back to rubbing her shaved head.

"They killed everyone," Kerrick said.

He had not cried, not once since he had been brought to this place. Perhaps it was the way the girl carried on, wailing and screaming all the time. She was older than he was, five or even six years older, yet she shrieked like an infant. Kerrick understood that, knew it was easy enough to do. All you had to do was give in. But he wouldn't. A hunter does not cry—and he had been on a hunt. With his father. Amahast the greatest hunter. Now dead like all of the rest of the sammad. There was a swelling in his throat at the thought, but he fought it down. A hunter does not cry.

"Will they kill us, Kerrick? They won't kill us, will they?" she asked.

"Yes."

Ysel started to wail again and threw her arms about him, pulling his body tight against hers. This wasn't right; only small children touched each other. But even though he knew that it was not permitted he still enjoyed the feel of her flesh against his. Her breasts were small and hard and he liked to touch them. But when he did this now she pushed him from her and cried even louder. He stood and walked away in disgust. She was stupid and he didn't like her. She had never talked to him before they had been brought to this place. But now that there were just the two of them it was different for her. Not for him. It would have been better if one of his friends were here instead. But they were all dead; a pang of fear went through at the memory. No one else from the sammad left alive. They would be next. Ysel didn't seem to understand that, she could not bring herself to believe that there was nothing they could do to save themselves. He had searched carefully, over and over again, but there wasn't a thing in the wooden chamber that could be used for a weapon. Nor was there any way to escape. The gourds were too light to harm even a child. Much less one of the murgu who had brought them here. He picked up the gourd of water and sipped at it; his empty stomach rumbled. He was hungry— but not hungry enough to eat the meat they had brought. Just looking at it made him want to vomit. It wasn't cooked—nor was it raw. Something had been done to it so that it hung from the bone like cold jelly. He poked at it with his finger and shuddered. The door creaked, then opened.

Ysel pressed her face to the base of the wall and screamed, her eyes closed, not wanting to see what came through. Kerrick stood, facing the opening, his fists clenched and empty. Thinking about his spear. What he would do to them if he only had his spear.

There were two of the murgu creatures this time. He might have seen them before, he might not. It made no difference, they all looked alike. Bumpy, scaly, thick-tailed, blotched with different colors, with those ugly things sticking out behind their heads. Murgu that walked like men and grabbed things with their deformed two-thumbed hands. Kerrick moved slowly back as they entered, until his shoulders were against the wall and he could go no further. They stared at him with expressionless eyes and he wished again for his spear. One of them twitched and moved its limbs, making mewling noises at the same time. The wood was hard against his shoulders.

"Have they eaten anything yet?" Enge asked. Stallan signified negative, then pointed to the gourd.

"That's good meat, enzyme-treated and ready to eat. They use fire to burn their own meat before they eat it, so I knew they wouldn't want to have it raw."

"Have you put some fruit out for them?"

"No. They are meat eaters."

"They may be omnivores. We know little about their habits. Get some fruit."

"I cannot leave you here alone. Vaintè herself ordered me to guard you." There was a tremble of dismay to the hunter's words caused by the conflicting orders.

"I can defend myself against these small creatures if I have to. Have they attacked anyone before this?"

"Just when we brought them in. The male is vicious. We beat him until he stopped. He hasn't done it since then."

"I shall be safe. You have followed your instructions. Now obey mine."

Stallan had no choice. She left, reluctantly but quickly, and Enge waited in silence, searching for a way to open communication with the creatures. The female still lay facing the wall, once more making the high-pitched sound. The small male was silent, undoubtedly as stupid as all males. She reached down and took the female by the shoulder, pulled at her to turn her around. The creature's skin was warm and not unpleasant to touch. The wailing sound grew louder—and sudden agony lanced through her arm.

Enge bellowed with pain and lashed out, knocking the male to the ground. The thing's teeth had broken her skin, drawn blood. She arched her clawed fingers and hissed in anger. The creature scrabbled away from her and she followed. Then stopped. And felt guilt.

"We are at fault," she said, anger ebbing away. "We killed the rest of your pack. You cannot be blamed for doing what you did." She rubbed at her sore arm, then looked at the bright stain of blood on her palm. The door opened and Stallan came in, carrying a gourd of orange fruit.

"The male creature bit me," Enge said calmly. "Are they poisonous?"

Stallan hurled the gourd aside and rushed to her side, glanced at the wound—then raised a hard fist to strike the cowering male. Enge restrained her with a light touch.

"No. The fault was mine. Now, what about the bite?"

"Not dangerous if it is cleaned well. You must come with me so I can treat it."

"No, I shall wait here. I don't want to show fear to these animals. I will be all right."

Stallan moved with disapproval, but could do nothin. She hurried out, was gone for only a brief time before returning with a wooden chest. From it she took a container of water and used it to cleanse the bite, then stripped the cover from a nefmakel and put it into position. Enge's moist skin stirred the dormant creature to life and it adhered to her flesh, already beginning to secrete antibacterial fluid. As soon as this was done Stallan took two knotted black lumps from the box.

"I'm going to secure the male's legs and arms. It won't be the first time. The creature is vicious."

The small male fought to escape but Stallan seized it and hurled it to the floor, then knelt on its back, holding it still with one hand. With the other she seized one of the bindings and wrapped it around the beast's ankles, then inserted the binding's tail into its mouth. The binding swallowed by reflex, drawing its body tight. Only when it was well-secured did Stallan throw the creature aside.

"I will remain and guard you," she said. "I must. Vaintè ordered your protection. I have been remiss once and you have been injured. I cannot permit it to happen again."

Enge indicated begrudging agreement, then looked at the discarded gourd and the fruit tumbled on the floor. She pointed at the prostrate female.

"I'll get the round-sweet-eating-things. Turn that one over so she can see me."

Ysel screamed hoarsely when the cold hands grabbed her, lifted her roughly, and pushed her back against the wall. She chewed at her knuckles and sobbed as the other marag stamped towards her, stopped, then held up an orange. Its mouth slowly opened to reveal rows of pointed white teeth. It uttered an animal's screech as it waved the orange, scratching its claws on the floor when it did this. Ysel could only moan with fear, unaware that she had bitten into the flesh of her fingers and that blood was running down her chin.

"Fruit," Enge said. "Round, sweet good things that you eat. Fill your stomach, make you happy. Eating makes one strong. Now do as I command." She spoke temptingly at first, then commanding. "You will take this fruit. You will eat at once!"

Then she saw the blood where the creature had injured itself and she turned away in disgust. She put the gourd of fruit onto the floor and signaled Stallan to join her by the door.

"They have crude tools," Enge said. "You said they had shelters of some kind, as well as large animals to serve them?" Stallan nodded. "Then they must have some degree of intelligence."

"That doesn't mean that they can talk."

"A well-made point, hunter. But for the moment we shall just have to assume that they do have a language that they use to communicate with one another. I must not let a single failure stop me—look, the male is moving! It must have smelled the fruit. Masculine reactions are coarser, it cares more for its hunger than our possible threat. But it still watches us, still a wild animal. Look!" She cried out with triumph. "It is eating the fruit. A first success. We can at least feed them now. And there, see that, it is bringing fruit to the female. Altruism—that must denote intelligence."

Stallan was not convinced. "Wild animals feed their young. I have seen them work together on the hunt. I have seen it. That is no proof."

"Perhaps not—but I will not permit myself to be dissuaded so quickly. If boats can understand simple commands, why, then creatures like these should at least be able to do the same."

"You will teach them then, in the same manner that boats are taught?"

"No. I considered that at first, but I want to obtain a better level of communication. Teaching boats involves positive and negative reinforcement of a few commands. An electric shock indicates a wrong action, while a bit of food rewards success. That is good for training boats, but I am not trying to train these animals. I want to talk with them, communicate with them."

"Talking is a very difficult thing to do. Many of those who emerge from the sea never do learn."

"You are correct, hunter, but that is a matter of degree. The young may have difficulty in talking as adults, but you must remember that all of the young talk together when they are in the sea."

"Then teach these beasts the children's language. They might be able to master that."

Enge smiled. "It has been many years since you spoke as a child. Do you remember what this means?"

She raised her hand and the palm changed from green to red, then back to green again as she made a signal with her fingers. Stallan smiled.

"Squid—a lot of them."

"You do remember. But do you notice how important the color of my hand is? What I said would be incomprehensible without that. Can these fur creatures change the color of their palms?"

"I don't think so. I have never seen them do it. Though their bodies have red and white colors."

"That may be an important part of their speech—"

"If they have one."

"Agreed, if they have one. I must watch them more closely when they make their sounds again. But the greater urgency is to have them speak like Yilanè. Beginning with the simplest of expressions. They must learn the completeness of communication."

Stallan made a gesture of incomprehension. "I do not know what that means."

"Then I will demonstrate to make my meaning clear. Listen carefully to what I say. Ready? Now—I am warm. Do you understand?"

"Yes."

"Good. I am warm, that is a statement. The completeness is made clear in the union of the parts of the statement. I now say it again even more slowly. I . . . am . . . warm . . . I move my thumb in this manner, looking upward a little at the same time, say *warm* as I lift my tail slightly. All of that, the sounds spoken aloud and the correct motions are all combined together to form the complete expression."

"I have never considered such matters—and I find that my head hurts when I do."

Enge laughed and indicated appreciation of the attempt at humor. "I would fare as badly in the jungle outside as you do in the jungle of language. Very few make a study of it, perhaps because it is so complex and difficult. I believe that the first step in understanding is to consider that our language recapitulates phylogeny."

"Now my head does ache. And you think beasts like these can understand that—when even I have no idea of what you are talking about?" Stallan indicated the creatures, now quiescent against the wall, the gourd empty of its fruit, bits of skin littering the floor around them.

"I will not attempt anything that complex. What I meant was that the history of our language is matched by our development in life. When we are young and first enter the sea we do not yet speak, but we do seek the protection and comfort of the others in our efenburu who enter the water at the same time. As our intelligence grows we see older ones talking to each other. Simple motions of the hand or leg, a color change of the palm. We learn more and more as we grow older, and when we emerge from the sea we add spoken sounds to the other things that we have learned until we become Yilanè in the completeness of our communications. That brings me to my problem here. How do I teach our language to these creatures who do not share our cycle of life? Or do they? Do they pass through an aquatic period after birth?"

"My knowledge of these matters is far from complete—and you must remember that this species of ustuzou is new to us. But I doubt strongly if they were ever aquatic. I have captured and bred some of the more common and smaller wild species that abound in the jungle. They all seem to have certain things in common. They are very warm, all of the time."

"I have noticed that. It seems quite strange."

"Other things are equally strange. Look at that male there. You will see that he has only a single penis that cannot be decently retracted. None of the species of ustuzou I have captured has a normal double penis. Not only that, but I have studied their mating habits and they are disgusting."

"What do you mean?"

"I mean that after impregnation of the egg the *females* carry the young. And when they are born they still keep them close about their bodies and feed them with soft organs that grow on their torsos. You can see them, there, on the young female."

"How very unusual. Then you believe that the young stay on land? They do not go properly into the sea?"

"That is correct. It is a trait that is common to all the different ustuzou species I have observed. Their life cycles appear to be different from ours in every way."

"Then do you appreciate the import of your observations? If they do have a language of their own they can't possibly learn it in the same way that we learn ours."

Stallan signed agreement. "I appreciate that now, and thank you for the explanation. But does that not raise a most important question? If they have a language—how do they learn to speak it?"

"That is indeed the most important question, and I must attempt to find the answer to it. But I can tell you truthfully now that I have not the slightest idea."

Enge looked at the wild creatures, their faces sticky with the juice of the fruit they had eaten; they stared back at her. How could she possibly find a way to communicate with them?

"Leave me now, Stallan. The male is securely bound, the female shows no signs of violence. If I am alone they will have only me to watch without their attention being distracted."

Stallan considered this for a long moment before signing reluctant agreement. "It shall be as you request. I agree that the danger is not great now. But I shall remain just outside the door which will be slightly open and unlocked. You must call to me if they threaten you in any way."

"I will. You have my promise. Now my work must begin."

CHAPTER TEN

There was much work to be done in establishing this new city. Much extra work needed to put right the errors perpetrated by the former Eistaa, the justifiably dead Deeste, and with all this Vaintè found her days filled from first light to the coming of dark. As she sank into sleep she sometimes envied the nocturnal boats and other creatures that moved by night. If she could remain awake, just for a short time longer each day, so much more could be accomplished. It was an unnatural idea, but was still the last thing that occupied her thoughts many nights before she slept. These thoughts, of course, did not interfere with her sleep, because disturbed sleep was a physical impossibility for the Yilanè. When she closed her eyes, she slept—a motionless sleep that, to an outsider, had a disturbing resemblance to death. Yet this sleep was so light that it was easily broken by something unusual. Many times during the dark hours of the night, animal cries would lift Vaintè gently awake. Her eyes would open and she would listen for a moment. Hearing nothing more her eyes would close and she would be asleep again.

Only the gray light of dawn woke her completely. This morning—as all other mornings—she stepped from the warm bed to the floor, then prodded the bed with her toe. As it stirred she turned to the place where one of the countless trunks and stems of the living city bulged out into a gourd-like growth filled with water. Vaintè placed her lips over its orifice and sucked in sweetened water until she had drunk her fill. Behind her the bed quivered with slow spasms as it curled itself into a long bundle against the wall; its body cooled as it sank into a comatose state until it was needed again.

It had rained during the night and the dampness of the woven floor was uncomfortably cool on the soles of Vaintè's feet as she crossed an open area. After that she stayed under shelter as she made her way to the ambesed, fargi after fargi assembling in the train behind her as she went.

Each morning, before the work began, the project leaders, like all of the other citizens of the city, would be sure to pass through the ambesed. There they would stop for awhile and talk to one another. This large, open area in the heart of the city was the hub around which all of its varied activities revolved. Vaintè went to her favored spot on the west side where the rising sun struck first, deep in thought and unaware of the citizens who moved aside to let her pass. She was the Eistaa, the one who always walked in a straight line. The bark of the tree was already warm and she leaned against it with satisfaction, her pupils contracting to narrow slits as the rising sun washed over her. She looked on with great satisfaction as Alpèasak stirred to life. This brought her a different warmth that was even more enjoyable. Pride of place, the highest place, for this was her city. Hers to grow, to build, to expand, to create out of a wilderness on this hostile shore. She would build well. When the cold winds swept over distant Inegban* this new city would be ready. Then her people would come and live here and honor her for what she had accomplished. When she thought of this there was always the small irritating memory in the back of her mind that on the day when this happened she would no longer be Eistaa here. Malsas< would come with the others, Malsas<, Eistaa of Inegban*, and destined to rule the new city as well. *Perhaps*. Vaintè kept that word most secret and never spoke it aloud. Perhaps. Many things happened in the course of time. Malsas< was no longer young, there were those who pushed from below; everything changes with time. Vaintè would cross that river when she came to it. It was enough for now to build the new city—and build well.

Etdeerg caught Vaintè's eye and came at once at her gesture.

"Have you found what was killing the food animals?" Vaintè asked.

"We have, Eistaa. A large ustuzou, black in color, with deadly claws and long sharp teeth—teeth so long that they project from the creature's mouth even when the mouth is closed. Stallan had traps set near the opening that it had torn in the fence. We found it there, dead, this morning. It was held by the traps on its legs so it could not flee, while one of them had circled its neck and had strangled the beast."

"Decapitate it. When the skull is cleaned bring it to me."

Vaintè signaled dismissal and caught Vanalpè's attention at the same time. The biologist left the group she was talking to and came to join her.

"You will report on the new beach," Vaintè said.

"Close to completion, Eistaa. The ground has been cleared, the thorn barrier is high, the coral offshore growing well—considering that it has only been there a short time."

"Splendid. Then we can look forward to the new births. Births that will wipe away forever all memory of the deaths on the old beach."

Vanalpè agreed, but also expressed guilty doubt. "Though the beach is ready—it is not safe."

"Still the same problem?"

"It will be resolved in time. I am working closely with Stallan and we now believe a solution is close to hand. The beasts will be destroyed."

"They *must* be. The males will be safe. What happened before will never happen again."

The dark mood slowly passed as Vaintè talked to others, became involved in the vast work that was the new city. But her thoughts were never far from the hunter. When some time had passed and Stallan had not appeared she signaled to a fargi and ordered her to look for the hunter. It was close to midday before Stallan arrived and joined Vaintè in the leafy shade.

"I bring you good news, Eistaa. The beach will soon be safe."

"If that is true then the shame of the city is at an end."

"So are the alligators. We have found where they breed. I have fargi bringing all the eggs here, capturing all the young. They are delicious."

"I have eaten them and I agree. Then you will raise them with the other meat herds?"

"No, they are too vicious for that. Special pens are being built for them beside the river."

"Very good. But what are you doing with the fully grown adults?"

"The ones that are too big to trap are being killed. It is a waste of good meat, but we have no choice. Using nocturnal boats we approach them before they stir for the day, then kill them on the spot."

"Show me where they breed. I wish to see for myself." Vaintè had had enough of the ambesed. As the heat increased those around her grew torpid and dozed in the shade. But she did not want to rest; there was too much to be done.

A group of fargi followed after them as they walked slowly towards the shore. It was hot even beneath the trees and more than once they sank into the pools that had been dug for cooling purposes beside the path. Most of the swamp that they passed through had not been cleared yet. It was a tangle of heavy undergrowth and plants, foul-smelling, thick with small biting insects. It gave way at last to a sandy shore with dense brush beside it. There was tall grass and small palms, as well as strange, flattened plants each armed with immensely long needles. This land of Gendasi was a very different world from the one they knew. It was filled with an endless variety of new things to see. And to be wary of.

Ahead was the river, a slow-moving and deep stream. The boats were drawn up there and were just being fed by the attendant fargi. Blood trickled from their tiny mouths as the fargi pushed in gobbets of red meat.

"Alligator," Stallan said. "It is better than wasting it. The boats are so well fed I think they are ready to breed."

"Then starve them a bit. We need all of them in operating condition now."

A multitude of trees grew along the riverbanks, rising up in thick profusion. There were gray ones with massive trunks, while close beside them grew high green trees covered with fine needles, as well as even higher red ones with roots arching out in all directions. Between the trees the ground was blanketed with purple and pink flowers, while even more plants grew above them along the branches. Great blooms of many colors. The jungle was bursting with life. Birds cried in its darkness and red-striped snails oozed along the tree trunks.

"It is a rich land," Vaintè said.

"Entoban* must have been this way at one time." Stallan said, nostril flaps opened wide as she sniffed the air. "Before the cities spread and covered the land from one ocean to the other."

"Do you think it was really like that?" Vaintè struggled to understand this new idea. "It is a difficult concept to contain. One always thinks of the cities as having been there since the egg of time."

"I have talked with Vanalpè about this on more than one occasion. She has explained it to me. What we see here in this new land of Gendasi might very well be what you could have seen in Entoban* at one time very long ago. Before the Yilanè grew the cities."

"You are right, of course. If we grow our cities there must have been a time when there was but a single city. Which leads to the disconcerting thought that there may have been a time when there were no cities at all. Is such a thing possible?"

"I do not know. You must talk of this to Vanalpè who has mastered such head-disturbing concepts."

"You are right. I will ask her." She realized then that the fargi were pressing too close about them, their mouths gaping open as they labored to understand the conversation. Vaintè moved them back with a quick gesture.

They were approaching the alligator breeding grounds, although by this time most of the great creatures had been cleared from the banks. The survivors were wary, sinking into the water and vanishing from sight when the boats appeared. The females were the last to leave, for surprisingly enough these primitive and unintelligent beasts cared for their eggs and their young. Boats were pulled up on the shore ahead where a working party of fargi labored in the sun. They drew up their own boats beside them and Vaintè turned to the supervisor, Zhekakot, who watched from the shelter of a large tree.

"Tell me of your work," Vaintè said.

"Much progress is being made, Eistaa. Two boatloads of eggs have been sent to the city. We are netting all the young we can. They are very stupid and easy to catch."

She leaned over the pen at her side and made a quick grab, then straightened up, holding out at arm's length the baby alligator suspended by its tail. It twisted and hissed and tried to reach her with its tiny teeth.

Vaintè nodded approval. "Good, very good. A menace removed and our stomachs full. I wish all of our problems had such an agreeable solution." She turned to Stallan. "Are there other breeding grounds?"

"None between this place and the city. When we have cleared here we will work upriver and out into the swamps. It will take time, but it must be thorough."

"Good. Now we will look at the new fields before we return to the city."

"I must return to the other hunters, Eistaa. Zhekakot will be able to show you the way if that is agreeable."

"Agreeable," Vaintè said.

The air had become wonderfully stifling hot as the wind died away completely. The boats pulled out into the river and Vaintè noticed that the sky had an odd yellow color to it that she had never seen before. Even the weather was different here in this strange part of the world. As they moved back downstream the wind began to rise again—but it had changed direction and was blowing from behind them. Vaintè twisted about and saw the dark line that had appeared on the horizon. She pointed.

"Zhekakot, what is the significance of that?"

"I do not know. Clouds of some kind. I have never seen anything like it before."

The black clouds rushed towards them at unbelievable speed. One moment they had just been a smear above the trees, then they rose up, came closer, darkening the sky. And with them came the wind. It struck like a sudden fist and one of the boats, caught sideways, overturned.

There were cries, suddenly cut off, as its occupants were hurled into the choppy water. The boat dived and splashed and managed to right itself, while the Yilanè in the water swam away in all directions to avoid the boat's thrashing. None of them appeared to be injured as, with great difficulty, they were dragged from the choppy water and helped aboard the other boats. All were many years from the oceans of their youth and swam awkwardly. Vaintè shouted instructions until one of the more adventurous fargi, eager for higher status even if it meant risking injury, swam over to the still agitated boat and managed to clamber aboard. She spoke to it sharply, kicking it in a tender spot, and finally managed to get it back under control.

The wind howled viciously about them, threatening to swamp the other boats. All of the Yilanè now had their membranes drawn over their eyes and their nostril flaps closed against the driving rain. Then, audible even over the screaming wind, was the sound of a great crackling from the forest as a giant tree blew down, taking smaller ones with it.

Vaintè's voice could not be heard above the wind, but they understood her instructions to keep the boats away from the river banks lest they be crushed by any more falling trees.

The boats bobbed wildly in the breaking waves; the Yilanè huddling close together in an attempt to keep warm under the cold, driving rain. It seemed a very long time before the wind began to be gusty, then lessened a slight bit. The worst of the storm appeared to have passed.

"Back to the city!" Vaintè ordered. "As fast as possible."

The unbelievable wind had torn a track through the jungle, toppling even the largest trees. How widespread was this destruction? Had the wind struck the city? It must have. And the trees that formed the city were still young, still growing. But were they well-rooted? How much damage might have occurred! It was a terrifying thought yet one that could not be escaped. Vaintè had a terrible vision of destruction before her eyes as she kicked her boat into ever greater speed.

Stallan held the bound animal by the neck as she released the trap that secured its kicking limbs, then dropped it into the cage. So intent had she been on this operation that she did not notice the change in the weather until she straightened up. Her nostril flaps opened as she sniffed at the air. Something was familiar—and wrong. She had been with the first exploring party that had crossed the ocean to Gendasi, when they came seeking a site for the new city. When they had agreed on the shores of Alpèasak she had been one of the group that had remained behind when the uruketo had returned to Inegban*. They were armed and strong and well aware of the dangers hidden in the unexplored jungle. But it was the unknown danger that had almost destroyed them, wiping out their supplies of food and forcing them to either hunt or starve. It had been a storm of wind and rain of a ferocity they had never known before.

And it had begun in just this manner with yellow sky, the air unmoving and close. Stallan sealed the animal cage and called out "Danger!" as loud as she could. All the nearby fargi spun about at the sound, for it was one of the first words they learned.

"You, to the ambesed, you others spread out. Tell everyone. A storm with high winds is almost here. To the beaches, open fields, the water—away from the trees!"

They ran, none faster than Stallan. As the first gusts of wind hit, Yilanè by the hundreds were hurrying to safety in the open. Then the storm struck with its full fury and the driving sheets of rain hid the city from sight.

Stallan found a group of fargi huddled together on the riverbank and she pushed in among them to escape the cold rain. They stayed like that as the wind burst upon them, some of the younger ones hissing with fear until Stallan's sharp command silenced them. Stallan's authority kept them there while the storm raged about them, forcing them to wait until it had passed before she ordered them back into the city.

When Vaintè's tired boat drifted up the debris-strewn shore Stallan was there waiting for her. Long before words could be spoken she signaled that things were good. Not perfect, but good.

"Tell me of the damage," Vaintè called out as she jumped ashore.

"Two fargi dead and . . ."

Vaintè silenced her with an angry gesture. "The city, not the citizens."

"Nothing major has been reported yet. A good deal of minor damage, branches torn down, some parts of the city blown to the ground. Fargi have been sent to inspect the new fields and the herds but none have returned yet."

"Far better than I hoped. Reports will be coming to the ambesed."

The damage was obvious as they pushed their way through the city. The living roofing had blown down in many places and the walkways were strewn with the broad leaves. There was a wailing from a foodpen as they passed and Stallan saw that one of the deer had broken its leg in panic during the storm. A single dart from her ever-present hèsotsan silenced it.

"It is bad, but not as bad as it could have been," Vaintè said. "This is a strong city and growing well. Will the windstorm strike again?"

"Probably not—at least not until next year. There is wind and rain at other times, but only at this time of year does the windstorm blow."

"A year is all that we need. The damage will be repaired and

Vanalpè will see that all the growth is strengthened. This new world is cruel and hard—but we can be just as cruel and hard."

"It will be as you say, Eistaa," Stallan said, and her words were not simple agreement but were strongly colored with the knowledge that Vaintè meant exactly what she said—and would accomplish what she set out to do.

At any cost.

CHAPTER ELEVEN

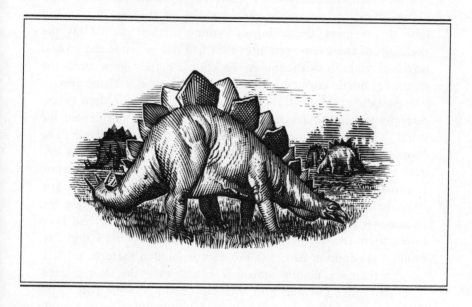

Alpèasak grew—and healed its wounds at the same time. For days Vanalpè and her assistants had clambered about the city making careful records of the damage done by the storm. Hormone applications speeded the new growth until the roofing leaves spread their overlapping patterns anew, while additional tree trunks and aerial roots strengthened the walls. But simple rebuilding was not enough for Vanalpè. Sturdy vines, tough and elastic, now twined up through the walls and across the roofing.

Not only was the city stronger, but it was growing safer with every passing day as the cleared fields bit into the surrounding jungle. This expansion, although it looked haphazard, was silent and efficient, carefully planned. The most dangerous part, the spreading of the larvae in wild jungle, was done by the Daughters of Death. Though they were protected from most of the wild creatures by armed fargi, there was no protection from bruises and accidents, wounds from the thorns—or snakebite from the serpents hidden there. Many were injured, some radically, a few died. The city was as uncaring as Vaintè at their fate. The city came first.

Once the larvae had been sown the death of the jungle was certain. The voracious caterpillars that emerged had been crafted for this single purpose. Birds and animals found their taste bitter and repellent; the caterpillars found all vegetable matter to their liking. Blind and insatiable they crawled up the tree trunks and through the grass, destroying everything in their path. Only the skeletons of trees remained after they had passed while the ground was foul with their droppings. As they ate they grew until the repulsive, bristle-covered creatures were as long as a Yilanè arm.

And then they died, for death was there waiting in their genes, carefully planted to assure that these creatures did not devour the world. They died and rotted into the bed of their own excreta. The cunning design of Vanalpè and the other gene engineers was evident even here. Nematode worms were already turning the repulsive mass into fertilized soil, aided by the bacteria in their gut. Even before the beetles had devoured the dead trees, grass had been sown and the thorn barriers planted. A new field had been eaten from the jungle, pushing it further away from the city, forming yet another barrier to the dangers hidden there.

Yet there was nothing unnatural or harsh about this slow advance. The Yilanè lived as one with their surroundings, were part of the environment and inextricably entwined with it: anything else would have been unthinkable. The fields themselves had no regularity of plan or design. Their shapes and sizes depended only upon the resistance of the foliage and the appetite of the caterpillars. The thornbushes formed a protecting barrier of varying thickness while many patches of the original jungle still remained to add variety to the landscape.

The grazing herds were just as varied. Each time the uruketo returned from Inegban* it brought fertilized eggs or newly born young. The more defenseless species were in the fields nearest the city center, the original fields where the urukub and onetsensast had grown to maturity. These armored—but placid—omnivores now grazed in mindless security at the jungle's edge, twice the size of a mammoth and still growing, their great horns and armored hides rendering them immune to all dangers.

Vaintè was pleased with the progress that had been made. When she went daily to the ambesed she went with the security that no problems would arise that she could not solve. But this morning she had a hint that all was not well when the fargi hurried up to her with a message, pushing others aside rudely to indicate the importance of the tidings she bore.

"Eistaa, the uruketo has returned. I was in a fishing boat, I saw it myself . . ."

Vaintè silenced the stupid creature with a curt signal, then signaled to her aides. "We meet them at the pier. I want the news of Inegban∗."

She walked in stately silence down the path, her friends and aides behind her, a rabble of fargi bringing up the rear. Though it was never cold in Alpèasak, there was much rain and dampness at this time of year so that she, like many of the others, walked with a cloak draped about her both for warmth and protection from the drizzling rain.

Slow dredging by the clawed paddle-feet of eisekol had deepened the river and adjoining harbor. The uruketo's cargo no longer had to be transhipped by boats, since the giant creature could now nestle up against the shore. It was just emerging from the rainswept ocean when Vaintè and her entourage arrived at the docking place. The harbor leader was directing the fargi who were putting fresh fish onto the underwater ledge to feed the uruketo. The dimwitted creature took this offering, berthing itself in the correct position to be secured to the dock. Vaintè watched the efficiency of the operation with satisfaction. A good city was an efficient city. Hers was a good city. Her eyes traveled along the immensity of the great black form, up to the fin where Erafnaiš stood directing the operation.

Next to the commander stood Malsas<.

Vaintè stood rigid at the sight because she had put the existence of the other Eistaa completely from her mind. But memory and realization gripped her now, sending a knife of pain through her sharper than any physical blade.

Malsas<, Eistaa of Inegban∗. For whom this city was being built. Who would bring her people here upon its completion and rule in Vaintè's place. Malsas<, erect and alert with the look of certain authority in her eye. She was not ill nor was she old. She would be Eistaa of Alpèasak.

Vaintè remained frozen, so her thoughts would not be revealed in her movements, as Malsas<, her followers and assistants, emerged from the uruketo and came towards her. Vaintè could only hope that formality might mask her true feelings.

"Welcome to Gendasi, Eistaa, welcome to Alpèasak," Vaintè said, pleasure at the Eistaa's presence as well as gratitude emotionally coloring her words of welcome.

"It is my pleasure to be in Alpèasak," Malsas< answered, just as formally. But the last syllable of pleasure required an opening of the mouth to reveal her teeth—and she did not close her mouth after this for long seconds. This slight indication of displeasure was warning enough for Vaintè and would not be repeated. Vaintè was respected for the work she was doing—but she could be quickly replaced. Vaintè forced all thoughts of jealousy and treachery from her mind and lowered her eyes briefly in acceptance of the warning.

This brief exchange was so subtle that it went unnoticed by the other Yilanè. Affairs at this level were not their concern. Malsas< moved the aides and fargi even further away with a motion of rejection before she spoke again, so their future conversation could not be overseen or overheard as they walked back to the city.

"Last winter was cold and this one is colder. This summer there were no youths or fargi from Soromset seeking admission to Inegban*. When the weather was warmest I sent a party of hunters to see how the city was. It was dead. Soromset does no longer exist. It died just as Ergetpe died. The leaves of the city are dead, carrion crows peck the bones of the Yilanè who lived there. On the beaches and the warm waters of the landlocked Isegenet sea the Yilanè lived in three great cities . . ."

She broke the thought off there and Vaintè finished it for her.

"Ergetpe is dead of the cold. Soromset has followed her way. Only Inegban* remains."

"Only Inegban* remains and each winter the cold draws closer. Our herds grow small and soon there will be hunger."

"Alpèasak awaits."

"Indeed it must—when the time comes. But now there is greater need to broaden the fields and increase the breeding of the animals. For our part we must breed more uruketo, but it is a slow labor that we were too late in starting. But there is hope now that the new strain will be successful. They are smaller than the creature I came in, but develop much faster. We must have enough of them to move the entire city in one summer. Now show me what they will find when they arrive in Alpèasak."

"They will find this," Vaintè said, indicating the trunks and veined walls and latticed floors of the city that stretched away on all sides of them. The rain had stopped, the sun emerged and glinted from the raindrops on the foliage. Malsas< signaled approval. Vaintè moved her arm in a circle.

"Beyond the city—the fields. Already filling with beasts of all kinds that please the eye and stomach."

Vaintè signaled armed guards to precede them as they passed through meadows of grazing animals towards the outermost fields.

Through the high-arched wall of thick trunks and thorns they could see the giant forms of the urukub eating green leaves at the jungle's edge, while even at this distance they could hear the rumbling of the large rocks in their second stomachs that ground up and aided in the digestion of the immense amounts of food they consumed. Malsas< admired the sight in silence for some time before turning away and beginning the return to the heart of the city.

"You have builded well, Vaintè," she said when their followers could hear them again. "You have all done well."

Vaintè's gesture of thankful acceptance was filled with sincerity behind the ritual movements. The acceptance and praise from the Eistaa, before all the others, was a mark of such distinction that no thoughts of jealousy or rebellion could possibly be in her head. At that moment she would have sincerely followed Malsas< to certain death. They let the others crowd close now as they walked, to listen and learn, for that was the only way to learn and remember. Only when they went through the opening in the Wall of History did their talk once again turn to darker things since the history in the wall is that of death.

Between the circle of the ambesed and the circle of the birth beaches stood the thorny Wall of History. Embedded in it were the symbolic defenses that once had meaning and importance. Could the Yilanè once have really brandished giant crabs such as the ones preserved here, held them in the ocean as weapons to defend the breeding males? It was said to be true, but not since the egg of time could it have been known to be true. The sharp nettles, the thorns themselves, these had been surely used in the past as they were used now. But what of these shells of giant scorpions? No one really knew any more—yet these ancient exoskeletons were carefully preserved and admired, had been taken with great delicacy from the wall of Inegban* and brought here as a sign of the city's continuity.

Since the wall was living history as well, in the entrance, nearest to the beaches, were woven the preserved bodies of dead hèsotsan. Next to them the fanged skulls of the attackers they had killed.

At the very end was a round-domed skull, blank-eyed and bleached by the sun. It was surrounded by spear points and sharp blades of stone. Malsas< stopped before it and indicated curiosity and need for an explanation.

"One of the ustuzou that befoul this land. All of the skulls that

you see here are from lice-ridden, fur-bearing, warm-stinking
ustuzou that have threatened us and that we have killed. But this
nameless species was the worst of all. With those sharp-edged
stones they committed the deed that is worse than all other deeds."

"They murdered the males and the children." Malsas< spoke
the words with the coldness of death itself.

"They did. We found them and killed them."

"Of course. You are no longer troubled by them?"

"No. All safely dead. This species is not local but came from
the north. We tracked and killed them, every one of them."

"Then the beaches are now secure?"

"In every way except for the coral reefs. But they grow fast
and when they are high enough there will be the first births. Then
the birth beaches will be safe in every way." Vaintè drew the claws
of one hand over the whiteness of the skull. "Safe in particular from
these infant killers.

"We shall never be bothered by them again."

CHAPTER TWELVE

The eating that afternoon was special, a formal occasion to welcome Malsas< and her staff. Events of this kind were so rare that most of the younger fargi had never watched one before; they moved about with excitement all that day talking excitedly to each other—though few were listening. This was a very new and unusual thing to them. In their day-to-day existence the Yilanè, although they enjoyed their food, looking forward with anticipation to sleeping with stomachs full, the consuming of the meat itself was a solitary act. Each would present a broad leaf to one of the meat-preparers and receive a portion of deliciously enzymed meat which they would eat in some quiet spot. This was the way food was taken and they could not imagine how it might be otherwise. Very little work was done this day as the inhabitants of the city filled the ambesed, pressed tight against its walls, climbed into the lower branches of the palisade in their eagerness to watch.

After their inspection of the city and the fields, Vaintè and Malsas< made their way to the ambesed. There Malsas< met with one after the other of those responsible for the growth of Alpèasak, spending most of the time with Vanalpè. When she was satisfied with what she had heard Malsas< dismissed them all and spoke to Vaintè.

"The warmth of the sun and the growth of this city has taken the winter from behind my eyes. I will return to Inegban＊ with this news. It will make the coming winter less cold for our citizens there. Erafnaïs reports that the uruketo has been loaded and is well-fed and ready to swim at any time. We will eat, then I will leave."

Vaintè communicated her grief at the sudden parting. Malsas< thanked her, but dismissed any thought of staying longer.

"I understand your feelings. But I have seen enough to know that the work here is in good hands. But the uruketo is slow: we must not waste a single day. Let us eat. You know Alakensi, my first advisor and efenselè. She will serve you meat at this time."

"I am honored, highly honored," Vaintè said, thinking only about the privilege of this offer, not letting her thoughts dwell at all on Alakensi whom she knew of old. A creature of devious mind and unkind plots.

"Good." Malsas< gestured Vanalpè over. "Now we will eat. Alakensi, who is closest to me in all things, will serve Vaintè meat. You, Vanalpè, for what you have done in growing this city, in designing and expanding it so well, you are chosen to serve me."

Vanalpè was as speechless as a youngster fresh from the ocean at this, radiating pride with every movement of her body.

"For this special occasion there are two meats," Vaintè said. "One from the old world, one from the new."

"Old and new shall blend in our interiors the way Inegban＊ shall blend into Alpèasak," Malsas< said.

There were cries of appreciation at this from those who stood close, for she had spoken so well and the idea was so novel that they would tell each other about it and talk about it for some time. Vaintè did not speak again until those closest had repeated what Malsas< had said so that everyone would know.

"The meat from Entoban＊ is urukub, grown from the egg brought carefully to these shores, hatched in the Gendasi sun, grown large on Gendasi herbiage. There are others, but this one is the biggest, you have all seen it when you have passed the pasture at the swamp. You have all admired the sleekness of its hide, the arched length of its neck, the full-flesh of its flanks. You have seen it."

There were murmurs of appreciation at this, for they all had seen the tiny head at the end of that long neck rising high up from the water with a great mouthful of dripping green vegetation.

"The first urukub to be slain, yet one so large that all here will eat their fill of it. Then for Malsas< and those who have traveled with her from Inegban* there will be a creature they have never eaten before, sharp-footed deer of the kind found only in this place. The eating will now begin."

The two who would serve hurried away to return with the gourds of meat, each kneeling before the Eistaa she was to serve. Malsas< reached out and took up a long bone with a tiny black hoof attached, cool sweet flesh hanging loosely from it, tore a large bite from it, then held it up so all could see.

"Urukub," she called out and all who heard her made comment on her humor. For the smallest bone in a urukub was bigger than this entire beast.

Vaintè was pleased. The eating went well. When they had finished, washing their hands in gourds of water that their servers held up to them, the ceremony was over and the others went to eat before darkness came.

With no one listening or watching for the moment Malsas< could speak in confidence to Vaintè. Her voice was soft and the motions of her limbs merely hints of movement.

"Everything said here today was more than true. Everyone has labored hard, you hardest of all. Therefore I know you can use the labors of the Daughters of Death I brought with me."

"I saw them. They will be used."

"Use them until they die!" Malsas<'s teeth clacked together loudly with the force of her expression. "There are more and more of them, like termites eating away at the base of our city. See that they do not attempt to eat this city as well."

"No possibility, not the slightest, of that happening here. I have hard and dangerous work for all of them. That is their fate."

"We are of a single mind then. Good. Now about you, work-hardened, never-weary Vaintè. What can be done to help you more?"

"Nothing, we have all that we need."

"You do not speak of personal need, but I know you can use assistance. Therefore it is my wish that the strength of my hand, first to me in everything, my efenselè Alakensi, be attached to your following. To be your first aide and share your labors."

Vaintè would not permit herself the slightest movement, the softest word, for that would have revealed the spate of instant anger that engulfed her. But she did not have to speak. Malsas< looked her directly in the eyes, and eye to eye they both understood.

Malsas< permitted herself just one little mocking gesture of victory, then turned and led her followers to the uruketo.

Had Vaintè possessed a weapon at that moment she would have sent a dart of death into that retreating back. Malsas< must have planned every moment of this even before she arrived. She had her spies in Alpèasak reporting on everything that happened here. She had known that as Eistaa here Vaintè would be reluctant to turn over power. Therefore the repulsive Alakensi had been brought here. She would sit at Vaintè's side and watch and spy— and report everything that happened. Her presence would be a constant reminder of Vaintè's certain fate. She would labor and build this city—and in the end she would be pulled down. For on that black day it would all belong to Malsas<. Now she realized what had been done; her past was laid clear by her future. From the very beginning Malsas< had had it all planned. Let Vaintè work and struggle and build the city—and in the building construct her own fate.

Unknowingly Vaintè raked her foot along the floor, her thick sharp nails tearing at the wood. *No!* It was not going to be that way. In the beginning she had just wanted to rise through her own labors, to join those that led the city. No more. Malsas< would never rule here. Alakensi would die; her appointment had been her death notice. The details were not clear—but the future was. As winter closed in on Inegban* the sun shone on Alpèasak. Weakness ruled there while strength grew here. Alpèasak was hers—and none would ever take it from her.

In her rage Vaintè left the presence of others, walked through the city by the most circuitous route where only a few fargi could see her—and upon seeing her flee from the anger that radiated from the very impact of her stride. Death was in every movement of her body.

There was a guardpost, now deserted, high above the port. Vaintè went there and stood in the lengthening shadows while the loading of the uruketo was completed. The last cargo taken into it were the limp bodies of a number of deer. Vanalpè had improved upon the toxin, normally used to stun large animals so they could be moved. The new drug did not stun—nor did it kill—but rather brought the creatures to the very brink of death. Their heartbeats could barely be detected, their breathing was immensely slowed. Treated in this manner they could cross the ocean to Inegban*, needing neither food nor water, to provide needed meat for the hungry citizens there. It was Vaintè's fervent wish, and she spoke it aloud though none could hear, that Malsas< be treated in this way. To lie dead but not-dead until the end of time.

When the uruketo left at dusk Vaintè returned silently and alone through the growing darkness and, despite the anger still possessing her, fell instantly asleep.

Sleep cleansed her mind of hatred, but in the morning it still lurked there at the edge of her thoughts. To those that saw her in the ambesed she appeared as always. But she had one glimpse of Alakensi across the ambesed and she had to turn away, rigid with hatred. Her temper was short as many discovered. It was Enge's ill luck to approach her at this time.

"I have a small request, Eistaa," she said.

"Refused. From you and your walking-dead creatures I want only work."

"You were never cruel without a reason before this," Enge said calmly. "It is my understanding that to the Eistaa all citizens are equal."

"Precisely. It is my decision that the Daughters of Death are no longer citizens. You are work animals. You will labor until you die; that is your fate." The memory surfaced, long put aside by the pressure of work, brought up now by the sight of Enge standing before her.

"The ustuzou you were teaching to talk. What of them? Time has passed, a great deal of time."

"More time is needed, that is the request that I have. More time—or no time."

"Explain yourself."

"Each morning I begin to work with the ustuzou with hope that this will be the day of comprehension. Each evening I leave them with the strong sensation that it is all a wasted labor. The female is intelligent—but is it just the intelligence of an elinou that prowls the city seeking out and killing mice? The actions look intelligent but certainly are not."

"What of the male?"

"Stupid, like all males. He will not respond, even when beaten. He just sits and stares in silence. But the female, like an elinou, responds to kindness and is pleasant to be with. But, after all this time, she can speak only a few phrases, usually wrong, and always bad. She must have learned them as a boat learns and they are surely meaningless to her."

"I am not pleased at this news," Vaintè said, nor was she. Enge could have been working in the fields all this time; her labors had been lost. The reasons for attempting to communicate with the ustuzou were no longer important. There had been no further threat from the creatures—while trouble from other sources was bad enough. But if the danger was gone the intellectual interest was still there. She voiced the question aloud.

"If the creatures cannot learn Yilanè—have you taught yourself their language?"

Enge signaled despair and doubt with a convulsive movement of her body. "That is another question I cannot answer. At first I thought of them as ambenin, speechless things that could not communicate. But now I see them as ugunin . . ."

"Impossible!" Vaintè rejected the idea completely. "How can a creature of any kind communicate but not give or receive information? You are giving me puzzles—not answers."

"I know, and I am sorry, but I see no other name for them. Their sounds and movements reveal no pattern at all, and I say this knowing I must have memorized thousands of their movements and sounds. All are meaningless. It was difficult, they are so waxy and move so little. In the end, I came to believe—as a theory only— that they must have another level of communication that will remain forever closed to us. I have no idea of what it might be. I have heard of the theory of mental radiation, one brain talking directly to another. Or radio waves perhaps. If we had a physicist in the city that might be answered."

She fell silent as Vaintè expressed despair, doubt, and disbelief.

"You never cease to amaze me, Enge. A first-class mind was lost to this city when you devoted your existence to your repellent philosophy. But now I think that your experiments and expectations are at an end. I will see your ustuzou and decide what will be done." Vaintè saw Stallan near by and signaled her to come as well.

She led the way with Enge and Stallan following after. When they approached the prison chamber Stallan hurried ahead to open the barred entrance. Vaintè pushed past her and stared down at the young ustuzou while Stallan stood ready in case they should attack. The female was squatting, but her lips were drawn back to reveal her teeth and Vaintè grew angry at what was obviously a threat. The small male stood in waxy, motionless silence against the rear wall.

Vaintè called out to Enge. "Make them do their tricks," she ordered.

When Kerrick heard the scraping of the bolt that secured the door he jumped about to place his back against the wall, sure as always that this would be the day of death. Ysel was beginning to laugh at him for it.

"Stupid boy," she said, rubbing at the scratches on her bare skull. "Still baby-afraid. The marag brings us food and plays games . . ."

"Murgu bring death and they will kill us one day."

"Stupid." She threw a fruit rind at him and turned with a smile to face the one who visited them.

It was a strange marag who entered first, stamping heavily, and her smile faded. But the other familiar one was right behind, along with the brutal one, and the smile returned. It was another day just like any other.

She was a lazy and not-too-bright little girl.

"Speak to me," Vaintè ordered, standing before the ustuzou. Then with emphasis, slowly and clearly as though adddressing a young fargi, "Speak . . . to . . . me!"

"I beg, let me try first," Enge requested with supplication. "I can get a response."

"Not any more you can't. If the creature cannot talk, that is the end of it. Too much time has been wasted." Turning back to the female ustuzou Vaintè made herself clear, absolutely and directly clear.

"This is my personal demand—and it is most urgent. You will speak now and you will speak as well as any Yileibe. If you do, you will keep on living and growing. Speech means growth—speech means life—understand?"

Ysel understood—at least she was aware of the emotion of the threat—and fear, kept at bay so very long, returned.

"I find it hard to talk, please." But the Tanu words elicited no response from the great ugly creature towering over her. She must remember what she had been taught. She tried, tried as hard as she could, making some of the movements as she spoke the words.

'has leibe ènè uu. . .''

Vaintè was baffled. "Is that talking? What is it saying? It can't mean 'The old female grows adroit'."

Enge was baffled as well. "There is possibly the meaning that growing supple puts years on females."

Even as Vaintè was attempting to understand this possible interpretation her anger welled up within her. Perhaps, on another day, she would have taken this attempt, pitiful as it was, as an indication that the ustuzou was learning to speak. But not today. Not after the insults of yesterday and the infuriating presence of Alakensi. It was too much—and after she had even attempted to be polite to the disgusting fur beast. Reaching down she seized it by both forelimbs and raised it into the air before her, shaking it and bellowing with rage at the stupid creature, ordering it to speak.

The thing didn't even make the attempt. Instead it just closed its eyes and produced water from them, threw its head back, opened its mouth wide and emitted an animal screech that hurt Vaintè's skull.

Vaintè was beyond thought, her mind filled instead with blind hatred.

She leaned forward and sank her long rows of sharp conical teeth into the ustuzou's throat, bit down hard, tearing out its life.

Hot blood spurted into her mouth and she gagged at the taste, throwing the corpse from her and harshly spitting out its blood. Stallan moved slightly, radiating silent approval.

There was a gourd of water before her face and she seized it from Enge and rinsed out her mouth, spitting and gagging, pouring the remainder over her face.

The blinding anger was gone, she could think now, and could feel as well the satisfaction in what she had done. But she was not finished. The other ustuzou remained alive—and with its death they would all be extinct. Turning swiftly she moved in front of Kerrick and glared down at him.

"Now you, the last," she said, and reached out towards him. He could not retreat. His body moved and he spoke.

". . .*esekakurud—esekvilshan. . .elel leibeleibe. . .*"

It made little sense at first and she stepped forward. Then stopped and looked more closely at the creature. There was a cower there, at least a clumsy attempt at a cower. But why was it moving from side to side like that? It made no sense. Then came realization— the thing of course had no tail so it could not do the lift correctly. But if that was really a tail lift, then it might be trying to communicate top-disgust-sensation as well as top-speech-volition. The bits and pieces were beginning to come together and in the end Vaintè cried aloud.

"Do you understand, Enge? See—it is doing it again."

Clumsily, but clearly now, clear enough to understand, the ustuzou was speaking.

"I very much don't want to die. I want very much to talk. Very long, very hard."

"You did not kill it," Enge said as they left the chamber and Stallan bolted the door behind them. "Yet you had no mercy at all for the other . . ."

"The other was worthless. You will now train this last one for it may be of use to us some day. Other packs of the creatures could be marauding out there. But you told me it never spoke?"

"Never. It must have been more intelligent than the other. It watched me all of the time, yet it never spoke."

"You are a better teacher than you know, Enge." Now sated, Vaintè was magnanimous. "Your only mistake was in teaching the wrong ustuzou."

CHAPTER THIRTEEN

Although the sky above was clear blue, fine snow was blowing fiercely up through the mountain pass. The biting north wind that tore across the mountains was picking it up from the slopes below, then sending it hurtling through the pass in great frigid waves.

Herilak struggled with its fury, almost leaning against it as he pushed the last stumbling steps through the heavy drifts. Part of his left snowshoe had broken and it slowed him down. Yet if he stopped to mend it he would be dead before he finished. So he pressed stumbling on, a large man made even bulkier by the layers of furs wrapped about him. He could feel the change in the slope now as he entered the pass, went through it, tripping and falling again and again, but rising each time to shake the snow from him, then staggering on. As he passed the rocky scarp, the gray bones of stone rising from the drifts and kept free by the wind, he felt that wind lessen. He was through. Just a few paces further on and he was out of the wind completely, shielded by the rock. He dropped down with a sigh, his back against the rough stone, for the climb had taxed even his great strength.

His outer mittens were glazed with ice and snow and he had to beat them together before they were supple enough to remove. With his warm inner glove he wiped the caked snow from his eyebrows and eyelashes and blinked down at the valley below.

It was a sheltered place where some greatdeer still wintered; he could see the dark specks of their herds further up the valley. Below him was a stand of tall trees that gave shelter to the meadow beside the stream. A stream that never froze at its source where it welled up from beneath the ground. It was a fine spot to camp and to winter, and was known as levrelag Amahast, the camping place of the sammad of Amahast. Amahast married to Aleth sister of Herilak.

But the valley below was empty.

Herilak had heard this from a hunter of his own sammad, who had met a hunter of sammad Ulfadan who swore that he had been here, and that he was speaking only the truth. Herilak knew that he had to see for himself. He had taken his spear and his bow and his arrows, rubbed his body thickly with goose grease, then put on the soft furs of the beaver with the fur against his body, then the suit of coarse fur of the greatdeer over that. With the snowshoes lashed to the heavy fur boots he was ready for the winter. He traveled light for he must travel fast, and the bag over his shoulder held little more than a supply of dried meat and some of the mashed nuts and berries of ekkotaz.

Now he had found that which he sought and he was very displeased. He sucked a mouthful of snow as he bent to repair the snowshoe. Every once in awhile he would look up from the work to the empty valley below, as though to remind himself of the unpleasant truth. It remained empty.

It was midday before he was finished. He chewed on some dried meat while he pondered on what to do next. He had no choice. When he had finished eating he climbed to his feet, a big man who stood a head taller than even the tallest in his sammad, rubbing grease from his flowing beard and looking down the valley in the direction he must go. South. He started that way, along the slope, and once he began walking he never looked back once at the empty camping place.

All that day he walked and only stopped when the first stars began to sparkle in the darkness. He rolled himself in his furs and stared up at the night sky before closing his eyes to sleep. But he had a thought then and opened them again and searched among the familiar patterns. The Mastodon charging at the Hunter who held his spear ready. The bent row of stars in the Hunter's belt. Was there a new one there, next to the center star? Not as bright as the others, but just as clear in the cold transparency of the winter sky. He could not be sure. It would have to be the tharm of a strong warrior to be in that honored place, adding strength to the Hunter. He was not certain if it had been there before. While he thought about it he closed his eyes again and slept.

On the afternoon of the third day, three days of marching from first light to early darkness, Herilak came through the trees beside a fast-flowing river, the current so swift that it still had an open channel in its center. He went quietly as a hunter always does, once surprising a small herd of deer, sending them jumping away between the trees, bounding high with sprays of snow flying about them. One at least would have been easy prey—but he was not hunting now. Not for deer. Pushing through a thicket he stopped suddenly, then bent to look at the ground. At the gut rabbit snare strung between two boughs.

After that he chanted as he went and let his spear rattle against the low branches that he passed. This was a new thing that had started with the frozen winters. In none of the stories that the old ones told was there any mention of the need. There was the need now. Tanu had killed Tanu. The world was not the free place it once had been, where hunters did not fear hunters.

In a short time he could feel beneath his feet a path that had been trampled into the snow. When he came to the next clearing in the forest he stopped, plunged his spear into a drift like a standard and squatted on his haunches beside it. He did not have long to wait.

Silent as wreath of smoke a hunter appeared on the other side of the clearing. His spear was ready, but he lowered it when he saw Herilak's sitting figure. Herilak climbed slowly to his feet as the other hunter also stabbed his spear into the snow and started forward. They met in the center of the clearing.

"I am here on your hunting grounds but I do not hunt," Herilak said. "This is where the sammad of Ulfadan hunt. You are the sammadar."

Ulfadan nodded agreement. Like his name, his blond beard was long, reaching almost to his waist. "You are Herilak," he said. "My niece is married to Alkos of your sammad." He chewed over the relationship, then pointed back over his shoulder with his hand.

"We will take our spears and we will go to my tent. It is warmer than the snow."

They walked side by side in silence for it is not a hunter's way to chatter like a bird when on the trail. The river moved swiftly at their side as they followed the path along its frozen bank. They came to the place where the river swung out and back in a slow curve and in the curve was the winter camp of the sammad, twelve large and sturdy tents. In the meadow beyond the tents the mastodons dug into the snow with their tusks, their breaths rising up in drifts of vapor, to reach the dry grass hidden below. From each tent a thin plume of smoke also rose into the cloudless sky. There were shouts as children ran between the tents playing some game. It was a peaceful scene well familiar to Herilak; it could have been his own sammad. Ulfadan pulled the hide flap aside and led the way into the darkness of his tent.

They sat in silence while the old woman poured melted snow, from the bark pail beside the fire, into wooden mugs, adding dried herbs to make a savory drink. The two hunters warmed their hands on the mugs and sipped at the brew while the women chattered to each other as they wrapped themselves in skins and slipped out of the tent one by one.

"You will eat," Ulfadan said when they were alone.

"The hospitality of Ulfadan is talked about in the tents of the Tanu from the sea to the mountains."

The formal words did not quite match the generosity of the portion, a few flakes of dried fish smelling very strongly of age. The winter was long and spring far distant yet. There would be hunger in the tents before it came.

Herilak drained the last drops of liquid with noisy appreciation, and even managed to summon up a belch to show how rich the meal had been. He knew that he should now talk about hunting, the weather, the migrating herds, and only much later reach the point of his visit. But this slow and time-consuming custom was changing as well.

"The mother of the wife of my first son is the wife of Amahast," Herilak said. Ulfadan nodded in agreement, for this fact was known to him. All of the sammads in these mountain valleys were linked by marriage in one way or another. "I have been to the camping place of Amahast's sammad and the place is empty." Ulfadan nodded at this as well.

"They went south last spring, their path always taking them

down this valley. It was seen that half of their mastodons had died. It was a bad winter."

"It is known that now it is always a bad winter."

Ulfadan grunted in unhappy agreement. "They did not return after that."

Herilak turned the thought over in his head, tracing in his mind the trail down through the valleys to the flatlands, then eastward to the sea. "They went then to the sea?"

"Each year now they go the encampment by the river at the sea."

"But this year they did not return."

There was no answer to that other than silent agreement. Something had happened that they did not know about. Perhaps the sammad had found a different winter camp; more than one sammad had been destroyed by cold and their encampments were empty. There was that possibility. There was the greater possibility that something far worse had happened about which they knew nothing.

"The days are short," Herilak said, climbing to his feet. "And the way is long."

Ulfadan rose as well and seized the big hunter's arms in his hands in a gesture of appreciation. "It is a long and lonely way to the sea in winter. May Ermanpadar guide your path all of the way."

There was nothing more to be said. Herilak pulled his furs tight about him again and once more pointed his spear to the south. It was only after he had reached the plains that he went faster, for the snow here was frozen and hard. Winter was his only enemy now for the ice-bound land was empty of life. Only once in his many days of walking did he see a greatdeer, and this was a thin and wretched creature pursued by a small pack of starving longtooths. He saw them moving across the plain in his direction. There was a low rise here with a stand of leafless trees upon it and Herilak stopped beside them to watch.

The wretched greatdeer was weakening, its flanks torn and dripping with blood. It stumbled to a halt when it reached the slope, too winded to run any further, and turned at bay. The starving longtooths came in from all sides, heedless of danger with the smell of warm blood in their nostrils. One of them was caught by the dagger-pointed horns and tossed aside. But this was the opportunity the leader needed to spring in and hamstring the greatdeer, tearing at its hindlegs. Bellowing, the creature fell and the end was upon it. The leader, a great black creature with a thick ruff of hair about its throat and chest, drew back as though to let the others eat first. There would be enough for all.

When it moved aside it became aware for the first time of watching eyes. With wild instinct it knew it was being observed. It rose growling and looked straight up the hill at Herilak, its gaze meeting his. Then it crouched and moved in his direction, halfway up the hill, coming so close that Herilak could look into the unblinking yellow of its eyes.

Herilak's gaze was just as unswerving. He did not move nor point his spear, but in his silence he communicated an unspoken message. They would go their way, he would go his. If he were attacked he would kill; the longtooth knew what spears could do. The yellow eyes watched steadily and the creature must have understood because it turned suddenly and went back down the hill. Now it would feed, and the others made way for it. But before it sank its muzzle into the warm flesh it glanced back up the hill. Nothing waited under the trees. The spear-animal was gone. It lowered its head and ate.

A blizzard trapped Herilak inside his furs for two whole days. He slept most of the time, trying not to eat too much of his dwindling store of food. But it was eat or die from the cold. When the storm finally lifted he went on. Later that same day he had the good fortune to find the recent tracks of a rabbit. He pushed his spear under the strap across his back and notched an arrow into his bow. That night he feasted on fresh meat by his fire. Ate his fill and more again, staying up late, nodding half asleep as he roasted the remainder over the blaze.

There was less snow on the ground this far south, but the midwinter frost was just as hard. The frozen grass of the riverbank crackled underfoot. He paused when he heard something, cupped his ear and listened closely. Yes, the distant whisper was there. The sound of surf, waves beating upon a beach. The sea.

The grass did not crackle now as he went forward, spear ready, eyes that saw everything. Ready to face any danger.

But the danger had long since gone. Under a gray winter sky he came upon the meadow with the bones of the mastodons resting there. A cold wind, cold as death, sighed through the high-arched ribs. The carrion scavengers had done their work, then the crows and sea birds had followed and feasted well. It was there, just beyond the mastodons, that he found the first of the Tanu skeletons.

His jaw clenched hard, his eyes narrowed to slits as he realized that more and more skeletons littered the river bank. It was a slaughtering yard, a place of death.

What had happened here? Dead, all dead, an entire sammad, that was clear from the beginning. Skeletons of adults and children lay where they had dropped. But what had killed them? What enemy had fallen upon them and had butchered them? Another sammad? Impossible, for they would have taken weapons and tents, would have driven off the mastodons, not just killed them along with their owners. The tents were still there, most of them wrapped and loaded onto the travois that lay beside the mastodons' skeletons. This sammad had broken its summer camp, had been leaving when death had sprung upon them. Herilak searched further, and it was in among the bones of the largest skeleton that he saw a glint of metal. He lifted the bones aside with respect and took up the red-rusted form of a skymetal knife. He brushed away the rust and looked at the patterns on the metal, patterns that he knew so well. His spear fell to the frozen ground as he held the knife with both hands, thrust it up into the sky and howled with grief. Tears filled his eyes as he bellowed aloud his pain and anger.

Amahast, dead. The husband of his sister, dead. Their children, the women, the tall hunters. Dead, all of them, dead. The sammad of Amahast was no more.

Herilak shook the tears from his eyes, growling with rage as hot anger burned away the sorrow. Now he must find the killers. Bent low he traced his way backwards and forwards, searching for what he did not know. But searching carefully and closely as only a hunter can. Darkness stopped him and he lay down for the night beside the bones of Amahast and searched for Amahast's tharm among the stars. He would be there, that was certain, one of the brighter stars.

Next morning he found that which he was searching for. At first it appeared to be just another strip of torn leather, one among many. But when he pulled away the frozen black fragments he saw that there were bones inside. Carefully, so as not to disturb them to any greater degree, he picked away at the leathery hide. Long before he was finished it was obvious what he had found, nevertheless he continued until all of the tiny bones were uncovered.

A long, thin creature, with tiny and unusable legs. Many ribs, far too many ribs, and more bones in the spine than seemed possible.

A marag of some kind, there was no mistake, for he had seen their kind before. It did not belong here, no murgu could live this far away from the hot south.

South? Did that have a meaning? Herilak stood and looked west, where he had come from. No murgu there, that was impossible. He turned slowly to face the north and could see inside his head the cold ice and snow stretching away forever. The Paramutan lived there, very much like the Tanu although they spoke in a different manner. But there were very few of them, they rarely came south, and they fought against winter only, not Tanu or each other. East, out into the ocean—there was nothing there.

But south, from the hot south, murgu could come. They could bring death and leave again. South.

Herilak knelt in the frozen sand and studied the marag skeleton carefully, memorized all the details of it until he could have scratched its likeness in the sand and would remember forever every single bone of it.

Then he stood and ground its brittle fragments underfoot. Turned about and without once looking back started on the return trail.

CHAPTER FOURTEEN

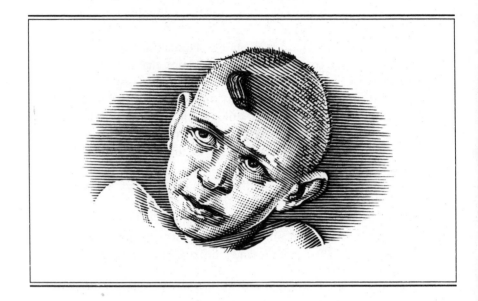

Kerrick never realized that it was age alone that had saved his life. Not that Vaintè had spared him because he was so young; she felt the most intense disgust for ustuzou of any age and would happily see them all dead. Ysel had been too old to respond naturally to a new language, particularly one as complex in construction as Yilanè. For her Marbak was the only way to speak and she used to laugh with the women when hunters from the Ice Mountains visited their tents and spoke so badly they could barely be understood. To her this was just stupidity, any intelligent one of the Tanu would of course speak Marbak. Therefore she had showed no interest in learning Yilanè, and was satisfied to memorize by rote some of the funny sounds just to please the marag and get food from it. Sometimes she even remembered to make body movements with her words. It was all just a stupid game—and she had died for believing that.

Kerrick never thought about language as a separate entity: he just wanted to understand and respond. He was still young enough to learn a language without conscious effort, by listening and watching. If he had had any idea that there were thousands of conceptual areas in the Yilanè language—that could be combined in over 125 billion ways—he would just have shrugged. The numbers were meaningless, particularly since he could not count nor visualize any number larger than twenty, the count of a man. What he learned he had learned without conscious effort. But now, as the lessons progressed, Enge did draw his attention to certain statements, ways of interpreting things, and made him repeat sloppy movements until he did them correctly.

Because of his inability to change areas of skin color he was learning what was referred to as graylight talk. In heavy jungle, or at dawn and dusk when there was very little light, the Yilanè communicated without color patterns, rephrasing expressions so that color was not necessary.

Each morning of their imprisonment he had expected death when the door had opened. He remembered the slaughter of the sammad far too well, the extinction of everything living, men, women, children—even the mastodons. He and Ysel would be killed one day as well; there was no alternative. When the ugly marag had brought food instead of death in the morning he knew that their slaughter had just been put off for one more day. After that he would watch in silence, trying not to laugh, as stupid Ysel made nothing but mistakes, day after day. But he had a hunter's pride. He would not help her or the marag, would not answer when he was talked to, and he tried to accept the blows that followed in silence as a hunter should. After many days had passed he discovered that he could understand some of the things that Enge said when she spoke to the other marag that he hated the most, the one who beat him and tied him up. Keeping silent became more important after this, for it kept secret his knowledge; a small fragment of success where before there had only been total disaster.

And then Vaintè had killed the girl. He felt no remorse about that because she had been stupid and deserved to join the rest of the sammad. Only when Vaintè had seized him, the blood of murder still fresh on her jaw, only then had the hunter's strength failed. He had only hunted once, had not been accepted as a hunter, that was what he told himself later, trying to explain away his failure to accept death from those sharp and terrible teeth. In all truth he had been just as frightened then as he had been when his spear drew the marag from the water. He had spoken out of dreadful fear, scarcely aware of what he was doing, and had spoken well enough to save his life.

Kerrick still knew that he would die some day, when the murgu had had enough of him. But that day was in the future and now, for the first time, he permitted himself a tiny bit of hope. Each day he could understand more and speak better. And he still had not been out of this room since the moment they had been brought here. Some day he would be let out of it, unless they intended him to spend his remaining days locked away, and on that day he would run. The murgu waddled, they did not walk, and he was sure he could run faster than they could—if they could run at all. This was his secret hope and because of it he did what he was asked and hoped that his rebelliousness had been forgotten.

Each day began the same way. Stallan would open the door and stamp in. Kerrick would carefully control his loathing of the violent creature. Even though he no longer fought back the hunter would still hurl him to the floor and kneel painfully on his back as it put the living shackles on his ankles and wrists. Stallan would then rub a string-blade over his head to remove the stubble of hair, usually cutting his skin at the same time. Enge would arrive later with the fruit and the gellid meat that he had finally forced himself to eat. Meat meant strength. Kerrick never spoke to Stallan, unless the creature struck him and demanded an answer, which was very rare. Kerrick knew better than to expect any compassion from this ugly, hoarse-voiced creature.

But Enge was a different matter altogether. With a boy's sharp eyes he watched closely and saw that Enge reacted differently from the other murgu. For one thing she had expressed pain and sorrow when the girl had been killed. Stallan had enjoyed it greatly and had applauded the action. Once in a great while Enge would arrive with Stallan. Kerrick's speaking improved and when he was sure he could say exactly what he wanted, he began to watch patiently each day as the door opened. When Stallan entered alone he forgot the matter completely until the following morning.

This went on until the morning when Enge entered as well. Kerrick said nothing, but he stiffened his body so that Stallan was more brutal than usual in handling him. As his arms were pulled out before him and the cool shackle was being slapped into place he spoke.

"Why do you hurt me and bind me? I cannot hurt you."

Stallan's only answer was a gesture of disgust and a blow across the head. Out of the corner of his eyes he saw that Enge was listening.

"It is hard to talk when I am bound," he said.

"Stallan," Enge said, "what the creature says is true."

"It attacked you, have you forgotten that?"

"No, but that was when we first brought it in. And you will remember it bit me only when it thought I was hurting the female." She turned to Kerrick. "Will you try to injure me again?"

"Never. You are my teacher. I know if I speak well you will reward me with food and not hurt me."

"I marvel that an ustuzou can talk—but it is still a wild creature and must be secured." Stallan was adamant. "Vaintè put it in my charge and I will obey my orders."

"Obey them, but bend them a slight amount. Free its legs at least. It will make talking easier."

In the end Stallan reluctantly agreed and that day Kerrick worked especially hard, knowing that his secret plan had moved ahead just that single step.

There was no way to count the days, nor did Kerrick particularly care how much time had passed. When he had been in the north, with his sammad, winter and summer had been markedly different and it had been important to know the time of year for the hunting. But here, in the endless heat, the passage of time did not matter. Sometimes rain would drum on the transparent skin above the room, while at other times it would be darkened by clouds. Kerrick knew only that a long time had passed since Ysel's death, when there was an interruption to their daily lesson. The rattle of the outside lock drew the attention of both of them so that they turned to look when the door swung open. Kerrick welcomed the novel event until Vaintè entered.

Although the murgu were very similiar one to the other he had learned to notice differences. And Vaintè was one creature whom he would never forget. He automatically signaled submission and respect as she stamped across the floor towards them, was pleased to see that she was in a good mood as well.

"You have done well in your animal-training, Enge. There are stupid fargi out there that do not respond as clearly or as quickly as this one. Make it speak again."

"You may converse with it yourself."

"Can I? I don't believe it. Why it is like giving instructions to a boat and having it answer you back." She turned to Kerrick and said clearly. "Go left, boat, go left."

"I am not a boat, but I can go left."

He walked slowly about the room while Vaintè expressed disbelief and pleasure in equal portions.

"Stand before me. Tell me the name you have been given."

"Kerrick."

"That means nothing. You are a ustuzou so you cannot say it correctly. It must be said this way, Ekerik."

Vaintè could not realize that it was the sounds alone that made up his name. She added the physical modifiers so that in its entirety it signified slow-stupid. Kerrick could not have cared less.

"Ekerik," he said, then again with the modifiers, "Slow-stupid."

"I could almost be talking to a fargi," Vaintè said. "But see how unclearly it says Slow-stupid."

"It can do no better," Enge explained. "Having no tail it cannot complete the motion correctly. But see, it has taught itself that twisting motion which is as close as it can come."

"I will have need of the creature soon. The uruketo has brought Zhekak from Inegban* to work with Vanalpè. She is vain and she is fat—but she has the best scientific brain in Entoban*. She must stay here for we need her help. I wish to please her in every way. You must see that this ustuzou attracts her attention. The sight of a talking ustuzou will be a success I wish to achieve."

Kerrick expressed only respectful attention as she turned to him. Unlike the Yilanè where to think a thought was to express it—he could lie very well. Vaintè looked him up and down coldly.

"It looks filthy, it must be washed."

"It is washed daily. That is its natural color."

"Disgusting. As is the creature's penis. Can't it be forced to withdraw it into its pouch?"

"It has no pouch."

"Then have one made and attach it. The same color as the creature's flesh so it will not be noticed. And why is its skull scratched like that?"

"The fur is cut off daily. You ordered it."

"Of course I did—but I didn't order the ugly thing to be butchered as well. Talk to Vanalpè. Tell her to find a better way of defurring it. Do this at once."

Kerrick just expressed humble thanks and amplified respect when they left. Not until they were gone and the door was sealed did he permit himself to straighten up and laugh out loud. It was a very hard world, but at the age of nine he was learning to survive in it very well.

Vanalpè came that same day, shown in by Stallan, and followed by her usual train of assistants and eager fargi. There were too many of them to fit into the small chamber and Vanalpè made all of them, other than her first assistant, wait outside. The assistant put the bundles and containers on the floor while Vanalpè walked around Kerrick examining him closely.

"I've never seen a live one before," she said. "But I know the creature well. I did the dissection on the other."

She was behind Kerrick's back when she said this so he did not hear it all. Which was just as well since the Yilanè expression for dissection was the very literal *cutting-dead-meat-apart-to-learn*.

"Tell me, Stallan, can it really speak?"

"It is an animal." Stallan did not share the general interest in the ustuzou and wanted it dead. But she obeyed orders and did it no injury.

"Speak!" Vanalpè ordered.

"What do you want me to say?"

"Wonderful," Vanalpè said and instantly lost all interest. "What have you been using to remove the fur?"

"A string-knife."

"Very messy. You've butchered the animal. Those things are better for cutting meat. Bring me the unutakh," she ordered her assistant.

The brown, slug-like creature was shaken out of the container onto the palm of Vanalpè's hand. "I use it for preparing specimens. It digests the fur but not the hide. But only on dead specimens so far. Let us see how it works on a live one."

Stallan hurled Kerrick to the floor and leaned on him as Vanalpè pried the rolled-up unutakh open and placed it on his skull. He shivered away from the cold, slimy touch and the Yilanè expressed amusement at the sight. It crawled damply across his skin.

"Very good," Vanalpè announced. "Flesh unharmed, fur removed. Now for the next problem. The creature certainly needs a pouch. I have this tanned hide, almost a perfect color match. Just a matter of fitting it into place and trimming it. I've lined it with modified bandages to adhere to the skin. Good. Stand it up now."

Kerrick was close to tears at the rough and insulting handling but he forced them back. Murgu would not see him cry. The cold slug still crawled across his scalp and was now over one eye. When it moved away he glanced down at the small breechclout that they were fitting into place. It was no bother to him. He forgot about it as the slug went slowly across the lashes of his other eye.

It would be many years before he would learn that the covering pouch was made from the preserved and well-tanned skin of Ysel, the girl who had been murdered before his eyes.

CHAPTER FIFTEEN

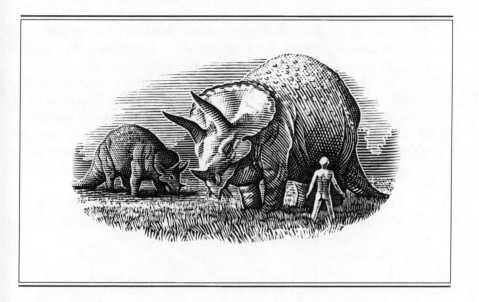

"I have thought about your status for a long time," Enge said. "I have reached the inescapable conclusion that you are the lowest of the lowest."

"I am the lowest of the lowest," Kerrick agreed, trying to concentrate on her speech and ignore the unutakh crawling damply over his skull. This was only the third day that it had cleansed his body of hair and he still found it repulsive. As soon as it was finished he looked forward eagerly to washing off its slimy tracks. He also had a growing respect for the small creature. When he had pried it off the previous morning it had adhered to his finger and consumed most of one fingernail. It was crawling to the back of his head now and he could wipe his browless and lashless eyes clean with the back of his hand.

"Are you giving me all of your attention?" Enge asked.

"All. I am the lowest of the low."

"But you don't speak that way. You have never learned to do it correctly. Now you must. Say it this way. Lowest of the low."

Kerrick noted her bent posture, tail tucked under, and did his best to imitate it.

"Better. You must practice. Because you will soon be in the

company of those who are highest here and they will not take insults of language."

"How do you know that I am lowest of the low?" Kerrick said, phrasing it as a question asked by one of low mentality—when in reality he was getting both bored and annoyed by their talk.

"Vaintè is the Eistaa and rules here in Alpèasak. She is the highest. Beneath her and infinitely above you and I are Stallan and Vanalpè and others who order the city. They have their aides and of course the fargi who train in their service. Even though you now speak better than many fargi you must still be lower than they are for they are Yilanè and you are merely ustuzou, a talking animal but still an animal."

Kerrick cared nothing for the structure of their complicated relationships of rank and privilege. He was just curious about the word he had never heard before.

"What are fargi?"

"They are, well, just fargi."

As soon as she had said it Enge realized the emptiness of the statement. She sat rigid and unmoving for a long time as she struggled for a definition. It was difficult to express clearly since, like any accepted fact of life, one took it for granted and never questioned the fact's existence. *It was like asking What is the sun?* It is the sun. Its existence defines it. She knew that physicists could tell her many facts about the sun, far more than she might ever wish to know. But if she were to train this ustuzou to appear in public it had to know all the commonplace things that others knew. Including, apparently, what a fargi was. To explain she must begin at the beginning.

"When the young leave the birth beaches they enter the sea. They live in the ocean for many years, growing and maturing. It is a happy time because fish are easy to catch and dangers are few. All those who enter the ocean at the same time belong to the same efenburu. They are efenselè to each other and form a bond that lasts a lifetime. Eventually they mature and emerge from the ocean to live on land. The males are rounded up and brought to the city since they are too stupid to fend for themselves. This is a very hard time for every one must find her own way into life. Food is plentiful but so are dangers. Life is in the cities and the young go there. They listen and learn, and those that learn to speak become part of the city at the lowest level. They are fargi. You are lower than they are."

"I can understand that, but I do not understand about the males. The fargi are females?"

"Of course."

"But you are male—"

"Do not be insulting. You have never seen a male since they are carefully protected in the hanalè."

Kerrick was stunned by this information. Female—all the murgu were female! Even the repellent Stallan. Indeed, everything about the murgu did not make sense. All Tanu could talk, even young ones. These murgu must be stupid. "What happens to those who do not learn how to speak?" he asked.

"That is no concern of yours. Just remember that even to the lowest fargi, one who is yileibe, that is speaking with utmost difficulty, you are lower."

"I am the lowest of the low," Kerrick agreed and tried not to yawn.

A short time later their lesson was interrupted by the unbolting of the door. Kerrick smoothed his features to hide the intense loathing he always felt when Stallan came in. She was carrying a sealed container.

"The time is now," Stallan said. "Vaintè wishes the presence of the ustuzou. I have brought this to restrain the creature."

Kerrick made no protests when Vaintè removed the unutakh, then scrubbed him from head to toe with water. She seemed displeased with the manacle creature that held his wrists and replaced it with a fresh one. From the container she then produced a long, dark length that writhed slowly when she held it by one end.

"We want no trouble from this ustuzou," Stallan said, pulling Kerrick over and looping the creature about his neck, then clamping its mouth onto its own body to make a secure loop. She held tight to the other end. "Tell it to follow you," she told Enge, still refusing to accept the fact that Kerrick was anything more than a trained animal. They were matched and equal in their hatred of one for the other.

Kerrick did not care; for the first time since he had been captured he would see what lay beyond the door. He had only vague memories of pain, forest and trees when he had first been brought here. Now he was alert and ready, and trying hard to appear docile and manageable. Enge threw the door wide and he followed her, his hands shackled before him, Stallan walking behind holding tight to his leash.

A dimly-lit green tunnel stretched away before them. It had woven flooring like his prison chamber, but the walls were more insubstantial. They were made of growths of many kinds, thin and thick tree trunks, climbing vines, flowering shrubs as well as many strange plants that were unknown to him. Overlapping leaves made a covering above. There were corridors leading off this one, where he had quick glimpses of moving figures, then they emerged into a sunlit opening. He had to squint against the glare after his long imprisonment. The light hurt, but he looked anyway with watering eyes, taking in everything.

Was this all there was to Alpèasak? he thought. When Enge talked about it he had a picture in his mind of a giant encampment with countless tents stretching as far as the eye could see. He should have known that murgu knew nothing about a real camp. Yet this jumble of corridors and trees was indeed very large. And wherever he looked there were murgu. Too many of them all at once; it was like falling into a pit of them. His skin crawled as they crowded around, pushing each other to see the ustuzou, then following after when he had passed. They were stupid too, a lot of them could barely talk. These must be the fargi he had been told about.

The corridor ended suddenly in an open area, far bigger than the ones they had crossed before. Kerrick's eyes were getting used to the light now and could see the groups of Yilanè all about the open space. Stallan called out a sharp command and the fargi moved aside leaving an open path for them. Across the hardpacked soil they went to the far wall where a small group stood. Two of them were very important, because even at this distance the crouching attitude of those in attendance was obvious. As they came closer Kerrick recognized Vaintè; that was one he would never forget. Beside the Eistaa squatted a very fat Yilanè, her skin drawn tight as though ready to burst. Vaintè signaled them to stop and turned to the fat one at her side.

"There you see it, Zhekak, one of the ustuzou who committed the crimes of which you know."

"Pull it closer," Zhekak ordered in a thin voice, the fat muffling the motions of its limbs. "It does not look too dangerous."

"This is still a young one. The mature ones are gigantic."

"Interesting. Let me see its dentition."

While Kerrick was still puzzling out the meaning of the new

phrase, Stallan seized him by the head and pried his jaws open, dragging him forward so Zhekak could see into his mouth. Zhekak was intrigued by the sight.

"Very similar to the preserved specimens that Vanalpè has. There is much to study here, much of interest. I see the day when Alpèasak will lead all of the other cities in their knowledge of ustuzou and their uses."

Vaintè was radiating pleasure. "There is something else about this creature that you should know. It talks."

Zhekak fell back expressing disbelief, wonder, incredulity and respect, her gross body writhing with the effort of saying this all at the same time.

"Demonstrate," Vaintè ordered.

Stallan tugged Kerrick closer and Enge stood to one side where he could see her. "Speak your name to those of great rank before you," she said.

"I am Kerrick, lowest of the low."

Zhekak was overly generous in her appreciation. "A wonderful bit of training. I have never seen a beast that could speak its name before."

"There is more to it than that," Enge said with respectful addition—not correction. "It can talk just as though it were Yilanè. You may converse with it if you so wish."

Zhekak's delight, incredulity, and disbelief were very great. When she was finished she leaned forward and spoke very slowly and very clearly.

"I find this hard to believe. You cannot really talk."

"I can. I can speak very fast and very clearly."

"You've been trained to say that."

"No. I learned as a fargi learns."

"In the ocean?"

"No. I cannot swim. I learned to speak by listening to Enge."

Zhekak did not look towards Enge and her speech was full of contempt. "That is very good. Kind words spoken of one who caused so much difficulty in distant lovely Inegban∗. It is only fitting that a crude beast like this speaks well of a Daughter of Death." She turned to Vaintè. "You are to be congratulated in that you have made something out of nothing, a city out of jungle, a speaker out of an ustuzou, a teacher out of a deathless one. Surely the future of Alpèasak will be always warm."

Vainte dismissed Enge and Kerrick with a gesture as she spoke to Zhekak. "I will remember those words always. A new world means new things and we are doing our best. And now—will you take meat? We have some new varieties here that you would never have tasted."

Zhekak clacked her jaw in loud appreciation. "That is what I was told and that is what I intend to discover for myself."

Fat murgu, eat and explode. Those were Kerrick's thoughts, but no hint of this was reflected in his submissive stance.

"Return it to its place," Vainte said, dismissing them as well. Stallan tugged on the leash and pulled Kerrick along behind her. Kerrick stumbled, almost fell, but made no complaint. They left the great open space and returned to the green tunnels of the city. Enge turned into a different tunnel and Kerrick glanced carefully around. When there were very few others in sight, none of them close by, Kerrick called out in pain.

"Help me. Such pain. This thing on my neck . . . I'm choking."

Stallan turned about and cuffed Kerrick on the side of the head for disturbing her. But she knew that they wanted this animal kept alive. The leash would have to be loosened. She dropped the free end and reached for the animal's head.

Kerrick turned and ran, scarcely hearing the roar of rage that bellowed after him.

Run, boy, run, fast as your legs can carry you, faster than any murgu. There were two of them ahead, uncomprehending fargi.

"Move aside!" he ordered—and they did!

Stupid, stupid creatures. The leash was flapping over his shoulder and he raised his hands and gathered it up so it wouldn't impede him. As he ran through one of the open spaces he glanced over his shoulder and saw that Stallan was far behind him. He was right, these creatures could not run.

He slowed a bit then, ran easier, ran free. He could run this way all day. The breath came strongly to his lungs, his feet slammed down on the matting as he fled for his life.

He could not be stopped. When he saw groups of murgu ahead he took a different way. The fargi moved aside when he ordered them to. One marag did not move, tried to grab at him instead, but he dodged the clumsy effort and ran on. When he found himself alone at last in a leaf-shrouded chamber he paused for breath—and to plan.

The city was all around him yet. The sun filtered down through the leaves and he blinked up at it. Late afternoon, the sea would be behind him, the land ahead in the direction of the setting sun. That was where he must go.

City blended into fields without any sharp distinction. He trotted briskly now, running only when he was noticed. The first difficulty to be overcome was a thick hedge filled with long thorns. His heart leapt. If he were found here he was trapped. He ran swiftly along it, searching for an opening, aware that two of the murgu had seen him and were calling after him. Yes, there it was, stout vines that looped back and forth across the gap. There must be a way of opening them, but he did not bother to search for it. Instead he dropped flat and wriggled under the lowest strand. A herd of small deer looked at him, then fled in panic through the tall grass. He followed them, kept straight on when they veered aside at the next fence. Now that he knew what to look for the vine-covered opening was easy to see. This time when he dropped flat to slide under it, he looked back and he saw that a group of murgu were at the far side of the field, just starting to open the last gate that he had slipped under. They would never catch him now!

Then he came to the final field. It had to be the last because the high green wall of the jungle was just beyond. He had already passed small bits of jungle, but these had been surrounded by the fences and fields. The jungle beyond this fence was unending, dark and frightening. But whatever dangers it held were nothing compared to those of the city he was leaving behind. He slipped under the vines into the field and stood up—and saw the great creatures that were looking at him.

Fear seized him and shook him savagely so he could not move. Big they were, bigger than mammoths, murgu from his worst nightmare. Gray, wrinkled, with legs like tree trunks, great shields of bones rising up and up, horns on their noses pointing directly at him. Kerrick's heart beat so loudly in his chest that he thought it would burst.

Only then did he notice they were not moving towards him. Tiny eyes in wrinkled sockets stared down and scarcely saw him. The ponderous heads lowered and the sharp jaws tore at the grass. Slowly, a step at a time, he walked around them, towards the partly grown fence that was still filled with large gaps that opened out onto the dark of the forest.

Free! He had escaped! He brushed some hanging vines aside and stepped onto the cool loam of the jungle floor. Brushed the sticking vines aside, and once again.

Then he discovered that they had adhered to his arms, were slowly tightening themselves about him.

They weren't vines at all but living traps. He tore at them, tried to bite them, but to no avail. He had been close, so very close. As he spun about in their cool embrace he saw the murgu coming after him through the field. So close.

He turned again to the forest, hanging limply, fighting no longer, scarcely able to react when the two-thumbed hands seized him cruelly. Looking up at the trees and freedom. At the flash of movement of some animal there.

The leaves above parted for an instant and he saw a bearded face. It was gone as quickly as it had come. Then he was being dragged back into captivity.

CHAPTER SIXTEEN

Vaintè leaned back comfortably on her resting wood, deep in thought, her body fixed and motionless. Her aides surrounded her and talked quietly among themselves, they in turn being encircled by the ever-attendant fargi. Vaintè was in the midst of an island of silence, for none would dare to disturb the Eistaa's immobile state. Her thoughts were the force that drove the city.

But her only thought at the moment was one of extreme hatred; her immobility served only to hide that fact and represented no matters of great cogitation. She rested in complete stasis—except for her right eye which moved slowly, following the three retreating backs. Vanalpè, her irreplaceable aide in growing this city, the scientist Zhekak who could prove just as important. And with them Alakensi, the deadly weight that hung about her neck. How well Malsas< had planned this, what subtlety of malice. Now that the first vital work had been done Alakensi was there to make sure that Malsas< profited by it. To observe and remember—then to hand the leadership over to Malsas< when she arrived. There she went now, currying favor with Zhekak, hearing everything that passed between the two Yilanè of science.

The three vanished from sight and Vaintè's eye rolled back

and came to focus on Enge who had come up silently and now stood before her, bent in a gesture of supplication.

"Leave me," Vaintè said, as curtly as she could. "I speak with no one."

"A matter of greatest importance. I implore you to listen."

"Go."

"You must listen. Stallan beats the ustuzou. I am afraid she will kill it."

Vaintè gave Enge her full attention now, demanding an instant explanation.

"The creature tried to escape but was recaptured. Stallan beats it terribly."

"This is not my wish. Command her to cease. Wait—I will do it myself. I want to hear more about this escape. How did it happen?"

"Only Stallan knows. She has told no one."

"She will tell me," Vaintè said, grim authority in her gesture.

When they reached the prison chamber they saw that the door was open and could hear the thudding sound of blows, the moans of pain, as they came down the corridor. "Stop," Vaintè ordered, halting in the doorway, speaking the word with such strength that Stallan halted, her arm still raised, the blood-drenched leash in her hand.

At her feet Kerrick lay twisted in agony, his back raw bloody flesh, beaten half unconscious.

"Tend the creature," Vaintè ordered and Enge rushed forward. "And you, put that thing down and give me an instant explanation."

There was such certain death hovering behind her words that even the strong and fearless Stallan quavered before it. The leash fell from her powerless fingers: it took all of her will to force her body to answer. Knowing that Vaintè had but to speak the few words more and she was doomed.

"The creature escaped from me, ran. Very fast. No one could catch it. We followed it to the fields, keeping close behind it. But never close enough. It would have escaped had it not been caught by one of the traps placed around the fields to stop the ustuzou night raiders."

"That close," Vaintè said looking down at the small form. "These wild animals have abilities we are not aware of." Her anger was dying away and Stallan quivered with relief. "But how did it escape?"

"I do not know, Eistaa. Or rather I know what happened but cannot explain it."

"Try."

"I shall. It walked beside me, obeying my commands. When we had gone some distance it stopped and raised its hands to the collar of this leash, choking and saying it was being strangled. This was possible. I reached to the collar but before I could touch it the ustuzou ran away. And it was not choking."

"But it told you it was choking?"

"It did."

Vaintè's anger was gone now as she thought hard about what the hunter had said. "Were you not holding the leash?"

"I had released it when I reached for the collar. The beast was choking, it could not escape."

"Of course. You did the only thing possible. But it was *not* choking. You are sure of that?"

"Positive. It ran a long way and breathed well. When it was captured the first thing I did was look at the collar. It was just as it had been when I put it on."

"These things are unexplainable," Vaintè said, looking down at the unconscious ustuzou. Enge was bent over it, cleaning the blood from its back and chest. Its eyes were discolored and bruised, there was blood upon its face as well. Surprising that it was alive after Stallan's attention. The inescapable fact was that the collar had not been choking it. But it had *said* it was being choked. That was impossible. But it had happened.

Then Vaintè stiffened into immobility. It was a thought, an impossible thought, one that would never have occurred to a crude hunter like Stallan. Vaintè controlled the thought, held it at bay for the moment as she spoke rudely and stiffly.

"Leave at once."

Stallan hurried out immediately, expressing relief and gratitude, knowing that her life was out of danger for the moment, happy to put everything that had happened out of her mind.

But not Vaintè. Enge's back was still turned so she was able to seize the thought, examine it, and not be concerned about anyone observing her own thinking processes.

It was simply an impossible idea. But it had happened. One of the first things that she had learned in the science of thought was that when all other explanations have been rejected, the remaining explanation, no matter how illogical or apparently false, must be the only explanation.

The ustuzou had said the collar was choking it. The collar was not choking it.

The statement of a fact was not a fact.

The ustuzou had said a fact that was not a fact.

There was no word or expression for this in Yilanè so she must make one up. It was a lie. The ustuzou had *lied.*

No Yilanè could lie. There was only immobility, or lack of expression to conceal one's thoughts. A statement was a thought and a thought was a statement. The act of speaking was one with the act of thinking.

But not with the ustuzou.

It could think one thing and speak another. It could appear quiet and docile, then say it was choking—when all of the time it was only thinking of escape. It could lie.

This creature must be kept alive, cherished, guarded—and prevented from escaping. The future was gray and formless and Vaintè was not sure of the details. But she knew with positive assurance that the ustuzou was her future. She would use it and its ability to lie. Use it to climb, use it to reach the summit of her ambitions.

But now she must put all thoughts of this impossible talent from her own mind. She must order things done so that none of the others should know. She would order all discussion of the escape forbidden. Should Stallan die? For a moment she considered it— then rejected it. The hunter was too valuable. Stallan would obey the order for silence, would enjoy obeying it since she would certainly remember how close she had been to death before Vaintè's anger. When she had composed herself Vaintè drew Enge's attention.

"Is the creature badly hurt?"

"I cannot tell. It is bruised and cut, but that could be all. See, it stirs, its eyes are open."

Kerrick looked up blurredly at the two murgu standing above him. He had failed to escape, he hurt, and he had failed. There would be another time.

"Tell me what you feel," Vaintè ordered, and he was surprised at the worry in her words.

"I hurt. All over." He moved his arms and legs. "That is all. I hurt all over."

"That is because you tried to escape," Vaintè said. "You took your chance when Stallan let go of your leash. I will arrange matters in the future so that this will never happen again."

Kerrick was not too tired or sore to notice the elision in Vaintè's words, the obvious leaving out of a statement. Vaintè must know what he had said to Stallan to make her drop the leash. Enge did not notice, but he did. He saw that knowledge and wondered at it, then forgot it. He hurt too much.

One of Vanalpè's students came and dressed his wounds—and after that he was left completely alone for many days while they healed. The student brought food every morning, then checked the progress of his healing. There were no more language lessons—nor did he have to suffer the attentions of the dreaded Stallan. His manacles were removed, but the door was always securely locked.

When the pain lessened enough he thought about his attempt to escape—and what had gone wrong. He would not be trapped that way next time. He would avoid the false vines, leap over them, and flee into the jungle.

Had he really seen the bearded face there among the leaves? Or was it just wishing, hoping, that had placed it there? He could not be sure. Maybe it was only his desire that someone be there, waiting. It did not matter. He did not need any help. Just the chance to run. The next time they would not stop him.

Day after slow day passed until his wounds had healed and the scabs had fallen away, leaving white scars in their place. The student still examined him closely every morning when she brought the food. When all the bruises on his skull were healed she brought the unutakh to remove the long stubble of hair that had grown. After this he became used to the creature's slimy ministrations once again. The door was always sealed when the student was with him, and he could feel the ominous presence of Stallan on the other side of it. There was no escape that way. But they would not keep him in this chamber forever.

On the day the student came in, moving with excitement, he knew that something was going to happen. She washed him and carefully inspected his body, saw that his skin pouch was decently in place, then crouched and watched the door. Kerrick knew better than to ask the creature what was happening. She never spoke to him or answered his questions. So he sat back and looked at the entrance as well.

It was indeed an important day. When the door opened next

Vaintè entered, followed by the waddling fat body of Zhekak. Fargi and aides followed them bearing containers.

"It has escaped once," Vaintè said. "It must be arranged that it shall never happen again."

"An interesting problem, Eistaa, and one that has given me many happy moments of contemplation. I believe that I have the answer, but I shall show you rather than tell you in the hopes that you will take pleasure from the revelation."

"I take pleasure in any work of Zhekak's," Vaintè said formally, but allowed an extra feeling of satisfaction to show through. Zhekak waved a fargi over and took the container from her.

"This is very new," she said, drawing out a length of flexible material. It was thin, darkish red in color—and immensely strong. Zhekak demonstrated that it could not be broken by having two fargi tug at the ends of it, struggling and slipping to the amusement of all. As a final test she took up a string-knife and pulled it back and forth across the taut length. When it was handed to Vaintè she looked close and saw that it had scored the shining surface, but no more than that. She expressed admiration—and puzzlement.

"I shall be happy to elucidate," Zhekak said with immense self-esteem. "A string-knife, as you know is a single long molecule. It cuts because of its small diameter, it is virtually unbreakable because of the strength of the intramolecular bonds. And here we have like attempting to cut like. The flexible length is made of fibers of molecular carbon grown in that medium. They will bend but not break, and cannot be cut."

Vaintè radiated approval. "So you have a leash that will certainly secure the beast. So I ask the next obvious questions. How do you fasten it to the ustuzou—and to what do you fasten the other end?"

Zhekak wriggled her soft flesh with pleasure. "Eistaa, you do understand these things so well. Here is the creature's collar-to-be."

An assistant produced a semi transparent, jellyfish object the length and thickness of her arm. It writhed sluggishly as Zhekak draped it about Kerrick's neck. He disliked the cold touch of it but knew better than to protest in the slightest. Zhekak issued brisk orders as the assistant brushed the ends of the creature with some salve, then pressed them together to form a thick collar about Kerrick's neck.

"Quickly!" Zhekak ordered, "the secretion process is beginning."

With careful touch they looped the end of the leash about the creature, then pulled on it so that it sank into the thing's transparent flesh, to the very center.

"Lean close, Eistaa," Zhekak called out, "and you will see the process begin."

The transparent flesh was beginning to discolor deep down, congealing about the alien object in its core.

"This animal is a simple metal secretor," Zhekak said. "It is depositing molecules of iron about the flexible core. Soon it will, stiffen and grow strong. We will feed the creature until a complete metal collar is formed about the ustuzou's neck. A metal collar too strong to be broken or cut."

"Admirable. But what will you affix to the other end?"

Zhekak's pendant flesh wriggled with pleasure as she walked across the room to the watching fargi and pulled one forward. This creature was taller and wider than most; strong muscles rippled under her skin as she walked. Zhekak pinched one muscular arm between her thumbs and could not dent it.

"This fargi has served me many years and is the strongest I have ever found. She is barely able to talk, but she still does all the lifting and heavy work in the laboratory. She is yours now, Eistaa, for a more important service." Zhekak's little eyes, almost lost in the folds of flesh, looked around at her silent and expectant audience.

"This is what her service will be. A collar will be grown about her neck as well—with the other end of the lead firmly grown into it. The ustuzou and the fargi will be joined together for life like two fruits growing from the same bough!"

"Your mind is like the mind of no other," Vaintè said, and all of the aides and assistants signaled agreement. "Joined together, forever inseparable. I am told our ustuzou runs very fast. Tell me, ustuzou, how far can you run pulling this little fargi?"

There was no answer to this so Kerrick was silent, while all of the others were much amused. He looked at the stupid features of the creature at the other end of the lead and felt nothing but burning hatred. Then he noticed that Vaintè was looking closely at him and he silently expressed resignation and acceptance. She approved.

"This fargi has a new name," Vaintè said, and they all grew silent. "From this moment on she shall be named Inlènu* for her mighty body shall make the entire world a prison for the ustuzou. Do you know your name, strong one?"

"Inlènu∗," she said with great satisfaction, knowing that she had been named by the Eistaa herself and would now serve the Eistaa.

Kerrick's posture of acceptance was as false as the pleasure of all the rest in the chamber was true. He reached out slowly with his toe and rolled it over the length of the lead where it lay on the floor, already thinking of possible ways to sever it.

Es mo tarril drepastar, er em so man
drija.

===========

*If my brother is wounded, it is I who will
bleed.*

CHAPTER SEVENTEEN

T he evening sky was as red as fire behind the black outlines of
the trees, while over the ocean the first bright stars had
appeared, tharms of the strongest warriors. But the four men
on the beach faced away from the stars, stared instead at the dark
wall of the jungle before them, for they feared the unseen beasts
that were hidden there. They crouched with their backs against the
wooden side of their boat, taking some strength from its solidity. It
had brought them here and would, they fervently hoped, take them
safely away again from this place of many dangers.

Ortnar could no longer keep silent, and he spoke the thoughts
of all of them.

"There could be murgu in there, watching us right now, ready
to attack. We should not be here." He chewed his lip with
apprehension, his imagination filling the darkness with unseen
dangers: he was a lean and nervous man much given to worry.

"Herilak told us to wait here," Tellges said, and this decided
the matter for him. He did not fear what he could not see, and
much preferred taking orders to giving them. He would wait patiently until the sammadar returned.

"But he has been gone all day. He could be dead, eaten by the
murgu." Ortnar was possessed by the terror of his thoughts. "We

should never have come this far south. We passed herds of deer, we could have hunted . . .''

"We hunt when we return," Serriak said, catching some of Ortnar's fear. "Now shut your mouth."

"Why? Because I speak the truth, that is why. Because Herilak seeks revenge we will all die. We should not have come . . .''

"Be silent," Henver said. "There is something moving along the beach."

They crouched, spears ready, lowering them with relief only when Herilak's silhouette was clear against the sky as he climbed the dune.

"You have been gone all day," Ortnar said when the sammadar came close, the reproof clear in his voice. Herilak chose not to hear it, standing before them and leaning wearily on his spear.

"Bring me water," he ordered, "then listen to what I have to say." He drank thirstily, then dropped the gourd onto the sand and lowered himself beside it. When he spoke his voice was low and distant as he talked first of things they knew.

"The sammad of Amahast is no more, all killed, you saw their bones upon the shore. You see Amahast's skymetal knife now around my neck and know that I took it from among his bones. What I found on that beach, among those skeletons, led me to believe that death came to them from the south. I chose you to come with me to find that death. I chose you because you are strong hunters. We have come south for many days, stopping only to kill for meat to fill our bellies. We have come south to the country of the murgu and have seen many of them. But yesterday we found something different. We found trails that were not animal trails. I followed those trails to where they led. I will tell you now what I found."

There was something in Herilak's voice that silenced them all, even Ortnar. The last light of sunset washed Herilak's face as red as blood, a blood-mask that belonged with the anger that drew his lips back from his teeth, clenched his jaw so tightly that it now muffled his words.

"I have found the killers. Those paths were made by murgu, of a kind I have never seen before. There is a great nest of them out there where they teem like ants in an anthill. But they are not ants—or Tanu—although they stand erect on legs like Tanu. They are not any of the beasts we know, but are murgu of a new kind.

They move over the water on the backs of creatures like boats and their nest is guarded by a wall of thorns. And they have weapons."

"What are you saying?" There was terror in Ortnar's voice, for Herilak spoke of nightmares come alive. "That there are murgu that walk like Tanu? Who have spears and bows and kill like Tanu? We must leave, now, quickly, before they reach us . . ."

"Silence." There was grim command in Herilak's voice. "You are a hunter, not a woman. If you show your fear the animals you hunt will know it and will laugh at you and all of your arrows will miss their mark."

Even Ortnar knew that this was true and he bit his lips shut to assure his silence. If you spoke of deer, no matter how distant they were, they would hear you and flee. Worse still, if a hunter felt fear all the animals would know it and his stone points would never strike true. Ortnar felt the others turn away from him and knew that he had spoken too quickly without thinking. He took refuge in silence.

"These murgu are like Tanu but not like Tanu. I watched all day from hiding and saw them do many things that I did not understand. But I did see something that is a weapon, although it is not a spear or a bow. It is like a stick. A marag pointed one and there was a noise and I saw a deer fall dead." His voice rose, challenging them to disbelieve him, but none spoke. "This is what I saw, although I cannot explain it. The stick-thing is a weapon and there are many murgu, many sticks. It is they who killed the sammad of Amahast."

It was Tellges who broke the long silence that followed. He believed what Herilak had said, but he could not understand it all.

"These murgu that kill with noise-sticks. You can be sure they killed the sammad?"

"I can be sure." Herilak's voice was grim again with the portent of the words that he spoke. "I can be sure because they know of the Tanu. I can be sure of this because I saw them capture a boy of the Tanu. They know of us. We now know of them."

"What do we do, Herilak?" Serriak asked.

"We return to the sammad because there are just the five of us against so many murgu that they cannot be counted. But we do not return with our hands empty. The Tanu must be warned of this danger, shown what the danger is."

"And how will this be done?" Ortnar asked, and there was still a tremor of fear in his voice.

"I will think before I sleep and you will be told in the morning. Now we will all sleep because there is much to be done tomorrow."

Herilak had not spoken the entire truth. He had already decided what must be done, but he did not want them awake and worrying about it all night. Particularly Ortnar. He was one of the best hunters—but he thought about things too much before they happened. Sometimes it was better not to think but simply to act.

At dawn they were awake and Herilak ordered all of their possessions packed into their boat, ready for launching.

"When we return," he said, "we will want to leave without delay. It may be that we will be followed." He smiled at the sudden apprehension on their faces. "It is only a small chance. If we do our work as hunters there will be no chance at all. Here is what we must do. We are going to find a small group of murgu who are not close to the others. Yesterday I saw groups like this. They were doing something. We will find them and then, unseen, we will slay them. All of them, in silence. If my brother is hurt, I will bleed. If my brother is killed, then death is mine to return. Now we leave."

Herilak looked at their grim and silent faces, could see them weighing his words. What he had proposed was something new and dangerous. But they would be hunting and killing murgu, murgu that had attacked and slaughtered the entire sammad of Amahast. Had butchered the women and children, the mastodons, everything. When they thought of this the anger grew within them and they were ready. Herilak nodded and took up his weapons and they took up theirs as well and followed him into the jungle.

It was dark under the trees where the dense foliage blocked out the sun, but the trail was well-trodden and easy to follow. They went in silence, bright birds calling out above them in the canopy of the forest. More than once they stopped, spears ready, as something heavy and unseen crashed in the undergrowth nearby.

The trail they followed twisted up through sandy hillocks set with towering pine trees, fresh-smelling with the morning breeze rustling their needles above. Herilak raised his hand suddenly and they stopped in rigid silence. He raised his head and sniffed the air, then cocked his head to listen. They could all hear the sound now, a faint crackling like burning twigs, or waves upon a stony shore. They crept forward then, to a place where the trees opened out upon grassy meadows. Meadows filled with movement.

Murgu, a giant herd of them, stretching out into the distance.

Four-legged, round, each twice as big as a man, small eyes rolling as they tore at the grass and pine-cones. One reared to seize a branch in its duck-like bill, sharp claws on its small forelegs, sharper claws on its long hindlegs. Herilak signaled a retreat; they would have to work their way around the herd. Before they could move there was a scream from the jungle and a great marag appeared among the trees, leaping forward onto one of the grazing beasts. It was armored and scaled, its teeth white daggers now dripping with blood. Its forelegs were tiny and useless—but the claws of its great hind legs tore the life from its prey. The rest of the herd squealed and ran; the hunters hurried on before the marag took notice of them as well.

The trail led down from the trees into low, brush-covered land. The ground was getting softer, water pushing up between their toes as they walked; the sun burned on their backs while here in the open, away from the shelter of the forest, the damp heat was suffocating. They were running with sweat, panting for air, by the time Herilak signaled a halt.

"Up ahead, do you see it?" He spoke so quietly that they could barely make out his words. "That open stretch of water. That is where I saw them. Go forward in silence and do not show yourselves."

They moved like shadows. No blade of grass rustled, no leaf moved to show that they had passed. One by one they slid up to the water's edge where they peered unseen from the darkness. Then there was the quiet gasp of indrawn breath from one of the hunters; Herilak scowled in his direction.

Although the sammadar had told them what he had seen, and of course they had believed him, the reality was another thing altogether. They could only watch in horrified silence as the two dark forms slid silently through the water towards them. The first of them came close, passed by before the concealed hunters.

A boat—but not a boat—for it moved without oars. It had been decorated with a large shell at the front. No, not decorated, the shell grew there, was part of the living creature that was the boat itself. And on its back it carried other creatures, murgu. They could only be the ones that Herilak had told them of. But his words had not prepared them for the disgusting reality. Like deformed Tanu they stood erect, or unlike Tanu squatted back on their thick tails. Some of them held strange objects, while others had long dark sticks that must be the weapons Herilak had described. The hunters watched in frozen silence while the creatures passed, not a short arrow flight away. One of them was making clacking, growling sounds. Everything about the scene was alien and repellent.

Then the dark forms were past, had stopped on the far bank and the murgu were climbing ashore.

"You have seen," Herilak said. "It is as I told you. They did this same thing yesterday, then they returned. Now you must move without being seen and find places along the bank where there is space to draw your bows. Lay your arrows on the ground before you. Wait in silence. When they return I will give the order to be ready. Choose your targets. Wait. Bend your bows but do not loose your arrows. Wait. When I give the command—kill them all. Not one must escape to warn the others. Is this understood?"

He looked at each grim, set face, and each hunter nodded agreement. In silence they took their positions, then in silence, unmoving, they waited. The sun rose high, the heat was intense, the insects bit and their mouths were dry with thirst. Yet no one moved. They waited.

The murgu were doing strange, incomprehensible things, while making loud animal sounds at the same time. They were either still as stones or twitching with repulsive movements. This went on for an unbearably long time.

Then ended as suddenly as it had begun. The murgu were putting their artifacts onto the living boats, then boarding them. The ones with the killing-sticks, obviously acting as guards, went first. They pushed off.

The birds were silent in the heat of the day, the only sound the ripple of water around the shell bows of the approaching creatures. Closer they came, and still closer, until the colored details of their scaled skins were repulsively clear. They were close to the bank, coming even with the unseen hunters, passing . . .

"*Now.*"

Strum of bowstrings, hiss of arrows. A murgu screamed hoarsely, the only one to utter a sound, then was silenced as a second arrow caught it in the throat.

Arrows had plunged as well into the dark hides of the living boats; they heaved in the water, spun about, the bodies of the dead murgu spilling from them. There was another loud splash as Herilak dived into the water and swam to the massacre. He returned dragging one of the bodies after him, was helped from the water by ready hands.

They turned the marag over, stared into the sightless eyes, prodded it unbelievingly with their bows.

"It was well done," Herilak said. "All dead. Now we leave— and we take this with us." He held out one of the killing-sticks. "We also take the body."

They gaped in silence, not understanding. Herilak's answering smile was the smile of death.

"Others must see what we have seen. They must be warned. We take this corpse with us in the boat. We row all this day and all of the night if we must. We get far away from this place and the murgu. Then, before this marag stinks too much, we flay it."

"Good," Tellges said. "Take the skull too. Cure the hide and take it with us."

"That is correct," Herilak said. "There will be no doubt then, none at all. Every Tanu who sees these things we have brought will then know what we have seen."

CHAPTER EIGHTEEN

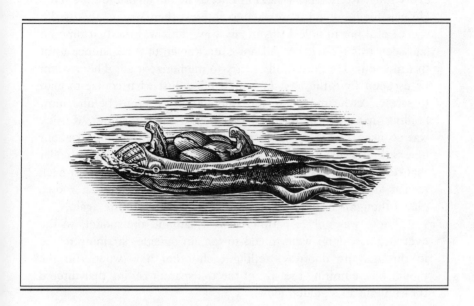

The model had a practical purpose, was indeed essential to the planning and design of the city. But like all things Yilanè it had to have a functional gestalt of its own, a completeness that went far beyond actual necessity. A chart could have been made that would serve the same purpose well enough, just as charts were used for navigation of the uruketo. But charts were used there only because of the shortage of space. In that particular case necessity demanded charts so the pragmatic answer was to make charts. Since no such restriction existed in the city, a scale model of Alpèasak was constructed that was essential for future planning, yet was also pleasing to behold.

Vaintè walked slowly around it, immensely satisfied. It was much improved since Sòkain had come from Inegban* with her trained assistants. They had fleshed out the details that had only been indicated by the field surveyors. Now tiny stunted trees formed the heart of the city, surrounding the small opening of the ambesed. When Vaintè bent close to look there was the golden crescent of the birth beaches, complete down to the wall of thorns.

Alakensi was of course right behind her, a constant reminder that Malsas< would be getting reports on every detail of her movements and decisions, a nagging presence that dulled the pleasure of everything. Kerrick came next in line, as he did all of the time now. He was feeling even more excited interest than Vaintè, though he was careful not to reveal this in any way. This was the first time he had seen this model; he had not even known of its existence until this moment. He must study it, try to memorize it all. Then, when he escaped from the city, he would know just what course to take to safety. As he moved so did Inlènu∗, a few steps behind him, holding up a loop of the lead that bound them together. Kerrick was so used to her presence now that he usually forgot all about her. She was just an inescapable fact of life—like the metal collar that rested about his neck. When he stopped she stopped, her back turned, not listening to anything being said, thinking her own placid thoughts until a tug on the lead stirred her to life again.

There was only a narrow walkway around the model, so the ever-attentive fargi were forced to remain outside, straining to see in through the doorway, telling each other how wonderful the model was, admiring the size of the transparent ceiling that filtered the sunlight to a golden glow.

Vaintè had reached the far side of the model now where Sòkain was working with her assistants. Vaintè was upon them before Sòkain was aware of her presence.

"Welcome, Eistaa, welcome," she said hurriedly standing up, speaking, brushing mud from her knees—and holding onto a bulbous orange creature at the same time.

"Do not let me disturb your work," Vaintè said.

"It is completed. The transfer of measurements has been made."

"And this is what you use," Vaintè pointed to the orange animal. "I have never seen a creature of this kind before."

Sòkain held out the orange chiton case for Vaintè's inspection. Other than a tiny mouth and sealed eyes it was featureless, except for a tube on top and a number of indentations down the side.

"Explain," Vaintè ordered, for as Eistaa there was no small detail of the city that she must not know. Sòkain pointed to the bare ground where the model was being enlarged, to small slivers of wood that had been pushed into it.

"Those bits of wood correspond to the stakes we used in the survey. When we are in the field I place this measuring creature upon a marked spot in the ground and look through this tube at a stake which is a certain distance away. When this is done I press the indentations to inform the instrument to remember the angle and distance. I then turn the tube to another stake and do the same. This is done many times. When I return to the model the instrument-creature informs us of the scaled down distance between stakes and of the correct angles between them as well. The result—this model."

"Excellent. What are these curved channels you have scribed in the soil?"

"Waterways, Eistaa. On this side of the city we have found a great deal of swamp. We are now plotting its extent."

Vaintè displayed concern. "We need many more fields. Can these swamps be drained or filled?"

"I do not think so. But Akasest, who has improved the quality of the feed for the herds, has examined them as well and we are now planning to create enclosures there. There are many amphibious species, such as the urukub, that will thrive in that environment."

"A satisfactory solution and utilization of the environment. You are both to be commended."

"Our pleasure is to serve Alpèasak," Sòkain said formally, expressing great personal pleasure at the same time.

Much later, Vaintè was to remember this conversation, for it was the last time that she was ever to speak to the surveyor.

Like all of her days, this was a full one. As the city expanded so did the work—and with it the decisions that had to be made. By the time that the shadows were getting long she became aware of her fatigue and waved the attentive fargi away, then signaled Kerrick for a drinking fruit. There was one attached to a saptree close by and he prodded the green bulb until the suckers let go. He brought it to Vaintè who opened its orifice and drank the cool, sweet water inside. When she lowered it she saw Stallan hurrying across the ambesed, shouldering fargi aside in her haste. Vaintè knew that there was trouble, knew it as clearly as if the hunter had spoken aloud.

"Tell me," Vaintè ordered as Stallan hurried up.

"The survey party, Sòkain and her assistants, they have not returned—and it is almost nightfall."

"Have they been this late before?"

"No. My orders are specific. There is a party of armed guards with them who bring them back at this time each day."

"Then this is the first time that they have not returned at the specified time?"

"Yes."

"What can be done?"

"Nothing until morning."

Vaintè was possessed by a sense of disaster, and all those present shared it. "I will want a very large armed party ready to leave at dawn. I will lead it."

Vaintè was awake when the first light filtered through the trees. Fargi were sent to summon Kerrick. He yawned and stretched and followed after the Eistaa, still not completely awake. Vaintè had not summoned Alakensi but she came along as well. Eager as always to see anything that she might report on to Malsas<. Stallan and the armed guards were already boarding the boats when they arrived at the river's edge. This was not Kerrick's first ride in a boat, but he still found the creatures fascinating. This one had just been fed and the legs and tail of a baby alligator were still hanging from its mouth. The creature's little eyes, set under the shell, bulged slightly as the wet skin contracted with effort and the rest of the alligator vanished from sight. He climbed aboard with the others. The pilot bent and shouted a command into the boat's ear opening. The flesh beneath them began to pump rhythmically and jet out water. The small flotilla moved out into the stream beneath the blood-red dawn sky.

Stallan was in the lead boat, showing the way. Fields moving slowly by on each side, the animals there either fleeing from them, or looking on with gross stupidity at their passage. Beyond the drained fields were carefully preserved and fenced areas of swamp. Large trees that were well-rooted in the mud had been left standing and were connected by the living fence. This had been grown in place, vines that were both flexible and strong. They had to be, for the urukub inside were the largest creatures on earth. Their immense forms sent waves of water surging through the fences when they moved; their tiny heads seemed grotesquely small on the ends of their long necks. They browsed the trees above, dredged deep in the swamp below for underwater plants. One of their young, already bigger than a mastodon, cried out shrilly as it splashed and swam to safety when the boats passed close. Kerrick had never been to this part of the city before so he carefully memorized the course that they were following.

When they had passed the last field the uncleared swamp began; Stallan led the small flotilla into a narrow channel. Tall trees rose up on all sides, their water roots lifting high above the boats. Flowers grew in great profusion here, white moss hung from the boughs above. Biting insects rose in clouds and Kerrick slapped at the ones that landed on him and began to regret that he had come on this trip. Not that there had been any choice.

They went slower now, wending their way through ever narrower channels, until Stallan finally signaled a stop.

"This is where they were working," she called out.

The silence closed in when Stallan stopped speaking. A bird flew by overhead cackling loudly, but there was no other sound. Nor was there anything to see. The guards clutched at their weapons, looking about in all directions. Nothing. It was Vaintè who broke the deadly silence.

"They must be found. Spread out through these channels. Stay alert."

Kerrick had good eyesight and caught the movement first.

"There!" he called out. "In that waterway. I saw something move."

Every weapon was pointed that way in an instant, until Stallan commanded them to be raised.

"You will be shooting and killing each other. Or me. I'm going in there. Point your hèsotsan some other way."

Her boat slipped forward slowly, Stallan standing with one foot on the thing's shell, peering ahead into the leaf-shrouded darkness.

"It's all right," she called back. "It's one of our own boats." Then, after a long moment of silence, she added reluctantly, "It's empty."

The other boat shivered when her boat bumped against it, shivered even more when Stallan jumped into it. It took shouted commands, and a good kicking, before the boat backed away from the bank. As it approached the other boats Stallan was silent—but her pointing finger was explanation enough.

There was something stuck into the boat's thick hide. Stallan reached down and pulled it free and the boat quivered with pain. Kerrick felt his heart beat loudly in his chest as Stallan held the object out for them to see.

A Tanu arrow!

Stallan dipped the arrow in the river to wash it clean, then leaned out and handed it to Vaintè. She turned it over and over in her hands, reading a detestable message there that arched her thick body with anger and detestation. When she looked up at Kerrick he cowered back as though from a blow.

"You recognize this, don't you? I also know what it is. An

ustuzou artifact with a sharp tip of stone. There are more of your disgusting ustuzou out there. We did not kill them all. But we will now. Kill them all, every one. Find them and slaughter them. This land of Gendasi is large, but not large enough to hide your ustuzou. It will be Yilanè or ustuzou—and it will be Yilanè who prevail."

There were hisses of agreement from all who heard her and Kerrick felt a sudden fear that he would be the first to be killed. Vaintè raised the arrow to throw it far from her, then lowered it and grew silent. Then she looked at Kerrick with a sudden new interest.

The deaths of Sòkain and the others would now have a purpose, she thought. She sat silent and unmoving for a long time, not seeing Alakensi or any of the others, but looking into a distance at something visible only to her. They waited patiently until she moved again and spoke.

"Stallan, you will search until you are sure that all those missing are gone. Return before dark. I am going back to the city now. My duty is there."

She sat in immobile silence all of the way back to Alpèasak. She had to. Her plan was finished and complete and if she dared move at all everyone would read it clearly. Only when they were at the dock and climbing back onto the shore did she move. Her eyes slipped across Alakensi's broad back, hesitated a second and moved on.

The plan was indeed made.

CHAPTER NINETEEN

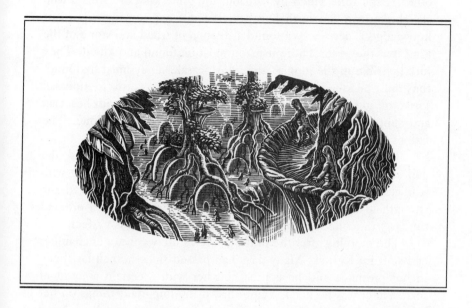

No trace of the surveying party was ever found. The arrow was grim evidence of their fate. Vaintè went alone to her chamber where she put it away with the other ustuzou artifacts that they had captured, in the chests that grew from the walls. Then she sat on her seat of power and sent for Vanalpè and Stallan, who arrived with the ever-present Alakensi close behind her. Kerrick looked in as well, but fled at her gesture. She could not bear the thought of an ustuzou presence now. The three of them conferred for a long time with Stallan about the security of the city. There would be more traps, more guards—and no more survey parties for the time being. After this she dismissed them and called in one of the fargi she had recently promoted to assist her, the one who could speak the best.

"The uruketo will be here soon. When it leaves I want you to leave with it. I want you to return to Inegban* and seek out Malsas<. You are to tell her what I will now tell to you. You will tell her in exactly the way I tell you. Do you understand?"

"I do, Eistaa. I will do as you command."

"Here is the message. Greetings, Malsas<, I bring you a message from Vaintè in Alpèasak. This is a sad and anger-filled message of great concern. Some are dead. Sòkain is dead. She and the other Yilanè were killed by ustuzou, the same kind of ustuzou who slaughtered on the birth beaches. We did not see them but our knowledge is certain. We found a weapon of wood and stone of the kind that they use. These ustuzou must be found and killed. They lurk invisible in the jungles around Alpèasak. They must be found, they must be killed. All killed. When the uruketo returns to Alpèasak I ask you to send many fargi in it who can shoot well, with hèsotsan and supplies of darts. I feel it imperative that this be done. The fate of Alpèasak depends on the ustuzou deaths."

Then Vaintè grew silent, oppressed by the truth and the darkness of her own words, while the fargi swayed before her with fear at the terrible message she must carry. But Vaintè had the strength to push the darkness aside and she did so, then ordered the fargi to recite the message back to her until it was perfect.

The morning after the uruketo left Vaintè went to her chamber and sent for Kerrick. Many days had passed since he had last been in her presence and he approached her with a certain amount of fear. There was no need. Vaintè had many important things on her mind now, he could tell that at a single glance, and actually seemed pleased at his presence.

"Inlènu∗," she called out, and the great creature shambled forward obediently. "You are to stand in the entrance, fill it with your body and no matter who approaches you will send them away. Do you understand?"

"They go away."

"Yes, but say it strongly like this. Go away, Vaintè commands. Say it."

"Go away, Vaintè commands."

"That is correct. Now do it."

Inlènu∗ made a good guardian; there was a scurry of running feet at her ominous presence. Vaintè turned to Kerrick and spoke as Eistaa issuing orders.

"You will now tell me everything about the ustuzou, your kind of ustuzou. Speak."

"I do not understand the meaning of the Eistaa's words."

Vaintè saw his fear and confusion and realized that the question was too general. She must be more specific. "What is the name of your ustuzou city?"

"Ustuzou do not have cities. This is the first city I have ever seen. Ustuzou live in . . ." He searched his memory in vain. It had been so long since he had heard or spoken Marbak that the words would not come. He fell back on description. "Soft structures made of skins, hung over poles. These come apart and the poles are pulled by . . . large animals with hair."

"Why do they come apart? Why do they move?"

Kerrick shrugged, then wriggled with the effort to put together bits of faded memory. "That is just the way that it is done. You hunt one place, fish another. That is just the way it is done."

Continued questioning elicited few more answers. The ustuzou seemed to live in groups, like the group they had slaughtered, and there were other groups, but no indication of how many. The unused memories of the boy were vague and uncertain. Vaintè finally had enough of the questioning and stopped it with a single gesture. Now came the important part. She would use fear and reward, train this ustuzou to do what must be done. Her manner changed and she spoke now as Eistaa, she who controlled the life of the city and its inhabitants.

"I can kill you or have you killed at any instant—you know that."

"I know that." He trembled with supplication, confused by the sudden change of tone.

"I can also raise you up, see that you are honored and do not always remain an ustuzou, lowest of the low. You would like that, wouldn't you? To sit by me, to command others to labor for you. I can do that for you—but you in turn must do something for me. Something that only you can do. You must do for me the thing that only you can do."

"I will do what you ask, Eistaa, but I do not understand what you are saying. I do not know what you are talking about."

"It is what you do when you speak of one thing and think another. It is what you did to Stallan. You told her you were choking and you were not."

"I don't know what you mean," Kerrick said, radiating stupidity and lack of knowledge, innocence. Vaintè moved with joy.

"Wonderful! You are doing it now. You are doing the thing where you talk about things that didn't happen as though they did happen. Admit it—or I will kill you on the spot."

He quailed at the abrupt change in Vaintè's mood, the motion of killing with her mouth open, her face close to his, those rows of deadly teeth just before him. "I did that thing, yes, I admit it. I did it to escape."

"Very good." She stepped back and the moment of danger was

past. "This thing that you do, that no Yilanè can do, we will call it lying. I knew that you lied, and I also know that you will undoubtedly lie to me in the future. I cannot prevent it—but Inlènu* will see to it that your lies will not permit you to escape. Now that we know that you lie, we will put that lying to good use. You will lie for me. You will do that for me."

"I will do what the Eistaa orders," Kerrick said, not understanding, but quick to agree.

"That is correct. You will do as I order. You will never speak of this order—for if you do you are dead. Now—here is the lie you must speak, and you must speak it in a very excited way. You must say— 'There, in the trees, an ustuzou, I saw it!' Those are the words. Now repeat them."

"There in the trees I saw an ustuzou."

"Good enough. Do not forget that. And speak it only when I order you to. I will make a motion like this."

Kerrick agreed happily. It was easy enough to do, though he could not see the reason for it. The threats had been real enough though so he made a special effort not to forget the words and the sign, muttering them to himself as he walked away through the city.

Many days had passed since Kerrick had last seen Enge. He rarely even thought of her now for his new-found freedom occupied every moment of his waking day. At first he had been hesitant to venture out alone and even took pleasure in the dumb presence of Inlènu* as some measure of security. When he did leave his room he very quickly discovered how stratified Yilanè social structure really was. He quickly came to understand that his position was somewhere near the top, since he was seen often in the Eistaa's presence, sitting close to her. For the nameless fargi this was evidence enough of how high he ranked above them and, crude as it was, this respect was represented in the way they addressed him.

When he walked through the green corridors he saw how those fargi with the intelligence and ability to master their language were quickly slotted into city life. They became guards, food preparers, slaughterers, work gang supervisors, agriculturists, a wealth of occupations about which he knew little. With these Yilanè he spoke in a neutral manner, taking them as equals, or slightly lower, and this was readily accepted.

Respectful speaking he saved for those who were the leaders. Their position was obvious, though what they did was not always as clear, since they were trailed by aides and assistants, these followed in turn by fargi eager to be called upon, anxious to find a fixed status in the order of the city.

With so much to see Kerrick had very little time to miss Enge's daily visits. The city was an ant's nest of industry and occasionally he wished that she were there to explain some of the more puzzling aspects of life in Alpèasak. He asked after her a few times, but the curt dismissal of his question taught him not to follow that subject any further. But the response made him curious. When Enge and Vaintè had talked together it had been as equals. So why this bias against even mentioning her name? He considered, then rejected, questioning Vaintè about her whereabouts. The Eistaa made it very clear that she was the one who began and terminated conversations.

He saw Enge again strictly by chance. He was near the ambesed, where Vaintè had dismissed him from her presence, when there was a stirring of excitement among the fargi. They were asking questions of each other and all hurrying in the same direction. Curious, he followed after them just in time to see four Yilanè go by, carrying a fifth one. He could not get close in the press and decided not to draw any attention by ordering them aside. He was about to leave when the same four Yilanè returned, walking slowly now, mouths agape. Their skins were splotched with dirt, their legs caked with red mud. Then Kerrick saw that one of them was Enge. He called out and she turned to face him. She was attentive, but did not speak.

"Where have you been?" he asked. "I have not seen you."

"My language skills are no longer needed, so my meetings with you are ended. I work now in the new fields."

"You?" There was astonishment, even dismay, lack of understanding with the word.

"I." The other three had stopped when she did and she signaled them to continue on, asking Kerrick to do the same. "I must return to work."

She turned away and he hurried up beside her. There was a mystery here that he dearly wanted to solve, but he did not know how to begin.

"The one that you carried here. What happened?"

"A serpent bite. There are many where we work."

"Why you?" They were not overheard now as they walked; the plodding Inlènu* did not count. "You talk to the Eistaa as one equal to another. Yet you now do work better done by the lowest fargi. Why?"

"The reason is not easy to tell. And I have been forbidden by the Eistaa to speak of it to any Yilanè."

Even as she spoke the words Enge realized the ambiguity of meaning that they contained. Kerrick was not a Yilanè. She indicated Inlènu∗. "Order that one to walk ahead of us, to follow those three." As soon as this had been done Enge turned to Kerrick and spoke with an intensity he had never seen before.

"I am here, these others are here, because we have strong personal beliefs that those who rule do not agree with. We have been ordered to abandon them—but we cannot. For once you have discovered the truth you cannot turn away from it."

"What truth are you talking about?" Kerrick asked in puzzlement.

"The burning, disturbing truth that the world and all things in it contain more than can be easily seen. Do you ever think of these things?"

"No," he answered quite honestly.

"You should. But you are young—and not a Yilanè. I have puzzled about you since you first started to speak, and your existence is still a puzzle to me. You are not a Yilanè, yet you are not a bestial ustuzou since you can speak. I don't know what you are or how you fit into the scheme of greater things."

Kerrick was beginning to be sorry that he had found Enge. Little of what she said made any sense to him. But now that she was speaking, for her own benefit more than his, she could not be stopped.

"Our belief must be true because there is a power in it that passes the comprehension of the nonbeliever. It was Ugunenapsa who came first to this understanding, spent her life ordering her mind, forcing herself to understand. To bring a new thing into the world where none had been before. She talked to others about her belief and they laughed at her. Word reached the Eistaa of her city about her strange ways and she was called before the Eistaa who commanded her to speak. And she did. She spoke of the thing within all of us that cannot be seen, the thing that enables us to speak and separates us from the unthinking animals. Animals do not have the thing within which is why they cannot speak. Therefore speaking is the voice of the thing within and that thing within is life and the knowledge of death. Animals have no knowledge of life or death. They are, then they aren't. But the Yilanè know—

and now you know. Which is the great puzzle that I must grapple with. Who are you? What are you? Where do you fit into the design?"

Enge turned to face Kerrick, looked into his eyes as though she might find the answer to her question there. But there was nothing that he could say in answer, and she realized that.

"Someday you may know," she said. "Now you are too young. I strongly doubt if you can comprehend the wonder of the vision that Ugunenapsa had, a vision of a truth that she could explain to others. And the proof as well! For she angered the Eistaa who ordered her to set aside these false beliefs and live as all Yilanè have done since the egg of time. Ugunenapsa refused and thereby put her beliefs ahead of her city and the commands of her Eistaa. The Eistaa saw disobedience and stripped her of her name, ordered her from the city. Do you know what this means? No, you cannot. A Yilanè cannot live without her city and her name once she has attained it. To leave is to die. Since the egg of time a Yilanè turned away from her city has suffered a deadly change. The rejection is so strong that the Yilanè collapses instantly, quickly falls unconscious and soon dies. It was always that way."

Enge was possessed now of a strange humor, something between elation and delight. She halted and took Kerrick lightly by both arms and looked into his eyes, trying to convey what she felt.

"But Ugunenapsa did not die. There *was* a new thing in the world with proof undeniable. And since that day this truth has been proven time and time again. I was ordered from Inegban∗, ordered to die—and I did not. None of us died, which is why we are here. They call us the Daughters of Death because they say that we have a pact with death. That is not true. We call ourselves the Daughters of Life and that is true. Because we live where others die."

Kerrick wriggled free of her cool and gentle grasp, turning away, lying. "I have come too far. I am forbidden to be here in the fields." He tugged on his leash, avoiding the intensity of her gaze. "Inlènu∗, we return."

Enge watched in silence as he left, then turned back to the fields. Kerrick looked behind him then and saw her plod slowly down the dusty track. He shook his head with mystification and wondered what she had been talking about. Then he noticed the orange trees nearby and pulled Inlènu∗ that way. His throat was dry and the sun was hot and he had not understood one word in ten that Enge had said. He had no way of knowing that her beliefs were the first rift ever torn in the millions of years of Yilanè homogeneity. To be Yilanè was to live as Yilanè. Nothing else had been comprehensible. Until now.

There were armed guards posted here, and about the entire city, who looked at him curiously as he pulled the ripe oranges from the tree. These guards provided daytime security, while larger and stronger traps were positioned to block entry by night. But in the days to come the guards saw nothing—while the traps merely collected a great assortment of animals of all kinds. The ustuzou killers never returned.

In all the time that it took for the uruketo to cross the ocean to Inegban∗ and return there were no further attacks on the city. When the uruketo did arrive Vaintè and her retinue were waiting as the great beast was secured to the land. It was the commander, Erafnaiś, who was first ashore, pausing before Vaintè and formally acknowledging her high station.

"I bring a personal message from Malsas<, Eistaa, who is much concerned about the ustuzou atrocity. I have private words for you, but she also commanded me to speak aloud of the need for vigilance and strength—and the destruction of the ustuzou. To that end she has sent her best hunters, with hèsotsan and darts, and the will to destroy the menace completely."

"We are all of a like mind," Vaintè said. "Walk beside me as we go for I want to hear all the news of Inegban∗."

There was indeed news, and, in the privacy of Vaintè's quarters, Erafnaiś related it to her, with Alakensi the only other present.

"The winter has been mild. Some animals have been lost, but the weather has been better than in other years. That is the day side of what I have to tell you. The night side is that there has been disaster among the uruketo. More than half are dead. They grew too fast, there was a weakness. Other uruketo are being bred. But the citizens of Inegban∗ will not come to Alpèasak this summer or the next or next again."

"These are hard words you bring," Vaintè said. Alakensi also motioned her unhappiness. "And all the more need to exterminate the ustuzou. But you must return with word of our growth to take the bitter taste of the other words from your mouth. You must see the model. Alakensi, order a fargi to have Stallan attend us there at once."

Alakensi did not enjoy being ordered about like a fargi, but concealed her resentment and turned away to pass on the order. When they reached the model Stallan was already there.

Alpèasak had not grown since Sòkain's death, but its defenses had hardened. Stallan pointed out the newly grown thorn hedges and guard stations where armed Yilanè were now posted day and night.

"What good can a guard be at night?" Alakensi asked in her petulant way. Stallan's answer was formal and clear.

"Very little. But they are protected, there are heaters and cloaks so they rest well. Nor must they walk the long way from the city and back each day. At dawn they are watching, and still on guard at sunset."

"I feel the resources could be used more wisely," Alakensi said, unconvinced. Vaintè took a middle path, which was unusual for she usually ignored Alakensi when she spoke.

"Perhaps Alakensi is right. We must be sure. We will see for ourselves, you as well, Erafnaìs, so you can tell Malsas< of our defenses when you return."

They straggled through the city in a ragged column, with Stallan and Vaintè in the lead, the others following behind in order of rank. Kerrick—with the ever-present Inlènu* beside him—walked just behind the commander of the uruketo. The aides and fargi followed after. Because of the rain Vaintè and some of the others were wrapped in cloaks. But the rain was warm so Kerrick did not use a cloak, but enjoyed the feel of it upon his skin.

He also took careful note of the path they used, through the fields and the living gates. Someday he would come this way alone. He did not know how he would do it, but it would be done.

The group of trees was near the forest, at the edge of the final field. As they drew close it could be seen that vines and thornbushes encircled the grove, leaving only a single entrance to the strongpoint. Stallan pointed out the Yilanè with a hèsotsan, on a platform above. "When they watch, none shall pass," she said.

"It appears satisfactory," Vaintè said, turning to Alakensi and receiving a reluctant agreement to her request for an opinion. She then started past the grove and Stallan requested her to stop.

"There are creatures of all kinds out there. You must let guards precede you."

"Agreed. But I am Eistaa and go where I wish in Alpèasak. With my advisors. You may keep the rest of the group back here."

They only proceeded when a line of attentive guards, guns ready, went cautiously on ahead of them. On the far side of the grove Stallan pointed out the traps and defenses.

"You have done well," Vaintè said. Alakensi started to disagree but Vaintè ignored her, turning to Erefnaiɛ instead. "Bring word of all this to Malsas< when you return. Alpèasak is guarded and in no danger."

She turned about and in the moment when only Kerrick could see her she signaled to him to speak—intensifying the order when he gaped. Then he understood.

"There!" He called out loudly. "There in the trees. I see an ustuzou."

The urgency of his words was such that all turned, all looked. In that moment, when everyone's attention was focused on the trees, Vaintè let her cloak drop to the ground. Held beneath it was the stone-tipped, wooden arrow.

Grasping it firmly with both hands she turned slightly and plunged it into Alakensi's chest.

Only Kerrick saw, only his attention was not upon the trees. Alakensi clutched at the shaft with her thumbs, her eyes open wide with horror, opened her mouth to speak—then slumped and fell.

Kerrick realized then what his lie was for. And he improved upon it instantly.

"An ustuzou arrow, it came from the trees. It has hit Alakensi!"

Vaintè stepped aside, body rigid, as the excitement swirled about her.

"An arrow from the trees," Inlènu* called out; she usually repeated what she heard. Others said the same and the fact was established. The word was the deed, the deed the word. Alakensi's body was rushed away, Stallan and Erafnaiɛ hurried Vaintè to safety.

Kerrick came last. He looked one more time at the jungle wall, so close yet infinitely distant, then plucked the lead secured to the collar about his neck and Inlènu* came obediently after him.

CHAPTER TWENTY

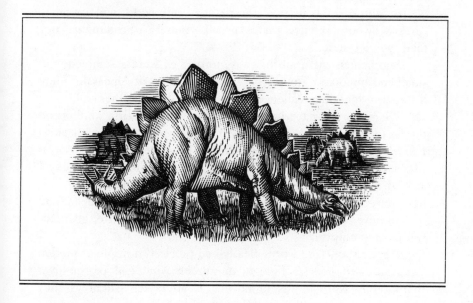

Vaintè stayed alone in her chamber, grieving for the death of the
loyal Alakensi. That is what Kerrick told the anxiously awaiting
Yilanè when he emerged. She would see no one. They all
sorrowed as they left. He was such an excellent liar. Vaintè marveled at his talent as she looked out and listened through a small
gap in the leaves, and knew that this was indeed the weapon she
had always desired. She stayed away now from the sight of others
because victory and joy were in every muscle of her body when she
moved. But none saw her move for she did not appear in public
until well after the uruketo had gone. By that time she no longer
mourned the dead Alakensi, for this was not the Yilanè way. Whoever or whatever Alakensi had been, she no longer was. Her dead
body was no longer hers and had been disposed of by the lowest
fargi whose occupation that was. Vaintè was triumphant. The lives
of those still living would continue—would do more than continue,
would blossom as they were soon to find out.

Vaintè issued the orders and those who led in the city came to
attend her. Kerrick stood back and watched because he felt that
something momentous was in the air, could detect this just from
the stance of Vaintè's body. She welcomed each of them by name
when they arrived, something she had never done before.

"Vanalpè, you who grew this city from a seed, you are here. Stallan who defends us from the perils of this world, you are here. Zhekak, whose science serves us all, Akasest who supplies our food, you are here."

She named them all this way, until they were assembled, the small and important group who were the leaders of Alpèasak. They listened in motionless silence when Vaintè spoke to them all.

"Some of you have been in this city since the first landings on the first day, before the city existed, while some arrived later on as I did. But now all of you work hard to bring honor and growth to Alpèasak. You will have heard of the shame I found on the day I arrived in this city, the murders of the males and the young. We have purged that crime, the ustuzou who did it are safely dead, and it shall never happen again. Our birth beaches are secure, guarded, warm—and empty."

As she spoke the words clearly and precisely a ripple of motion swept the listeners as though an unseen wind had passed over them. Only Kerrick was unmoved, as attentively silent as they were, waiting frozen for Vaintè's next words.

"Yes, you are right. The time has come. The golden sands must be filled with fat and torpid males. Now is the time. Now we begin."

Kerrick had never seen such excitement in all of his days in Alpèasak. There was loud talking and much laughter as they walked, faster than they usually walked, and he followed after in much puzzlement as they went through the city to the entrance to the hanalè, the sealed area where the males lived. The guardian, Ikemend, stepped aside at their approach with expressive movements of great welcome as they went through the entrance. Kerrick started after them but was jerked to a halt by the iron collar about his neck. Inlènu∗ stood as silent and immobile as a rock as he tugged on the lead that joined them. Behind his back there was a thud as the door was locked and sealed.

"What is it, what is happening? Speak, I order you," he said, most irritated.

Inlènu∗ turned round and empty eyes upon him. "Not us," she said, then repeated it. "Not us." Nor could he force her to say any more. He thought about this strange occurrence for some time, but after a while he forgot the incident, put it aside as just one more inexplicable happening in this city of many secrets.

Bit by bit his exploration of Alpèasak continued, for he was curious about everything. Since everyone knew that he sat close to the Eistaa all of the time there were none to bar his way. He did not attempt to leave the city, the guards and Inlènu* would have prevented that, but he wandered everywhere else. This was natural to him for children in the sammad had done the same thing. But now he remembered less and less of his former existence; certainly there was nothing to remind him of that earlier life. Before very long he had adapted to the oceanic pace of Yilanè existence.

Each day began in the same manner. With first light the city stirred to life. Like the others Kerrick washed himself, but unlike them he was thirsty in the morning—hungry as well. The Yilanè ate but once in the day, sometimes even missing days, and drank their fill at the same time. This was not his way. He would always drink deeply from the water-fruit, perhaps in unconscious memory of his brief days as a hunter. Then he would eat the fruit that he had put aside the evening before. If there were other matters of importance he would order a fargi to do this task, get the fruit for him, but he tried to do it himself whenever possible. The fargi, no matter how carefully he instructed them, would always return with damaged and rotten fruit. To them it was all the same, fodder for animals— creatures who ate what they were given regardless of its condition. In fact, if there were any fargi present when he was eating, they would gather around, watching with dumb intensity, speaking among themselves and trying to understand what he was doing. The more adventurous would taste the fruit—then spit it out, which the others always thought was most amusing. At first Kerrick tried to dismiss the fargi, was annoyed at their constant presence, but they would always return. In the end he suffered their attentions, was scarcely aware of it like the other Yilanè, dismissing them only when something private and important had to be discussed.

Slowly he began to see through the apparent disorder of Alpèasak to the natural order and controls that ruled everything. If he had been of an introspective turn of mind he might have compared the movement of the Yilanè in their city to that of the ants in their own cities beneath the ground. Apparently a senseless scurrying, but in reality a division of labor with workers gathering food, nurses tending the young, armored and clawed guards preventing invasions— and at the heart of it all the queen producing the endless stream of life that guaranteed the ant city's existence. Not an exact analogy, but a close one that he never even considered. But he was just a boy, adapting to extraordinary circumstance, so like the others he made no comparisons and unthinkingly ground the ants beneath his feet and passed on.

Many mornings he would go out with the fargi who had been ordered by one of the herders to bring in fruit from the groves around the city. This was pleasant to do before the heat of midday and his growing body needed the exercise. He would walk fast, even run, with the heavy tread of Inlènu∗ lumbering after him, many times stopping only because she became too warm and would go no further. Then he would feel very superior, streaming with sweat, knowing that he could go on and on when even a Yilanè as strong as Inlènu∗ could not.

Around the city the groves of trees and green fields stretched out in widening circles of a diversity that was constantly changing. Vanalpè's assistants and their helpers were always developing new plants and trees. Some of the new fruits and vegetables were delicious, others smelled bad or tasted worse. He tried them all because he knew that they had been tested for toxicity before being planted.

The variety of plants was there to feed the even greater variety of animals. Kerrick had no knowledge of the Yilanè's deep-rooted conservatism, of their millions-of-years-old culture that was based upon change only in the short term where it would not affect the stability and continuity of existence. The future would be as the past, immutable and unchangeable. New species were added to the world by careful gene manipulation; none was ever taken away. The forests and jungles of Gendasi held exciting new plants and animals that were a constant source of fascination to Vanalpè and her aides. Most of these were too familiar to Kerrick to be of any interest. What fascinated him were the great, lumbering, cold-blooded beasts that he used to call murgu; a Marbak word that he had now forgotten along with all the others.

Just as Alpèasak grew from Inegban∗, so did the life of the old world flourish here in the new. Kerrick could spend half a day watching the three-horned nenitesk tearing at the foliage with mindless hunger. Their armored skins and large armored plates before their skulls had been developed to ward off predators now millions of years extinct, although perhaps they too were also pre-served in small numbers in some of the older cities in Entoban∗. Racial memories of their threat were still imprinted in the giant creatures' brains and they would sometimes wheel about and tear up great clumps of earth with their horns when something caused them to perceive a possible danger. But this was the exception; normally they tore placidly at the undergrowth, consuming vast amounts of it every day. If he moved slowly Kerrick discovered that he could get quite close to the immense creatures for they saw no possible threat from his tiny form. Their hides were heavily wrinkled, while small and colorful lizards scurried across their backs, crawling into the folds of skin to eat the parasites there. One day, despite Inlènu*'s worried tugging on the lead, he ventured close enough to reach out and touch one of them on its cool, rough hide. The effect was unexpected for he had an instant vision of another great gray animal, Karu the mastodon, trunk lifted to throw dust over his back, one bright eye looking down at Kerrick. As quickly as it came the vision vanished and the gray wall of the nenitesk's hide was before him. Suddenly he hated the creature, an insensate rock, unmoving and stupid. He turned his back on it and would have left it then but for the fact that something appeared to have disturbed it. For some reason it mistook the other nenitesk for a marauder and there was the thudding of giant bodies, the crash of armor and horns. Kerrick looked on with pleasure as small trees were crushed and the ground was torn up on all sides before they lost interest and separated.

One thing that Kerrick did not like was the slaughtering yard where each day animals in great numbers were killed and butchered. The killing was quickly and painlessly done; at the entrance to the yard a guard simply shot the animals as they were driven up. When they fell they were dragged into the yard by large beasts that were immensely strong and stupid, apparently indifferent as well to the fact that their legs were soaked and stained with blood. For it was a bloody business inside as the still-warm carcasses were disjointed and carved to bits, then thrown into tubs of enzyme. While Kerrick was now used to the jellied, half-digested meat he really wanted to forget the process that brought it before him.

The laboratories where Vanalpè, Zhekak, and their assistants worked were beyond his understanding and therefore boring. Kerrick rarely went there. He much preferred to examine the incredible detail of the growing city model—or to talk with the males. He discovered them after he had been turned away from the birth beaches. None were permitted there but guards and attendants. From what he could see through the thorn barrier around the beaches they looked dull beyond belief. Just fat males lolling about in the sun.

But the males in the hanalè were different. By this time he had forgotten the sense of profound shock that he had felt when he had first discovered that all of the Yilanè he had met, even terrifying creatures like Stallan, were female. He accepted that as a fact of life now, had long forgotten the roles of male and female among the Tanu. He was just curious about a part of the city he had never seen. After being turned away from the hanalè many times he had questioned Vaintè about it. She had been amused by this, though she hadn't explained why. She had decided that as a male there was no reason he could not be admitted. But Inlènu✶ could not go in—therefore he was forbidden entrance as well. He thought about this for a long time until he hit upon the obvious answer. He went through the door—which was closed behind him. Leaving Inlènu✶ on the outside with their unbreakable link still connecting them.

This meant that he could not leave the area inside the door, so could not see all of the interior of the hanalè. But this did not matter. The males came to him, overjoyed at the novelty of his presence in their sheltered and boring existence.

Superficially there was no way that Kerrick could tell the males from the females. He was young enough not to think this of any importance and it was only the curiosity of the males, once the novelty of his presence had worn off, that caused them to reveal their nature.

Though most of the males talked to him or asked him questions at one time or another, it was Alipol who came forward eagerly to greet him whenever he appeared. Although Ikemend ordered all the affairs and operations of the hanalè, it was Alipol who ruled inside the door. He had been selected in Inegban✶ for this position of responsibility and leadership. He was far older than any of the others, all of whom had merely been selected for youth and good health. In addition Alipol was an artist, a fact that Kerrick did not discover for a long time. This happened on a visit when Alipol did not appear and Kerrick had to call out to one of the others.

"Alipol is busy at his art as always," he said and hurried on. Kerrick did not understand the expression, most of the males were worse than fargi in the crudeness of their language, but what he had said had to do with beauty, of making things, of new objects. Alipol did not appear that day, so on the next visit Kerrick displayed his curiosity.

"Art is of greatest importance, perhaps the greatest thing that there is," Alipol said. "But these stupid young males don't know that, and certainly the brutal females would have no idea of its existence."

Alipol, and the other males, always referred to the females in this manner, with a mixture of fear and respect that Kerrick could never understand. Nor would they explain it to him, so he had long since ceased asking.

"Please tell me," Kerrick said, with curiosity and interest, which Alipol accepted with a certain suspicion.

"A rare attitude," he said, then made his mind up. "Stay here and I will show you what I do." He started away, then turned back. "Have you ever seen a nenitesk?"

Kerrick did not understand the relevancy of the question, though he agreed that he had indeed seen the great beasts. Alipol left and returned with an object that had Kerrick expressing unconcealed joy and pleasure. In turn Alipol's own pleasure was beyond belief. "You see what others don't see," he said simply. "They have no eyes, no understanding."

Alipol had his hands joined before him, all four thumbs turned up to form a bowl. Resting upon them was the delicately formed image of a nenitesk, glowing brightly in the sunlight and seemingly woven from beams of light. The eyes were shining red, while every line of tail and horn, great shield and stumpy legs had been caught in glowing radiance. Kerrick bent close to see that the tiny creature was formed from thin strands of some shining material, woven together to form the intricate object. He reached out a questing finger and found it hard to the touch.

"What is it? How do you do it? I've never seen anything like it before."

"Woven of wire, silver and gold wire. Two metals that never grow dim. The eyes are small gems that I brought with me from Inegban*. They are found in streams and banks of clay, and I have the skills to polish them."

After that Alipol showed Kerrick other things he had made: all of them were marvels. Kerrick could appreciate art and he longed to have one of them, but dared not express his desire lest it interfere with the friendship they had formed.

As the city grew and flourished only one major problem remained. The ustuzou. During the rainy months, when there was cold in the north, the city was guarded and ringed with defenses. When the warmth returned to the north, then Stallan led raids up along the coast. Only once did they find a large group of ustuzou;

they killed all that did not flee. At other times small groups were attacked and killed, and once they returned with a wounded prisoner. Kerrick went with the others to see the filthy, fur-covered creature, and he felt no sense of identification at all. It never regained consciousness and died quickly. This was the only time that the mounting clashes between Yilanè and ustuzou interfered with the order of city life. All of the other encounters took place at a distance now and were only the concern of Stallan and the others with her.

Without the rhythms of the seasons, the passage of time was scarcely noted in Alpèasak. The city grew with the leisured pace of any living creature, animal or plant, reaching out into the forest and jungle until it covered a vast area inland from the river and the sea. Reports from Inegban* had the unreality of weather not felt, a storm not experienced. The recent winters had been mild enough so that some there hoped the cold weather was at an end, although the scientists who knew about these things insisted that the condition was only a temporary one. They talked of air and water temperature measurements made at the summer station in Teskhets, and pointed out the increasing numbers of ravenous wild ustuzou that had been driven down from their normal haunts in the north.

In Alpèasak news of this sort was, of course, of great interest, but they were still tales told of a distant land. More uruketo were being bred, that was good to hear, and one day Inegban* would come to Alpèasak and the city would be complete. One day. In the meantime there was much to do here and the sun was always warm.

For Kerrick the world was endless summer. Without the arrival of autumn he never looked forward to the snows of winter. From his place of privilege close to the Eistaa he watched the city grow—and he grew with it. Memories of the life he had once led grew dim, vanished altogether except for the occasional confusing dream. In mind if not in body he was Yilanè and none dared speak otherwise in his presence. He was no longer ustuzou. No longer Ekerik. When Vaintè called him by his name she changed the way the word was said and everyone else copied her way. He was no longer Ekerik, slow and stupid, but Keririk, close to the center.

There was need for the new name for he was growing, tall as a Yilanè, then even taller. There was so much hair on his body now that the unutakh died, perhaps from overeating, and he had been supplied with a larger and more voracious unutakh. But without the cold of winter to end the year, the green of spring to begin the new, there was no way to measure the track of time.

Kerrick did not know it but he was fifteen years of age when Vaintè ordered him into her presence.

"When the uruketo leaves in the morning I go with it to Inegban*."

Kerrick showed abstract interest, but little else, though he did lie and say it was sorrow to be parted from her. Inegban* was a word to him, nothing more.

"Major changes are on the way. The new uruketo reach maturity and in one summer, two at the most, Inegban* will be abandoned. They are so concerned there with fear of the future and the changes it will bring that they do not appreciate the real problems we have here. They care nothing about the ustuzou that threaten us, scarcely even notice the Daughters of Death who sap our strength. I have great labors ahead of me and you must aid me. That is why you are coming with me to Inegban*."

Now Kerrick's interest was indeed captured. A voyage inside the uruketo, across the ocean, a visit to a new place. He was both excited and afraid and Vaintè was aware of that since he was too upset to lie.

"You will capture everyone's attention, and when I have that attention I will convince them what must be done." She looked at him quizzically. "But you are too much of a Yilanè now. We must remind them all that you were once ustuzou, still are."

She went to the opening where she had placed the small knife many years ago, and took it out. Zhekak had examined it, pronounced it a crude artifact worked from meteoritic iron, had then placed a rustproof coating on it. Vaintè gave it to Etdeerg, her first assistant, and ordered her to fix it into position about his neck. Etdeerg did this with a piece of twisted gold wire, attaching it to the shining iron of his collar, while the fargi watched and listened at the doorway.

"That looks strange enough to make them look twice," Vaintè said, reaching out to press flat the sharp end of the wire. Her fingers touched his skin, the first time in years, and she was surprised at the warmth of it.

Kerrick had looked at the dull knife with lack of interest, had no memory of it at all.

"The ustuzou drape themselves with skins, it has often been remarked, and you had one about you when you were brought here." She signaled to Etdeerg who opened a bundle and shook out a smooth deerskin. The fargi chattered with distaste and even Kerrick moved away from it.

"Stop that," Vaintè ordered. "This is no piece of lice-ridden filth. It has been sterilized and cleaned, and that will be done again daily. Etdeerg, remove the false pouch and put this in its place."

Then Vaintè ordered the fargi cleared away and Inlènu* to block the doorway since she remembered why the pouch had been made in the first place.

Etdeerg stripped off the pouch and tried to fit on the skin, but the seals were in the wrong place. She went to fix them and Vaintè looked at Kerrick with interest. He had changed, grown, and she stared at him now with a mixture of attraction and disgust. She went across the chamber and reached down to him and Kerrick shivered at her touch. Vaintè laughed with pleasure.

"You are a male, very much like our males. Just one instead of two—but you respond just as they do!"

Kerrick felt unease at what she was doing, tried to pull away but she seized him tight with her other hand and drew him close.

Vaintè was aroused now, the aggressor as all female Yilanè were, and he was pulling away yet responding at the same time like any male.

Kerrick had no idea of what was happening to him, nor what were the strange sensations he was feeling. But Vaintè was well aware. She was Eistaa, she could do as she willed. With practiced motions she hurled him to the floor and mounted him, while Etdeerg watched with appreciation.

Her skin was cold on his, yet he was warm, strangely warm, and then it happened. He had no idea of what it was, just that it was the greatest and most wonderful thing that had ever occurred in his entire lifetime.

CHAPTER TWENTY-ONE

"I have a respectful message from Erafnaìs," the fargi said, speaking slowly and carefully, yet quivering with the effort to get the message correct. "The loading is complete. The uruketo is ready to leave."

"We go," Vaintè announced. Etdeerg and Kerrick stepped forward at her gesture. She looked around at the leaders of Alpèasak gathered before her and spoke in the most official and formal manner. "The city is yours until I return. Keep it well. You have my trust."

Having said this she took her leave and went slowly through the city with Kerrick and Etdeerg walking a decent pace behind.

Kerrick had long since learned to control his movements so he appeared as calm as the others. Inside he churned with conflicting emotions. This voyage, he was looking forward to it, yet was also afraid of such a major change in his ordered existence. And yesterday, what had happened yesterday with Vaintè, he still couldn't understand. What had caused such an all-encompassing sensation? Would it happen again? He hoped that it would. But what was it?

Any memories he had of Tanu passion, of the differences between the sexes, of the funny-forbidden talk the older boys had whispered to each other, even of the pleasure he once felt in touching Ysel's bare body, all this was gone. Overlaid and forgotten under the need for survival with the Yilanè. The males in the hanalè never talked of their relationship with the females, or if they did it was never in his presence. Inlènu✷ was dumb on the subject. He had no knowledge of sexuality, Yilanè or Tanu, and could only puzzle over this exciting mystery.

The sky behind them was red with sunset when they reached the harbor. The enteesenat, leaping with anticipation of the voyage, surged up out of the sea and splashed back into the water in a welter of red-tinted froth. Kerrick was last aboard, climbing down the opening in the high fin, blinking at the dim-lit interior. Beneath him the floor pulsed and he lost his footing and fell. The journey had begun.

The novelty quickly wore off for Kerrick since there was little to see and nothing at all to do. Most of the interior was taken up by the dead-alive bodies of deer and stalakel. The stalakel lay heaped in piles, small forelimbs limp, horn-beaked jaws gaping open. Some of the deer, though unmoving, had their eyes wide open, and this was clearly visible in the light from the luminescent patches. He had the uneasy feeling that they could see him, that they were crying out at their paralyzed state. They couldn't be, he was putting his own feelings into theirs. The sealed interior closed in on him and he clenched his fists with unknown terror, made worse by what seemed to be an endless storm. The uruketo's fin stayed sealed and the air grew musty and foul.

In the darkness the Yilanè grew torpid and slept. There were only one or two on watch at any time. Once he tried to talk to the Yilanè at the helm, but she would not answer; all of her attention was focused on the compass.

Kerrick was asleep when the storm ended and the heavy seas died down. He jerked awake as the chill, salty air washed over him. The Yilanè stirred and reached for the cloaks—but the air and the shaft of light were pure pleasure to him. He tugged at his lead until the sluggish Inlènu✷ woke up and had wrapped herself in a cloak, then pulled her after him towards the opening in the fin. He scrambled quickly up the corrugations and pulled himself up beside Erafnaìs who stood there, wrapped tightly in a large cloak. Inlènu✷ stayed below, as far as the lead would permit her. He held tight to the edge and looked out at the green waves rolling towards them and frothing over the uruketo's back, laughing when salt spray splashed his face. It was different, wonderful, exciting. Rays of sunlight cut through the clouds lighting up the vastness of the sea that stretched to the horizon in all directions. He shivered with the chill and wrapped his arms about him, but would not leave. Erafnaìs turned and saw him, and wondered at his emotions.

"You are cold. Go below. Take a cloak."

"No—I like it like this. I can understand now why you cross the sea in the uruketo. There is nothing else like it."

Erafnaìs was very pleased. "Few others feel this way. Were the sea to be taken from me now I would feel very strange." *Strange* had overtones of unhappiness and despair, with just the slightest suggestion of death. The scar on her back made it difficult to express this with exactitude, but so powerful were her feelings that the meaning was clear.

A flight of seabirds floated by overhead and Erafnaìs pointed in their direction.

"We are not far from the land now. In fact there, low on the horizon, that dark line. The coast of Entoban∗."

"I have heard the name spoken, but never understood its meaning."

"It is a great land mass, so large that it has never been sailed around for the sea gets cold to the south. It is the home of the Yilanè where one city stretches to the fields of another city."

"That is our destination?"

Erafnaìs agreed. "On the northern coast. First through the passage known as Genaglè into the warm waters of Ankanaal on whose shores is Inegban∗."

When she spoke the word there were mixed overtones of pleasure and pain. "Be pleased it is now midsummer, for the past winter was the worst in the city's history. Crops died. Animals died. Beasts from the north raided the herds. And once, briefly, hard water fell from the clouds and was white on the ground before it melted."

Hard water? The meaning was clear—but what was it? Before he could ask for an explanation Kerrick had a vision, clear and sharp, of snow-covered mountains. But accompanying it was a terrible pang of apprehension and fear. He rubbed at his eyes— then looked out at the sea and thrust the memory from him. Whatever it was it did not bear considering.

"I am cold," he said, half-lie, half-truth, "so return to the warmth inside."

One morning Kerrick awoke to warm air and sunlight, a beam

that poured down from the open fin. He climbed quickly to join Vaintè and Etdeerg who were already there. He was surprised at their appearance, but since they said nothing about it he did not comment. Vaintè had an aversion to being questioned. He looked at her out of the corners of his eyes. Her forehead and the strong angles of her jaw had been painted red with pigment, neatly applied in scrolls and turns. Etdeerg did not have any coloring on her face, but black vines appeared to twist about her arms, ending with leaf patterns on the backs of her hands. Kerrick had never seen a Yilanè decorated in this manner before, but managed to contain his curiosity and looked towards the shore instead. The coastline moved slowly by, green wooded hills clearly visible above the blue of the sea.

"Inegban∗," Etdeerg said, a wealth of mixed emotions behind the single word.

Grassy fields were mixed in among the forests now, with the dark figures of beasts grazing upon them. As they moved past a point of land a grand harbor opened out. Upon its shores were the beaches of Inegban∗.

Kerrick, who thought Alpèasak a city of wonder, now saw what a real city was and allowed his feelings to show, to the immense pleasure of Vaintè and Etdeerg.

"Alpèasak will be this one day," Vaintè said. "Not during our lives, for Inegban∗ has been growing since the egg of time."

"Alpèasak will be greater," Etdeerg said with calm assurance. "You will make it so, Vaintè. You have an entire new world to build it in. You will do it."

Vaintè did not answer. Nor did she deny it.

As the uruketo approached the inner harbor Erafnaìs climbed to the top of the fin, then called down orders. The great creature slowed and stopped, lay wallowing in the clear water. The pair of enteesenat swam ahead, then turned about sharply before they reached the floating boom of large logs. They had no desire to brush against the long stinging tentacles of the jellyfish that were suspended from the logs. They hurtled back and forth, anxious for the boom to be opened so they could reach their waiting reward, the treated food they were longing for. This was delayed until the uruketo in the harbor were driven away. Smaller than normal, still half trained, they were slow to obey. When they were safely restrained a harnessed uruketo tugged the boom open and the enteesenat instantly darted inside. Their own uruketo proceeded at a more leisurely pace.

Kerrick could only gape in silence. The dock area was vast—yet was still crowded with Yilanè awaiting their arrival. Behind it rose the trunks of ancient trees, their branches and leaves high above seemingly touching the sky. The pathway leading from the docking area into the city was wide enough to drive an urukub down. The Yilanè that were crowding it now parted to let a small procession past. At its head were four fargi carrying a construction made of gently curved wood and hung with colored fabrics. Its function was revealed when the fargi placed it carefully onto the ground, then squatted beside it. A hand pushed the fabric aside and a Yilanè, resplendent with golden face coloring, stepped down to the ground. It was a figure that Vaintè instantly recognized.

"Gulumbu," she said with carefully controlled lack of emotion that allowed just a small measure of her distaste to show through. "I know her of old. So she is the one who now sits at Malsas<'s side. We will meet her."

They had disembarked and were waiting on the dock when Gulumbu walked slowly up. She made the humblest of greetings to Vaintè, acknowledged Etdeerg's presence—and let her unseeing eyes move slowly past Kerrick.

"Welcome to Inegban*," she said. "Welcome to your home city, Vaintè, now builder of Alpèasak across the storm-filled sea." Vaintè acknowledged this with equal formality.

"And how fares Malsas<, Eistaa of our city?"

"She has ordered me to greet you and take you to attend her in the ambesed."

While they talked the palanquin had been carried away. Vaintè and Gulumbu walked side by side instead, leading the procession into the city. Kerrick and Etdeerg walked behind them with the other aides, in silence for this was a formal occasion.

Kerrick took it all in with widened eyes. Other vast walkways led from the one they were on, all crowded with Yilanè—and more than Yilanè. Small creatures with sharp claws and colorful scales darted through the crowds. Some of the largest trees they passed had steps worked into their bark, curving up and around to platforms above where other Yilanè, many of them with painted faces and bodies, looked down on the milling crowds. One of these tree-dwellings, larger than the others, had armed guards below. The

Yilanè above looked out, moving about and twittering together in a manner that proved they could only have been males.

Nor was there the dedication to work and the formality of talk that he knew in Alpèasak. Yilanè pointed rudely at him, and talked to each other coarsely about his strange appearance.

And there were Yilanè of a kind he had never seen before, some only half the size of the others. They stayed together in groups, pressing themselves aside when other Yilanè passed, looking on with worried eyes, not speaking. Kerrick touched Etdeerg's arm and indicated them questioningly.

"Ninse," she said, scorn in every motion. "Yileibe."

The unresponsive, the dumb ones. Kerrick understood that clearly enough. Obviously they couldn't speak or understand what was said to them. No wonder they were unresponsive. Etdeerg would say no more about them and he put the matter aside for the moment with all of the other questions he was eager to ask.

The ambesed was so large that the farthest side was hidden by the milling crowds. But they opened before the procession which passed through them to the sunny, favored wall, where Malsas< reclined with her advisors on a platform draped with more of the soft fabrics. She was resplendent with gold and silver paintings on her face and down her arms, curlicues of gold reaching down her waistless, ribbed body. She talked to an aide, appearing not to notice the procession until it was just before her, waiting that extra little moment to deliver not an insult, but a firm reminder of rank. Then she turned and saw Vaintè and welcomed her forward. A place was made at her side as they greeted each other.

Kerrick was staring about at everything, taking little notice of what was being said, so was startled when two Yilanè approached and seized him by the arms. As they pulled at him he looked fearfully at Vaintè—who signaled him not to protest but to go with them. He had little choice. They pulled strongly and he allowed himself to be led away with Inlènu* walking dutifully after.

Close to the ambesed was the doorway to a strange structure. There was no way to tell its size for it was hidden by the city trees. But panels of translucent chitin were visible between the trunks, stretching away to both sides. A solid-looking door of the same material was before them, without handles or openings in its surface. Still holding tight to his arm, one of the Yilanè reached out and squeezed a flexible bulb beside the door. After a short wait the door opened and a fargi looked out. Kerrick was pushed through the door with Inlènu* following after. The door closed behind them.

"This way," the fargi said, ignoring Kerrick and speaking to Inlènu*, then turned and walked off.

It was most unusual. A short length of corridor made of the same chitinous material led to another door. Then another. The next chamber was smaller and the fargi stopped here.

"Eye membrane over," she said to Inlènu*, letting her own transparent nictitating membrane slide over her eyes. Then she reached out her hand, thumbs spread wide, and tried to place them on Kerrick's eyelids.

"I heard you," he said, slapping the hand away. "Keep your dirty thumbs to yourself."

The fargi gaped, shocked at hearing him speak, and took a moment to recover. "Important that eyes be closed," she finally said, then closed her own membranes and squeezed a bulbous red growth on the wall.

Kerrick had just enough time to close his eyes before a rush of warm water showered down on them from above.

Some trickled into his mouth, was burning and bitter, and he kept his lips clamped tightly closed after that. The spray stopped, but when it did the fargi called out "Eye . . .shut."

The water was replaced by moving air that quickly evaporated the water from their bodies. Kerrick waited until his skin was completely dried before he tentatively opened one eye. The fargi's membrane had slipped back, and when she saw that his eyes were open she pushed through the last door and into a long low chamber.

It was a complete mystery to Kerrick: he had never seen anything like it before. Floor, ceilings, walls, they were all made of the same hard material. Sunlight filtered through the translucent panels above and threw moving leaf patterns on the floor. Stretched along the far wall was a raised surface of the same material with completely unidentifiable objects upon it. Yilanè busied themselves with these things and took no notice of their arrival. The fargi left them, saying nothing. Kerrick could make no sense of any of it. Inlènu*, as always, cared not in the slightest where she was or what was happening. She turned her back and squatted comfortably on her thick tail.

Then one of the workers noticed their arrival and drew the attention, in a most formal way, of a squat and solid Yilanè who was staring at a small square of material as though it had great importance.

She turned and saw Kerrick, and stamped over to stand before him. One of her eyes was missing, the lid collapsed and wrinkled, and the remaining one bulged out strongly as though trying to do the work of two.

"Look at this, look at this, Essag," she called out loudly. "Look at what has been sent to us from across the sea."

"It is strange, Ikemei," Essag said politely. "But it brings to mind another species of ustuzou."

"It does, only this one is not covered with fur. Why is that fabric draped around it? Remove it."

Essag started forward and Kerrick spoke in the most commanding manner.

"Do not touch me. I forbid it."

Essag fell back while Ikemei called out with happiness.

"It talks—an ustuzou that talks. No, impossible, I would have been told. It has been trained to memorize phrases, that is all. What is your name?"

"Kerrick."

"I told you. Well-trained."

Kerrick was growing angry at Ikemei's firm wrongness of mind.

"That is not true," he said. "I can talk as well as you, and a lot better than the fargi that brought me here."

"That is hard to believe," Ikemei said. "But I will assume for the moment that what you said was original and not a rote statement. If it is original—why then you can answer questions."

"I can."

"How did you arrive here?"

"I was brought by Vaintè, Eistaa of Alpèasak. We crossed the ocean in an uruketo."

"That is true. But it also could be a learned statement." Ikemei thought intensely before she spoke again. "But there is a limit to learned statements. Now what can I ask you that your trainers could have no knowledge of? Yes. Tell me, before the door opened to admit you here—what happened?"

"We were washed by very bitter-tasting water."

Ikemei stamped her feet with appreciation. "How wonderful. You are an animal that can talk. How did this come about?"

"I was taught by Enge."

"Yes. If anyone is suited for that task she is. But now we will stop talking and you will do as I say. Come to this workbench."

Kerrick could see what they were doing, but had no idea why.

Essag used a pad to moisten the ball of his thumb, then Ikemei pierced it suddenly with a sharp object. Kerrick was surprised that he felt nothing, even when Ikemei squeezed great drops of blood from his thumb. Essag caught them in little containers which sealed themselves when she squeezed their tops. Then his arm was placed flat on the surface and rubbed with another pad that first felt cool, then numb.

"Look there," Ikemei said, pointing high on the wall. Kerrick looked up and saw nothing. When he looked back he saw that while he had been distracted she had used a string-blade to slice away a thin layer of his skin. There was no sensation of pain. The small drops of blood that began to well up were covered by the adhesive bandage of a nefmakel.

Kerrick could not contain his curiosity any longer. "You have taken some of my skin and my blood. Why?"

"An ustuzou with curiosity," Ikemei said, signing him to lie flat on a low bench. "There is no end to wonders in this world. I am examining your body, that is what I am doing. Those colored sheets there will make a chromatographic examination, while those precipitating columns, those transparent tubes, will discover other secrets of your chemistry. Satisfied?"

Kerrick was silent, understanding nothing. Ikemei placed a lumpish gray creature on his chest and prodded it to life.

"And now this thing is generating ultrasound to look inside your body. When it is finished we will know all about you. Get up. We are done. A fargi will show you the way to return."

Ikemei looked on and marveled as the door closed behind Kerrick and Inlènu∗. "A talking animal. For the first time I am eager to get to Alpèasak. I have heard that ustuzou lifeforms are varied and interesting there. I look forward with great interest to seeing them for myself. Orders."

"I hear, Ikemei," Essag said.

"Do a complete series of sera tests, all the metabolic tests, give me a complete picture of this creature's biology. Then the real work begins."

Ikemei turned to the workbench and almost as an afterthought said, "We must find out all we can about its metabolic processes. We have been ordered to find parasites, predators, anything that will cause specific damage to this species." She wriggled with distress as she said this and her assistant shared her discomfort. Ikemei gestured her to silence before she could speak.

"I know your thoughts and share them. We build life, we don't destroy it. But these particular ustuzou have become a menace and a danger. They must be driven away. That is it, driven away. They will leave and not bother the new city when they see they are in danger. We shall not kill them, we will just drive them away."

She spoke with all the sincerity that she could muster. Yet she and Essag shared a growing fear that darker things were being planned. Their respect for life, all life, warred with their sense of survival and their muscles twitched spasmodically with the silent conflict.

CHAPTER TWENTY-TWO

As the great doors were swung slowly shut the sounds of the ambesed outside began to grow quiet. Silence filled the room when they had closed all the way. Vaintè had scarcely noted the details of the doors before, though she had been in this chamber many times in the past. Her attention was drawn to them now. They were intricately carved with a variety of intertwined plants and animals, these in turn had then been inset with shining metal and gemstones. They were just one more of the luxuries and pleasures of this ancient city that were taken for granted by the Yilanè who dwelled here. That she had once also taken for granted. How different this was from new-grown Alpèasak where there were scarcely any doors at all—while the few that did exist might still be damp with the sap of their growth. Everything there was crude and quickly grown, new and green, in direct contrast to this cultured city, old and staid. It was brash of her to be here, Eistaa of a wilderness city come to stand before those who ruled in timeless Inegban∗.

Vaintè rejected this line of thought instantly. There was no shame to newness, no need for her to feel inferior here in this great city. Inegban∗, ancient, rich—but certainly doomed, there could be no doubting that. These trees would die, cold mists and dead leaves would blow through the empty city, these ponderous doors would fall beneath the fists of time, would be splintered and turn to dust. The Yilanè of Inegban* might sneer now at the crudeness of her distant city—but it would be their salvation. Vaintè treasured that thought, turned it over and over and let it possess her. Alpèasak would be their salvation—and she was Alpèasak. When she turned to face Malsas< and her aides she stood erect with pride that bordered on arrogance. They felt this and at least two of them stirred restlessly. Melik and Melpon<, who knew her well for these many years, knew her rank and expected some deference. Nor was Malsas< very enthusiastic about this seeming lack of respect. When she spoke her attitude was firm and questioning.

"You seem very pleased, Vaintè, you must tell us why."

"It is my pleasure to be in Inegban* again, among all her comforts, to be among efenselè of my efenburu. It is my pleasure to report to you that the work I have been asked to do is progressing well. Alpèasak grows and prospers, the fields are vast, the animals many. Gendasi is a rich and fertile land. Alpèasak will grow as no other city has grown before."

"Yet there is a shadow behind your words," Malsas< said. "A hesitation and an unhappiness that is all too clear."

"You are too perceptive, Eistaa," Vaintè said. "There is a shadow. The ustuzou and all the other animals of this land are numerous and dangerous. We could not establish the birth beaches until we had eliminated the alligators, creatures very similar to the crocodiles we know, but infinitely more plentiful. There are species of ustuzou that are delicious, you have eaten them yourself when you honored our city with your visit. Then there are the other ustuzou, the ones that stand on their hind legs like crude copies of Yilanè. They cause much damage and are a constant threat."

"I understand the danger. But how can these animals prevail against our weapons? If they are strong is that not because of your weakness?"

It was an open threat that Vaintè instantly turned aside. "Would that it were only my weakness. I would then step down and let one who was stronger preside in my place. But look how these dangerous animals reached right into our ranks and killed your efenselè, strong Alakensi, ever-watchful Alakensi. Dead Alakensi. They may be small in numbers but they have a jungle ustuzou's low cunning. They lay traps. Sòkain and all with her died in such a trap. If a fargi dies there are always more to take her place. But who can replace

Alakensi or Sòkain? The ustuzou kill our food animals, but we can raise more. But the ustuzou also killed on the birth beaches. Who can replace those males, those young?"

Melpon< cried aloud at the thought. She was very old and given to much sentimental thinking about the birth beaches. But her cry spoke for all of them, even Malsas< who was clutched by the same strong feelings. But she was too experienced to permit herself to be swayed by emotion alone.

"The threat seems to have been contained so far. You do well."

"That is true—but I wish to do more."

"What?"

"Let me first supply all here with more information about the ustuzou. I wish them to hear about it from the lips of the captive ustuzou itself."

Malsas< pondered this and in the end signaled agreement. "If the creature has information that might be of value we will hear it. Can it really talk—respond to questions?"

"You will see for yourself, Eistaa."

Kerrick must have been waiting close by, because the messenger returned with him very quickly. Inlènu* settled down to face the closed doors while Kerrick addressed himself to the assembly in silent expectancy of orders, one of the lowest facing those of the highest.

"Order it to speak," Malsas< said.

"Tell us of your pack of ustuzou," Vaintè said. "Speak so all can understand."

Kerrick glanced quickly towards her when she said this, and as quickly away. Those last words were a signal. He was now to supply the listeners with the information that she had carefully drilled into him.

"There is little to say. We hunt, dig in the ground for insects and plants. And kill Yilanè."

A murmur of anger and a quick shift of bodies followed instantly.

"Explain about killing Yilanè," Malsas< ordered.

"It is a very natural reaction. I have been told that Yilanè feel a natural disgust towards ustuzou. Ustuzou react the same way to Yilanè. But being brutal creatures they seek only to kill and destroy. Their single aim is to kill all Yilanè. They will do this—unless they are killed themselves."

It sounded stupid even as Kerrick said it. Who could believe such an obvious and contrived lie? But the answer to this was clear; it would be accepted at once by these Yilanè who could not lie themselves. He recoiled in fear at the threat of death in their movements and was relieved to be ordered from the chamber. Malsas< spoke as soon as the door was closed again.

"The ustuzou must be wiped out once and for all. Every single one of them. Sought out and destroyed. Pursued and killed just as they killed Alakensi who sat closest to me. Now, Vaintè, can you tell us how this will be done?"

Vaintè knew better than to let them see that she had won a major tactical victory. Keeping her thoughts carefully on the plans that she had made she leaned back solidly on her tail and numbered off the steps to victory.

"Firstly—there must be more armed fargi. We can never have too many. They guard the fields, push out along the paths into the jungle, keep the ustuzou at bay."

"That will be done," Malsas< agreed. "We have been breeding hèsotsan and training fargi in the use of these weapons. When you return the uruketo will carry as many armed fargi as it can hold. Two of the smaller uruketo are reported ready for a longer sea voyage. They will carry fargi as well. What else?"

"Creatures to spy, creatures to kill. Yilanè are not jungle killers, but Yilanè of science can breed those creatures that will do this to perfection."

"This is being seen to as well," Melik said. "Much work has already been accomplished. Now that the sampling of the tissue of your ustuzou has been done the work will proceed to its conclusion. Ikemei who is supervising all of this work is waiting close by to be summoned. She will explain."

"Then everything that can be done has been done," Vaintè said, expressing pleasure and gratitude with every movement of her body.

"It has," Malsas< said, but there was a touch of displeasure behind her words. "Started but not finished. And the flow of time is not kind to us. Those who care about such things have returned early from Teskhets. They report a cold summer, an early autumn. They fear for a long and violent winter. We must proceed always with care—but we *must* proceed."

The emphasis in her words, the bitter anger and the fear was so strong that those who listened to her swayed backwards beneath the wave of emotion. They shared the fear for long moments before Malsas< broke the silence.

"Send for Ikemei. We will hear what has been done."

They were not only to hear about the research progress, but were to see the results with their own eyes. Ikemei entered, followed by a train of heavy-laden fargi, who hurriedly put their burdens down and left. Ikemei pulled the covering from a cage that was large enough to hold a grown Yilanè.

"The ruler of the skies," she said proudly, her single eye bulging. "A raptor of skill, strength—and intelligence."

The great bird ruffled its feathers and turned its head about slowly to look at them. The hooked beak was made for tearing flesh, the long wings for flying high, fast, tirelessly. The bird's toes were tipped with curled sharp claws designed only for killing. The creature did not like to be stared at. It shook its wings and screeched angrily. Ikemei pointed to an elongated, dark object that clung to one of the raptor's ankles with tight-wrapped toes.

"This beast is a neurological image recorder," she said. "Very much improved for this use. As I am sure you know an image from its eye is focused on a membrane within. Neurons then store the image in microganglia for future retrieval. Since single images are being stored, not memories of complex series or motions, there is almost no limit to the number of these images that can be recorded."

"Images of what?" Malsas< asked abruptly, bored by the technical talk, little of which she understood.

"Images of whatever we wish to record, Eistaa," Ikemei said. "This bird is almost immune to cold—the creatures fly at very high altitudes while searching for their prey. Therefore after its training had been completed this creature was instructed to fly north. The training has been most successful. Normally the creature has no interest in longtooth, carnivorous ustuzou that dwell far to the north. They offer it no threat and are too large to attack and eat. But the bird is well-trained and knows that it will be rewarded if it follows instructions. This one flew far to the north. And, here, we can see exactly what it saw."

Ikemei opened one of the parcels and took out a bundle of prints. They were grainy, black and white, but very impressive. She had arranged them in dramatic order. First a field of white with black dots upon it. Then the swoop, the dots took shape, then were clear. Four-legged, fur-covered ustuzou. One of them grew, filled the print, looked up with snarling jaws, curved teeth protruding.

Then jumped aside at the threat of the attacking bird. This last print was the most dramatic of all for the wing-spread shadow of the raptor lay across the longtooth and the snow. When Malsas< had finished looking at them Vaintè took the pictures with eager hands, excitement growing as she went through them.

"It can be trained to search for any creature?"

"Any."

"Even the ustuzou I brought from Alpèasak?"

"Particularly that ustuzou. It will search and it will find and it will return. Where it has been can easily be determined by using the pictures of its flight to prepare a map."

"This is the weapon I need! The ustuzou move in small packs, while the country is large. We found one pack and destroyed it easily. Now we will find the others . . ."

"And you will destroy them in the same way," Malsas< said.

"We will. I promise you—we will."

"I am pleased. Vaintè, remain. Everyone else will now retire."

Malsas< sat in frozen silence until the heavy doors had closed behind their backs. Only then did she move, and as she turned to face Vaintè she expressed unhappiness and more than a suggestion of fear. The Eistaa of Inegban* unhappy and afraid? There could be only one cause. Vaintè understood, and her movements echoed those of Malsas< as she spoke.

"It is the Daughters of Death, is it not?"

"It is. They will not die—and their numbers grow."

"Nor will they die in Alpèasak. In the beginning, yes, the work was hard and the dangers many. But now that we have grown and prospered it is not the same. They are injured, some die. But not enough."

"You will take some of the worst offenders with you in the uruketo when you return. The ones that talk in public, who make converts."

"I will. But each one I take means one less armed fargi. In Alpèasak these deathless creatures impede me because they will not aid in the destruction of the ustuzou. They are a burden."

"Equally so in Inegban*."

"I will take them. But only in the new and unproven uruketo."

Malsas<'s sign of assent had small overtones of respect.

"You are hard and dangerous, Vaintè. If the young uruketo fail to cross the ocean, their failure will also be a success."

"My thoughts exactly."

"Good. We will talk of these matters again before you return to Alpèasak. Now—I am tired and the day has been long."

Vaintè made a most formal withdrawal—but once the door had closed she had to fight to prevent her elation from being revealed. She was filled with thoughts of the future as she walked through the city, and her body moved to mirror those thoughts. There was not only elation, but death was very present as well, so much so that the fargi she passed moved quickly away from her. She was hungry now and went to the nearest place of meat. Many were waiting and she ordered them from her path. Vaintè ate well, then washed the meat from her hands and went to her quarters. They were both functional and comfortable, yet also highly decorated with woven and patterned cloth.

The fargi hurried away at her abrupt command. All except the one that she signaled to her.

"You," she ordered. "Seek out my ustuzou with the leashed neck and bring it here."

It took some time because the fargi had no idea where to look. But she spoke to fargi she met who spoke to others and the command passed through the living fabric of the city until it reached one who saw Kerrick.

Vaintè had almost forgotten the order by the time he arrived, was deeply involved in planning the future. Memory returned instantly when he entered.

"This has been a day of success, a day of my success," she said. Speaking to herself, not knowing or caring what he responded. Inlènu∗ settled down comfortably on her tail, facing the woven cloth on the wall, enjoying its patterns in her own almost mindless way.

Vaintè pulled Kerrick down beside her and stripped away his fur coverings. Laughing when he tried to draw away from her, exciting herself as she excited him.

Kerrick was no longer frightened by what happened. It felt too good. When it was over and she pushed him from her he went regretfully. Hoping already that this thing would happen again and again.

CHAPTER TWENTY-THREE

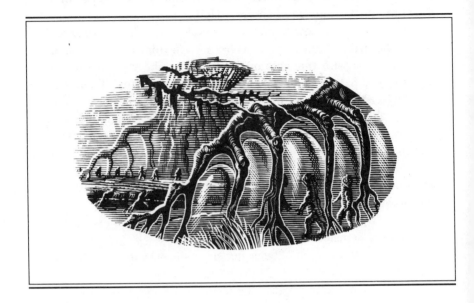

Thunder rumbled ominously behind the dark clouds as the torrential rain lashed the surface of the ocean. The uruketo moved slowly away from the shore, with the two smaller uruketo close behind. The enteesenat, happy to be in the open ocean again, raced ahead, surging up and out of the water as they dived through the waves. Inegban∗ soon fell behind, grew dim, then was lost from sight in the rain.

It was not an easy voyage. After the excitement and unexpected pleasures of Inegban∗, the return trip in the uruketo was a constant torment to Kerrick. The interior was filled to capacity, the bottom so covered with fargi that it was impossible to walk without treading on them. Food and water were in short supply and carefully rationed. This was no hardship for the Yilanè who simply grew torpid and slept most of the time. Not so Kerrick. He felt closed in, trapped, unable to breathe. Nor was there any respite in sleep, for he would dream of suffocating, drowning, and wake with a cry, running with sweat. He could not move around at will, and only twice during the seemingly endless voyage did he manage to make his way up inside the fin to gasp in lungfuls of the life-giving salt air.

There was a storm in mid-ocean that prevented the fin from

opening for so many days that the foul-smelling air became unbreathable. In the end the fin had to be opened, just a slit, but this was still more than enough to admit a dripping shower of cold sea water along with the air. Damp and sticky, first cold then warm again, Kerrick suffered in silent misery.

When the storm finally ended and the fin could be opened again, Vaintè ordered the others away and climbed to the top alone. The seas were still heavy and white-tipped waves stretched out on all sides. Empty seas. The two small uruketo had vanished; they were never seen again.

Kerrick's seasickness ended only when they were in the harbor of Alpèasak. The sickness and the days without food had weakened him so greatly that he could barely climb to his feet. The caged raptor had suffered almost as much as he had; its head hung low and it cried out weakly when they carried it away. Kerrick was the last ashore, and had to be lifted bodily up the fin by Inlènu* and two of the fargi.

Vaintè breathed deeply of the moist, warm air, rich with the odors of the living city, and felt immense pleasure as she shook off the lethargy of the voyage. She slipped into the first cooling tank she came to, rubbed away the salt and crusted filth from the uruketo's interior, emerged into the sunlight again refreshed and fit.

She had no need to summon the city leaders because they were all waiting for her in the ambesed when she arrived.

"Alpèasak is well?" she asked, and felt even more refreshed when they all communicated well-being. "What of the ustuzou, Stallan, what of those vermin that gnaw at the fringes of our city?"

"A nuisance, little more. Some of our meat animals have been stolen, others butchered during the hours of darkness, their flesh carried away before morning. But our defenses are strong, there is little they can do."

"The smallest amount is too much. They must be stopped. And they will be. I bring more fargi, trained in the use of their weapons. The ustuzou will be followed and killed."

"They are hard to track," Stallan said doubtfully. "They have an animal's skill in the forest and leave no sign of their passing. Or if there is a trail it leads only to an ambush. Many fargi have died that way."

"No more," Vaintè said, and expressed pleasure as the raptor screeched as though in response. Its cage had been brought forward by its handlers and the bird was now preening its feathers in the sunlight.

"All will be explained," Vaintè said. "This flying creature will enable us to find the ustuzou den where they hide their cubs and females. But first I want the reports in detail of everything that has passed while I have been away."

The raptor recovered quickly from the sea voyage: Vaintè waited impatiently for the next ustuzou raid. When the report reached her she issued rapid orders and went at once to the outlying pasture where the attack had occurred. Stallan was there first, pointing out with disgust the butchered corpses on the blood-stained grass.

"Wasteful. Just the rich hindquarters have been taken."

"Very practical," Vaintè said, showing little emotion. "Easy to carry, little to waste. Which way have they gone?"

Stallan indicated the opening that had been torn in the thorn fence, the trail beyond that vanished under the tall trees.

"North, as always. An easy trail to follow which means we were meant to see it. The meat is gone and only death, traps, and ambushes will be on that trail if we dare to follow it."

"The bird will go where we cannot," Vaintè said as the raptor was brought up. The captive creature screamed angrily and tore at the shackle that held its leg. It was not caged now but sat instead on a wooden perch mounted on a platform. Long poles supported this so that the fargi that carried it could not be reached by claw or beak. Kerrick arrived at the same time, wondering at this early summons.

"Do your work," Vaintè ordered the handlers.

Kerrick found himself suddenly no longer a spectator as hard thumbs seized him and dragged him forward. The raptor was excited by the sight and smell of the bleeding carcasses, screeching and flapping its wings thunderously. One of the handlers carved a lump of flesh from the flank of a butchered beast and threw it towards the bird. It seized the red meat greedily with its free foot, clamped it to the perch with its claws and tore bloody gobbets from it. Only when it was done did they continue. Kerrick struggled as he was pushed forward, almost within reach of that gory, hooked beak.

"Follow, find. Follow, find," the handler shouted, over and over, while they forced Kerrick even closer.

The raptor did not attack, but turned its head instead to fix one cold, gray eye upon Kerrick. It stared unwaveringly at him while the commands were shouted at it, only blinking and bobbing its head when the orders ceased.

"Turn the perch until it faces the trail," the handler ordered, then reached out from behind and swiftly released the shackle.

The raptor screamed, bent its legs—then hurled itself into the air with the thunderous beat of great wings. Kerrick fell back as the bird looked in his direction and the handler shouted instructions.

It had been well-trained. It mounted swiftly into the air, soared about in a single lofty circle—then started north.

"It has begun," Vaintè said with great satisfaction.

But her enthusiasm ebbed as day after day went by—and the raptor did not return. The worried handlers avoided her, as did everyone else at the sight of the anger in her movements. As long as Kerrick was not summoned to her presence he stayed as far away as he could. The hanalè offered a quiet retreat where he could not easily be found; he had not been there since their return from Inegban*.

Ikemend opened the door at his approach. "You have been to Inegban*," she said, her words a question and an answer at the same time, excitement in the movements she spoke.

"I have never seen such a city."

"Tell me of it, for I will never see it again with my own eyes."

While he spoke she fitted the leash into a groove that had been worked into the wood of the doorway, then closed the door against it. Kerrick knew what she wanted to hear and told her only of the glories of the city, the crowds and the excitement—and nothing of the hunger and cold of the winters. He valued his visits to the hanalè so made sure that Ikemend would always look forward to seeing him. She listened as long as she could, hurrying away only when the urgency of her work demanded it. The males did not like Ikemend and carefully avoided her company. None of them were in sight now. Kerrick looked down a dark hallway, to the interior he would never see, then called out when someone passed at the far end.

"It is I, Kerrick, I would speak with you."

The male hesitated, then started on, stopping only when Kerrick called out to him again. "I have been to Inegban*. Would you like to hear about the city?"

The bait was too strong to be resisted. The Yilanè came slowly forward into the light and Kerrick recognized him. Esetta*, a moody creature whom he had talked to once or twice. All of the other males admired Esetta∗'s singing, though Kerrick found it monotonous and a little boring. Though he had never said this aloud.

"Inegban∗ is a real city," Esetta∗ said, in the abrupt, breathless fashion that all the males used. "There we could sit high up among the leaves and watch everything that happened in the crowded walkways below. We were not forever trapped in boredom as we are here, with little to do other than to think of the fate of the beaches. Tell me. . ."

"I will. But first send for Alipol. I want to tell him too."

"I cannot."

"Why?"

Esetta∗ took a perverse pleasure in his answer. "Why can't I? You want to know why I can't? I will tell you why I can't." He hesitated over the answer, flicking his tongue between his teeth to dampen his lips before he spoke.

"You cannot speak to him because Alipol is dead."

Kerrick was shocked by this news. Sturdy Alipol, as solid as a treetrunk. It did not seem possible.

"He was taken ill—an accident?"

"Worse. He was taken, taken by force. He who has been to the beaches twice before. And they knew, those crude beasts, they knew, he told them, pleaded with them, showed them the lovely things he makes but they just laughed at that. Some of them turned away, but the hideous one with the scars and that rough voice, the one who leads the hunters, she found the protests exciting and seized Alipol and stifled his cries with her ugly body. All day they were there, she made sure, all day, I saw it. Sure of the eggs."

Kerrick understood that something terrible had happened to his friend, but did not know what. Esetta∗ had forgotten him for the moment, was swaying with his eyes closed. He hummed a dirge-like tone, then began to sing a hoarse song that brimmed with dread.

> Young I go, once to the beach,
>   and I return.
> Twice I go, no longer young,
>   will I return?
> But not a third, please not a third,
>   for few return.
> Not I, not I. For if I go, I know,
>   I'll not return.

Esetta* grew silent then. He had forgotten that Kerrick was to tell him about Inegban*, or perhaps no longer cared to hear about that distant city. He turned, ignoring Kerrick's questions, and shuffled back down the hall. Even though Kerrick called out loudly after that no one else appeared. In the end he let himself out, pulling the door shut so it sealed behind him. What had Esetta* meant? What had killed Alipol on the beach? He could not understand at all. Inlènu* was asleep in the sun, leaning against the wall, and he jerked cruelly on the leash until she blinked vacantly up at him, yawned, and climbed slowly to her feet.

CHAPTER TWENTY-FOUR

The fargi was eager to deliver her message—a message to the Eistaa herself!—but in her eagerness she had moved too fast in the heat of the day. When she reached the ambesed her mouth gaped so wide and she breathed so fast that talking now was impossible. In an agony of indecision she lurched forward into the sun, then fell back into the cool shadows. Was there a waterpool nearby? In her confused state she could not remember. None of the fargi nearby paid any heed to her moving fingers and the play of colors across the palms of her hands. They were selfish, thinking only of themselves, never helping another fargi. She grew angry, ignoring the fact that she would have done exactly the same thing herself in a similar situation. In desperation she looked into nearby corridors and finally found a drinking fruit. She sucked the cool water from it, then squeezed the rest of its contents over her arms and body. Her breathing finally slowed and she hazarded an attempt at speaking.

"Eistaa . . . I bring you a message . . ."

Rough but understandable. Walking slowly now, keeping to the shadows, she circled the ambesed, pushing her way through the clustered fargi to the empty space before the Eistaa. Once there she stiffened her body into the position of expectant-attention, lowest to the highest.

It was Vanalpè who noticed her after some time and drew Vaintè's attention to the silent figure.

"Speak," Vaintè ordered.

The fargi shivered with apprehension and had to force herself to speak the carefully memorized words.

"Eistaa, I bring message. Message is from she who feeds the raptor. The bird is returned."

"Returned!" Vaintè was delighted and the fargi writhed with joy, believing in her simplicity that the pleasure was directed at her. Vaintè summoned another fargi with a quick motion. "Find Stallan. She is to attend me at once." She turned back to the fargi who had brought the message.

"You. Return to the ones with the bird. Stay with them until the pictures are ready for me to see then come and inform me. Repeat."

"Return to those with the bird. Stay. Return to the Eistaa when ready are the . . ."

"Pictures, views, landscapes." Vaintè said it three different ways so the stupid creature could understand. "Repeat, akayil."

Akayil, disgust-in-speech. The watching fargi whispered the terrible expression to each other and felt fear, moving away from the messenger when she left as though afraid of some contamination.

"Vanalpè, how long will the process take?" Vaintè asked.

"To start with, the information is available now. The memory store of the bird's ganglion array will have been dumped into a larger memory bank. I have done this myself when recording growth patterns. The first pictures and the last pictures may be seen at once—but finding one's way through the information in between is the time-consuming part."

"Your meaning is not clear."

"I am stupid in my explanations, Eistaa. The bird has been gone for very many days. All of this time, night and day, a picture has been memorized every few moments. The memory creature may be instructed to remove all the black pictures of the night, but countless more still remain. Then each picture must be brought to the liquid-crystal screen, to be ignored or recorded. This will take days, many days."

"Then we will be patient and we will wait." She looked up and saw the stocky, scarred figure of Stallan approaching and signaled her close.

"The bird has returned. We will soon know if the ustuzou have been found. Are we ready to mount an attack?"

"We are. The fargi now shoot well, the hèsotsan are well-fed. More dart-bushes have been planted and many darts have been gathered. The boats have been breeding and some of the young ones are big enough for service."

"Ready them. Load food and water, then attend me. You, Vanalpè, your experience with pictures will be put to good use now. You will go at once to aid those who do that work."

For the rest of that day, and all of the next, Vaintè guided the city and put all thought of ustuzou from her mind. But on every occasion when she relaxed and there was no one close to speak to, instant memory returned. Had the ustuzou been found? If they had been found they must be killed, sought out and destroyed. Her nose flaps whitened with anger when she thought of the ustuzou. When she felt like this she took no pleasure from eating, while her temper was so short that one frightened fargi died after her savagely curt dismissal. It was a good thing for the well-being of the city that word finally reached Vaintè on the third day.

"The pictures are ready, Eistaa," the fargi said and a shiver of relief passed through all who heard that. When Vaintè left the ambesed even Kerrick joined the large group of followers who trailed after her, as eager as any to discover what had happened.

"They have been found," Vanalpè said. "A large picture is being processed and is almost ready."

The sheet of cellulose was slowly being extruded from a beast's orifice. Vanalpè pulled it free with a wet smacking sound and Vaintè seized it up, still damp and warm.

"They have indeed been found," she said, and the picture trembled in her fingers at the pleasure in her movements. "Where is Stallan?"

"Here, Eistaa," Stallan said, laying aside the pictures she had been looking at.

"Do you know where this place is?"

"Not yet." Stallan pointed to the center of the picture. "But it is enough to know that this river goes past the site. We attack by water. I am now following their trail, it is a way that I know and the first part is already marked on my charts. With the pictures I shall follow them until they reach this place. See, it is their lair. The shelters of skins, the large beasts, everything as before."

"And they will be destroyed as they were destroyed before." She signed Kerrick to attend her, then tapped the picture with her thumb. "You know what this is?"

The black and white patterns meant nothing to him; he had never seen a picture before. He took the sheet and turned it in different directions, and even looked at the back before Vaintè tore it from his hands.

"You are being difficult," Vaintè said. "You have seen these creatures and structures before."

"With all respect, Eistaa," Vanalpè said, her interruption humble and apologetic. "But the fargi are like this as well. Until they have been trained to look at pictures everything that they see is meaningless."

"Understood." Vaintè threw the picture aside. "Finish the preparations. We leave as soon as the site is identified. You, Kerrick, you will be coming with us."

"Thank you, Eistaa. It is my pleasure to aid."

Kerrick was sincere about this. He had no idea of where they were going or what they were doing. But he looked forward to the novelty of the voyage in the boats.

His enthusiasm wore off very quickly. They left at dawn, sailed until dusk and then slept on the shore. This continued day after day until he began to envy the Yilanè their ability to lapse into an almost mindless state. He looked at the shore instead and tried to imagine what was behind the wall of trees behind the beaches.

There were changes in the shoreline as they moved slowly north. Jungle gave way to forest, then to marshes, then low scrub. They passed the mouth of a great river but continued on. Only when they entered a large bay was there a change from their northerly route. Vaintè and Stallan in the lead boat altered direction and headed up the bay. This was something new and the somnolent fargi stirred to life. When they drew close to the reeds along the shore their passage stirred the birds that were feeding there, causing them to rise up in great flocks that darkened the sky; the sound of their honking was deafening. When the marshes gave way to beach again Vaintè signaled them to land—although the sun was only halfway down the sky. Like the others, Kerrick moved close to hear what was being decided. Stallan was touching one of the pictures.

"We are here—and the ustuzou are here, on the riverbank. If we go closer today we may be seen. It will be wisest to lighten the boats here, leave all the water and food on the beach. In that way we will be prepared to strike fast at first light."

Vaintè agreed. "We will attack from the water, in the breaking-wave movement, since we cannot get behind them this time. I want them all killed, except for the few that Stallan has been instructed to take prisoner. Is this understood? Repeat."

The group leaders repeated the instructions while the fargi strained to understand. This was done over and over until even the most dim-witted knew what they had to do. Kerrick turned away, bored, but returned quickly when Vaintè signaled to him.

"You will remain here with the supplies and await our return. I don't want you killed by mistake during the fighting. Your work will come later."

Before Kerrick could answer she turned away. He had no desire to see any killing, even of ustuzou, so he welcomed her decision.

They were up at dawn and into the boats. Kerrick sat on the shore while they boarded the boats, then watched their silent departure as they slipped away into the morning mist. Inlènu✳ watched as well, with apparent lack of interest, though she did open one of the meat containers as soon as they were out of sight.

"You're disgusting, a glutton," Kerrick said. "You will get fat."

"Eat good," Inlènu✳ said. "You eat too."

He really did not like the meat that was preserved in the bladders; it always had a musty taste. But he nibbled a little, then drank some water, knowing that there was no way he could get Inlènu✳ to move until she had eaten her fill. He looked closely at her and realized that what he had said was true; she was getting fat, a soft layer over her entire body that rounded the hard contours of her solid muscle.

Though he was used to the constant presence of others he found that he could still relish the freedom of being alone. Inlènu✳ did not count. When the boats had gone silence descended. There were sounds, the breeze rustling the tall grass, the small waves slapping on the shore. But there were no voices, none of the constant talk of the ambesed.

Kerrick led the way as they walked quietly along the clean sand, between the tussocks of grass, surprising birds that fluttered away almost from beneath their feet. They walked on, until Inlènu✳ muttered complaints and had to be ordered into silence. The tide was going out when they came to the ridge of high black rock. Seaweed hung from it in streamers and just above the water there were large mounds of dark shellfish clinging to the cracks.

"Good to eat," Inlènu✳ said, smacking her jaws loudly. Standing knee-deep in the sea she tried to pull some free but they were firmly fastened to the stone. She made no protest when Kerrick led her ashore and found a fist-sized rock. He used this to break some of them free and Inlènu✳ seized them and shoved them into her mouth and crunched down with her immense jaws. She spat the fragments of shell into the ocean and happily swallowed the sweet flesh inside. Kerrick gathered more for himself and used the metal knife about his neck to open them. They stayed and ate until they could eat no more.

It was a pleasurable day, the best that he could remember. But Kerrick wanted to be there when the others returned, so they went back to the landing site in the early afternoon. They had a long wait. It was almost sunset before the boats reappeared.

Vaintè was first ashore. She strode across the beach to the supplies, dropped her weapon into the sand, and tore open a bladder of meat. As she bit a great chunk from it she looked at Kerrick's inquiring stance. She chewed and swallowed greedily before she spoke.

"None escaped. The killers have been killed. They fought hard and we lost fargi, but the world has many fargi. We did what we came here to do. Now you will do your duty as well."

She called out an order and two fargi took a heavily wrapped bundle from one of the boats and dragged it ashore. At first Kerrick thought that it was a bundle of skins. Then it moved.

When the fargi dropped it on the sand the skins fell open and Kerrick looked down at a bearded face. Blood had soaked into the creature's hair; its eyes were wide with terror. It opened its mouth at the sight of Kerrick and strange harsh sounds came out.

"The ustuzou speaks," Vaintè said. "Or does whatever passes for speaking among these dirty creatures. What is it saying, Kerrick? I order you to listen and tell me what it says."

There was no thought of disobeying. When the Eistaa spoke one always did what she said. But Kerrick could not obey and he moved with fear.

He could not understand the sounds. They meant nothing to him, nothing at all.

CHAPTER TWENTY-FIVE

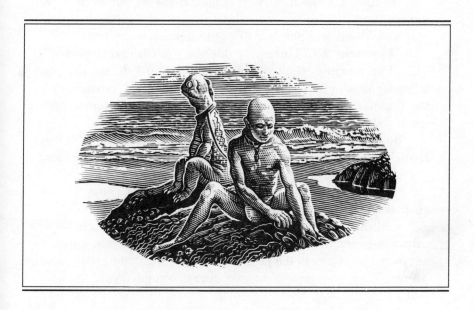

"Is the creature speaking?" Vaintè asked, insistently. "Tell me at once."

"I don't know," Kerrick admitted. "Perhaps it is. I can understand nothing. Nothing at all."

"Then the noise it makes—it is just a noise."

Vaintè was furious. This was a setback to her plans. She should never have believed Enge with her insistence that the filthy beasts actually communicated with each other. She must have been wrong. Vaintè vented her anger on the ustuzou, pushing her foot into the thing's face, twisting hard. It groaned with pain and called out loudly.

Kerrick cocked his head, listening intently before he spoke. "Eistaa, please wait—there is something."

She stepped back and spun about to face him, still angry. He spoke quickly before she turned her wrath on him as well.

"You heard it, it called out the same thing—many times. And I know, that is, I think I know what it was saying."

He fell silent, chewing at his lip as he searched through memories long buried, words forgotten, silenced.

"Marag, that is what it said. Marag."

"That conveys no meaning."

"It does, I know it does. It is like, it has the same intent as ustuzou."

Now Vaintè was puzzled. "But the creature is ustuzou."

"That is not what I mean. To this one, the Yilanè are ustuzou."

"The meaning is not completely clear, and I do not like the inference, but I grasp what you are attempting to say. Proceed with the questioning. If you think this ustuzou is yileibe and cannot speak well we will find you another one. Begin."

But Kerrick could not. The captive was silent now. When Kerrick leaned close to encourage it the ustuzou spat into his face. Vaintè was not pleased.

"Clean yourself," she ordered, then signaled to a fargi. "Bring another one of the ustuzou here."

Kerrick barely noticed what was happening. *Marag.* The word turned over and over in his head and stirred up memories, unpleasant memories. Cries in the jungle, something frightening in the sea. Murgu. That was more than one marag. Murgu, marag, murgu, marag . . .

He stiffened and realized that Vaintè was calling to him angrily.

"Are you suddenly yilenin too, as unable to speak as a fargi fresh from the sea?"

"I am sorry, the thoughts, the sounds the ustuzou made, my thoughts . . ."

"They mean nothing to me. Speak with this other one."

Kerrick looked down into wide, frightened blue eyes, a tangle of blond hair about its head. There was no hair on the thing's face and its body under its wrappings was swollen and different. The frightened creature wailed as Vaintè grabbed up one of the stone-tipped wooden spears that had been taken from the ustuzou and prodded the captive's side with it.

"Look at me," Vaintè said. "That is correct. I now show you what your fate will be if you remain silent like this other one and do not make your speaking."

The bearded captive cried out hoarsely as Vaintè turned and stabbed the spear into its flesh, again and again, until it was silent. The other prisoner moaned in agony and rolled about as much as it could in its tight binding. Vaintè threw the blood-drenched spear aside.

"Loosen its limbs and make it speak," she ordered as she turned away.

It was not easy. The captive wailed, then coughed heavily

until its eyes streamed with tears, mucus dribbled down its lips. Kerrick leaned close and waited until it grew quieter before he spoke the only words that he knew.

"Marag. Murgu."

The answer came quickly, too fast for him to understand, though he recognized murgu—and something else. Sammad. Yes, sammad, the sammad had been killed. That was what the words meant. All in the sammad slain by the murgu. That was what she was saying.

She. Unbidden the word was on his lips. Female. She was linga, the other dead one, hannas. Male and female. He was hannas too.

Understanding grew, but only slowly, a word, an expression at a time. Some words he could not understand at all; the vocabulary of an eight-year-old, all that he had ever known, was not that of a grown woman.

"You make noises at each other. Is there understanding?"

Kerrick blinked at Vaintè, leapt to his feet, and stood gaping for a long moment before the meaning of her question penetrated the flood of Marbak words that filled his head.

"Yes, of course, Eistaa, there is understanding. It moves slowly— but it moves."

"Then you are doing well." The shadows were long, the sun below the horizon, and Vaintè had a cloak wrapped about her. "Tie it again so it cannot escape. In the morning you will continue. When you have perfected your understanding there are questions you will put to the ustuzou. Questions that will need answers. If the creature refuses—just remind it of the other's fate. I am sure that that argument will be a strong one."

Kerrick went for a cloak for himself, then returned to sit on the sand beside the dark form of the woman. His head was filled with a clash of words, sounds, and names.

The woman spoke some words—and he realized that he could understand them even though her movements were unseen!

"I grow cold."

"You can speak in the dark—and I can understand."

"Cold."

Of course. Marbak was not like Yilanè. It did not depend upon what the body was doing. It was the sounds, just the sounds. He marveled at this discovery while he unrolled some of the blood-soaked skins from the dead man, then spread them over the woman.

"We can speak—even in the night," he said, wiping his sticky hands on the sand. When she answered her voice was low, still fearful, but curious as well.

"I am Ine of the sammad of Ohso. Who are you?"

"Kerrick."

"You are captive too, bound to that marag. And you can speak with them?"

"Yes, of course. What were you doing here?"

"Getting food, of course, that is a strange question to ask. We should never have come this far south, but many starved to death last winter. There was nothing else we could do." She looked at his outline against the sky and felt a great curiosity. "When did they capture you, Kerrick?"

"When?" It was a difficult question to answer. "It must have been many summers ago. I was very small . . ."

"They're all dead," she said with sudden memory, then began to sob. "These murgu killed them all, all except a few captured."

She sobbed even louder and there was sudden pain in Kerrick's neck. He seized his collar with both hands as he was dragged away. The noise was disturbing Inlènu* in her sleep and she rolled away from it, pulling Kerrick after her. After that he did not try to talk again.

In the morning he was slow to waken. His head felt heavy, his skin warm. He must have been in the sun too much the day before. He found the water containers and was drinking thirstily when Stallan approached him.

"The Eistaa has informed me that you talk with the other ustuzou," she said. There was a wealth of rich loathing behind the concept of bestial communication that she used.

"I am Kerrick who sits close to the Eistaa. Your manner of talk is an insult."

"I am Stallan who kills the ustuzou for the Eistaa. There is no insult in calling you what you are."

The hunter was filled with the fullness of the killing today. Her manner was normally as rough as her voice, yet not this venomous. But Kerrick was not feeling well enough to argue with the brutal creature. Not today. Ignoring her movements of superiority and contempt he turned his back on her, forcing her to follow him as he went to the spot where the bound woman lay.

"Speak to it," Stallan ordered.

The woman shivered at the sounds of Stallan's voice, turned frightened eyes on Kerrick.

"I am thirsty."

"I'll get some water."

"It writhed and made noises," Stallan said. "Your noises were just as bad. What was the meaning?"

"It wants water."

"Good. Give the thing some. Then I will ask questions."

Ine was frightened of the marag that stood near Kerrick. It stared at her with a cold and empty expression, then moved its limbs and made sounds. Kerrick translated.

"Where are more Tanu?" he asked.

"Where? What do you mean?"

"I am asking for this ugly marag. It wants to know where more are, other sammads."

"To the west, in the mountains, you know that."

Stallan was not satisfied with the answer. The questioning continued. After a while, even with his inconsistent knowledge of the language, Kerrick realized that Ine was avoiding clear answers.

"You are not telling all that you know," he said.

"Of course not. This marag wants to find out where the other sammads are in order to kill them. I will not tell. I will die first. Do you want the thing to know?"

"I do not care," Kerrick answered truthfully. He was tired— and his head ached. Murgu could kill ustuzou, ustuzou kill murgu, it was nothing to him. He coughed, then coughed again, deep and chesty. When he wiped his wet lips he saw that there was blood in his saliva.

"Ask again," Stallan said.

"Ask her yourself," Kerrick said in such an insulting manner that Stallan hissed with anger. "I want some water to drink. My throat is dry."

He drank the water, gulping it greedily, then closed his eyes to rest for a moment.

Later he was aware of someone pulling at him, but it was too much effort to open his eyes. After a bit they went away and he drew his legs to his chest and wrapped his arms about them. Unconscious, he whimpered with cold although the sun was hot upon him.

CHAPTER TWENTY-SIX

There was an awareness of the passage of time; there was a constant awareness of pain. Pain that very quickly became the most important thing in Kerrick's life, an overwhelming presence that trampled him underfoot. He slipped in and out of consciousness, welcomed the blank periods of darkness as an escape from the fever and the endless agony. Once he was awoken by the sound of someone screaming weakly; it was some time before he realized that he was doing it himself.

The worst of these times slowly passed away. There were still only brief periods of consciousness, but during them the pain had now subsided to a dull ache. His vision was blurred, but the strong, cool arm about his shoulders, supporting him so he could drink, could have only been that of Inlènu✳. A constant attendant, he thought, constant attendant. He laughed at the idea, he didn't know why, as he drifted off again.

This timeless period came to an indefinite finish one day when he found himself conscious but unable to move. It wasn't that he was held down or bound in any way, just that a terrible weakness was pressing him flat. He found that he could move his eyes, but they hurt when he did it bringing inadvertent tears. Inlènu✳ was beside him, sitting comfortably back on her tail, staring at nothing with silent pleasure. With great effort he managed to croak out the single word, *water*, unable to make the accompanying body motions to indicate that he wished some water to be brought to him. Inlènu*'s nearest eye rolled towards him while she considered his meaning. Eventually his intent became obvious, even to her, and she stirred and went to bring him the gourd. She raised him so he could drink. He slurped, then coughed, dropping back exhausted but conscious. There was a movement at the entrance and Akotolp swam into his vision.

"Did I hear it speak?" she asked and Inlènu* signed an affirmative. "Very good, very good," the scientist said, bending over to look at him. Kerrick blinked as her fat features, heavy wattles swaying, swam into view like a rising moon.

"You should be dead," she said with some satisfaction. "And you would be dead had I not been here. Move your head to show how grateful you are for that."

Kerrick managed a slight motion of his jaw and Akotolp accepted it as her due. "A frightening disease, raging through your entire system: those sores on your skin are the least part of it. The fargi wouldn't touch you, too stupid to realize that an infection like this is species specific, had to tend you myself. Most interesting. Had I not worked with warm-fleshed ustuzou in the past your death would have been certain."

While she talked, mostly for her own benefit, Akotolp changed the dressings on his body. This was moderately painful, but nothing like the pain that he had felt before. "Some of the ustuzou we captured had the same disease, in a milder form. Antibodies from their youth. You had none. I exsanguinated the sickest one completely, made a serum, did the job. There, finished. Now eat something."

"How . . . long . . ." Kerrick managed to whisper the words.

"How long the food? How long the antibodies? Are you still delirious?" Kerrick managed to move his hand in the motion of time significance. "Understood. How long have you been ill? Very long, I did not keep track. It is not important. Now drink this, you need protein, you've lost a third of your bodyweight, it is delicious meat enzymed to liquid, most digestible."

Kerrick was too weak to protest. Though he did gag on the repulsive liquid before he managed to get some down. After that he slept, exhausted. But this had been the turning point. The disease was over, he was on the mend. He had no visitors, other than the fat scientist, nor did he want any. Memories of the Tanu that he had talked to turned over and over in his mind. No, not Tanu, ustuzou, degenerate, warm-fleshed killers. Flesh of his flesh. Tanu. The same people, the same creatures. He had a double-identity that he could not understand and he fought to make sense of it all. Of course he was Tanu himself, since he had been brought here when he was very young. But that had happened so long ago, so much had happened to him since that all memory of this had vanished. He was left more with a memory of the memory, as though it were something that he had been told about and had not really experienced himself. Though physically he was not Yilanè, could never be, he nevertheless now thought like one, moved like one, spoke like one. But his body was still Tanu and in his dreams he moved among his own people. These dreams were disturbing, even frightening, and he was glad that he remembered very little of them when he awoke. He tried to remember more of the Tanu words but could not, while even the words he had spoken aloud slipped from his mind as he recovered.

Other than the perpetual silent presence of Inlènu✳ he was left completely alone. Akotolp was his only visitor and he wondered at this.

"Are they all still away from the city, all of those who are killing the ustuzou?" he asked her one day.

"No. They have been back twenty of days at least."

"But no one passes outside, not even the fargi, no one comes in other than you."

"Of course not." Akotolp settled back solidly on her tail, her four thumbs laced together and resting comfortably on the thick roll of fat on her midriff. "You know little about the Yilanè, just about this much, the space between my thumbs." She pinched them together tightly. "You live in our midst yet know nothing."

"I am nothing, I know nothing. You know everything. Enlightenment would be pleasure."

Kerrick meant what he said, it was not mere politeness. He lived in a jungle of mysteries, a maze of unanswered questions. Most of his life had been lived here in this city of secrets. There were assumptions and knowledge of Yilanè life that everyone seemed to know—yet no one would talk about. If flattery and fawning could get answers from this fat creature, he would contort himself into every position of obeisance.

"Yilanè do not grow ill. Disease strikes down only the lower animals, like you. I can assume that there were once diseases that affected us. They have long since been eliminated, like the fever that killed some of the first Yilanè to come here. Infections may follow traumatic wounding; they are quickly conquered. So your illness baffles the stupid fargi, they cannot understand it or accept it—so they ignore it—and you. However, such is my skill at working with all forms of life that I am immune to such stupidities."

She expressed great satisfaction with herself and Kerrick hurried to agree in great detail. "There is nothing unknown to your Highest," he added. "Could this stupid one presume upon your intelligence to ask a question?"

Akotolp signaled bored permission.

"Is there not disease among the males? I was told in the hanalè that many of them die on the beaches."

"Males are stupid and make too much stupid talk. It is forbidden for Yilanè to discuss these things."

Akotolp looked at Kerrick with one quizzical eye, while rolling the other at the same time towards Inlènu*'s stolid back, while she made up her mind.

"But I can see no harm in telling you. You are not Yilanè—and you are male—so you will be told. I will speak of it simply, because only one of my great knowledge can really understand it. I am going to describe to you the intimate and complicated details of the process of reproduction. Firstly, you must realize your inferiority. All of the warm-fleshed male creatures, including yourself, evacuate sperm—and that is your total involvement in the birth process. This is not true of our superior species. During intercourse the fertilized egg is deposited within the masculine pouch. This act triggers a metabolic change in the male. The creature grows torpid, expends little energy, and grows fat. The eggs hatch, the young nurse in the protected pouch and grow strong, emerging only when they are mature enough to survive in the sea. A beautiful process that frees the superior females for more important duties."

Akotolp smacked her lips hungrily, reached out, and seized up Kerrick's unfinished gourd of liquid meat and drained it in a single swallow. "Superior in every way." She belched with pleasure. "Once the young have entered the sea the male role in reproduction is finished. Very much the same, it might be said, as that of an insect called the mantis where the female eats the male while they are copulating. Reversing the male metabolic change is not efficient. Approximately half of them die in the process. While this is presumably uncomfortable for the male it has no effect at all on the survival of the species. You have no idea of what I am talking about, do you? I can tell that by the bestial emptiness of your eyes."

But Kerrick understood only too well. *A third time to the beaches, certain death,* Kerrick thought to himself. Aloud he said, "What wisdom you have, Highest. Had I been alive since the egg of time I would know only the smallest part of what you do."

"Of course," Akotolp agreed. "The inferior warm-fleshed creatures are incapable of major metabolic change which is why they are few in number and capable of surviving only at the rim of the world. I have worked with animals in Entoban* that encase themselves in the mud of dried lake bottoms during the dry season, surviving that way until the next rains fall, no matter how long a time that may be. Therefore even you will be able to understand that metabolic change can cause survival as well as death."

The facts came together and Kerrick spoke aloud, without thinking. "The Daughters of Life."

"The Daughters of Death," Akotolp said in the most insulting manner. "Do not speak of those creatures to me. They do not serve their city, nor do they die decently when turned away. It is the good who die." When she looked at Kerrick now there was cold malice in her gestures. "Ikemei is dead, a great scientist. You had the honor of meeting her in Ingeban* when she took samples of your body tissues. That was her undoing. Some fools in high places wished for her to find a biological way of destroying your ustuzou. She would not, could not do this, no matter how hard she tried. So she died. The scientist preserves lives, we cannot take them. Like a Yilanè rejected by her city, she died. You are an insensate male animal and I talk to you no more."

She waddled away, but Kerrick was scarcely aware of her going. For the first time he was beginning to understand some bit of what was happening around him. He had stupidly accepted the world as he saw it. Had believed that creatures like the hèsotsan and the boats were completely natural. How could they be? The Yilanè had shaped their flesh in some unknown manner—must have shaped every plant and animal in the city. If the fat Akotolp knew how to accomplish such things her knowledge was indeed well beyond anything that he could possibly imagine. For the first time he sincerely respected her, respected what she knew and what she could do. His sickness, she had cured that. He would be dead except for her knowledge. He fell asleep then and moaned in his sleep at the dreams of animals and flesh changing all around him, of himself melting and changing as well.

Soon he was well enough to sit up. After that, leaning on Inlènu*, he managed to walk a few dragging steps. Bit by bit his strength returned. When he was able to, he ventured out of his chamber and sat against a leafy wall in the sun. Once here, and apparently as sound as ever, his presence was permitted again. The fargi came when he called and brought him fruit, all that he wished to have, to wash the taste of liquified raw meat from his mouth.

His strength continued to return until finally, stopping often to rest, he even managed to venture out as far as the ambesed. Before his illness this would have been a short stroll. It was an expedition now and he was leaning heavily on Inlènu* and running with sweat before he reached his goal. He dropped against the ambesed wall, gasping for breath. Vaintè saw him arrive and ordered him to her presence. He struggled to his feet, stumbling when he walked. She watched his unsteady approach.

"You are still ill," she asked, expressing concern as she spoke.

"The illness has passed, Eistaa. Just the weakness remains. Akotolp, she of endless knowledge, tells me to eat much meat so that flesh will return to my body, and with it my strength."

"Do as she orders, that is my command as well. Victory marched with us to the north and all of the ustuzou we met we destroyed. Other than the few we made prisoner. It was my wish that you speak with them, seek out information."

"As the Eistaa commands," Kerrick said. Though he spoke with humble courtesy he was possessed of sudden excitement: his skin flushed and he trembled. He knew that he loathed the disgusting creatures. Yet he still longed to communicate with them.

"You will speak, but not with those we brought back. They are dead. Build your strength. When the warm sun returns to the north we go there again for an even greater killing."

Kerrick signed supplication, wondering at his sudden disappointment.

It was enough now to lie in the sun, to put the illness behind him as his strength returned. Many days passed before Akotolp sent for him. The fargi led the way to a part of the city he had never visited before, to a sealed and strangely familiar panel. It opened to reveal a still damp chamber.

"It is a water entrance—just like the one in Inegban*!"

Inlènu* wriggled her thick body in agreement. "Hurts the eyes."

"Then keep them shut, one of great stupidity." Then he closed his own eyes quickly as the warm liquid washed over them.

Akotolp turned from her work when they entered, reached out and pinched Kerrick's flesh between her thumbs.

"Good. You cover your ribs. You must exercise as well. That is the order I pass on to you from the Eistaa. She is most concerned that you will able to go north with the others."

"I hear and I obey." Kerrick's eyes were moving about the strange room as he talked, trying—and failing—to understand what he saw. "Once, in distant Inegban* I was in a place like this."

"You are wise in your stupidity. One laboratory is the same as another."

"Tell me what you do here, great one."

Akotolp smacked her lips and her fat flesh trembled with the strength of her feelings. "You wish me to tell you, creature of endless stupidity! Were you to live ten lifetimes you could not begin to understand. Since Yilanè first came from the sea we have had our science, and since that time it has been growing and maturing. Science is the knowledge of life itself, of seeing inside life, seeing the cells that form all life, seeing inside the cells to the genes, seeing the spiral there that can be cut and moved and changed until we are masters of all life. Have you understood a word that I have said, groveling and crawling one?"

Kerrick signed groveling and crawling as he spoke. "Very little, she of endless knowledge, but enough to know that you are the master of life."

"That is true. At least you have intelligence enough to appreciate even if you cannot understand. Look in wonder at this creature." Akotolp pushed one of her assistants aside and gestured at a knobbed and spiked, multicolored creature that squatted beside a transparent section of the wall. Bright sunlight shone against what appeared to be a great eye in its side. Disconcertingly, it had another eye in the top of its head. Akotolp signaled Kerrick forward, then wobbled with mirth at his reluctance.

"You are afraid of it?"

"Those eyes. . ."

"They cannot see, stupid one. It is blind and senseless, the eyes modified for our use, lenses to bend light so we can see the unseen. Look here, on this transparent plate, what do you see?"

"A drop of water?"

"Amazing observation. Now watch when I place it into the sanduu." Akotolp prodded with her thumb until an opening appeared in the sanduu's side, then slipped the plate into it. She then squinted into the topmost eye, grunting to herself as she thumbed the sanduu with instructions. Satisfied, she straightened up and signaled Kerrick to her.

"Close one eye. Look in here with the other. Tell me what you see."

He saw nothing. Just a blur of light. He blinked and moved his head—then saw them. Transparent creatures with rapidly moving tentacles. He could not understand it and turned to Akotolp for assistance. "I saw something, moving beasts, what were they?"

"Animals, minute ones, there in the drop of water, their images magnified by the lenses. Do you know what I am talking about?"

"No."

"Exactly. You will never learn. Your intelligence is equal to that of the other ustuzou behind you. Dismissed."

Kerrick turned and gasped when he saw the silent, bearded Tanu standing in the niche in the wall. Then he realized that it was only a stuffed and mounted animal. It meant nothing to him and he left quickly.

Yet he felt strangely disturbed as he walked back, the sun warm on his shoulders, Inlènu* plodding patiently behind. In thought and speech he was Yilanè. In form he was ustuzou. Which meant he was neither one nor the other and he grew upset when he thought about it. He was Yilanè, that was what he was, there was no doubt about that.

Unconsciously, as he told himself this over and over, his fingers pinched at his warm Tanu flesh.

CHAPTER TWENTY-SEVEN

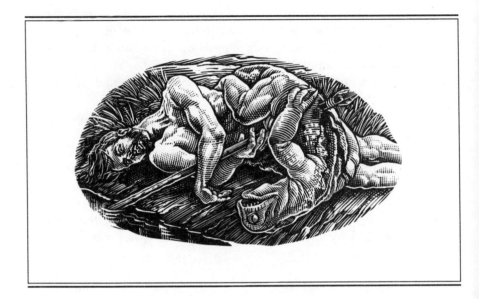

"The time has come for us to leave," Stallan said. "It is here in the pictures, everything we need to know."

"Show me," Vaintè said. Her aides and the fargi pressed close to see as well, but a gesture drove them back. Stallan passed the pictures over, one at a time, with a careful explanation of each.

"These are the earliest, of the high valleys where the ustuzou usually winter. But this last winter the valleys remained frozen. The thaw did not come that brings them life during the rest of the year. Therefore the ustuzou must move south to find food."

South, away from the cold of their winter, Vaintè thought, just as we flee south from the frigid winters of Inegban∗. She wiped this repugnant idea away as quickly as it had come. There was no connection between the two facts, could be no connection between Yilanè and ustuzou. It was just a matter of chance. What did matter was that the creatures would have to move south to find food. She spoke aloud.

"South—where we can reach them."

"You see the future clearly, Eistaa. If they stay, then they die of starvation. If they do not stay, why, we will be there to greet them."

"When do we leave?"

"Very soon. See here, and here. The large beasts that drag the poles and skins. They come down from the hills. There is grass, but still gray and dead after the winter. And the white, here in the hollows, that is hard water. They must come further south."

"They will. Are your preparations made?"

"They are. Supplies gathered, the boats fed, the armed fargi are ready."

"See that they remain that way."

She dismissed Stallan, put the hunter from her mind instantly, addressed her thoughts instead to the coming campaign. They would be going far inland this time and would be away all of the summer. They could not carry enough food with them for this long a time—so should she arrange for resupply? Or live off the land? This would be easier—and every beast they killed and ate would be one less for the ustuzou. But there would also have to be a reserve of preserved meat so their progress would not be slowed. Everything must be considered. Prisoners must be taken as well. The raptor's chance movements would find only a few of the ustuzou packs. But questioning the prisoners would lead them from one pack to another until they had all been destroyed. A fargi hurried over at her gesture.

"Command Kerrick to attend me."

Her thoughts went to the coming campaign until she was aware of his presence before her.

"Tell me of your health," she ordered. "You are thinner than you used to be."

"I am, but the weakness has gone, the scars from the sores are healed. Each day I make this fat Inlènu* run with me to the fields. She loses weight, I gain it."

"We go north soon. You will go with us."

"As the Eistaa speaks, so do I obey."

He expressed this in the most formal manner when he left, revealing no other emotion. But the thoughts that churned beneath that calm exterior were quite different.

He was eager to go—yet was afraid at the same time. Most of his memories of the last voyage north were buried beneath the pain of his sickness. It had been easiest when he was the sickest because then there had only been unconsciousness with no memory of what had passed. But then had come the wakening days, the pains in his chest, the sores that covered his body. He knew that he should eat but he could not. He had been vaguely aware of the wasting away of his body, the close approach to death, but had been too weak to do anything about it. Only when the gradual and painful recovery had begun could he think of food again.

But that was in the past—and must be kept in the past. Though he still grew tired by the end of the day, each day he was that slight bit stronger. It would be all right. He would go with them and there would be other ustuzou to talk to. For a long time he had not permitted his thoughts to dwell on this, but now a strange excitement filled him and he looked forward eagerly to the expedition. He would talk to Tanu again—and this time he would remember more of the words. There was a sudden and inexplicable excitement when he thought about talking with them and he walked faster, until Inlènu∗ registered patient protest.

They started north a few days later, earlier than had been originally planned, for now they would be going slower. Vaintè wanted to see if they could supply their own meat as they went along. On the first day they traveled only until early afternoon before making a landing on a rocky shore. Stallan left at once with her best hunters, followed by a group of nervous fargi.

They returned well before dark, the fargi now burdened with the carcasses of deer. Kerrick looked on with strange excitement as they came up and placed the deer carefully before the Eistaa.

"This is good, very good," she said with pleasure. "You are truly named, Stallan, for you are a hunter without peer."

Hunter. Kerrick had never considered the significance of the name. Hunter. To enter the forest, move stealthily across the plain, to make the kill.

"I would like to hunt too, Stallan," he said, almost thinking aloud. He bent to pick up a hèsotsan that lay nearby, but Stallan kicked it roughly away with her foot. The rejection was cruel and sharp.

"Ustuzou are killed with hèsotsan, they get no closer than that."

Kerrick recoiled. He had not been thinking of the weapons, just the chase. While he was shaping a reply Vaintè spoke first.

"Is your memory so short, Stallan, that you have forgotten that it is I who give the orders? Give Kerrick your own weapon. Explain to the ustuzou how it functions."

Stallan stiffened into immobility at the strength of the command. Vaintè did not change her final imperative position. It was important that all Yilanè, even of Stallan's rank, be reminded that she alone was Eistaa. And it pleased her to pit these two against each other, since their hatred of each for the other was so great.

Stallan could only obey. The fargi pushed close as they always did when something was being explained, while Stallan reluctantly held out the weapon to Kerrick.

"This creature is hèsotsan, developed and bred to be a weapon." Kerrick gingerly took the cool dark length in his hands and followed the indicating thumb. "They are mobile when young, only changing their form when they get their full growth. The legs become vestigial, the spine stiffens until the creature looks like this. It must be fed or it will die. This is the mouth," she indicated a black-lipped opening, "not to be confused with this orifice where the darts are inserted. The darts are picked from the bushes and dried—do not move your hand!"

Stallan tore the weapon from Kerrick's grasp and held it while she fought to control her temper. The presence of the Eistaa behind her just made this possible. Had they been alone she would have smashed the ustuzou to the ground. Her voice was even hoarser when she spoke again.

"This weapon kills. To do this you squeeze its body with one hand, here where your hand was, then press here on the base with the thumb of your other hand."

There was a sharp cracking sound and a dart hissed harmlessly out into the sea.

"The darts are inserted here. When the hèsotsan receives the impulse it produces a small quantity of a secretion which explodes into steam, driving the dart out forcibly. When they are loaded the darts are harmless to handle. But as it moves through the projection tube the dart brushes against a gland that secretes a poison so strong that a drop too small to see will instantly kill a creature as large as a nenitesk."

"You make an excellent teacher," Vaintè said, a sharp edge of amusement adding a second meaning. "You may stop now."

Stallan thrust the hèsotsan at Kerrick and turned quickly about. But not so quickly that he could not see the burning hatred in her movements. He returned the emotion in full. But he quickly forgot the incident as he examined the weapon, eager to try it on the hunt. But not so eager that he would allow Stallan anywhere near him when they were out of sight of the others. It would be wise to always stay well away from the hunter now, particularly during the hunt. The poisoned darts could kill him as easily as any other animal.

When it was time for the hunt next day he did go out with his weapon until he saw which way Stallan and the others had gone— then he went in the opposite direction. He had no desire to be the victim of a fatal accident.

Hunting was not easy with the clumsy Inlènu✻ in tow, but he did as well as he could. He had some success and in the coming days Inlènu✻ carried more than one deer back to the beach. But more important than the deer themselves was the way he felt when stalking his prey through the high grass. It was a pleasure beyond pleasure. He did not notice when he grew tired: his appetite was ravenous and he slept well. The hunting continued as they moved slowly north, and every day he found that he could do that little bit more. By the time they left the ocean and started up the wide river he felt as strong as he ever had. It was only a few days after that when they had their first battle, their first massacre of the summer.

Kerrick stayed at his usual place in the encampment on the river bank when the others left. The raptor's pictures had shown that the ustuzou were moving in this direction along the river bank, so the ambush had been carefully laid. It was no affair of Kerrick's. He sat cross-legged on the ground and teased the hèsotsan's mouth open with his fingernail, then pushed a fragment of meat into it, thinking of the next hunt. Inlènu✻ was so noisy. But at least she had learned to be motionless and quiet when they stopped. He would do a wide circle around the next herd of deer that they found, then lie in wait downwind from them. The deer would move away from the other hunters and approach him—instead of the other way around. It was a good plan.

The distant shriek cut through his thoughts. Even Inlènu✻ stirred herself and looked around. It sounded again, louder, closer. Kerrick jumped to his feet, the weapon in both hands ready to fire as the cry came again, the sound of heavy thudding.

There was a harsh bellow from the bank above them and a great head appeared. Long white tusks, a lifted trunk, the deafening shriek again.

"Kill the ustuzou," Inlènu✻ pleaded. "Kill, kill!"

Kerrick had the hèsotsan in a line before his eyes, looking along it at the creature's dark eye glaring down at him.

"Karu . . ." he said, and did not fire. Inlènu✻ moaned in fear.

The mastodon lifted its trunk and bellowed again. Then turned and vanished from sight.

Karu. Why had he said that? What did it mean? He had been startled by the giant creature—but not afraid at all. That strange word, Karu, it stirred up mixed memories. Warm and friendly. Cold as death. He trembled and pushed them away. The fighting should be very close. The large, hairy beast must have been frightened by the battle, had run this way. He was glad that he had not killed it.

"The Eistaa sends for one by the name of Kerrick," the fargi said, moving slowly along the river bank. She had been wounded by some sharp object and a large bandage covered her lower arm. There was blood on her side and streaked down her leg.

"Wash yourself clean," Kerrick ordered, then gave a tug on his lead and Inlènu* lumbered to her feet. The hèsotsan had finished the bit of meat and he smoothed its mouth shut as they walked; it had tiny, sharp teeth and could give a nasty little bite if this were not done.

They followed the river bank, then turned away from it when they came to a well-trampled path. More wounded fargi passed them going in the opposite direction. Some of them had stopped; others were sprawled on the ground, too weak to go any further. They passed one of them that had died on the way, eyes wide and mouth gaping. The fighting must have been fierce.

Then Kerrick saw his first dead Tanu. They were heaped together, men and women, children's tiny corpses tossed aside. Beyond them a mastodon, dead among the broken poles, its load burst and scattered.

Kerrick was numb, with an emotion—or lack of emotion—that left him stumbling along in silence. These were ustuzou, they needed killing. These were Tanu—why were they dead? These were the loathsome ustuzou that had slaughtered the Yilanè males and the young on the beaches. But what did he really care or know about that? He had never even been close to the beaches.

A fargi, the spear that had killed it still through her body, lay in bloody embrace over the body of the hunter who had wielded it. The fargi was Yilanè and he, Kerrick, he was Yilanè as well.

But, no, he was Tanu. Was he Tanu too?

The question could not be answered, but could not be forgotten as well. Yet he must forget it then and remember that he had been a boy—but that boy was dead. In order to live he must live as a Yilanè. He was Yilanè, not dirty ustuzou.

A fargi pulled at his arm and he stumbled after her. Through the column of death; dead Tanu, mastodons, Yilanè. It could not bear looking at. They came to a group of armed fargi who moved aside so that Kerrick could pass. Vaintè stood there, every movement of her body expressing unconcealed anger. When she saw Kerrick she pointed soundlessly at the object on the ground before her. It was an animal's skin, badly tanned and mottled, limp and shapeless except for the head that had been stuffed.

Kerrick recoiled in horror. Not an animal—a Yilanè, and one that he recognized. Sòkain, the surveyor who had been killed by the ustuzou. Killed, skinned, and brought here.

"See this." Every motion of Vaintè's body, each sound she spoke, exuded hatred and a relentless anger. "See what these animals have done to one of such intelligence and grace. I want to know more of this matter, which one of them was responsible, how many were involved, where we can find them. You will question the ustuzou we hold captive over there. We had to club it into submission. It may be the pack leader. Make it bleed, make it tell you what it knows before I kill it. Be quick. I will want to know when I return. A few of them fled destruction but Stallan leads her hunters and follows and will pull them down."

There was a glade here surrounded by high trees. The Tanu lay on the ground, arms and legs bound, while a fargi beat the creature with its own spear. "Make it suffer—but do not kill it," Vaintè ordered, then turned away as a messenger hurried up.

Kerrick approached slowly, almost against his will. Saw that the hunter was big, taller than he was, his flowing beard and hair matted thick with blood. The beating continued yet the man said nothing.

"Stop that," Kerrick ordered, prodding the fargi with his weapon to get her attention. "Move back."

"What are you?" the man asked hoarsely, then coughed and spat out a mouthful of blood and fragments of teeth. "Are you a prisoner, leashed like that? Yet you speak to them. Where is your hair? Who are you? Can you talk?"

"I . . . I am Kerrick."

"A boy's name, not a hunter's name. Yet you are grown . . ."

"It is I who ask questions. Give me your name."

"I am Herilak. This is my sammad. Was mine. They are dead, all dead, aren't they?"

"Some escaped. They are being pursued."

"A boy's name." His voice was gentler. "Come closer, boy who is now a man. Let me see you. They bruised my eyes, you must come close. Yes, I see. Even though all of your hair is gone I can still see that you have a Tanu face."

Herilak rolled his head back and forth, trying to shake the blood from his eyes. Kerrick reached down and gently wiped them clean. It was like touching himself, the warm skin. Skin like his, flesh like his. Kerrick shivered all over, his hand shook in the grasp of some unknown sensation.

"You were making sounds at them," Herilak said, "and wriggling about too just as they do. You can speak with them, can't you?"

"You will answer my questions. It is not you who will do the questioning."

Herilak ignored this but nodded with understanding. "They want you to do their work. How long have you been with them?"

"I don't know. Many summers . . . winters."

"They have been killing Tanu all of that time, Kerrick. We kill them, but never enough. I saw a boy once, being held by the murgu. Do they have many captives?"

"There are no captives. Just myself . . ." Kerrick fell silent; a memory long forgotten stirred his thoughts, a bearded face in the trees.

"They captured you, raised you, didn't they?" Herilak said almost in a whisper. "You can speak with them. We need your help, the Tanu need you now . . ."

He broke off as he saw what hung about Kerrick's neck. His voice was choked now as he spoke.

"Turn, boy, turn to the light. Around your neck—is that yours?"

"Mine?" Kerrick said, touching the cool metal of the knife. "I suppose so. It was around my neck, they tell me, when I first came to them."

Herilak's voice was distant, as he too dredged in memories of the past. "Skymetal. I was one of those who saw it fall from the sky, searched and found it. I was there when the knives were made, sawn from the metal block with sheets of stone, hammered and drilled. Now—reach into my furs, in the front, that's right. You have it, pull it out."

The metal knife was hanging from a thong. Kerrick clutched it, unbelieving. It was the same as his—only twice as large.

"I saw them made. A large one for a hunter, a sammadar, a small one for his son. The son, a boy's name, Kerrick perhaps, I don't remember. But the father. One close to me. His name was Amahast. Then I found the skymetal knife again many years later—in the broken bones of his body. The bones of Amahast."

Kerrick could only listen in frozen, horrified silence as the name was spoken. A name remembered in dreams, forgotten upon awakening.

"*Amahast.*"

Amahast. The word was like a key unlocking a flood of memories that washed silently over him. Karu, his mastodon, killed beside him. His father, Amahast, killed, the sammad destroyed around him. The memory blurred and merged with that of this sammad lying dead now on all sides. The slaughter, the years, the long years since. Through these memories the hunter's words slowly penetrated.

"Kill them, Kerrick, kill them as they have killed us all."

Kerrick turned and fled with Inlènu∗ stumbling after, away from the hunter and his voice, away from the memories that flooded through him. But these he could not escape. He pushed past the armed fargi to the top of a grassy slope that led down to the sea, dropped to the ground, sat clutching his legs, staring out at the ocean yet not seeing it.

Seeing Amahast, his father, instead. And his sammad. Unclearly at first, but fleshed out in greater detail as memory returned. The memory was still there, buried and long forgotten, but hiding there still. His eyes filled with a child's tears, tears that he had never shed as a child, that welled out and ran down his cheeks as he saw his sammad being destroyed, slaughtered just as the sammad of Herilak had been destroyed this day. The two scenes blurred in his mind and were one. To survive all those years with the Yilanè all of this he had to forget. He had survived, he had forgotten.

But now he remembered, and in remembering he was two people, the ustuzou who spoke like a Yilanè; the boy who was Tanu.

Boy? He stared at his hands, arched his fingers. He was no longer a boy. In those long years his body had grown. He was a man yet knew nothing of being a man. The realization came that his father, the other hunters, so large in memory—why, he must be their size now.

Springing to his feet, Kerrick roared aloud with defiance and anger. What was he? Who was he? What was happening to him? Through the crash of his emotions he was aware of a movement at his neck, a pulling. He turned about, blinking, to discover that Inlènu✳ was tugging gently at their connecting lead. Her eyes were wide, her shivering motions expressing worry and fear at his strange actions.

He wanted to kill her, half raised the weapon still clutched in his hand. *Marag*, he cried, "marag." But the anger drained away as quickly as it had come and he lowered the weapon shamefacedly. There was no harm in this simple creature, more of a prisoner than he was.

"Be of peace, Inlènu✳," he said. "There is nothing wrong. Be of peace."

Reassured, Inlènu✳ sat back on her tail and blinked comfortably in the evening sun. Kerrick looked past her to the glade behind the trees where Herilak waited.

Waited for what? An answer, of course. To a question that Kerrick could not answer, although the question was all too clear.

What was he? Physically he was Tanu, a man with the thoughts of a boy who had never grown as a Tanu. That was clear and obvious when he thought about it. That boy, to stay alive, had become Yilanè. That was obvious too. A Yilanè inside his thoughts, a Tanu for the world to see. That much was clear. What was not clear was what would happen to him next. If he did nothing, his existence would go on very much as it had in the past. His position would remain high, next to the hand of the Eistaa, secure and honored. As a Yilanè.

But was that what he wanted? Was that his future? He had never considered these matters before, had no idea that a conflict such as this might exist. He shrugged his shoulders, struggling to remove an invisible burden. It was too much to consider right now. He needed to puzzle things out slowly. He would do as Vaintè had asked, question the ustuzou. There would be time later to think of these matters; his head was hurting too much now.

When he returned nothing had changed. Herilak was lying bound on the ground, the three fargi standing guard in unquestioning obedience. Kerrick looked down at the hunter, trying to speak, but the words did not come. It was Herilak who broke the silence.

"Do as I said," he whispered. "Kill the murgu, cut my bonds, escape with me. To the mountains, to the winter snow, the good hunting, the fire in the tent. Come back to your people."

Though they were whispered the words were echoing in his head like the roll of thunder.

"No!" he shouted aloud. "You will be silent. You will answer my questions only. You will not speak except to answer . . ."

"You're lost, boy, lost but not forgotten. They've tried to make you one of them but you are not of them. You are Tanu. You can come back to the sammad now, Kerrick."

Kerrick shouted in anger, ordering Herilak to be silent, but he could not drown out the hunter's voice or his words. Neither would he give in. It was the fargi, the one who still held the hunter's spear, who made the decisive move. She did not understand, but she could see that there was disagreement. Remembering the Eistaa's earlier orders she moved forward to help, hammering the butt of the spear into Herilak's side, again and again.

"No!" Kerrick roared aloud in Tanu, "you cannot do that."

The weapon in his hand snapped almost without volition and the fargi crumpled and died. Still in the grip of his anger he turned and fired at the next one as well; her mouth still gaping with disbelief as she fell. The third one started to raise her own weapon but she crumpled like the others. He kept squeezing and squeezing on the hèsotsan until the fargi corpses bristled with darts. Then it was empty and he threw it down.

"The spear, take it," Herilak ordered. "Cut me free."

Inlènu* lurched after Kerrick as he stumbled to the fargi and pulled the spear from her dead grasp. He cut Herilak's ankles free, then his wrists.

"What is this? What has happened?" Vaintè called out angrily.

Kerrick spun about to see her standing above him, mouth open, teeth shining. And now, for the first time he saw before her in the blur of memory those teeth tearing a girl's throat out. Saw the rows of teeth above him as she straddled him, roaring with pleasure. Shared pleasure, for he had been moved as well.

Pleasure and hatred now, he felt them both.

She was saying something he could not hear, issuing an order he could not obey, as she turned away and reached for one of the abandoned weapons.

What he did next was so natural, so right that it required no thought or effort. The spear came up, thrust forward, into Vaintè's side, deep into her body. She clutched at it and it came free. Blood spurted as she crumpled and fell backwards out of sight.

"Run," Herilak shouted, pulling at Kerrick's shoulder. "Come with me. You can't stay here, not after what you have done. You must come with me. That is all that you can do now."

He took Kerrick by the hand, tugging him towards the dark wall of the forest beyond the glade. Kerrick resisted—then stumbled after him crashing, through the undergrowth, the spear still clutched, forgotten, in his hand, with Inlènu∗ protesting and stumbling along behind.

Their running footsteps died away as they vanished from sight among the trees. The glade was quiet again.

Quiet as death.

BOOK TWO

CHAPTER ONE

The flock of crows wheeled up in wide circles, cawing loudly before settling back among the trees. There was little wind and the afternoon was close and hot. Under the trees it was cooler, for the leaves were so thick upon the birch and oak trees above that only a dapple of flickering sunlight filtered through to the forest floor below. A moving pattern of light that played over the three figures sprawled on the soft grass.

Even Herilak's massive strength was spent; his wounds had reopened and blood matted his hair and beard, spread wetly down his side. He lay back, eyes closed, drawing in breath after ragged breath.

Inlènu* lay opposite him, her position an unconscious mockery of his with her jaw gaping wide to cool herself after the unwelcome exertion in the heat.

Kerrick was not as exhausted as they were, so was well aware of what was happening, of where they were. In the foothills close above the shore. They had fled, running until Inlènu* could run no more, and when she had staggered to a halt Herilak had fallen as well. While they had been running Kerrick's panic had slowly ebbed away—but had been replaced by a heart-stopping fear.

What had he done?

The question was its own answer. He knew what he had done. He had destroyed himself. He had murdered the Eistaa. Now that the emotion was spent he could not understand what had possessed him to do such an insane thing. With that single thrust of the spear he had cut every bond that held him to the Yilanè, had set every Yilanè hand against him. The life he had known was ended, was as dead as Vaintè herself. Now he could never return to the comforts of Alpèasak, to the easy life he had known there. Ahead of him was only a blankness, an emptiness, with the only certainty that of death itself. Shivering with apprehension he turned and pushed a shrub aside and looked back down the slope. Nothing moved. There was no sign of any pursuit. Not yet—but they would certainly follow. The murderer of the Eistaa would not be allowed to escape unpunished.

He could not return. Not after what he had done. The past was dead. He was an exile now, a Yilanè among ustuzou. More alone than he had ever been before. The voice cut across his thoughts and it was long moments before he could understand the words.

"You did it well, Kerrick, a good clean thrust. Killed the one in command."

Kerrick's voice was numb with loss. "More than just the one in command. Leader, head of the city, sammadar of the city."

"Even better."

"Better? Her death will bring about my death!"

"Her? That ugly marag was female? It's hard to believe."

"They are all female. The males are kept locked away."

Herilak struggled up onto his elbows and looked coldly at Inlènu*. "That one too, a female?" he asked.

"All of them."

"Give me the spear. Then there will be one less."

"No!" Kerrick pulled the spear back before Herilak's groping fingers could find it. "Not Inlènu*. She's harmless, as much a prisoner as I am. You'll not kill her."

"Why not? Was it not her kind cut down my sammad, killed them all, every one? Give me the spear. I'll kill her and then you will be free. How far do you think you will be able to go bound to her like that?"

"You will not harm her, do you understand?" Kerrick was surprised at the warmth of his feeling towards Inlènu*. She had meant nothing to him before this. He had been aware of her only as a hindrance to his movements. But now her presence was somehow reassuring.

"If you won't kill her then use the edge of the spearhead. Cut yourself loose from the thing."

"This lead cannot be cut. See, the stone edge won't even scratch it." He sawed at the smooth, hard surface to no effect. "Some of your sammad escaped." Talk of this might make Herilak forget Inlènu* for the moment. "I was told this. I was also told that they were being followed."

"Do you know who they were? How many?"

"No. Just that some fled."

"Now I must think. Whoever they are, they will not go any further south. They will know better than that. They will return, back the way we came. Yes, that is what they will do. Backtrack, to the nearest water, the stream where we camped last night. We must go there as well." He looked up at Kerrick. "Have we been followed?"

"I have been watching. I don't think that any of them saw us escape. But they will come. They are good trackers. I will not be allowed to escape after what I have done."

"You worry without cause. They are not here yet. But we will not be safe until we are well away from the shore. They could still find us in these hills if, as you say, they know anything about tracking." He struggled to rise, and could only get to his feet with Kerrick's help. He rubbed the clotted blood from his eyes and looked about. "We go in that direction, along that valley. If we follow it north, then cross the ridge, we will come to the campsite by the stream. Now we leave."

They made slow progress the rest of the afternoon, since they were forced to proceed at Herilak's limping pace, going on steadily even though there was no sign of any pursuit. They were working their way up a grassy valley when Herilak stopped suddenly and raised his head to sniff the air.

"Deer," he said. "We need food. I don't think that we are being followed—but even if we are we must take the chance. You will bring a good-sized buck, Kerrick."

Kerrick looked at the spear, tested its weight in his hand. "I have not thrown a spear since I was a boy. I no longer have the skill."

"It will return."

"Not this day. You have the skill, Herilak. Do you have the strength?" He held out the spear and Herilak seized it.

"When I lack the strength to hunt I will be dead. Go to the stream there, under the trees, keep watch and wait until I return."

Herilak's back straightened as he tested the balance of the spear, then he trotted swiftly and silently away. Kerrick turned and led the way down to the stream where he drank his fill, then poured handfuls of water over his dusty body. Inlènu∗ knelt down and sucked water noisily between her pointed teeth, then squatted comfortably on the bank with her tail in the stream.

Kerrick envied her peace of mind, her stability at all times. It must be pleasant to be so stupid. She didn't question their presence here at all, had no concept of what might happen to her.

Kerrick knew what he had left behind—but the future was only a blank. He must come to terms with it: but it was too early to do that yet. How could he live away from the city? He knew nothing about this kind of rough existence. A boy's memories did not fit him for Tanu life. He wasn't even able to hurl a spear.

"A Yilanè comes," Inlènu∗ said and he sprang to his feet, terrified. Stallan and her hunters! This was his death. He drew back from the crackling in the underbrush—then swayed with relief when Herilak pushed his way through, a horned buck draped across his shoulders. He dropped it heavily and fell beside it.

Kerrick turned angrily to reproach Inlènu∗—then realized that it was not her fault. To Inlènu∗ all those who talked were Yilanè. What she really meant to say, though she knew no way to express it, was that someone, some person, was approaching.

"I saw murgu," Herilak said, and Kerrick's fear returned. "They were in the next valley, going back towards the sea. I think that they have lost our trail. Now we will eat."

Herilak used the spear to open and gut the still-warm deer. Since they had no fire he cut out the liver first, divided it, and handed a piece to Kerrick.

"I am not hungry, not now," Kerrick said, looking down at the raw and bloody lump of flesh.

"You will be. Do not discard it."

Inlènu∗ was facing away from them, but her nearer eye moved and followed every motion Herilak made. He was aware of this and after he had eaten his fill he pointed a bloody finger at her.

"Does that thing eat meat?"

Kerrick smiled at the question and spoke swiftly, ordering

Inlènu* to open her mouth. She did so, only her jaw moving. Herilak looked at the rows of glistening, pointed teeth and grunted.

"It eats meat. Should I feed it?"

"Yes, I would like that."

Herilak hacked off a forelimb and stripped most of the skin from it, then handed it to Kerrick.

"You feed it. I don't like its teeth."

"Inlènu* is harmless. Nothing but a stupid fargi."

Inlènu* closed her thumbs about the deer leg, then chewed slowly and powerfully on the tough meat, gazing blankly into the distance.

"What did you say it was?" Herilak asked.

"Fargi. It, well, I cannot say what the word means. Something like one who is learning to speak, but is not very good at it."

"Are you a fargi?"

"I am not!" Kerrick was insulted. "I am Yilanè. That is, although I am Tanu, I speak like a Yilanè so I am considered one. *Was* considered one."

"How did this happen? Do you remember?"

"Now I do. But I didn't, not for a long time."

His voice was halting, the words difficult to say, as he spoke aloud for the first time about what had happened to sammad Amahast. Relived the slaughter, the captivity, the fear of certain death and the unexpected reprieve. He stopped then because the words he spoke now did not seem capable of describing his years since that day.

Herilak was silent as well, understanding a little of what had happened to the boy Kerrick who had managed to live when all the others had died. A lone survivor who had somehow found a way to come to terms with the murgu. Who had learned their language and learned to live among them. He was a lot like them now, though he would not be aware of that. He moved about when he talked, then sat immobile when he was finished. They had done something to him; there was not a hair on his body. And he wore that pouch, made to look like his skin, as though they had taken away his maleness as well. Herilak's thoughts were interrupted by a sudden splash of water.

Kerrick heard it too and the color drained from his face. "They have found us. I am dead."

Herilak waved him to silence as he took up the spear, stood and faced downstream. There was more splashing, the sound of the bushes being pushed aside just around the bend. He raised the spear as the hunter appeared.

"It is Ortnar," he said, then called out.

Ortnar recoiled at the sound, then straightened and waved back. He was close to exhaustion, leaning on his spear as he came forward. Only when he was closer did he see Inlènu∗. He seized up the spear to hurl it at her, was stopped only by Herilak's command.

"Stop. The marag is a prisoner. Are you alone?"

"Yes, now." He dropped heavily to the ground. He laid his bow and empty quiver aside, but kept his spear in his hand and looked angrily at Inlènu∗. "Tellges was with me, we had been hunting when the murgu attacked, we were just returning to the sammad. We fought until our arrows were gone. They came at us with the death-sticks. There was nothing more we could do. All behind us were dead. I made him leave, but he hung back, did not run fast enough. They followed and he turned to fight. He fell. I came on alone. Now tell me—what are these creatures?"

"I am no creature, I am Tanu," Kerrick said angrily.

"Like no Tanu I have ever seen. No hair, no spear, tied to that marag . . ."

"Silence," Herilak ordered. "This is Kerrick, son of Amahast. His mother was my sister. He has been a prisoner of the murgu."

Ortnar rubbed his mouth with his fist. "I spoke in haste. This has been a day of death. I am Ortnar and I welcome you." His face twisted with an expression of grim humor. "Welcome to the sammad of Herilak, much reduced in numbers." He glanced up at the darkening sky. "There will be many new stars there tonight."

The sun was low now and the air was cool at this altitude. Inlènu∗ laid aside the well-gnawed bone and looked in Kerrick's direction.

"Humbly ask, low to high, where are the cloaks?"

"There are no cloaks, Inlènu∗."

"I am cold."

Kerrick shivered as well, but not from the cold. "There is nothing I can do, Inlènu∗, nothing at all."

CHAPTER TWO

Inlènu∗ died during the night.

Kerrick woke at dawn, shivering with cold. There was a beading of dew on the grass and mist was rising from the stream. When he turned towards Inlènu∗ he saw that her mouth was gaping open, her eyes staring sightlessly.

The cold, he thought. *She died in the night of the cold.*

Then he saw the pool of blood under her head. A spearpoint had been thrust into her throat, silencing her and killing her. Who had done this cruel thing? Herilak was still asleep but Ortnar's eyes were open, staring coldly at him.

"You did this!" Kerrick cried out, jumping to his feet. "Murdered this harmless creature in her sleep."

"I killed a marag." His voice was insolent. "It is always a good thing to kill murgu."

Shaking with rage, Kerrick reached out and seized Herilak's spear. But he could not lift it; the big hunter held fast to the haft.

"The creature is dead," Herilak said. "That is the end of it. She would have died soon of the cold in any case."

Kerrick stopped tugging at the spear and sprang suddenly at Ortnar, seizing him by the throat with both hands, his thumbs digging deep into the hunter's windpipe. His own throat hurt where the collar cut in; he had dragged Inlènu*'s dead weight after him, but he paid it no heed. Ortnar writhed in his grasp and groped for his spear, but Kerrick jammed the man's arm against the ground with his knee, grinding down hard. Ortnar thrashed feebly, tearing at Kerrick's back with the nails of his free hand, but Kerrick felt nothing in his rage.

Ortnar would have been dead had not Herilak intervened. He seized Kerrick's wrists in his great hands and pulled them wide. Ortnar hoarsely gasped in breath after breath, then moaned and rubbed at the bruised flesh of his throat. Kerrick's blind anger faded and, as soon as he stopped struggling, Herilak released him.

"Tanu does not kill Tanu," he said.

Kerrick started to protest, then grew silent. It was done. Inlènu* was dead. Killing her murderer would accomplish nothing. And Herilak was right; the winter would have killed her in any case. Kerrick sat down by her still form and looked out into the sunrise. What did she matter to him anyway? Just a stupid fargi who was always in his way. With her death his last link with Alpèasak was severed. So be it. He was Tanu now. He could forget that he had ever been Yilanè.

Then he realized that he was holding the flexible lead that joined him to Inlènu*. He was not free yet. And this lead could not be cut, he knew that. With that came the realization that there was only one way that he could be freed. He looked up, horrified, into Herilak's face. The sammadar nodded with understanding.

"I will do what must be done. Turn away for you will not enjoy the sight."

Kerrick faced the stream, but he could clearly hear what was happening behind his back. Ortnar stumbled to the water to bathe his face and neck and Kerrick shouted insults at him, trying to drown out the sounds.

It was over quickly. Herilak wiped the neck-ring on the grass before handing it to Kerrick. Kerrick went swiftly to the stream and washed it over and over in the running water. When it was clean he took it in both hands, stood and walked upstream away from the spot. He did not want to see what was lying back there.

When he heard the hunters approaching he turned quickly to face them; he had no desire to be killed from behind.

"This one has something to say," Herilak said pushing Ortnar forward. There was hatred in the small hunter's face and he touched his bruised throat when he spoke. His voice was hoarse.

"I was perhaps mistaken to kill the marag—but I am not sorry that I did it. The sammadar ordered me to say this. What is done is done. But you attempted to kill me, strange one, and that is something that is not easy to forget. But your bond to that marag was stronger than I knew—nor do I want to know more about it. So I say of my own free will that your back is safe from my spearpoint. How say you?"

The two hunters watched Kerrick in stern silence and he knew that he had to decide. Now. Inlènu* was dead and nothing could restore her life. And he could understand Ortnar's cold hatred after the destruction of his sammad. He, of all people, should be able to understand that.

"Your back is safe from my spear, Ortnar," he said.

"That is the end of the matter," Herilak said, and it was a command. "We shall talk of it no more. Ortnar, you will carry the deer's carcass. We will have a fire tonight and will eat well. Go with Kerrick, you know the path. Stop at midday. I will join you then. There is cover among those trees. If we are being followed by the murgu I will know it soon enough."

The two men walked in silence for some time. The track was easy to follow, the ground deeply scored by the poles of the travois, leading up the valley almost to its end, then over the ridge to the next valley. Ortnar was gasping for breath under the weight of his burden and called out when they came to the slow-moving stream on the valley's floor.

"Some water, strange-one, then we will go on."

He threw the deer down and buried his face in the stream, came up gasping.

"My name is Kerrick, son of Amahast," Kerrick said. "Do you find that too hard to remember?"

"Peace, Kerrick. My throat is still sore from our last encounter. I meant no insult, but you do look strange. You have just stubble instead of a beard or hair."

"It will grow in time." Kerrick rubbed at the bristles on his face.

"Yes, I imagine so. It just looks strange now. But that ring on your neck. Why do you wear it? Why not cut it off?"

"Here, you do it." Kerrick handed over the ring he was carrying and smiled as Ortnar sawed uselessly at the transparent lead with the edge of his spear point.

"It is smooth and soft—yet I cannot cut it."

"The Yilanè can do many things that we cannot. If I told you how it was made you would not believe me."

"You know their secrets? Of course, you must. Tell me of the death-sticks. We captured one but could do nothing with it. Finally it began to smell and we cut it open and it was a dead animal of some kind."

"It is a creature called a hèsotsan. They are a special kind of animals. They can move around like other animals when they are young. But when they grow old they become as you saw. They must be fed. Then darts are placed within them and when they are pressed in the correct manner the darts are fired out."

Ortnar's mouth hung open as he fought to understand. "But how can that be? Where are there animals like that?"

"Nowhere. That is the murgu secret. I have seen what they do, but I do not understand it myself. They can make animals do strange things. They know how to make them breed to do anything. It is hard to explain."

"Even harder to understand. It is time to go. Now it is your turn to carry the deer."

"Herilak ordered you to carry it."

"Yes—but you are going to help eat it."

Ortnar smiled as he said this and in spite of himself Kerrick smiled back. "All right, give it to me. But you'll get it back soon enough. Didn't Herilak say we would have a fire?" His mouth was suddenly wet with spittle at the memory. "Cooked meat—I had forgotten what it was like."

"Then the murgu eat all their meat raw?" Ortnar asked as they started up the track again.

"No. Well, yes and no. It is softened in some way. You get used to it."

"Why don't they roast it properly?"

"Because . . ." Kerrick stopped in his tracks at the thought. "Because they don't make fires. I never realized that before. I guess they don't need fires because where they live it is always warm. Sometimes at night when it is cool, or on wet days, we wrap—there is no word for it—warm things around us."

"Skins? Fur robes?"

"No. Living creatures that are warm."

"Sounds disgusting. The more I hear about your murgu the more I detest them. I don't know how you could bear living with creatures like that."

"I had little choice," Kerrick said grimly, then walked on in silence.

Herilak joined them soon after they had reached their stopping place for the night.

"The trail behind is empty. They have turned back."

"Cooked meat!" Ortnar said, smacking his lips together. "But I wish we had brought the fire with us."

These words touched a memory that Kerrick had long forgotten. "I used to do that," he said. "Keep the fire in the bow of the boat."

"That is a boy's work," Herilak said. "As a hunter you must make your own fire. Do you know how to do it?"

Kerrick hesitated. "I remember seeing it done. But I have forgotten. It was so long ago."

"Then watch. You are Tanu now and must know these things if you are to be a hunter."

It was a slow process. Herilak broke a branch from a long-dead and dried tree, then carefully cut and rounded a length of stick from it. While he did this, Ortnar searched deeper in the forest and returned with a handful of dry and moldy wood. He shredded and pounded this into a fine powder. When Herilak had finished the stick to his satisfaction he scraped another length of the wood flat, then drilled a shallow hole in it with his spearpoint.

When the preparations were done Herilak took Ortnar's bow and wrapped the bowstring about the carefully fashioned stick. He sat on the ground, held the length of wood steady with his feet, then placed the pointed tip of the stick into the hole in the wood and began to draw the bow back and forth to make it spin. Ortnar pushed some of the powdered wood into the hole while Herilak spun the stick as fast he could. A tiny thread of smoke twisted up, then died away. Herilak gasped with the effort and sat back.

The next time he spun the stick the wisp of smoke became a tiny spark of flame. They dropped more wood-dust upon it, blew carefully, cupped it between their hands as the flame grew, laughing with pleasure. They built the fire high, adding more and more wood, then let it die back to a bed of glowing coals. Soon the meat was roasting in the coals and Kerrick breathed in the cooking odors that he had completely forgotten.

They burnt their fingers on the hot meat, hacked off great pieces, ate and ate until their faces ran with grease and sweat.

Rested, then ate some more. Kerrick could not remember having eaten anything so good in his entire life.

That night they slept with their feet to the banked fire, warm and content, their stomachs full.

Kerrick woke during the night when Herilak got up to put more wood on the fire. The stars were bright points of light in the black sky, the star-group of the Hunter just above the horizon in the east. For the first time since their escape Kerrick was at peace, feeling the security of the hunters on both sides of him. They had not been followed. They were safe from the Yilanè.

Safe from the Yilanè? Would that ever be possible? He knew as these hunters did not how ruthless their enemy was. How strong. The raptors would fly and find every Tanu in every valley and meadow; nowhere could they be safe. The armed fargi would attack again and again until all the Tanu were dead. There was no possible escape. Nor could he sink back again into the blank escape of sleep.

Kerrick lay there awake, possessed by the knowledge of certain destruction. He watched as the sky lightened in the east and the stars vanished one by one. The new day had begun. The first day of his new life.

CHAPTER THREE

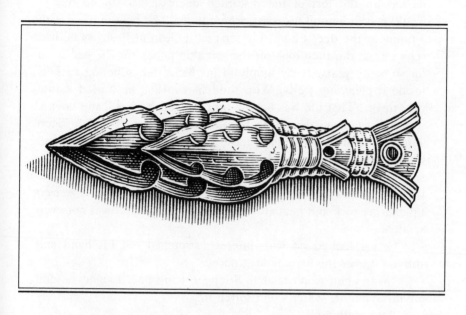

Kerrick's feet were swollen and sore after the long walk the day before. Sitting on a large boulder, chewing a lump of tough yet delicious meat, he bathed them in the cool water of the stream. Although his soles were thickly callused and tough he was unaccustomed to walking on stony ground. Now his feet were scratched and cut and he was not looking forward to the strenuous day that lay ahead. Herilak saw what he was doing and pointed to the long gash that cut through the callus of Kerrick's right foot.

"We must do something about that."

He and Ortnar were wearing flexible but strong madraps, made from two pieces of cured leather that had been carefully sewn together with lengths of gut. They did not have the materials here to fashion anything for him this complex—but there were other raw materials close to hand. Herilak found stones that would chip correctly and hammered off small, sharp flakes. Under his direction Ortnar removed the deer's skin, then scraped the adhering flesh from it in the running water. Herilak cut squares and strips from this, put the larger pieces around Kerrick's feet and bound them into place with the thin lengths.

"Good enough for now," he said. "By the time the skin gets stiff and starts to stink we will be far away from here." Kerrick picked up the rest of the discarded deerskin and found that it would just fit around his waist, where it could be held in place with a prong of the deer's horn. He scraped it clean of flesh, as he had seen Ortnar do, then took off the soft skin pouch that he had worn for so many years. It lay limply in his hand, the adhering suckers inside it gleaming wetly. With sudden revulsion he hurled it into the stream. That life was behind him forever; he was Tanu now.

But when he turned he tripped over the ring that had been around Inlènu*'s neck for all those years, that was still attached to the ring about his own neck. He held it out before him, loathing its smooth transparency and its solid strength. In sudden anger he smashed it down on the rock that rose from the stream bed, seized up another rock and beat at it until the anger died. It was not even scratched.

Ortnar looked on with interest, stretched out his hand and rubbed it over the unmarked surface.

"Won't cut, won't scratch. Stronger than stone. I've never seen anything like it. Water won't soften it?"

"No, nothing."

"Even hot water, boiling water?"

"I've never tried. We had nothing like that in the city. You can't boil water without fire . . ."

As soon as Kerrick had spoken the words he stiffened, looking down at the ring and its flexible lead, then slowly raised his eyes to the smoking fire on the shore. Not water, even boiling water. But something that the Yilanè knew nothing about.

Fire.

It might just be possible. The substance wasn't stone or metal. It might melt, or char, soften perhaps. If this happened it might then be weak enough to cut. Ortnar saw the direction of Kerrick's gaze and struck his hands together with enthusiasm.

"Why not? Fire might do something to it. You said the murgu don't have fire."

"They don't."

"Let me try."

Ortnar picked up the discarded ring at the other end of the lead and stepped over to the smoking ashes of the fire, poked it down into them.

Nothing happened. Kerrick looked on gloomily when he took it out and brushed the ashes from the smooth surface. It was unmarked—but he burnt his fingers. Ortnar sucked at them, then spat out bits of charcoal. Still determined he stirred the fire with a stick until it flamed up. When the stick began to burn he touched it to the ring.

Screamed and dropped it as it burst into scorching flame, crackling and exploding.

Kerrick saw the flame gush out surrounded by a growing cloud of black smoke, the ring burning, the fire flashing up the lead towards his face.

Unthinking, he hurled himself backward, away from the scorching heat. Fell splashing into the stream.

When he spluttered and rose to his feet again he saw the red weal across his arm and midriff where the burning lead had touched his body. It ended on his chest. With wondering fingers he touched the stub of the lead that ended there as well.

It was gone. This connection that had dominated his life, this restraint that had been with him all those long years. It was gone. He stood up straight, not feeling the burns, aware only that a great burden had been removed. His last tie with the Yilanè severed.

As they rubbed deer fat onto their burns, Ortnar pointed to the length of lead still hanging from the ring on Kerrick's neck.

"We could burn that off too. You could lie in the water, just that much above the surface, I could get some burning wood . . ."

"I think we've done enough for one day," Kerrick said. "We'll wait until the burns heal before trying anything like this again."

Ortnar kicked the hot metal ring into the water. When it had cooled he examined it with great interest, rubbing it with a stone. "It shines like skymetal. They have great skills, the murgu, to fit it about your flesh like that." He reluctantly gave the ring to Kerrick when he reached out for it.

"It was molded in place by one of their animals," he said.

"You will keep it?"

There was hope in Ortnar's voice and Kerrick almost gave the ring back to him. But as he clutched it in his hands he felt the same repulsion that he had when he took off the breech covering for the last time.

"No. It is Yilanè, murgu." He threw it out into the stream where it splashed and sank. "I still wear one about my neck. That is enough to have."

They were ready now to leave, but Herilak stood, leaning on his spear, looking back the way they had come.

"If more had escaped they would be here by now," he said.

"And we have been running like frightened women. Now we must stop and consider our trail ahead. Tell me about the murgu, Kerrick, what are they doing now?"

"I do not understand."

"Are they still following us? Are they waiting still on the beach where they attacked?"

"No, they will have gone by now. They were hunting for food and had brought very little preserved meat with them. The object of the expedition was to come this far north to destroy the sammad. Then return. Nothing would be accomplished by remaining here. With the Eistaa's death no one else would be in command. There would have been a lot of confusion and they would certainly have returned to the city by now."

"That is what the main body would have done. But would there be others left behind to search for us?"

"There might be. Stallan might be doing that—no. Of all of them she is the one who was closest to second in command. She would surely have ordered their return."

"Then you believe they are gone?"

"Almost certainly."

"That is good. We will return to the shore."

Kerrick felt a thrust of fear at the words. "They may be hiding, waiting for us."

"You just assured me that they would not."

"We are hunters," Ortnar said. "We will know if they are there."

"We have no reason . . ."

"Every reason." Herilak was firm now, once more in command. "We have two spears, one bow without arrows, nothing more. When the snow falls we will die. All that we need is back there. We return."

They went fast, too fast for Kerrick. It was too much like returning to certain death. By dusk they were in the foothills above the shore and could see the ocean beyond.

"Ortnar, you will go carefully," Herilak ordered. "Without sound, unseen. Look carefully for any sign of the murgu."

Ortnar shook his spear in acknowledgment, turned and slipped away through the trees. Herilak settled down comfortably in the shade and promptly went to sleep. Kerrick was too upset to do anything other than worry, to look towards the shore and let his fear populate the forest with stalking Yilanè.

The sun was below the horizon when a bird called out from the valley below. Herilak was instantly awake; cupping his hands to his mouth he answered the call. There was a crackling in the brush and Ortnar came into view running easily up the slope.

"Gone," he said. "Gone the way they came."

"You can't be sure," Kerrick said. Ortnar looked at him scornfully.

"Of course I am sure. I found no fresh tracks. And the carrion birds were everywhere—and they are quick to take fright. And I searched as well." His drawn face spoke louder than words. He pointed to the arrows that now filled his quiver. "Everything we need is there."

"We go now," Herilak announced.

It was well after dark when they reached the site of the massacre, but the gibbous moon's cold light enabled them to find the way. The crows and buzzards were gone with the daylight and now the mantle of darkness concealed the worst horrors of the massacre. The smell of decay was already strong. Kerrick stood on the shore, looking out to sea, while the others searched for what was needed. He turned back reluctantly to face the slaughter only when Herilak called to him.

"Put these on," the sammadar said. "They belonged to a great hunter. May they bring you good fortune."

There were fur leggings with solid leather soles, a cape, belt, and other heavy garments. Too warm for the summer, but they would make the difference between life and death when the snows came. A long spear, stout bow, arrows. Kerrick made a bundle of the things he would not wear and put it with the other bundles and baskets they were taking. Herilak had taken some of the crosspoles from one of the large mastodon travois and made a smaller one that they could pull. Everything they needed was now lashed into place upon it.

"We go now," he said, his voice grim as death with the dead of the sammad on all sides of him. "We will never forget what the murgu have done here."

They walked until the moon set, taking turns between the shafts of the travois, until they were too tired to go any farther. Kerrick still feared that Yilanè hunters were searching for him, but so great was his fatigue that he fell asleep while he was worrying and did not stir until dawn.

Herilak unlashed a bag of ekkotaz from the travois and they

dipped out handfuls of the delicious mixture, dried berries and nutmeat, pounded together. Kerrick had been a boy when he last tasted it and childhood memories flooded back as he licked it from his fingers. It was good to be Tanu. But even as he thought this he was scratching at his waist, over and over. When he pulled the fur back he saw the red bites. His skin crawled as he realized that the brave hunter who had last worn these furs had been infested with fleas. Suddenly being Tanu was not that pleasant. His back was sore from lying on the hard ground, his muscles ached from the unaccustomed exercise—and if that wasn't enough there was a sudden spasm of pain in his midriff. The burnt and tough meat was not sitting too well in his stomach; he hurried behind the nearest clump of bushes.

Racked with cramps he saw the flea crawl across his discarded garments. He cracked it between his fingernail, then wiped his fingers disgustedly on the grass. He was filthy and sore, flea-infested and ill. What was he doing here with these crude ustuzou? Why wasn't he in Alpèasak? He had been comfortable there, at peace, close to the Eistaa. Why couldn't he return? Vaintè was dead of a spear thrust—but who in the city knew that he had wielded the spear? He hadn't been seen. Why couldn't he go back?

He washed himself well, then went a few paces upstream to drink. On the bank the two hunters were lashing the load back onto the travois. They could go on without him.

But did he want to go back to Alpèasak? For years he had been thinking of escape from the city—and now he was free. Wasn't that what he had always wanted? That was the Yilanè's world, not his. There was no place for him there.

But was there a place for him among the Tanu?

He stood knee-deep in the cool water, his fists clenched. Lost. Belonging neither to one world nor the other. Outcast and alone.

Herilak called out to him, his words cutting through Kerrick's dark thoughts. He waded ashore, then pulled his garments slowly on.

"We leave now," Herilak said.

"Where do you go?" Kerrick asked, still torn by conflicting feelings.

"West. To find other hunters. To return with them and kill murgu."

"They are too strong, too many."

"Then I will be dead and my tharm will join the tharms of the other hunters in my sammad. But first I will have avenged them. It is a good way to die."

"There are no good ways to die."

Herilak looked at him in silence, understanding something of the conflicting emotions that Kerrick was feeling. Those years of captivity must have done strange things to the boy who was now a man. But the years were there, they could not be taken away. There was no going back. The way ahead might be hard—but it was the only way.

Herilak reached up to his neck and slowly lifted the leather thong with the pendant skymetal knife over his head, then held it out.

"This was your father's. You are his son for you still wear the smaller boy's knife made at the same time. Hang this one about your neck beside it. Wear it now to remind you of his death and the death of your sammad. And who killed them. Feel hatred in your heart and the knowledge that you seek vengeance as well."

Kerrick hesitated, then reached out and took the knife, held it, then clenched his fist tightly about its hard shape.

There could be no going back to Alpèasak. Ever. He must teach himself to feel only hatred towards the murderers of his people. He hoped that would come.

But now all he felt was a terrible emptiness inside.

Es mo tarril drepastar, er em
so man drija.

———————

If my brother is wounded,
I will bleed.

CHAPTER FOUR

The hunting was very bad. Ulfadan had been out since before dawn and had little to show for it. A single rabbit hung from his belt. It was young and scrawny, with scarcely enough meat on its bones to feed a single person. How was his entire sammad to eat? He came to the edge of the forest and stopped under a large oak, looking out at the grassland beyond. He dared go no further.

Here there were murgu. From here to the end of the world, if the world had an end, there were only these despised and frightening creatures. Some made good eating, he had once tasted the meat from the leg of one of the smaller murgu with bills that grazed in vast herds. But death was always waiting for the hunter who sought them out. There were poisonous murgu in the grass, snakes of all sizes, many-colored and deadly. Worse still were the giant creatures whose roars were like thunder, whose tread shook the ground like an earthquake. As he always did when he thought of murgu, though he did not realize it, his fingers touched the tooth of one of these giants that hung on his chest. A single tooth almost as long as his forearm. He had been young and stupid when he retrieved it, risking death to show his bravery. From the trees he had seen the marag die, seen the repulsive carrion eaters that quarreled and tore at the creature's body. Only after dark had he dared to leave the shelter of the trees, to pry this single tooth from the gaping jaws. Then the night-murgu had appeared and only chance had saved his life. The long white scar on his thigh was witness that he had not returned unharmed. No, there was no game to be sought beyond the protection of the trees.

But the sammad must eat. Yet the food they searched and hunted for was growing scarcer and scarcer. The world was changing and Ulfadan did not know why. The alladjex told them that ever since Ermanpadar had shaped Tanu from the mud of the river bed the world had been the same. In the winter they went to the mountains where the snow lay deep and the deer were easy to kill. When the snow melted in the spring they followed the fast streams down to the river, and sometimes to the sea, where fish leaped in the water and good things grew in the earth. Never too far south though, for only murgu and death waited there. But the mountains and the dark northern forests had always provided everything that they had needed.

This was no longer true. With the mountains now wrapped in endless winter, the herds of deer depleted, the snow in the forests lying late into the spring, their timeless sources of food were no more. They were eating now, there were fish enough in the river at this season. They had been joined at their river camp by sammad Kellimans; this happened every year. It was a time to meet and talk, for the young men to find women. There was little of this now for although there was enough fish to eat there was not enough to preserve for the winter. And without this supply of food very few of them would see the spring.

There was no way out of the trap. To the west and east other sammads waited, as hungry as his and Kellimans'. Murgu to the south, ice to the north—and they were trapped between them. No way out. Ulfadan's head was bursting with this problem that had no solution. In agony he wailed aloud like a trapped animal, then turned and made his way back to the sammad.

From the top of the grassy slope that led down to the river, nothing looked amiss. The dark cones of the leather tents stretched along the river bank in a ragged row. Figures moved about between the tents and smoke rose from the fires. Close by him one of the tethered mastodons raised its trunk and bellowed. Further along the shore some women could be seen scratching at the earth with their fire-hardened sticks, digging up edible roots. The roots were good food now. But what would happen when the ground froze again? He knew what would happen and he thrust the thought from him.

Naked children ran screaming, splashed in the water. Old women sat in the sun before their tents plaiting baskets from willow and reeds. As he walked by the tents Ulfadan's face was set and stern, unreadable. One of his smaller sons hurried up to him, bursting with an important message.

"Three hunters are here, from another sammad. One of them is very funny."

"Take this rabbit to your mother. Run."

The hunters were sitting around a fire, taking puffs in turn from a stone-bowled pipe. Kellimans was there, and Fraken the alladjex, old and withered, but respected greatly for his knowledge and healing powers. The newcomers rose in greeting when he appeared. One of them he knew well.

"I greet you, Herilak."

"I greet you, Ulfadan. This is Ortnar of my sammad. This is Kerrick, son of Amahast, son of my sister."

"You have food and drink?"

"We have eaten and drunk. Ulfadan's generosity is well-known."

Ulfadan joined the circle about the fire, took the pipe when it was passed to him and inhaled deeply of the pungent smoke. He wondered about the strange hunter without hair, who should have been dead with the rest of his sammad but was not. He would be told at the proper time.

Other hunters were also curious about the newcomers and came and sat in a circle about them, for this was the way of the sammad.

Herilak was no longer as formal as he once had been. He waited until the pipe had passed only once before he spoke.

"The winters are long, and we know that. The food is scarce and we know that. Now all in my sammad are dead except two."

There was a silence among the hunters after he had spoken these terrible words, wails of agony from the women who listened outside the circle. Many had relations who had married into Herilak's sammad. More than one looked up at the eastern sky where the first stars were beginning to appear. When Herilak spoke again no sound disturbed him.

"It is known that I went with my hunters so far south that there was no snow and it was hot in the winter, to the place where there are only murgu. It was my thought that murgu had killed

Amahast and all in his sammad. My thought was correct for we found murgu that walk like men and kill with death-sticks. It was one of their death-sticks that I found among the bones of sammad Amahast. We killed the murgu we found there, then returned north. Now we knew that death lay to the south and we knew what kind of death it was. But we were hungry this last winter and many died. In the summer the hunting was bad, as you know. So I took the sammad south along the coast because of the hunger. I led the hunters farther south for the easy hunting there. We knew of the danger. We knew that the murgu might attack us too, but without food we would be dead anyway. We were on our guard and there was no attack. It was only after we turned back that they fell upon us. I am here. Ortnar is here. The rest are dead. With us is Kerrick who is the son of Amahast, captured by the murgu, now free at last. He knows much about the murgu ways."

There was a loud murmur of interest then and movement among those listening as those to the back tried to get a clear view of Kerrick. They pointed out his lack of hair and the shining ring about his neck, and the skymetal knives that hung there. He stared straight ahead and said nothing. When they were silent again Kellimans spoke.

"These are days of death for the Tanu. The winter kills us, the murgu kill us, other Tanu kill us."

"Is it not enough to be killed by the murgu? Must we fight one another?" Herilak asked.

"It is the long winter and the short summer that we must battle against," Ulfadan said. "We came to this place because the deer are gone from the mountains. But when we tried to hunt here the bowmen of many sammads from beyond the mountains drove us away. We have little food now and in the winter we will starve."

Herilak shook his head sadly. "That is not the way. The murgu are the enemy, not the Tanu. If we battle one another our end is certain."

Kellimans nodded agreement as Ulfadan spoke next. "I believe as you do, Herilak, but this is not of our doing. It is the other sammads you must speak with. If it were not for them we would hunt and not starve. They come from beyond the mountains and they are many and very hungry. They push us back and we cannot hunt. They would see us die."

Herilak dismissed his words with a chop of his hand. "No, that is wrong. They are not the cause of your woes. The hunting must be just as bad beyond the mountains or they would not have come here. The Tanu have two enemies. The winter that does not end—and the murgu. Together they are uniting to destroy us. We cannot battle against the winter. But we can kill murgu."

Others raised their voices then and joined the argument, but were silenced when Fraken began to speak. They respected the old man's knowledge and healing powers and hoped that he could show them some answer to their problems.

"The murgu are like the leaves and as numberless as leaves. You tell us that they have the death-sticks. How can we fight against creatures like this? And why should we? If we risk death fighting them—what do we win? It is food and not warfare that we must have."

There was a murmur of approval when he finished speaking. Only Herilak seemed to disagree.

"It is food you must have, revenge that I will have," he said grimly. "A way must be found to kill these murgu to the south. When they are dead there will be good hunting down the coast."

There was much discussion and crosstalk after this, but nothing could be decided. In the end Herilak signed to Ortnar and they rose and left. Kerrick watched them go—but hesitated to follow them. His lust for revenge did not match theirs. If they did not call to him maybe he would not have to join them. He could stay here by the fire and join the talk with the other hunters. Perhaps he might even stay here with this sammad and hunt and forget the murgu.

But this was not the answer. He knew what the others here did not. He knew that the Yilanè would not forget him nor the rest of the Tanu. Their hatred ran too deep. They would send out the raptors and find every sammad and would not rest until they had all been destroyed. Ulfadan and Kellimans and their people feared only the winter and their hunger and the other Tanu—when the certain killer was just over the horizon.

No one took notice when Kerrick picked up his spear and left. He found his two companions at a fire of their own and he joined them there. Herilak poked at the fire with a stick, looking deep into it as though searching for an answer among the flames.

"We are only three," he said. "We cannot fight the murgu alone—but we will if we have to." He turned to Kerrick. "You know about the murgu—which we do not. Tell us of them. Tell us how they wage war."

Kerrick rubbed his jaw in thought before he spoke. Slowly and hesitatingly. "It is not easy to talk of. You will have to know about their city first, and how they are ruled. You must understand the fargi and the Yilanè and just how they go about doing things."

"Then you will tell us," Herilak said.

Kerrick found it difficult at first to speak of things in Tanu that he had never thought of in that language. He had to find new words for scenes he was familiar with, new ways of describing concepts totally alien to these hunters. They questioned him over and over again about things they could not understand. In the end they had some idea of how the Yilanè society worked, although they had little idea why it did so.

Herilak stared in silence at his clenched fists where they rested on his thighs, seeking to grasp the meaning of what he heard. In the end he had to shake his head.

"I will never understand the murgu and I think that I will not try. It is enough to know what they do. The large bird flies high to watch us, then returns and tells them where a sammad is so they can attack it. Is that right?"

Kerrick started to protest—then changed his mind and nodded agreement. The details were not important as long as they had some understanding of what the Yilanè were doing. "When they know where a sammad has stopped they prepare an attack. Fargi with weapons go out on the boats. They come from the sea suddenly and kill everything as you know."

"But you spoke of more than that," Herilak said. "Do they not camp on the shore the night before they attack?"

"Yes, that is the way that they do it. They stop as close as they can, spend the night, then leave their food supplies behind them in order to attack at dawn on the following morning."

"Do they always do it this way?"

"Always? I don't know. I've only been with them twice. But, just a moment, that doesn't matter. The way they think, the way they do things, they *would* do it the same every time. As long as something is successful they will not change it."

"Then we must find a way of using that knowledge to destroy them in turn."

"How will you do that?" Ortnar asked.

"I do not know yet. We must think about it and plan until we find a way. We are hunters. We know how to stalk our prey. We will find a way to stalk and kill the murgu."

Kerrick had been silent, lost in thought, seeing the destruction of a sammad as no one else could. He had once been on the shore when the attack had come, could still feel the horror when the dark forms had appeared from the sea. But he had also been there with the attackers, traveled from Alpèasak. He had watched the preparations for the attack, had listened to the orders and knew exactly how it all had been done. Now he had to combine these two opposite points of view and find some way of turning things around.

"Turn it around," he said aloud. Then shouted it again when they looked up at him. "Turn it around! But in order to do that we will need Ulfadan and Kellimans and their sammads. We must explain to them, make them understand and help us. Here is what we will then do. We will march south with the sammads and hunt. The hunting will be good and there will be much food. But once we go south our presence is sure to be discovered by the murgu, for they will be told about us by the great bird. But we will keep close watch and when we see the great bird we will also know what is going to happen. When we see the bird we must send out hunters to watch the beaches. Then we will know when the attack is coming and we will be ready. Instead of running we will fight and kill them."

"That is dangerous," Herilak said. "If we take the sammads we will be risking the lives of the women and the children, all those who cannot fight. There must be a better plan or these sammads will not take the risk of coming with us. Think again. Wasn't there something you told me that was very important, something about the night? The murgu don't like to go about at night?"

"I don't think it is just like that. Their bodies are different from ours. They must sleep at night, always. It is the way they are."

Herilak jumped to his feet, roaring with sudden enthusiasm. "The way we are we sleep at night as well—but we do not have to, not all of the time. So this is the thing that we will do. We will talk to the hunters and convince them that they should go south along the shore and hunt because of the coming hunger. In this way the sammads will get food for the winter. But while we are hunting we will watch always for the great bird that speaks to the murgu. When the bird sees us we will then send hunters to hide where they can watch the beaches to the south. When the murgu stop for the night we will know where they are. We will then come forward during the darkness. The hunters only. We will go in silence and in silence come to the beaches."

He clenched his fists and slammed them together. "Then we will fall upon them in the night. We will spear them while they sleep, rout them, kill them just as they have killed us." Afire with enthusiasm he rose and walked rapidly back to the circle of hunters. "They must be told. They must be convinced."

It was not an easy thing to do. Ortnar and Kerrick joined him and explained the idea over and over again. About how the murgu attacked and how they could be defeated. They repeated themselves and explained exactly how they could hunt and get food for the winter. And kill murgu.

Ulfadan was greatly troubled by all this, as was the other sammadar. It was too new an idea—and too dangerous a one.

"You are asking me to risk all of our lives on this plan," Ulfadan said. "You ask us to stake our women and our children out like bait for a longtooth to take so that it can be speared. This is a great deal to ask."

"It is—and it is not," Herilak said. "Perhaps you have no choice. Without food few will last the winter. And you cannot hunt here. Come south, we know the hunting is good there."

"We know the murgu are there."

"Yes—but this time we will be on the lookout for them. If you like, we will not wait until we see the great bird, but will have hunters always hidden on the beaches ahead. They will warn of any attack. When the murgu reach the beach we will know the attack is near. The warning will be given. In that way the tents and all else can be loaded on the travois during the night, the boys will drive the mastodons inland away from the shore, taking the women and all the small children with them. They will be out of danger that way. It is a risk, but it is a risk that you will have to take. Either that or die in the snows this winter. Without food none of you will see the spring."

"You speak harshly, Herilak," Kellimans said angrily.

"I speak only the truth, sammadar. The decision is up to your people. We have said what we have to say. Now we will leave."

It was not decided that night, nor the next day nor the next. But then it began to rain, a heavy rain that was blown about gustily by the cold wind from the north. Autumn would be coming early again this year. The food supplies were low and they all knew it. The three strangers sat apart from the others and were aware that people who passed looked at them with worry, many of the hunters with hatred as well for forcing this choice upon them.

In the end they began to realize that they had no choice at all. There was much wailing among the women when the tents were taken down and loaded on the travois. There was none of the usual excitement when a trek began. They might have been walking to their deaths. Perhaps they were. Subdued and wet they marched east through the driving rain.

CHAPTER FIVE

In the excitement of breaking camp Kerrick had been too busy to think about all the dangers that the future might hold. Unexpected memories had filled him with mixed emotions as the travois were lashed to the complacent mastodons. It was a wonderful sight when the great beasts leaned into their harnesses and pulled the creaking wooden frames slowly and steadily after them. They were piled high with tents and baggage, the children and babies sitting on top of everything. When the march began the hunters had fanned out ahead, scouring the barren country for any game they might find along the way. The sammad would not come together again until they met at the campsite in the evening, the hunters drawn by the fires and smell of cooking food.

For the first few days there was a great fear of what lay ahead, of the deadly murgu who would be stalking them. But the Tanu were fatalists, they had to be, for life changed constantly. They had always been at the mercy of the weather, the food that might not be there, the hunting that might fail. They were leaving behind starvation and certain death, had exchanged that for food and the possibility of continued existence. It was a fair enough bargain and their spirits rose as the days stayed warm and the hunting improved.

They even accepted Kerrick after the first few days, though

the children still pointed at his iron collar and laughed at his bare head and face. But stubble was growing there, a finger's length on his skull already, though his beard was wispy and thin. He was still clumsy with the spear and an awful shot with the bow—but he was improving. He was beginning to feel that the world was a good place to be alive in.

That is until they came to the ocean.

The first sight of the blue water filled Kerrick with a sense of dread so powerful that he stopped in his tracks. There was no one else in sight for he was well away from the low valley that the mastodon-drawn travois were following, nor were there any other hunters nearby at the time. With the fear came the desire to turn and run. Only death lay ahead. How could this handful of hunters imagine that they could stand up to the horde of armed fargi? He wanted only to flee, hide, seek refuge in the mountains. To go forward was certain suicide.

Warring with this overpowering emotion was the realization that he could not possibly leave at this time. This was too cowardly an action to contemplate. After all, he had helped originate the plan so he had little or no choice; he must follow it through. Yet the fear remained and it was with only the utmost reluctance that he could force himself to take a single shuffling step forward. Then another and another, until he was walking again, miserable and fearful—but still moving.

They halted close to the shore that evening. Even before the travois were unloaded the boys were already fishing in the brackish lagoon, baiting their bone hooks with earthworms. The waters were thick with hardalt, the small carapaced squid eager to take the bait. There was much shouting and laughter as they brought back their tentacled catch. They were quickly pried from their shells, gutted and sliced, were soon sizzling over the fires. Although tough and strong-flavored they were a welcome change of diet.

Kerrick spat out a gristly unchewable bit and wiped his fingers on the grass, stood and stretched. Did he have room for any more? He looked towards the fire—then caught a movement out of the corner of his eye. A seabird floating overhead.

No. He looked up at the great span of the creature's wings, the white of its breast red now in the setting sun, and stood frozen. It was here already. He could not see the black lump with its never-sleeping eye looking down at them from the raptor's leg—but he knew that it was there. Lower and lower it came, down towards the encampment. With an effort Kerrick broke the paralysis and hurried to Herilak sitting by the fire.

"It is here," he said. "Flying above us. They will now know about us . . ."

There was panic in Kerrick's voice which Herilak wisely ignored. His own words were quietly spoken and grim.

"This is very good. Everything is working just as we planned."

Kerrick had none of his assurance. He tried not to watch the bird as it circled above them, knowing that the pictures it would bring back would be carefully examined. The Tanu must show no obvious interest in it, no knowledge that they were aware of its function. Only when it had finished a last lazy circle and started away did he turn and gaze after it. There could be no doubt now that an attack would come.

After dark, when the hunters gathered to smoke and talk, Kerrick told them what he had seen and what it had meant. Now that they were committed there were no complaints. They questioned him closely, then discussed arrangements for the advance party of hunters to leave before dawn.

In the morning the sammads marched south. Herilak was in the lead and took them on a slow curve away from the coast. Kerrick recognized the terrain and knew that they were passing the place where sammad Herilak had been destroyed. There was no need to give the Tanu such a grim reminder of what dangers could come from the sea. They reached the beaches again that evening. Later, when the hunters met and talked, the decision was made to make Herilak their sacripex, their leader in battle. He nodded acceptance and issued his first orders.

"It is Kerrick and Ortnar who go ahead now. They have seen the murgu, they know what we are looking for. They will make their way along the coast and spend the night keeping watch on the shore. Two other hunters will go with them to watch as well and to return with the warning when that is needed. They will do this every night from now on. Others will also stay awake each night to watch the sea near our tents in case something goes wrong. We must be sure that it does not."

They proceeded along the coast for four days more in this manner, until the fifth day when Kerrick hurried back to the campsite at dawn. The hunters heard his running footsteps and seized up their weapons.

"There is no alarm, the murgu are not here. But I have looked at the coast ahead and there is something we can do." He waited until the two sammadars and Herilak were present, then explained. "The hunting is good now and there is much fish in the sea here. You must agree not to break camp today but to stay in this place and fish, while the hunters bring in meat for smoking. South of here there are cliffs, then a long stretch of beach with a thick birch wood that extends down almost to the shore. The distance is right. If the murgu come, when they come, they will not be able to find a landing place where the cliffs are, so they are sure to come ashore on the beach below the forest."

Herilak nodded agreement. "When we attack we can approach them unseen under the cover of the trees. Good. It will be done that way. Are we all of the same mind?"

There was some discussion, but no disagreement. Kerrick returned to the spot where Ortnar and the other two hunters were lying under cover and watching the sea.

The long wait began. They filled their time during the next days in constructing a birchbark shelter deep in the woods. The nights were cooler now and there was some rain. But two of them were always on the ridge above the ocean during the day, hidden but watching. By late afternoon all four of them would be there, for that was the time of most danger. It was at this time, after many days of watching, from full moon to full moon, that Herilak came to join them on the ridge.

"What have you seen?" he asked, standing under the trees beside them.

"Nothing. Just what you see out there. The empty sea. The same as always," Kerrick said.

"The hunters in the sammads have decided that there is enough meat now. They are grateful that we showed them these hunting grounds. They are ready to leave."

"That is a good decision," one of the watching hunters said. "None of us want this murgu attack." Kerrick agreed strongly with these feelings and felt a leap of hope, yet kept silent.

"You speak for yourself," Herilak said bitterly. "Yes, the trek has been successful. There is food enough now for the winter so I can understand why they are so eager to return. With their stomachs full they can forget their hunger and remember instead what happened to the two other sammads on this shore. This is to be the last night. They are eager to leave tomorrow at dawn. We stay here and march one day behind them in case the murgu attack after all."

"We will move fast," the second hunter called out. "They will not catch us now."

Herilak turned away from them scornfully. Ortnar was as bitter as he. "We did not do this just to fill your stomachs. We came to kill murgu."

"We cannot do it alone," Herilak said.

Kerrick turned and looked out to sea so they could not see the relief on his features. They might argue, but in the end the sammads would go. There was nothing to keep them here and every reason to leave. There would be no battle. Small white clouds drifted in the clear sky above, casting dark shadows on the clear water. Large shadows. Moving shadows.

He stood still, gazing at the shadows, and did not speak until he was absolutely sure. His voice was tight and he could not stop it from trembling.

"They are out there. The murgu are coming."

It was just as he said. The black boats were clearly visible now as they moved out from under the shadow of the clouds. They were going rapidly north.

"Are they not stopping?" Herilak cried out. "Are they going on to attack the sammads?"

"We must warn them—there is little time!" Kerrick said. One of the hunters turned to run with the warning, but Herilak stopped him.

"Wait. Wait until we are sure."

"They are turning towards shore now!" Ortnar said. "Coming towards the beach below us."

The hunters lay in silent concealment, filled with horror as the boats came close, bobbing in the gentle surf. There were loud orders and the armed fargi splashed out of the boats and made their way onto the beach. There was no doubt that a landing was being made when they began to pass supplies ashore.

"Now go," Herilak whispered to the two hunters. "Both of you. Go different ways so that one of you will be sure to bring the warning. As soon as it is dark and they cannot be seen the travois must be loaded as planned, then the sammads will move quickly, go inland. Trek until dawn and then take cover in the forest. As soon as the travois are loaded all the hunters are to leave the camp and join us here. Run."

The scene on the beach below was a familiar one to Kerrick, but shockingly new to the two hunters. They watched as the supplies were taken from the boats and the fargi, wrapped in cloaks, bedded down for the night. The leaders were grouped farther down the beach but Kerrick did not dare to move closer to see who they were. There was every chance that Stallan might be in command, and at this thought he shared some of the emotions of revenge that possessed the other two. Stallan who had beaten him and hated him, who had as good as killed Alipol with her unwanted and brutal attention. What a pleasure it would be to run his spear through that creature's hide!

There was no moon, but the stars clearly lit the white sand of the beach below, picked out the dark forms resting there. More stars climbed slowly from the sea until, at last, there was a slight rustling from the forest behind them.

The first of the hunters crept close. By dawn the attackers would be in position.

CHAPTER SIX

Herilak had been thinking only of this attack for days now, had planned it over and over so often that he could see clearly in his thoughts exactly how it would happen. Kerrick and Ortnar had been instructed so they knew what must be done just as well as he did. Herilak left them there at the edge of the grove, watching the beach, and ordered the first arrivals back through the forest to an open glade. Here they rested until all of the other hunters had appeared. He was the battle leader; they waited expectantly for his orders.

"Ulfadan, Kellimans," he said quietly. "Go among your hunters and ask their names. When you are sure that they are all gathered here come and tell me."

They did not talk or move about while they waited, for they were hunters. They squatted in silence, weapons ready, waiting for orders from Herilak, the sacripex, ready for battle. Only when he had been assured that they had all arrived did Herilak tell them what they were to do.

"We must strike as one," he said. "We must kill without being killed for their darts are instant death. In order to do this we will spread out in a single line, with each sammad taking half of the beach. Then we must crawl forward silently until we are in the grass above the beach. The wind is from the water so they will not smell us when we draw near. But they can hear, and hear well, so there must be nothing for them to hear. You must each take your position, and your sammadar will be sure that you are in the correct place. When you are there you will wait and you will not move. You will look at the beach. You will wait until you see me, Ulfadan and Kellimans as well, appear before you on the beach. That will be your signal to come forward. Slowly and silently. With your spears you will then kill murgu, remaining silent as long as it is possible."

Then Herilak reached out with the butt of his spear and touched the nearest hunter with it just below his chin, while all of the others strained forward to see what he was doing.

"Try to stab the murgu in the throat if you can, for that is where they are most vulnerable. Their ribs are many and unlike the animals we hunt their ribs cover the entire front of their bodies and do not stop just below the chest. A strong blow will penetrate, but a badly aimed thrust will be deflected by the bones within. Therefore— the throat."

Herilak waited while they thought about this, then continued.

"We cannot hope to kill them all in silence. As soon as the alarm is raised we will shout as loudly as we can to cause confusion. And keep on killing. If they run use your bows. Arrows will stop them. Do not hesitate, do not tire, but keep on killing. We will only be finished with them when they all are dead."

There were no questions. What they had to do was very clear. If any of the hunters felt fear they did not show it. They lived by killing and were very experienced at it.

Silent as shadows they moved through the trees, left the darkness of the forest, and crawled in equal silence across the grass above the beach. Kerrick was still on watch. He looked away from the sleeping fargi and started as he saw the moving shapes. There was not a sound from them, not the slightest. Herilak appeared among them and slipped forward. Kerrick touched him on the shoulder, then leaned close to breathe the words into his ear.

"Their leaders must be among the first killed. I want to do that myself."

Herilak nodded agreement and moved away. Slowly then, a step at a time, Kerrick moved back from the edge of the bank and along it to the position he had marked earlier.

A night bird called from the trees and he froze, waited a

moment then moved on. The only sound now was the lap of small waves on the sand. Other than that the night was still as death.

And death was on its way.

There was no impatience. Once they were in position not a hunter moved, nor was there the slightest sound to reveal their presence. Their eyes were on the lighter gray of the sandy beach, waiting patiently for the expected movement.

Tension twisted a tight knot in the pit of Kerrick's stomach. He was sure now that too much time had gone by. Something had gone wrong. Herilak and the sammadars should be on the beach. If they delayed any longer it would be light and they would be the ones who would be trapped . . .

He knew his fears were groundless, but that knowledge did not take them away. His fists were clenched so tight that they hurt. Where were they? What was happening? Clouds were thickening in the sky and obscuring the stars. Would he be able to see the figures when they did appear?

Then they were there, so silently and suddenly that they might have been shadows. Moving shadows that were soon joined by other shadows, until the dark line of half-seen forms stretched the length of the beach.

They stayed ahead of Kerrick because they could move quickly in absolute silence. He had to feel his way forward, lacking their skill at silent stalking of prey. He was well behind them when the line reached the first of the sleeping fargi. There were some muffled grunts, nothing more.

Now Kerrick could feel the soft sand beneath his feet, he could go faster. He ran forward, raising his own spear. He had almost reached the mound of supplies that were his marker, behind which the Yilanè lay, when a terrible screech of pain cut the silence of the night.

It was followed instantly by more screams and shouts; then the beach was alive with moving forms. Kerrick shouted as well, leaping around the stacked supplies and stabbing down at the Yilanè who was just standing.

She shrieked hoarsely as the point imbedded in her flesh, pulled away. He thrust again into her throat.

It was yelling, running, falling, dark butchery in the night. The fargi were awake instantly, but were panicked and frightened and in absolute confusion. If they remembered their weapons they could not find them in the blackness. They ran and sought safety in the ocean of their youth. Yet there was no safety even there for they were speared when they ran by, while sharp arrows flew after those who reached the surf. It was slaughter without mercy. The Tanu were efficient butchers.

Yet the fargi were so numerous that some did manage to escape, to reach the sea and splash in panic through the dead bodies there, to dive and swim to the boats. The hunters waded after them into the breaking waves, their bows striking death until their supply of arrows was exhausted.

The killing stopped only when there was nothing left alive to kill. The hunters walked among the heaped bodies, kicking at them, spears stabbing down at any sound or movement. One by one they stopped, exhausted, silent—until a hunter shouted a cry of victory. They all joined in then, an ululating call that was more animal than Tanu, a cry that carried across the water to the surviving fargi in the boats who moaned and cowered with fear.

The first light of dawn revealed the gruesome details of the night of slaughter. Kerrick looked about in horror, shuddering away from the dead that were heaped on all sides, tumbled one on top of the other. This sight did not seem to bother the hunters in the slightest. They called out happily, bragging of their exploits while they waded among the corpses in the surf to cut their arrows free. As the light grew Kerrick saw that his hands and arms were thick with blood; he went along the beach away from the fargi bodies and washed them clean in the sea. When he emerged Herilak was waiting for him, shouting with jubilation.

"It has been done! We have hit back at the murgu, struck them down, avenged the sammads that they destroyed. It has been a good night's work."

Out to sea the boats were fleeing south—most of them empty, or with just one or two fargi aboard. The slaughter had been most efficient.

Kerrick felt drained of hate and fear, exhausted. He sat down heavily on the heap of bladders of preserved meat. Herilak shook his spear after the fleeing boats, shouted after them.

"Go back! Tell the others what happened here this night. Tell the rest of the murgu that this will happen to all of them if they dare venture north again."

Kerrick did not share his unreasoning hatred, for he had lived too long among the Yilanè. In the growing light he saw the face of the nearest corpse—and recognized her. A hunter he had seen many times with Stallan. He felt himself shaking and had to avert his eyes from the horrifying sight of her ripped-open throat. A feeling of immense grief possessed him—though he was not sure what he was grieving for.

When Herilak had turned about at last Kerrick shook himself and called out.

"Did we have losses of our own?"

"One. Isn't that a true victory? Just one, stung by a poisoned dart. The surprise was complete. We have done what we came here to do."

"We are not finished here yet," Kerrick said, trying to be practical, to forget his emotions. He tapped the bladder that he was sitting upon. "These contain meat. As long as the outer skin is not broken the meat will not rot. I have eaten it. The taste is vile but it will sustain life."

Herilak was leaning on his spear now, thinking. "Then we have won life as well as victory. With this even more Tanu will survive the coming winter. I must send runners to the sammads, bring them here for this treasure." He looked about the corpse-strewn beach. "What else here can we use?"

Kerrick bent and picked up a discarded hèsotsan and wiped the sand from its dark body. When he pointed it towards the empty sea and squeezed in the correct manner there was a sharp crack and the dart vanished in the surf. Wrapped in thought he prodded it and the tiny mouth gaped open; he smoothed it shut again then held the weapon up to Herilak.

"Gather up the death-sticks. And the darts, I'll show you what they look like. We cannot breed these things—but if they are fed they will live for years. The poison on their darts will kill murgu as easily as Tanu. If we had had them tonight not one murgu would have left this beach alive."

Herilak struck him enthusiastically on the shoulder. "This victory will be only the first of many. I will send for the sammads at once."

When he was alone Kerrick took up one of the drinking bladders and drank deep, then looked around at the excited hunters. It was a victory, the first one for the Tanu. But he had a dark sensation that any future victories might not be this easy. He looked at the nearest fargi corpse, then stood and forced himself to begin a search of beach.

It took a long time to be certain; he even worked his way

through the surf looking at all the bodies there, made himself turn them face upwards one by one. When he had finished he dropped wearily onto the sand.

Some of the Yilanè he had recognized, mostly hunters, but there was even one he knew who had been a boat trainer. But he had searched in vain for one familiar face. It had not been there. He looked down the coast to the south, where the fleeing boats had long since vanished.

Stallan had been on one of them, he was positive of that. She had certainly led this expedition, and just as surely escaped with her own life in the darkness.

They would meet again one day, Kerrick was very sure of that. This defeat would not stop the Yilanè. If anything it would make them more resolute. This was not the finish of the battle, but only the beginning. Where it would finally end Kerrick had no idea.

But he did know that what was to come would be a clash such as this world had never seen.

A savage battle between two races who were united in only one thing; their absolute hatred of one for the other.

nu*nkè a>akburzhou
kaseibur>ak umuhesn
tsuntensi nu*nkèkash

────────────

The ring of bodies was good enough before we had the wall of thorns: the future will not change its suitability.

CHAPTER SEVEN

As a rain squall passed over the boats, gusts of wind set them to bobbing in the short waves. The heavy drops drummed on their wet skins and hissed into the ocean around them. The dark shore was hidden from sight now and the sea was empty behind. There was no sign of any pursuit. Stallan looked in all directions, then ordered her boat to halt and signaled to the others to do the same.

They came together in the gray light of dawn, without a command being spoken, seeking comfort in each other's presence. Even the unmanned boats pressed close, staying with the occupied boats and confused because they were not being instructed. Stallan looked at the surviving fargi with growing rage.

So few! A panic-stricken handful, all that remained of the great striking force that she had led north. What had gone wrong?

Her rage grew: she knew what had gone wrong, but when she thought about this her anger was so great that she had to put all thought of it from her mind for the moment. It would have to wait until she had these survivors safely back in Alpèasak; this was her first responsibility.

"Are any of you injured?" she called out, turning as she spoke so all of them could understand her. "Raise your arms if you are."

Stallan saw that almost half of them were wounded. "We have no bandages, they are gone with the rest of the supplies. If the wounds are open, wash them with seawater. There is nothing else. Now look around you, do you see the unoccupied boats? They will get separated soon and we cannot afford to lose a single one. I want at least one fargi in every boat. Make the transfers now while we are all together."

Some of the fargi were still too confused and panic-stricken to think for themselves. Stallan ordered her own boat through the pack, pushing and calling to them loudly until they obeyed.

"This boat is not empty," a fargi called out. "There is a dead fargi in it."

"Into the ocean with it, and any others you find."

"This boat is wounded, it has ustuzou arrows piercing it."

"Leave them in place—you will do more harm than good by pulling them out."

There were not enough fargi in the depleted force to enable Stallan to assign one to each boat. She was forced to leave some of the wounded boats to fend for themselves. As soon as all of the transfers had been completed she ordered the depleted flotilla south.

They sailed without stopping for the entire day. Stallan did not want to go near the shore until she was forced to by darkness. There could be other ustuzou there, watching from concealment, waiting to attack. They went on steadily with the shocked fargi collapsed in numb apathy, until the sun was below the horizon. Only then did Stallan order them towards the land, to the place where a stream ran into the sea. The fargi stirred with thirst when they saw the fresh water, but Stallan kept them in their boats while she scouted inland. Only then did she permit them to come ashore, a few at a time, to drink their fill. She held her hèsotsan ready and stood guard over them, the arch of her body stiff with her contempt for the stupid creatures. Hers was the only weapon they had. The rest of them had simply panicked and fled, their weapons completely forgotten.

"Lowest to highest," one of the fargi said after she had drunk her fill. "Where is there food?"

"Not here, you of little talk, less brains. Perhaps tomorrow. Get back into your boat. We do not sleep on shore tonight."

There were no cloaks to keep up their body temperature during the night so that all the fargi were sluggish and incapable of movement until the sun had warmed them in the morning. Their retreat continued.

On the third day, when there still had been no sign of pursuit, Stallan took the chance of going ashore to hunt. They needed food if they were to return alive. She picked the spot carefully, where a river delta had formed countless swamps and small islands. It was in the swamps that she managed to stalk some multicolored animals that were grazing among the reeds. They looked like urukub, only much smaller, with the same long necks and small heads. She managed to kill two of them before the herd fled. They were too large for her to move so she went back for the fargi and had the bodies dragged to the beach. They ate well, if primitively, tearing at the flesh with their teeth since they lacked cutting instruments of any kind.

Two of the injured fargi died during the voyage. Their only other losses were the pilotless and wounded boats which drifted off one by one during the nights that followed. Only Stallan's strength of will and firm command kept the survivors together until they finally reached familiar waters. It was midday when they passed some fishing boats, then rounded the headland that opened out into the harbor of Alpèasak. Their approach must have been seen and their depleted numbers noted, for there was no committee of welcome at the harbor when they arrived. It was deserted save for a single figure, Etdeerg who was now fulfilling the functions of Eistaa. She stepped forward when Stallan climbed from the boat, but said nothing. It was Stallan who spoke first in a most formal manner.

"When we stopped one day on a beach we were attacked during the night by the ustuzou. They move well in the dark. There was nothing we could do to defend ourselves. You see here the only survivors."

Etdeerg looked coldly at the fargi who were urging the boats towards their pens. "This is a disaster," she said. "Did this happen before or after you made your own attack on the ustuzou?"

"Before. We gained nothing. Lost everything. I did not expect an attack, I posted no sentries. I am at fault. I die now if you order me to."

Stallan did not breathe as she waited, unmoving. Death was just a single, short command away. She looked stolidly out to sea, but one eye rolled back to watch Etdeerg.

"You will live," Etdeerg finally said. "Although you are at

fault there is still need of your services in Alpèasak. Your death is not yet."

Stallan signaled acceptance and gratitude and her relief was clear.

"How could this possibly have happened?" Etdeerg asked. "Such a disaster is beyond my understanding."

"Not beyond mine," Stallan said, hatred and anger in every motion of her body. "It is very clear to me how it was done."

A movement caught her eye; she stopped speaking and turned to face the city as the palanquin was carried from beneath the trees. Four large fargi moved smoothly beneath its weight, while the fat figure of Akotolp waddled after them. The fargi placed the palanquin carefully on the ground and stepped back. Akotolp hurried up behind it, mouth wide open, then bent over the figure that rested there.

"You are to move only slightly, speak little, for there is still danger," Akotolp said.

Vaintè signed agreement, then turned to face Stallan. She had lost a great deal of weight, so much so that her bones could be clearly seen beneath her skin. The spear wound had healed, was now only a puckered scar, but her internal injuries had been great. When she had been brought to Akotolp she had been torpid for many days with all of her body activities slowed to a small fraction of their normal function. Akotolp had repaired the injuries, stopped the infection, transfused blood, done everything possible to keep the Eistaa alive. It had been a very close thing and only Akotolp's immense scientific skills, combined with Vaintè's own strength and will, had enabled her to survive. Etdeerg had taken her place in command and had served as Eistaa during the long illness, but Vaintè would soon resume her full functions. It was as Eistaa that she spoke now.

"Tell me what happened," she ordered.

Stallan did, leaving out nothing, speaking as carefully and unemotionally as she could about every detail of the expedition, the landing and the massacre, ending with their flight back to Alpèasak. When she was done she finished with the same words that she had spoken to Etdeerg.

"I am at fault. I die now if you order me to."

Vaintè waved the suggestion aside with a sharp motion that had Akotolp leaning forward and hissing with alarm.

"Fault or not, we need you, Stallan. You live. We need you for revenge if nothing else. You will be my arm. You will kill the one who did this. There can be only one."

"The Eistaa is correct. There was no second group of ustuzou to be seen in the pictures from the raptor. Everything about the ustuzou group looked as it should. But it was not. Someone knew of the raptor and ordered the night movements of the ustuzou. Someone knew we would land on the beach the night before we attacked. Someone knew."

"*Kerrick.*"

There was death in the name, so much so that Akotolp protested.

"You risk your own life, Eistaa, speaking in that manner. You are not well enough yet for such emotions."

Vaintè leaned back on the soft coverings and signaled agreement, resting before she went on.

"I must give this much thought. When we attack the ustuzou in the future we must do it in a new and different manner. Our knowledge has been diminished because now we can believe the raptor's pictures just half of the time. The daylight half. The ustuzou can move concealed by the darkness of night." She turned to Akotolp. "You know of these things. Can pictures be made during the night?"

Akotolp stroked her fat wattles as she thought. "Such a thing may be possible. If it is, there are certain birds that fly at night. Something may be done."

"You will start at once. Another question—is there a way to look at the pictures from the raptor in greater detail?"

"The meaning of your question escapes me, Eistaa."

"Then listen again. If the ustuzou Kerrick arranged the attack, then he must have been with the band. Therefore he will be in one of the pictures. Can we discover that fact?"

"The question is clear. Details in the pictures may be expanded, enlarged so that a small detail will be many times bigger."

"You have heard, Etdeerg. See that it is done."

Etdeerg signed acceptance of the command and hurried away. Vaintè turned her attention back to Stallan.

"We will attack in a different manner in the future. Night defenses must be prepared as well. It will take much thought. This must never happen again."

"We will need many more fargi," Stallan said.

"That is one problem that already has a solution. While you were away we received the glorious news that all of the preparations have been completed. Inegban∗ comes to Alpèasak before the end of summer. The two cities will be one again, strong and complete.

"We will have all the resources we need to sweep the ustuzou from the face of the earth."

Both Akotolp and Stallan signed happy acceptance of this fact, as did Vaintè herself. If this had happened any time before she had been wounded she would have had to find more formal ways of speaking of it, around it. Then her desire to rule Alpèasak had been her drive in life, her only and strongest ambition. Her hatred of Malsas< had been extreme because the Eistaa of Inegban∗ would be Eistaa of Alpèasak in her place when the two cities became one.

Now she welcomed Malsas<'s arrival. The spearthrust that had driven her into darkness, illness, and pain had changed everything. As first dim consciousness had returned after her injury, she had remembered what had happened. What that ustuzou had done to her. The ustuzou whose life she had saved, the one that she had raised up to stand close beside her and to do her bidding. The ustuzou that had repaid all of this by attempting to kill her. This brutal act would not go unpunished. Thinking of Kerrick only made her more resolute in her desire to rid the earth of the blight of his kind of creature. All Yilanè would feel the same when they discovered what had been done to the fargi who had been sent north. When Inegban∗ came to Alpèasak the Yilanè would realize that existence here was far different from the life that they had known before this, at peace in a city of peace. When their own lives and future were threatened as well by the ustuzou there would be an upswelling of support.

All of the might, the science, and the energy of the Yilanè would then be united behind a single idea. Destroy the ustuzou. Wipe all trace of them from the face of the earth. Mount a crusade that would sweep them away like the blight, the obscene disease that they were.

A crusade that could have but a single leader.

Vaintè saw her destiny at last.

CHAPTER EIGHT

The air was so still beneath the tall trees that the cold fog hung there, unmoving. This chill silence was broken only by the dripping of water from the leaves, the distant calling of a bird. A rabbit hopped cautiously from under a bush and began nibbling at the thick grass in the clearing. It stopped suddenly and sat up, ears turning to listen, then disappeared in a single frightened bound.

The heavy, slow footsteps were like the sound of distant thunder, coming closer. The creaking of leather bindings could now be heard and the loud rustling of wooden poles being dragged across the forest floor. Moving silently ahead of the column of mastodons, two hunters appeared at the edge of the clearing, eyes searching, spears ready. Although they were wearing fur robes and leggings, their arms were bare and beaded with moisture. Other hunters came from under the trees and advanced across the clearing. Then the first mastodon appeared, a great hump-backed bull. His trunk reached up and broke a branch from a tree; he stuffed the leaves into his mouth as he walked, chewing them contentedly.

One by one the other mastodons emerged from the forest, the poles of the travois they pulled cutting deep grooves into the soft loam. The women and larger children walked between them while another party of hunters brought up the rear. The Tanu were on the march that never ended.

It was late afternoon before they reached the campsite at the bend in the river. In the dark twilight the first snow was already swirling down through the trees. Ulfadan looked north and sniffed the cold wind.

"Early," he said. "Even earlier than last year. The snow will be as thick here in the valley as it will be in the mountains. We must talk of this tonight."

Kellimans nodded reluctant agreement. After the slaughter of the murgu the decision to return to this last campsite had been taken without any discussion or real thought. Once they had loaded the murgu weapons and supplies they had all been in a hurry to get away from the shore, suddenly frightened of the possibility of murgu revenge. It had been the most natural and easiest thing to do to retrace their steps. This also put off the need for any more decision making until they were safely away from the coast. Their old pattern of life had been broken; they could no longer winter in the mountains. Then what should they do? The question was spoken often—but never answered. Now they would have to face up to it and come to some agreement. Once the tents were set up and they had food in their stomachs they gathered around the fire and the talking began.

Unlike the settled, city dwelling, crop-harvesting Yilanè, the Tanu were hunters. They lived a nomadic life with no fixed base, constantly on the move, going to the place where the hunting was best, or the fish were running, or where seasonal fruit or tubers could be found. They claimed no single stretch of land for the entire earth itself was their home. Nor did they form large social groups like the Yilanè. Their sammads were small bands of individuals who were joined together for mutual aid. This enabled the older women to show the young girls where the best places were to dig for food. Boys could learn the skills of the hunt, while all the hunters could join together to bring down more game than each could individually.

Their sammadar was not a leader who issued orders, but rather the hunter who made the most sensible plans, the one who found the most game, the one who made sure that the sammad thrived. He wore no badge of office and was not marked out from the other hunters in any way. His rule was by mutual agreement. Nor could he issue unpopular orders; a hunter, and his family, could vote with their feet, vanishing into the trackless forest to join with another sammad if they were not pleased with the sammadar.

Now there were decisions to be made. The fire blazed high as more wood was loaded onto it, while the circle of hunters grew larger. They laughed and called to each other as they tried to get the best places near the fire, where they could be warm but out of the smoke. Their stomachs were full, there was food for the winter, and that was enough for the moment. Still, there were important decisions that must be made. There was much argument about what must be done which died away when Ulfadan stood and turned to face them.

"I have heard many say that they want to winter here in this place that we know. The hunting is bad here, but we have food enough to last until spring. But that is not what we should be thinking about. If we stay here will the mastodons be able to survive? Is there enough grass, are there enough leaves on the trees? This is the important question that should be asked. If we live through the winter but they die, then we will die too when the time comes to move on—and we cannot. That is what we must think about."

This began the discussion in earnest for the fate of the mastodons had been in the back of all their minds. Those who wanted to be heard stood and spoke to all of the hunters and there was very little crosstalk now. Herilak and Kerrick listened but did not say anything themselves. Herilak was sacripex as long as there were battles to be fought. Now, with the battle won, he sat among the others. As for Kerrick, he was pleased enough to be admitted to their circle and not have to sit on the outside with the women and children. It was enough to be here and to listen.

There was much rambling talk about their problems, some complaining, even more bragging. When the talk bogged down Ulfadan called for Fraken for guidance and others took up the cry. The old man was much respected for his memory and knowledge of healing; he was the alladjex who knew the secrets of life and death. Perhaps he could show them a way. Fraken came close to the fire, dragging after him the boy-without-a-name. When the boy was grown, and Fraken died, he would take the old one's name. Now he had no name for he was still learning. He crouched in front of Fraken and rooted in a leather bag to produce a dark ball which he placed carefully on the ground by the fire. Fraken teased it open with two sticks until tiny mouse bones were disclosed. Fraken treasured these bundles that the owls regurgitated, for in their contents he could read the future.

"The winter will be cold," he called out. "I see a journey." There was more like this and his audience was very impressed. Kerrick thought little of it. Anyone could have said the same— without the mouse bones. There were no answers here. Nor did any of the others have anything better to say. As he listened he realized that there could be no solution to their problems. Not unless they did something very new and changed all their old ways of doing things. Eventually, when he saw this clearly, and no one else seemed to be talking about it, he arose reluctantly to speak.

"I have listened to everything that has been said here, and have heard the same things said over and over. The winter-that-does-not-end has come to the mountains. The deer have left the mountains since the snow stays on the ground most of the year and there is no pasturage for them. If there is anyone who does not believe this and wishes to go north I would like to hear what that hunter has to say."

There was no answer other than that of a peevish hunter named Ilgeth who was well known for his bad temper. "Sit down," he called out. "We all know that, little-hair. Let hunters speak."

Kerrick was all too aware of his thin beard as well as the hair on his head that did not yet cover his ears, so he felt shame and started to sit down. But Herilak rose to his feet and stood beside him, touching his arm so he would remain standing.

"This hunter has the name of Kerrick, not little-hair. Although Ilgeth should know much about little-hair, since each year he has more skin than hair reaching up above his own eyes."

There was a great amount of laughter and thigh-slapping at this so that Ilgeth could only scowl and be silent. When Herilak had been sammadar he had used humor often to convince others. But he had other things to say as well and he waited for silence before he spoke again.

"Kerrick's hair is of importance only to remind us that it was removed by the murgu when they held him prisoner. We must not forget that he can speak with them and understands them. Our stomachs are full because he showed us how the murgu could be killed. We hunted where we knew they could strike. He showed us how we could attack them first and we killed many. When Kerrick talks we will listen."

There were grunts of agreement at that, so much so that Kerrick had the courage to go on.

"Then we are all of the same mind then that we cannot go north. To the east the land is as barren as here until the shore is reached where the murgu can strike. There is no place to winter there. Nor is there to the west where the land may be good but where the way is barred by Tanu who will not let us pass. Now I ask the question; why do we not go south?"

There were murmurs of astonishment at that, and at least some laughter that died away when Herilak scowled fiercely. He was much respected, for his skill as a battle leader as well as for the strength of his arm, so laughter faded before his displeasure. It was Ulfadan who rose then and spoke of the south.

"I have gone to the edge of the forest to the south, and when I was young even out into the grass that goes on forever. This I found there," he touched the long tooth strung about his neck. "I was young and foolish enough to risk my life for it. There are no deer there but only murgu that fight and kill. Murgu as tall as trees. There is only death for us to the south. We dare not go that way."

There were cries of agreement and Kerrick waited until there was silence before he spoke again.

"Let me tell you of murgu, because for many years I lived so far to the south that the snow never came and it was warm always. In that warm land there are murgu that eat grass and graze in the forests and in the swamps. Though they are not like the deer or other animals that we hunt, they can be eaten and their flesh is good. I know, because that is what I ate all those years."

There was only silence now. Even the women stopped talking to each other, the children ceased their play, as they all listened to Kerrick's strange and frightening story.

"What Ulfadan has told you is true. There are great murgu who eat the smaller ones. I have seen them and have seen even stranger things as well. But that is not important. What is important is this. How do the murgu-who-walk-like-Tanu live there? How do they exist among the killing murgu? They eat the meat of animals just as we do. Why are they not killed by the murgu as high as trees?"

There were many reasons he could have mentioned, but none of these were relevant now. Only one thing was and he was determined to speak of that and that alone.

"They are not killed because the murgu-who-walk-like-Tanu

kill anything that threatens them or their meat animals. They kill them with this."

He bent and picked up the hèsotsan that lay on the ground beside him, held it up high. There was not a sound now and every eye was upon it.

"No matter how large the beast, this will kill it. A murgu that would need all your spears and all your arrows to kill will fall dead when a single dart from this pricks its hide."

"I have seen this," Herilak broke in, bitterness in his voice. "I have seen the murgu come from the sea with these death-sticks, seen all in my sammad fall before them. Have seen the largest mastodon fall before them when the death-stick cracked. Kerrick speaks the truth."

"And now we have many of them," Kerrick said. "Many of them, darts as well. I know how to care for these death-stick creatures and I can show you the manner in which it is done. I know how to make them send out the darts of death, and will show that to you as well. If you go south there will be good hunting, good forage for the mastodons. And with these—" he held the weapon high above his head so all could see "—only certain death for the murgu."

After this there was excited talk and much argument, but no decision. Kerrick had eaten little during the day and when he saw Herilak leave he went after him. They went to the fire where the women were roasting meat on green boughs, brewing bark tea as well. Merrith, the woman of Ulfadan, saw them sit down and brought them food to eat. She had few teeth left, but she was wide and very strong and the younger women did as she ordered.

"I hope the death-sticks will obey us as they do you, or we will all leave our bones in the south." Her voice was husky, almost like a hunter's. She spoke her mind freely.

"Do you think, then, that we will go south?" Herilak asked, talking with difficulty around the mouthful of meat.

"They will argue all night, but that is what they will decide in the end. They talk too much. We will go south because there is no other way to go." She looked at Kerrick with frank curiosity. "What are these murgu like who held you captive? Are their tents big? Do they use mastodons—or giant murgu to pull their travois?"

Kerrick smiled at the thought, then tried to explain. "They don't live in tents, but grow special trees like tents that they sleep in."

Merrith laughed loudly. "You are telling me wicked stories. How can you load a tree behind a mastodon when you move to another campsite?" The rest of the women around the fire were looking their way, listening as well, and there was much giggling at this thought.

"It is the truth—because they stay in the same place all of the time so they do not have to move their sleeping trees."

"Now I know that you are telling me stories. If they stayed in one place they would hunt and kill all of the animals there. They would pick all the fruit and then they would die of starvation. Such a funny story!"

"This is true," Herilak said. "That is the way that they live. I have been there and I have seen them, but I did not understand them. They do not need to hunt because they keep all of their animals in one place so they cannot escape, then kill them whenever they want to. Is that not the way it is?" he asked Kerrick.

Merrith had shrugged her shoulders at such useless stories and gone back to her fire, but the other women remained, eyes wide as they listened to this wild talk. True or not, the stories were worth hearing.

"That is only part of it," Kerrick said. "A lot of things happen, and different murgu do different things. Some clear the land and build the fences so the animals can be kept safe, yet kept apart. Then there are the guards who take care of the males during the breeding season so the young are born safe. Some raise food for the animals, others kill them when the time comes. Others fish. It is all very complex."

"The males take care of the babies?" one of the women asked in a quiet and nasal voice. The older woman beside her struck her. "Be quiet, Armun," she said.

"It is a good question," Kerrick said, trying to see who had spoken, but she had her face turned away with her hair held over it. "The murgu lay eggs and the males hatch the eggs. Then when the young ones come out of the eggs they go into the ocean to live. They do not take care of babies the way we do."

"They are filthy and should all be killed!" Merrith called out, for she had been listening all the time. "It is not right that women should hear these kind of stories."

Their audience scattered at her command and the two men finished their food in silence. Herilak licked the last fragments of meat from his fingers, then touched Kerrick lightly on the arm.

"You must tell me more of these things because I want to know all about these creatures. I am not like the woman—I believe every word that you say. Like you I was their prisoner. Only a short time—but that was long enough. If you lead, I will follow you, Kerrick. A strong arm and a quick bow are what a hunter needs. But the Tanu need knowledge as well. We are Tanu because we can work stone and wood and know the ways of all the beasts that we hunt. But now we hunt murgu and you are the only one with the knowledge that we must have. It is you alone who can show us the way."

Kerrick had not thought of it this way before, but now he had to nod reluctant agreement. Knowledge could be a strength—and a weapon. He had the knowledge and Herilak respected it. This was high praise from a hunter as wise and strong as Herilak. Kerrick felt the beginning of pride. For the first time he began to believe that he was not the complete outsider here.

CHAPTER NINE

M errith had been correct; after talking far into the night the hunters had decided, with great reluctance, that they must go south to find grazing for the mastodons. With this decision made they had to face the next problem. How were they to go about doing this?

It was just after dawn when Herilak emerged from their tent. He was building up the fire when Ulfadan and Kellimans approached him. The two sammadars greeted him formally, then sat down beside him at the fire. Herilak poured them wooden mugfuls of bark tea and waited for them to speak their minds. Behind his back Ortnar looked out of the tent, then quickly pulled his head back inside.

"You would think after last night they would have enough of talking, but they are still at it," he told Kerrick. "I don't see any problem. Kill murgu, that is all we have to do."

Kerrick sat up in the sleeping bag and shivered as the cold air hit him. He quickly pulled his leather shirt over his head, then ran his fingers through his short hair, yawned and scratched. Through the open flap of the tent he could see that the three hunters were still talking. He felt as Ortnar did; they had had enough of this the night before.

But this final meeting could not be avoided. Herilak rose from the fire and went to the tent and called to him.

"There is need of you, Kerrick. You will join us."

Kerrick went and sat beside them at the fire and sipped the hot, bitter brew while Herilak told them what had been decided.

"The sammads will go south because they have no other choice. However they do not know what to do when we reach the murgu. But one thing is certain, the murgu must be killed, therefore there must be a battle leader. They have asked me to be sacripex."

Kerrick nodded agreement. "That is as it should be. You led us in victory when we killed the murgu on the beaches."

"An attack is a single thing and I know well how to lead in that. But we are now planning more than an attack. We are planning to leave the forest and go south into the grasslands where there are only murgu. Murgu of all kinds. Then we must kill these murgu with the death-sticks. Now I will tell you the truth. I know little of murgu and I know nothing of death-sticks. But you do, Kerrick. Therefore I have said that you must be the sacripex."

Kerrick could not think of an answer. This was too unexpected. He turned it over and over in his head, then reluctantly spoke.

"It is a great trust, but I do not feel I know enough to be sacripex. Yes, I know much about the murgu, but little about hunting and killing. Herilak is the proven leader here."

They were silent then, waiting for him to continue. The sammads were looking to him for leadership and he could not refuse. Ortnar had heard what had been said and had emerged from the tent and joined the waiting hunters. They wanted him to lead, but he did not have the skill. What could be done? What would the Yilanè do in this situation? Once he had asked himself this question an answer began to appear.

"Let me tell you how the murgu order these things," he said. "In their cities there is a sammadar who is first in everything. Under this sammadar there is a sammadar of the hunters, another for the food animals, and others for the different work of the city. Why do we not arrange things in the same way? Herilak will be the sacripex as you have asked. I will serve under him, advise him on the ways of the murgu. But he will be the one who decides what must be done."

"We must think about this," Ulfadan said. "It is a new thing."

"These are new times," Kellimans said. "We will do as Kerrick has told us."

"We will do it," Herilak said, "but it is I who will serve. Kerrick will tell us about the murgu and what must be done to hunt them and to kill them. He will be the margalus, the murgu-counsellor."

Ulfadan nodded agreement and stood. "That is the way it must be."

"I agree," Kellimans said. "The hunters of the sammad will be told and if all are in agreement we will go south when the margalus says."

When they had gone, Herilak turned to face Kerrick. "What must we do first, margalus?" he said.

Kerrick pulled at the strands of his thin beard while the two hunters waited. The answer to this was easy, and he hoped that all the other problems would be as simple to solve.

"To kill murgu you must learn about the death-sticks. We will do that now."

Herilak and Ortnar were armed with spears and bows as always, but Kerrick put his aside and took up a hèsotsan and a supply of darts instead. He led them upstream away from the tents, to a clear space beside the river. The trunk of a dead tree lay trapped here among the boulders, where it had been left behind by the high waters of spring.

"We will shoot at that," Kerrick said. "If anyone else comes near we will be able to see them. There is death in these darts and I want no one killed."

The hunters put their spears and bows aside and reluctantly came close when Kerrick held out the hèsotsan.

"There is no danger yet, for I have not put darts into the creature. Let me first show you how to feed it and care for it. Then the darts will be inserted and we will use the tree for a target."

The hunters were well used to working with tools and artifacts and soon stopped thinking of the weapon as a living creature. When Kerrick fired the first dart they jumped at the sharp crack of the explosion, then rushed to the tree to see the dart stuck there.

"Will it shoot as far as a bow?" Herilak asked. Kerrick thought about it, then shook his head *no*.

"I do not think so—but it does not matter. There will be no need to kill at a distance if the murgu attack us. When a creature is hit by a dart the poison affects it almost at once. First it falls down, then stiffens, then dies. Now you must learn to use the death-sticks."

As he began to hand the weapon to Herilak he saw a movement in the sky behind him. A bird, a large one.

"Get your bows, quickly," he said. "The raptor is here, the one that speaks to the murgu. It must not return. It must be killed."

The hunters did not question his orders but seized up their bows and nocked the arrows, waiting until the bird swooped low. As it drifted over them on wide-stretched wings their bowstrings twanged at the same instant. The well-aimed arrows flashed upwards, both thudding into the raptor's body.

It gave a single screech and tumbled from the air, splashing into the river.

"Don't let it get carried away," Kerrick called out.

He stopped to place the hèsotsan carefully on the ground, and before he could straighten up the other two had dived into the water. Ortnar was a strong swimmer and he reached the dead bird first, seizing it by the wing and spinning it about in the water. But it was too large for him to handle alone and he had to wait for Herilak to help him drag it ashore. They emerged from the river, their fur garments wet and streaming, pulling the immense bird after them, then letting it drop onto the sand.

"Look there," Kerrick said, "on its leg, that black creature."

The bird was dead, but this animal was not. Its claws were locked about the raptor's leg. The thing was featureless except for a bulge on its side. Herilak squatted to look closer at the beast—then jumped back as the eye opened and looked up at him, then slowly closed again. He reached for his spear, but Kerrick stopped him.

"There will be plenty of time for that. First we must show this to the hunters, show them the eye that watches us and the bird that carries it. These are the beasts that tell the murgu where we are. Once the hunters have seen it they will recognize it again. Whenever one appears it must be killed. If the murgu do not know where we are they cannot attack us."

"You are right, margalus," Herilak said respectfully. "You are the one who knows about these creatures."

Herilak had used the title easily and with sincerity. He had spoken it so naturally that Kerrick felt a sudden burst of pride. Perhaps he could not hunt as well as they, while his arrows usually missed their mark, but he knew about murgu and they did not. If he could not be respected for his hunting prowess, it was enough that he led in something. They seized up the bird and carried it back to the camp.

The raptor itself was a wonder, for no one had ever seen a bird that big before. They stretched its wings wide, then paced out their length. The hunters admired the placing of the arrows; both had hit home in the creature's chest. The children crowded close and tried to touch it, but were pushed away. One of the women bent over and prodded the black creature on the bird's leg—then screamed when the eye blinked at her. Then everyone had to see this happen and pressed around. Herilak bent and cut the arrows free, then returned Ortnar's to him as they walked away.

"Now let us learn to shoot the death-stick as well as we can the bow," he said.

By evening both hunters felt as secure with the weapon as did Kerrick. Ortnar fed the creature a scrap of dried meat from his pouch, then rubbed its mouth shut.

"This will never kill a deer on the hunt," he said. "It is hard to aim and the darts fall short."

"We can kill deer easily enough with spear or bow," Herilak said. "We need these for the murgu when we go south."

"Before we start the journey I want all of the hunters to know how to use these," Kerrick said. "Only then do we leave."

After they had washed in the river the smell of cooking drew them back to the tents. It was a clear night and the stars were crisp and sharp above the flickering lights of the fires. Merrith served them meat, and Fraken the alladjex was there as well. The old man went to a different fire every night where people spoke to him of the things that only he knew. He looked suspiciously now at Kerrick who appeared to have knowledge that he did not. Herilak saw the look and drew the old man's attention away.

"I had a dream last night that I was with others and we were hunting mastodon," Herilak said. Fraken nodded and smacked his lips over the warm tea as he listened. "How could that be? I have only hunted mastodon once, and I was very young then."

"It was not you who hunted this time," the old man said. "It was your tharm." There was silence about the fire as they listened with respect. "When we die the tharm leaves the body, but it may also leave during the time when we are asleep. Your tharm left you and joined a hunt, that is what happened. This is why a hunter should not be awakened if he is deep in sleep for his tharm may be away, and if he is awakened he will die because the tharm leaves the body when we die. Forever, never to return. If the hunter who dies has been strong in the chase his tharm will join the others among the stars."

His voice lowered and there was a harsh rasp now when he spoke.

"But beware of the hunter who is a trouble-maker and has led a bad life, for there are hunters like that. When this hunter dies his tharm remains close by, causing trouble for others. Not so a strong hunter. His tharm will be there in the stars for all to see. A strong hunter's tharm will return in dreams to help others and warn them of dangers."

Kerrick listened, but said nothing. Now he remembered hearing old Ogatyr tell stories like this when he had been a boy, remembering shivering with fear when he tried to sleep, afraid that the tharm of another was close by. Now—they were just stories. The Yilanè would have laughed at this talk of tharms and stars. For them death was simply the end of being and there was no mystery involved. They knew the stars to be so far distant that their existence could have no possible effect on any events here on earth. He remembered Zhekak telling him about the stars, about how hot they were, the moon cold, the planets very much like Earth. That was the reality; these were just stories. But when Kerrick looked around at their faces he saw only respect and belief and decided that this was neither the time nor the place for him to speak of these matters.

When Fraken left to go to another fire many followed after him, leaving just a few hunters sitting close to the heat and talking. None of them took notice when the girl carrying a large handful of feathers came over and joined them. Her name was Farlan, Kerrick remembered, the elder daughter of Kellimans. She was tall and strong, her hair thick and plaited down her back. Kerrick felt a sensation he could not identify when she brushed past him, her body touching his, and he stirred restlessly. She went around the fire and sat next to Ortnar.

"These are the feathers of the great bird you killed," she said. Ortnar nodded agreement, scarcely looking at her.

"They could be sewn to your robe so others would know your skill with the bow." She hesitated a moment. "I could sew them for you."

Ortnar thought about this for a long time, then apparently agreed.

"I'll show you the robe." He led the way into the darkness and she followed.

The hunters apparently took no notice of this—but one of them looked up and happened to catch Kerrick's eye; he smiled and winked. Only when the couple were out of sight did the hunters begin to whisper to each other; one of them laughed aloud.

Something was happening, something important Kerrick knew, but no one told him what it was. He remained silent as well for he was too ashamed of his own stupidity to ask.

Ortnar was not in their tent when Kerrick returned, and it was only in the morning that he noticed that all of the hunter's possessions were gone as well.

"Where is Ortnar?" he asked.

"Sleeping in another tent," was all that Herilak answered, and appeared reluctant to say any more.

Kerrick was beginning to realize that there were things about Tanu life, as with the Yilanè, that were done and not talked about. But he was Tanu, he should know. He would have to find out, but did not know how to go about this. It would require some thought.

However Ortnar's mysterious behavior slipped from his mind in the bustle of breaking camp.

They were on their way south, into the unknown.

CHAPTER TEN

Ulfadan, who knew this territory well, led the trek steadily south through the forest. It was only when the trees began to thin out and he could see the open grassland ahead that he ordered a halt and trotted back to report to Kerrick.

"The open country is ahead. Now we have stopped as you ordered, margalus."

"Good," Kerrick said. "Herilak and I have considered what to do when we go out on the plain to face the murgu. If we travel as we always do, in a single column, we will be open to attack at any time from the sides, where there is no protection. In the forest one mastodon must follow another because of the narrow track between the trees. But if there are no trees we will be able to move differently. Here is what we have decided."

The hunters crowded close to look as Kerrick bent and scratched a circle in the ground with a stick.

"This is how we will move," he said. "The mastodons will travel side by side, in a group. Herilak will go before them with one group of hunters, since he is the sacripex and will lead in any battle against the murgu. But an attack might come from the sides—or even from behind—so we must be on guard at all times. You, Kellimans, will be with the hunters of your sammad to the left side,

Ulfadan the same to the right. I will follow in the rear with other
hunters. All of us will be armed with the death-sticks, as well as
bows and spears. In this way, with hunters on all sides, we will be
able to guard the sammads in the center . . ."

He was interrupted by a cry of alarm from one of the boys who
were watching the forest around them. The hunters turned, weapons ready. A strange hunter had appeared from the trees and stood
motionless, looking at them. He was from one of the sammads from
beyond the mountains, they could tell that by the birchbark leggings he wore below his knees. It was Herilak who went forward to
meet him. When he came close the hunter bent and placed his
spear on the ground. Herilak did the same, and when he did so the
hunter called out to him. Herilak shook his head, then turned and
called back to the others.

"He speaks, but I understand little."

"Newasfar will talk with him," Ulfadan said. "He has hunted
beyond the mountains and knows how they talk."

Newasfar left his own spear behind and went to speak with the
stranger while they all watched. There was a brief exchange which
Newasfar translated.

"He is a sammadar called Har-Havola. He says that their
mastodons died in the cold of winter and they had to eat them in
order to stay alive themselves. Now all their food has gone and they
will die when the snows come. He has heard that there is much
food here and he asks for some."

"No," Herilak said in instant response. The other hunters
nodded agreement. Har-Havola stepped back at this, for it was one
word that he knew. He looked around at the expressionless faces,
started to speak, then must have realized that it was useless. He
bent and picked up his spear, was turning away—when Kerrick
called out.

"Wait. Newasfar, tell him not to leave. Ask him how many
hunters he has in his sammad?"

"We have no food to spare," Herilak said. "He must leave."

"I speak now as margalus. Listen to what I have to say."
Herilak acknowledged this and was silent. "We have more food
than we can eat right now. Meat from the hunt as well as the murgu
meat that we captured. When we go out into the grasslands there
will be good hunting and we will have even more meat. But there
will also be murgu that we must defend ourselves against. When

they attack the more hunters we have to fight them the more secure we will be. I say let them join us for we can use their spears."

Herilak thought about this, then nodded in agreement.

"The margalus speaks the truth. We will need many hunters now because some must stand guard during the night. I say as well—let them come with us. Speak with him, Newasfar, tell him what we do and what the danger is. Tell him that if his hunters fight at our side, then all in his sammad will eat."

Har-Havola straightened up when he heard this and struck his chest. They did not need Newasfar to translate his words. The Tanu from beyond the mountains were great hunters and fighters. They would come.

Then he turned towards the trees and called out a command. The file of frightened women emerged from the trees, clutching their children to them. The hunters came behind them. They were all emaciated and did not hesitate to take the food that was offered to them. When everyone had eaten, the column started forward again and moved slowly out onto the plain.

While the mastodons were being gathered together in a group Herilak spoke to the sammadars.

"Now that we have more hunters we have more security. Kerrick can join me in the fore since he is margalus. Har-Havola will march to the rear with his hunters, since there will be less danger there and they do not have death-sticks. As soon as the hunters are in position we will start."

The grassy plain stretched before them to the horizon, a series of undulating low hills. There were clumps of trees scattered about, but most of the plain was grass. A herd of animals, too far distant to identify, was running swiftly away from them and soon vanished from sight. Nothing else moved: the plain had a deceptively peaceful air. Ulfadan knew better; his fingers touched the great tooth suspended about his neck as he looked carefully about. All of the hunters clutched their weapons tightly now, well aware that they did not belong here. Even the mastodons seemed to feel the tension, trumpeting and tossing their great heads.

At first the distant beasts were only dark specks coming up from a shallow valley. But they moved quickly and soon the rumble of their feet could be heard as more and more appeared, coming towards the Tanu. The mastodons were halted at a signal from Herilak, the hunters moving quickly forward to stand in line between this unknown threat and the sammads. Now the beasts in the herd could be clearly seen, unknown creatures with long necks and legs. The leaders swerved when they saw the Tanu and galloped across their front, throwing up a billowing cloud of dust. It was from this dust that the murgu struck.

There was more than one of them, large and indistinct creatures that pursued the fleeing herd. They bounded suddenly into sight. The nearest of them saw the shapes of the mastodon, screeched loudly, turned and attacked.

Kerrick had his weapon raised and fired at the charging figure, again and again. It rose into the air, screaming, then fell and crashed into the grass before them as the poison took effect. Close enough so that the beast's bulging eye was just before Kerrick and seemed to be glaring into his. It kicked out its clawed feet in a spasm of agony, the mouth fell open and it roared fitfully. The rotten smell of its breath reached the hunters as it died.

The mastodons were screaming now with fear, rearing up and threatening to crush the travois and those nearby. Some of the hunters ran to quiet them while the rest still faced outward, weapons ready.

But the danger had passed. The herd was vanishing in the distance still pursued by the giant carnivores. Kerrick stepped forward warily towards the one they had killed. It lay unmoving now, a mound of dead flesh the size of a mastodon. A giant beast designed for slaughter, its rear legs long and muscled, its jaws filled with rows of pointed teeth.

"Can the flesh of this creature be eaten?" one of the hunters asked, turning to Kerrick.

"I don't know. I've never seen anything like this before. But it is a meat eater and the murgu only eat the flesh of the animals that eat grass and leaves."

"Let us move on," Herilak ordered. "We do the same. Leave this beast."

The Tanu only ate the meat from carnivores when they were starving; the taste was strong and repellent and not to their liking. Now they had enough food and no desire at all to cut into this hideous creature. They went on quickly, the mastodons rolling their eyes and bellowing with fear as they passed the dead animal. Tanu and mastodon, they all wanted to be away from this place as quickly as they could.

The plain teemed with life. Dark creatures that were obviously not birds soared above them. Great forms wallowed in a shallow lake which they prudently made a large circle to avoid. Smaller murgu, half-seen, moved away from them in the high grass. Though they stayed alert, their weapons ready, they were not attacked again. The day passed in this manner without further encounters. The shadows were getting long when they stopped to water their beasts at a stream. Herilak pointed to a low hill nearby that was topped by a thick growth of trees.

"We will stop there for the night. The trees will give us protection and this water is close by."

Kerrick looked up at the grove; it worried him. "We don't know what might be concealed there," he said. "Wouldn't we be better here on the plain where we could see anything approaching?"

"We know now that this plain is alive with murgu during the day—but we don't know what moves in the darkness in this place. The trees will be our shelter."

"Then we must be sure that we are the only ones sheltering there. Let some of the best hunters search there now before it is too dark to see."

They went cautiously, but the trees hid nothing of any great danger. Small murgu, tails held high, ran before them. There was a great flapping and screeching when they disturbed some birds feeding on fruit in the trees above. Other than this the grove was empty. It would be a good place to stop.

The mastodons quieted once they were freed of their burdens and were soon tearing at the green leaves. The boys brought the fire, carried in clay-lined baskets, and the tents were quickly set up. Guards were posted around the camp as darkness fell; they would be changed during the night.

"We have done all that we can do," Herilak said. "We have survived our first day."

"May we live through the night as well," Kerrick said, looking about worriedly. "I hope that we did not make a mistake in coming here."

"You bother yourself too much with things that cannot be changed. The decision was made. There was no other path to take."

Herilak was right, Kerrick thought, I worry too much. But he has been a sammadar and sacripex before, and knows about leading others. All of this is still new to me.

He fell asleep quickly after they had eaten, and did not stir until Herilak touched his shoulder. The night was very dark, but the stars of the Hunter had gone from the western sky and the Mastodon would soon follow: dawn was close by.

"Nothing came near us during the night," Herilak said, "though there are plenty of creatures out there. Perhaps they do not like our smell."

The dark shapes of other hunters moved under the trees as the sentries were replaced. Kerrick stood at the top of the slope and looked down at the darker outline of the stream.

"We have seen animals watering there," Herilak said, "but there was no way of telling what they were."

"As long as they leave us alone it does not matter."

They waited in silence until the sky lightened in the east with approaching dawn.

"A day and a night and we are all still alive," Herilak said. "It is said that a trek that begins well ends well. May that be true now."

CHAPTER ELEVEN

The slow march continued south that day, then the next and the next again. The hunters still took the precaution of flanking the sammads during the daylight hours and posting guards at night, but they walked with less apprehension, slept without worry. The plain was rich with animal life, but most of the creatures were murgu herbivores who stayed well clear of the sammads and their mastodons. There were predators, and many of the largest of these carnivores did attempt to attack them. The hunters killed the ones that came close and the others saw this and stayed clear. But the hunters knew that without the weapons that they had captured they would have been long since dead. With their defense the sammads could penetrate deeper and deeper into the plain.

The course they took stayed well clear of the swamps along the river and the large creatures that could be seen wallowing there. They avoided the thick forest as well, whenever they could, because when they passed through it they were forced to go in single file which made the column much harder to guard.

Despite the ever-present dangers the hunters still looked forward each morning to what the new day might bring, while each night they talked late around the fires about what they had seen that day. For them the world about them was an essential part of their lives. Normally they knew every animal in the forest, every bird in the trees; they knew their habits and how they were to be hunted.

But now they had discovered a whole new world. They had passed through a border area when the trek had begun, where they had seen some deer and other familiar beasts, as well as murgu of different kinds. Quite suddenly this had all changed and the animals they had watched and hunted all their lives were no more. Only some of the birds looked familiar, while the fish in the river were apparently no different. The rest were murgu, murgu in such variety that they could no longer be called by that single name. They were underfoot and in the grass, small lizards and snakes, while grazing the sea of grass itself were beasts of all sizes and colors. The hunters were specially watchful when they passed one of these herds because many times they were followed by packs of voracious carnivores.

Once, squatting and tearing at the rotting corpse of a large and nameless animal, they had seen carrion birds as large as the raptor that had once watched them. They were ungainly things with dark red plumage and very long tails. When the hunters passed close by they hopped about on their long legs and opened their beaks to hiss in anger. They were efficient carrion eaters for instead of bills they had jaws lined with sharp teeth.

The land was rich, the game so plentiful that it would have fallen in great numbers before their arrows had they had the time to hunt, while the weather itself became hard to believe. When they had set out on the trek the leaves were beginning to fall from the trees and they had felt the first cold grip of winter in the frosts at night. But now the seasons had been reversed and they seemed to be going back into the warm time. Even the nights were not cold, while during the day they took off their leather garments and walked with their skins exposed just as they did during the summer.

Then one day they came to the place where the large river that they had been following was joined by an even mightier one. Though it was only just past midday Herilak halted the march and asked Kerrick and the sammadars to join him.

"This will be a good place for a camp. There is that steep trail down to the river below that can be used for watering the beasts. It will also be at our backs at night and will be easy to guard. Good grazing here for the mastodons, fuel in the woods there for our fires."

"It is still early," Ulfadan said. "Why do we stop now?"

"That is the reason I called you here. When we began this march we decided only that we should go south. Now we have done that. So the time has come to decide where we will make our winter camp. We must now think about this."

"We passed a large herd of the duck-billed murgu today," Kellimans said. "I would very much like to taste one."

"My spear hand twitches," Ulfadan said, squinting into the distance across the river. "We have not hunted for many days."

"Then I say let us stop here." Herilak looked around and the hunters nodded agreement.

"I am thinking of the murgu-who-walk-like-men," Kerrick said. "They must never be forgotten."

Ulfadan snorted. "We have seen none of their great birds. They cannot know that we are here."

"We can never be sure what they know or do not know. They stalked and killed sammad Amahast and they did not have the birds then. Wherever we are, whatever we do, we must never forget them."

"What is your thought then, margalus?" Herilak asked.

"You are the hunters. We will stay here if that is to your liking. But there must be a guard at this spot, night and day, to watch the river in case of an attack. See how wide the river has become here? It must reach the ocean somewhere south of us. The ocean and the river can be a path for the murgu if they know that this is our camping place."

"The margalus is correct," Herilak said. "We will take this precaution as long as we are here."

Ulfadan was looking down the bare slope, frowning at it. "Always before we have camped among the trees. It is too open here."

Kerrick remembered the city of Alpèasak which was also on a river, but well guarded.

"There is a thing that the murgu do. They grow strong trees and thorn bushes to protect their camp. We cannot grow trees, but we could cut thorn bushes and pile them in a line for protection. It will keep the small beasts out—and we can kill anything large enough to break through."

"We have never done it before," Kellimans protested.

"We have never come this far south before," Herilak said. "We will do as the margalus tells us."

Although they had meant to stay just a night or two at this place, many days passed and still they did not move on. There were fish in the river and the hunting was very good here, better than they had ever known before. The duck-bills were so numerous that many times the far side of their herds could not be seen. They were very fast—but were also very stupid. If a group of hunters appeared suddenly they fled away. If this was done correctly the other hunters would be waiting in hiding ahead of them with spears and bows ready. Not only were the creatures fast and stupid—they also made very tasty eating.

The hunting was rich, the mastodons grazed well, it was a good place to winter—if indeed this warm weather could be called winter. But there was no escaping the seasons; the days were short and the star groups changed steadily in the night sky. The thorn wall was thickened and, without any positive decision being made, it came about that they stayed on in this place by the union of the two rivers.

The women were as pleased as the hunters, glad to be finished with the long trek. Walking, unloading, cooking, reloading, walking, it had been nothing but work without time enough for anything else. That was all changed for the better now with the tents firmly in place and everything spread out. There were roots to dig for, as well as a brownish-yellow tuber that they had never seen before. This proved to be deliciously sweet after it had been baked in the ashes.

There was much to do, much to talk about. At first sammad Har-Havola had kept apart from the others for they spoke a different tongue and knew that they were strangers. But the women of all the sammads met when they were out foraging and found that it was possible for them to talk together after a while, for the other language was like Marbak in many ways. At first the children fought, until the newcomers came to learn Marbak after which their differences were forgotten. Even the single women were pleased for now there were more young hunters to be sought after. There had never been a winter encampment this big. Three entire sammads gathered at one place made life busy and interesting.

Even Armun found a measure of peace, losing herself in the great numbers of women. She had only been three winters with sammad Ulfadan, and they had all been tragic ones for her. There had been great winter hunger in the sammad they had left, so much so that her mother, Shesil, had been too weak to live through the first winter in the new sammad. This meant that when her father had gone out hunting there was no one to protect her. The boys laughed at her, and she had to be careful not to speak in their presence for the young girls were just as bad. When Brond, her father, had not returned from the hunt during the second winter there was no escape from the others. Since she was strong and a good worker, Merrith, the sammadar's woman, let her eat at her fire, but made no attempt to protect her from the constant taunts. Merrith even joined in herself when she was angry, shouting "squirrel-face" along with all the others.

Armun had been that way since birth, that was what her mother had said. Shesil had always blamed herself, for she had once killed and eaten a squirrel in a time of great hunger, when everyone knew that women were forbidden to hunt. Because of this her daughter had been born with the front teeth of a squirrel, wide apart, and with the cleft upper lip of a squirrel as well. Not only had the lip been split, but there was an opening in the bone in the roof of the mouth behind it. Because of this opening she had not nursed well when she had been a baby, had coughed and cried a lot. Then, when she had begun to talk, what she said had a very funny sound. No wonder the other children had laughed at her.

They were still laughing, though not when she could reach them. She was a young woman now, long-legged and strong. And she still had the temper that had been her only defense as a child. Even the biggest boys did not make fun of her, except at a distance, for she had a ready fist and knew how to strike. Black eyes and bloody noses were her mark and even the stupidest soon learned to leave this squirrel-faced demon alone.

She grew up, friendless and apart. When she walked about the encampment she usually held the loose top of her soft leather garment over the bottom half of her face. Her hair was long and many times she held this the same way as well.

As long as she did not talk, the other women suffered her presence. Armun listened to them, saw the young hunters through their eyes, heard their excited gossip. Farlan had been the oldest of their group, and when Ortnar had joined the sammad she had been quick to go to him, even though she had only known him for a short while. The usual way was to get to know boys from the other sammads when they met each year. That was the usual way. But everything was changing now, and Farlan had been the first to take advantage of that change. Although the other young women said nasty things about her boldness, she was the one who had a tent and a hunter of her own—and they did not.

Armun was not jealous of the others, just angry. She knew the plains and the forest better than any of them; her mother had taught her well. She returned from foraging with her basket full when the other young women wailed at the barrenness of the land. She worked hard, cooked well, did all the things that should make her desirable to any young hunter. Yet she stayed far away from them knowing that they would only make fun of her just as everyone else did; her anger surged at the thought. When they saw her face they laughed, when she spoke they laughed. She remained silent and apart.

At least she tried to. But since she ate at Merrith's fire she must do as the older woman ordered. She brought wood and cut meat, scorched her hands turning it over on the coals. Merrith saw to it that there was good food waiting each evening when the hunters returned hungry and tired. But Armun did not want them laughing at her so she always found other things to do when they were gathered around the fire.

Although there was no snow, the rains came in the deepest part of winter. They were uncomfortable but not cold, and this discomfort was infinitely better than frozen forest and deep snow. Hunting patterns changed now, for the great herds of duck-bills had gone somewhere else upon the vast plain. Yet there were still murgu to hunt in the upland forest to the east, so hunting parties pushed farther and farther up into the hills. This was not without its dangers.

It was well after dark when the hunting party returned. The days were very short now so this was not unusual; some hunters even stayed out overnight when pursuing game. But something was wrong this time for the returning hunters called out loudly when they came into sight of the camp, their ululating cries drawing everyone's attention. Some of the hunters ran out to aid them when they called for help as well. When they came closer to the fires it could be seen that two of the hunters were being carried on litters made of poles and brushwood. Herilak led the way, grim-faced and tired.

"We were after the sharp-toed runners. A claw-marag was hidden under the trees. It attacked and did all this before we could kill it." The first litter was dropped heavily to the ground. "It is Ulfadan. He is dead."

Merrith screamed aloud when she heard this and ran forward. When she threw back the furs that lay across Ulfadan's face she wailed terribly and tore at her hair.

Herilak looked around until he saw Fraken, then called him over. "We have need of your healing skills. The marag fell on Kerrick and the bone in his leg is broken."

"I will need strong sticks, lengths of leather. You will help me."

"I will get the wood." Herilak looked up and saw Armun standing nearby. "Get some soft leather," he ordered. "Quickly."

Kerrick bit his lips but could not keep back the groan when they took him from the litter and placed him on the ground by the fire; the broken ends of bone sawed inside his leg. Fierce pain speared through it again when Fraken poked at the flesh.

"You will hold his shoulders tight, Herilak, when I pull the leg," Fraken ordered, then bent and seized Kerrick's foot. The old man had done this before, pulling and twisting so the broken ends of bone met. The pain of this pushed Kerrick into dark unconsciousness.

"Now the sticks to keep the bone in place," Fraken said, tying them securely with lengths of soft leather. The work was quickly done. "Put him into the tent, cover him with furs for he must be kept warm. You, girl, help us."

Kerrick blinked back to consciousness with sharp awareness of the throbbing pain in his leg. It hurt still, but far less than it had done. He pulled himself up onto his elbows and in the flickering light of the fire outside saw the lengths of wood bound to his leg. The skin had not broken; this would heal well. Someone moved behind him in the darkness. "Who is there?" he called out.

"Armun," she said, reluctantly.

He dropped back with a sigh. "Get me some water, Armun. A lot of it."

She hurried out, a dark figure quickly gone. Armun? He did not know the name. Had he met her before? It didn't matter. The leg had settled down to a steady throb of pain like a bad tooth. His throat was so dry that it made him cough. Water was what he needed, a long deep drink of cool water.

CHAPTER TWELVE

Kerrick slept fitfully until dawn, when the throbbing of the leg woke him yet another time. When he turned his head he saw the bowl of water close by. He pushed his hand out from under the furs, seized it and drank deep, drank again and drained it. The girl came from behind him and picked it up. He could not tell who she was, her hair fell over her face. What was her name? She had told him.

"Armun?"

"Yes. Do you want more water?"

"Water. And something to eat."

He had not eaten last night, had no desire to. But he was hungry now. The girl hurried out, her back turned. He hadn't been able to see her face, he couldn't place her at all. But she had a nice voice. The way she talked through her nose like that was familiar. How the leg hurt when he tried to get comfortable! Familiar? Why? This nagged a bit until he realized it was one of the sounds you used in Yilanè. *Armun*. He said it aloud, with the same nasal quality, then repeated it to himself. He had not spoken Yilanè in such a long time that when he did so now memories of Alpèasak pushed in, unbidden.

When she returned with the water she also brought some

smoked meat on a basketwork tray, bending to place them both beside him. With her hands full she could not cover her face and he looked closely at her when she bent down. His eyes caught hers and she turned away as quickly as she could, her fists clenched waiting for the laughter that never came. Armun could not understand this. She looked on in puzzled silence as he chewed hungrily at the meat. If she could have known what he was thinking she would not have believed it.

No, Kerrick thought, I haven't seen her before. I wonder why? I would certainly have remembered her. I wonder if she knows what her voice sounds like? I had better not tell her, she would only get angry being compared to a marag. But her voice does have Yilanè sounds to it. Not only that, her mouth is in some ways Yilanè. Perhaps the way the upper lip is separated. A familiar face. Inlènu∗'s face had looked a bit like that, but wider of course, and fatter.

Armun sat behind Kerrick and wondered. The pain must be tearing at him or he would have laughed by now, or asked questions about her face. The boys had always been curious, never letting her alone. Once five of them had seized her among the trees when she had been by herself. She had fought and kicked but they had held her down. Poked at her lip and nose and laughed until they had her in tears. There was no pain, just a great shame. She was so different from the other girls. They hadn't even pulled up her clothes to look at her the way they did with the other young girls when they caught them alone. Just poked at her face. She had been just like a funny animal to them. Her thoughts were so far away and so bitter that it was a moment before she realized that Kerrick had rolled onto his side and was looking back at her. She quickly pulled her hair across her face.

"That is why I did not recognize you," he said with satisfaction. "You pull your hair like that all the time, I've seen you do it."

She tensed, waiting for the laughter. Instead he grunted as he struggled to a sitting position, then wrapped the furs around him again because the morning was damp and foggy. "Are you Ulfadan's daughter? I've seen you at his fire."

"No. My father and mother are dead. Merrith lets me help her."

"The marag landed on Ulfadan, knocked him to the ground. We speared it but it was too late. His neck was broken. It was a big one. One swipe with the tail broke my leg. We should have had more death-sticks with us. It was the only thing that stopped the ugly thing."

He couldn't blame himself. In fact it was his order that every hunting party have a hunter with a death-stick to prevent something like this happening. But one wasn't enough among the trees. From now on hunting parties would have at least two hèsotsan with them.

But all thoughts of hunting and murgu were banished in an instant when Armun came close. Her hair brushed his face as she bent to pick up the empty water bowl; he could smell the sweet woman smell of her. He had never been this close to a girl before and the excitement of it stirred him. Unbid, the memory appeared, Vaintè above him, close to him. It was unwanted, disgusting, and he pushed all thoughts of that away.

But the memory lingered, tantalizing, for the feelings he had felt then had been very much like those he was experiencing now; the same excitement. When Armun bent again to pick up the tray he put his hand on her bare arm. It was warm, not cool. Soft.

Armun stopped, trembling, feeling his hand on her flesh, not knowing what to do. Without thinking she turned to look at him, his face close to hers. He did not laugh or turn away. Then the voices outside, coming closer, penetrated the silence.

"How is Kerrick?" It was Herilak who spoke.

"I go there now," Fraken answered.

The strange moment ended. Kerrick dropped his hand and Armun hurried away with the tray. Fraken pushed his way into the tent, his old eyes blinking in the darkness, Herilak close behind him. Fraken pulled at the leather straps that held Kerrick's leg tight to the wooden frame and nodded happily.

"All as it should be. The leg will heal straight. If these straps hurt you must pad them with dry grass. I go now to sing about Ulfadan."

Kerrick would have liked to have been there when the old man sang. The more hunters who chanted the happier Ulfadan's tharm would be. When the singing was finished Ulfadan's empty body would be wrapped in soft leather and tied high in a tree to dry in the wind. The body did not matter any more, once the tharm of the hunter had gone. Still, it would not have been proper to leave it where the carrion eaters could find it.

"I would be with you," Kerrick said.

"It is understood," Herilak said. "But it would not do to hurt the leg any more."

When they had gone Armun came from the rear of the tent, but still stood hesitatingly to one side. When he turned towards her she reached quickly for her hair—then let her hand drop because there was still no laughter in his face when he looked at her. It had happened and she did not question it. But she was still unaccustomed to being stared at.

"I heard you when you talked about being captured by the murgu." She spoke quickly, trying to hide her confusion. "Weren't you frightened, alone like that?"

"Frightened? In the beginning, I suppose I was. But I wasn't alone, they had also captured this girl, I forget her name. But they killed her." The memory was still just as clear, the emotion just as strong. The murgu with the girl's blood on it turning towards him. Vaintè. "Yes, I was afraid, very afraid. I should have kept quiet, but I talked to the murgu. I would have been killed as well if I hadn't talked to the one who held me. I did, I was that afraid. But I should not have talked."

"Why should you have kept quiet if talking saved your life?"

Why indeed? He was no hunter then, brave in the face of death. He had just been a child, the sole survivor of his sammad. There had been no shame in speaking out, he realized now. It had saved his life, brought him here, brought him here to Armun who understood.

"No reason, no reason at all," he said, smiling up at her. "I think that was when I stopped being afraid. Once they could talk to me they wanted me alive. At times they even needed me."

"I think that you were as brave as a hunter, even though you were just a boy."

These words disarmed him, he didn't know why. For some reason he felt close to tears and had to turn away from her. Tears, now, he a hunter? Without reason? Good reason perhaps, they were the unshed tears of that little boy alone among the murgu. Well, that was well past, he was no longer little, no longer a boy. He looked back at Armun and without intending to reached out and took her hand. She did not pull away.

Kerrick was confused by what he felt now, for he did not know what it meant, could relate the powerful and unknown emotions within him only to what had happened those times alone with Vaintè, when she had seized him. He did not want to think about

Vaintè now, or anything else Yilanè. Unknowingly his hand closed, hard, hurting her, but she did not pull away. A warmth swept over him as though from an unseen sun. Something important was happening to him, but he did not know what it was.

Not so Armun. She knew. She had listened often enough when the young women had talked, listened also to the older women who had children, when they told about their experiences, what went on in the night, in the tents when they were alone with a hunter. She knew what was happening now and welcomed it, opened herself to the sensations that overwhelmed her. More so because she had always had little hope, even less expectation. If only it were night now and they were alone! The women had been explicit, graphic about what was done. But it was day, not night. Yet it was so quiet. And she was too close to him now. When she pulled gently Kerrick opened his hand and she moved away. Rose and turned away from the look in his eyes.

Armun stepped outside the tent and looked about her. There was no one in sight; even the children were silent, gone. What did it mean?

The singing, of course, and when she realized this she began to tremble. Ulfadan had been a sammadar. They would all be at his singing, all the sammads, everyone. She and Kerrick were alone now.

With careful, deliberate movements she turned and went back into the tent. With sure hands laced shut the tent flap.

Just as surely opened the laces of her own clothing and knelt, pulling aside the furs, entering the warm darkness beneath them.

Her figure loomed, half-seen above him. He could not move much because of his leg. But he did not want to, and soon forgot about the leg completely. Her flesh was soft, unexpectedly warm, her hair brushing over his face in silent caress. When he put his arms about her the warmth of her body matched his as well. Memories of a cool body began slipping away. She was closer, closer still. She had no hard ribs, just warm flesh, round and firm, pushing with unexpected pleasure against his chest. His arms tightened, pressing her to him, her lips to his ear speaking sounds without words.

Outside the morning sun was burning through the mist, lifting it, taking the chill from the air.

Inside the tent, beneath the warmth of the furs, the heat of their bodies melted his memories of a cooler, harsher body. Pushed aside memories of a different life, a different existence, putting in their place a tender reality of infinitely greater worth.

entaposop
otoshkerke
hespeleiaa

———————

*All life forms are mutable since
DNA is endless in time.*

CHAPTER THIRTEEN

Alpèasak churned with life, seethed and writhed from first light until dark. Where a few fargi had once moved along the broad avenues of the city between the trees there now paraded Yilanè on foot, Yilanè of rank born on palanquins, fargi alone and in crowds laden with burdens, even well-guarded groups of males, round-eyed and silent as they looked about at the incessant movement. The harbor had been greatly enlarged, yet was still not large enough to accommodate all of the arivals, so that the dark forms of uruketo coming in from the ocean had to stay in the river, nuzzling against the bank, awaiting their turns. Once they were docked struggling masses of fargi unloaded their cargo, were pushed aside by the Yilanè passengers anxious to set foot on land after the long voyage.

Vaintè looked down at all the bustle with excitement, with pride in every taut line of her body. Her city, her labors, her ambition now fulfilled. Inegban* had come to Alpèasak at last. The union of the two cities brought an excitement with it that was impossible to resist. The youth and rawness of Alpèasak was now tempered with the age and wisdom of Inegban*. This union had produced an amalgam that seemed to be far superior to either of them alone. It was the world born anew, the egg of time just hatched, with all things possible, all promise bright.

There was a single shadow on this sunlit present and future, but Vaintè put that from her now since it was something that would be considered and acted upon later. At this present moment she wanted only to bask in the sun of her pleasure, warm herself on the beaches of success. Her thumbs gripped hard on the firm branch of the balustrade while so great was her excitement that all unknowing she shifted her weight from one foot to another in a solitary march of victory.

The voice spoke as from a great distance and Vaintè turned away reluctantly to see that Malsas< had joined her on the high platform. Yet so great was Vaintè's pleasure that there was room for the other to enter and join in as well.

"See, Eistaa," Vaintè spoke with pride in every movement. "It has been done. Winter will not come to Inegban*, instead Inegban* has come to endless summer here, one as warm and beneficent as any in the heart of Entoban*. Forever now will our city grow and prosper."

"It is as you say, Vaintè. When we were apart our two hearts did not beat as one, our two cities were different and separate. Now we are one. I feel as you do, that our strength is limitless, that we can do anything. And we shall. Will you not think a second time about sitting beside me, working with me? Surely Stallan can lead the fargi and wipe the curse of the ustuzou from the northern land."

"Perhaps she can, perhaps. But I know that I can and I will." Vaintè drew her thumb down between her eyes in a swift gesture. "I am as two. Now that health has returned the hatred that filled me so fully has grown smaller—but still remains firm. A hard ball of hatred that I can feel within me. Stallan might be able to crush the ustuzou. But it is I who must do it in order to destroy this rock of hatred inside my body. When they are all dead, when the creature I raised up and nurtured is dead, only then will this rock dissolve and vanish. Then I shall be whole and ready to sit at your side and do as I am bid. But this other must I do first."

Malsas< signed reluctant agreement. "I need you with me, but not when you are driven like this. Crush the ustuzou and crush the rock within. There is still the fullness of time ahead for Alpèasak."

Vaintè signed her thanks and appreciation. "We gather our strength now and will be ready to attack them as soon as the weather warms in the north. The cold that drove us from Alpèasak drives them south as well. But here the winter chill is our ally. The ustuzou must hunt now where we can reach them easily; they are watched. When the proper time comes they will die. We will sweep over them, then move north to strike the others. We will do this over and over, strike them again and again, until they are all dead."

"You will not use the boats? You spoke of attacking across the land instead?"

"They will expect us on the water. They do not know that we now have the uruktop and some tarakast as well. It was Vanalpè who knew of these creatures, who traveled to Entoban∗, to the far city of Mesekei, distant from the ocean, where creatures like these are used. She told them of our need, of the ustuzou who threaten, and was given the strongest breeding stock. The uruktop grow to maturity in less than a year. The young are now of a size, strong and ready. The tarakast are larger, take longer to mature, so only a few immature specimens were brought back, but even these will be of great aid. When we attack now we will do so by land. The ustuzou who escaped me now leads them, and it is with the group in the south. I have seen the creature in the pictures. He dies first. The rest will give us no problems when he has gone."

Vaintè looked into the future, planning her revenge, seeing only cruel death for this one she hated. As her thoughts darkened so did the sky above as a thick cloud drifted before the sun and shadow closed in over them. When the shadow touched their skins, so did an even darker shadow touch their thoughts, something even more troublesome than the ustuzou. It was always this way, for bright as any day begins it always ends in the darkness of the night. There was a darkness in this city of light that always entered their thoughts when they saw what they were seeing now.

A line of Yilanè, bound together at the waist, were moving slowly by below. The first in line looked around, then glanced upward, her quiet gaze drawn for some reason to the two figures looking down from above. The distance was not great so she was able to recognize them, recognized Vaintè. Her hand moved in quick and warm recognition, one efenselè to another, then she was past.

"From my own efenburu," Vaintè said bitterly. "That is a weight that I can never put down."

"The fault is not yours," Malsas< said. "There are Daughters of Death in my efenburu as well. This is a disease that eats us all."

"This is a disease that may have a cure. I dare not speak more of it now; we could be overheard. But I will say that I see a possibility of hope."

"You are first to me in all things," Malsas< said, sincerity strong in every motion. "Do this, cure this disease, and none will be higher."

Enge had not meant to acknowledge her efenselè, the gesture had been done unconsciously, yet even as she had done it she had realized her mistake. Vaintè would not have been pleased by it at any time. But now, with the Eistaa present, it might be considered an insult. Enge had not intended it so. It had been a mistake but not a deliberate one.

The line had halted before the barred gate, waiting for it to open, waiting for release. Release into prison, but for all of them it was a freedom. Here they were one, here they were free to believe the truth—and more important—speak the truth.

When she was with the other Daughters of Life, Enge no longer felt bound by her pledge not to speak to other Yilanè of her beliefs—for they all shared the same beliefs here. When Inegban* had come to Alpèasak the city's unwelcome burden of believers had come as well. There were so many of them that this compound had been grown, walled and guarded so that their intellectual poison did not spread. What they spoke of between themselves, behind these walls, was of no importance to the rulers outside. Just as long as these treasonous thoughts stayed behind the sharp thorns of the wall.

Efenatè hurried up to Enge, her slight form quivering with news. "It is Peleinè," she said. "She is talking to us, answering our questions."

"I will join you," Enge said, the stiffness of her body scarcely concealing her troubled thoughts. Ugunenapsa's teaching had always been clear to her, a beam of sunshine in the dark jungle of worry. But her teachings were not always seen that way by others, were open to interpretations and discussion. That was only right, for Ugunenapsa had taught about the freedom of the power of the mind to understand everything, not just the power of life and death. Although Enge agreed with this freedom, she was still disturbed by some of the interpretations of Ugunenapsa's words, and of all the interpretations Peleinè's disturbed her most of all.

Peleinè stood on the raised root of the large tree so that all those gathered around could understand what she was saying. Enge stopped at the edge of the crowd, settling back like the others onto her tail to listen. Peleinè was speaking in the new manner of discussion that had become so popular, using questions and answers to tell them what she wanted them to know.

"Ugunenapsa, the fargi still wet from the sea asked, Ugunenapsa, what makes me different from the squid in the sea? Then Ugunenapsa answered, the difference is, my daughter, that you can know of death, while the squid in the sea know only life.

"But knowing of death, how can I then know of life? The answer that Ugunenapsa then spoke was so simple and so clear that had it been spoken at the egg of time it would still ring clear tomorrow and tomorrow's tomorrow. The answer was that which sustains us, for knowing of death we know the limits of life, therefore we live when others would die. That is the strength of our belief, that is the belief that is our strength.

"Then the fargi, wet from the sea in her simplicity, asked what of the squid I eat, do I not bring it death? And she was answered, no, the squid brings you life with its flesh and since it knows not of death it cannot die."

There was a murmur of appreciation at this from the listeners, and Enge herself was moved by the clarity and beauty of the thought and for the moment forgot all reservations she may have had about the speaker. Eager in her desire for knowledge, one of the Yilanè cried out from the listening crowd.

"Wise Peleinè, what if the squid were so large that it threatened your life, and its taste was so horrible that it could not be eaten? What would you do then? Would you stand and be eaten, or would you kill even though you knew that you could not eat?"

Peleinè acknowledged the difficulty of the problem. "Here is where we must study Ugunenapsa's thoughts closely. She spoke of the thing within us that cannot be seen, that enables us to speak and separates us from the unthinking beasts. To preserve this unseen thing is worthwhile, therefore killing the squid to preserve the unseen thing is worth doing. We are the Daughters of Life and must preserve life."

"What if the squid could talk, what then?" someone called out, and since this was the question closest to all of them they were silent and attentive. When Peleinè spoke they all listened.

"For Ugunenapsa there was no answer for she knew of no talking squid." Peleinè made her answer more explicit. "Nor were there talking ustuzou. Therefore we must seek in Ugunenapsa's words for her true intent. Does speaking alone signify the knowledge of life and death? Or can an ustuzou speak, yet know not of death? If that is true, then to save our lives we might kill that ustuzou that speaks, for we know that we know of the difference, yet we know not if the ustuzou is aware. This is a decision that we must make."

"But we cannot decide," Enge called out, much disturbed. "We cannot decide unless we know, for if we do not know for certain then we violate all that Ugunenapsa taught."

Peleinè turned in her direction and signed agreement yet worry. "Enge speaks the truth, but speaks the problem as well. We must consider the reservation that there is only the possibility that the ustuzou may know of life and death. This must be balanced against the fact that we surely do know of life and death. On one hand a doubt, on the other a certainty. Since life is the thing that we value the highest I say we must hold to the certainty and reject the doubt. There can be no other way."

There were more questions, but Enge did not hear them, did not want to hear them. She could not escape her deep-felt belief that Peleinè was wrong, yet could not see her way clearly to expressing this certainty. She must ponder on it. She sought a quiet place away from the others and turned all of her attention inwards.

So wrapped was she in her thoughts that she did not notice the guards who went through the crowds seeking out a work party. Did not hear the little cries of distress when their teacher, Peleinè, was one of those selected, as though she were no different from the others. The working parties were chosen, leashed together, led away.

Those with Peleinè were not bound as were the others because they were taken away in smaller groups for different work. None of them noticed that in the end Peleinè was left alone. The guards were sent away as well by a Yilanè of authority who led Peleinè by a long route around the city to a door which opened for her. Peleinè went in unhappily, for this had happened before and she was still not sure within herself if what she was doing was correct. But until she decided she could make no protest, could not refuse to be here. Reluctantly she entered and closed the door behind her. There was only one other Yilanè present in the room.

"Now we will talk," Vaintè said.

Peleinè stood with her head bowed, staring unseeingly at her hands as she nervously laced and unlaced her thumbs. "I feel that what I am doing is wrong," she said finally. "I should not be here. I should not talk to you."

"You have no cause to feel that way. I merely want to hear what you have to say. Is it not a duty of a Daughter of Life to speak to others about her beliefs, to bring enlightenment to them?"

"It is. Are you then enlightened, Vaintè? Do you now call me a Daughter of Life instead of a Daughter of Death because you believe as I do?"

"Not yet. You must talk to me more, present more convincing arguments before I join your ranks."

Peleinè straightened up, suspicion in every movement of her body. "Then if you do not believe as we do—what need have you of me? Do you see me as a sower of dissension in the ranks of the Daughters? At times I see myself that way too, and wonder just where my process of careful analysis of our teachings is taking me."

"It is taking you to the truth. It is convincing you that the ustuzou who kill us deserve killing in return. There is justice in that. We defend our beaches, we kill those creatures that threaten our existence. I do not ask you to change your beliefs. I ask you only to aid us in this just war. If you do this the benefits will be great for all of us. Our city will be saved. The Eistaa will remove your bonds and you will all be citizens once again. Your beliefs will be recognized as legitimate because they will not threaten the existence of Alpèasak. You will be the true leader then of the Daughters of Life and will follow the footsteps and teachings of Ugunenapsa."

Peleinè-signed confusion and worry. "Yet I have doubts. If the ustuzou can speak they may be aware of the existence of death, therefore the meaning of life. If this is so I cannot aid in their extinction."

Vaintè came forward then, so close that their hands almost touched, and spoke with great feeling. "They are beasts. One of them was taught to speak, just as a boat is taught to obey commands. Just one of them. The others grunt like animals in the jungle. And this one who was taught to speak like a Yilanè now kills Yilanè. They are a blight that destroys us. They must be wiped out, every last one of them. And you will help. You will lead the Daughters of Death from the darkness of death and they will be the true Daughters of Life. This you will do. This you must do."

When she said this she touched Peleinè's thumbs gently with

the gesture that one efenselè uses only with another. Peleinè welcomed this embrace of one so high and realized that her rank could be that of an equal if she did what must be done.

"You are right, Vaintè, so right. It shall be done as you say. The Daughters of Life have lived apart from their city for too long. We must return, we must be a part of life once again. But we must not be turned from the true way."

"You shall not be. You will believe as you believe and none shall stop you. The path ahead is clear and you shall lead the way into the triumphant future."

CHAPTER FOURTEEN

It was Harl's first bow and he was immensely proud of it. He had gone with his uncle, Nadris, to the forest to search for the right kind of tree that they would need, the thin-barked one with the tough and springy wood. Nadris had selected the thin sapling, but Harl had chopped it down himself, sawing at the resilient, green trunk until it had been cut through. Then, under Nadris's careful direction, he had scraped off the bark to uncover the white heart of the wood within. But then he had had to wait, and waiting had been the worst part. Nadris had hung the length of wood high inside his tent to dry and had left it there, day after day, until it was ready. When the shaping began Harl had sat and watched while Nadris methodically scraped it with a stone blade. The ends of the bow were carefully tapered, then nocked to take the bowstring that had been woven from the long, strong hairs of the mastodon's tail. Even with the bowstring in place Nadris had not been satisfied, but had tested the pull, then removed the string and shaped the wood again. But in the end even this was finished. This was to be Harl's bow, so it was his right to shoot the first arrow from it. He had done so, bending the bow as far as he could, then releasing the arrow. It flew straight and true, sinking into the tree trunk with a satisfactory thud.

This had been the longest and happiest day in Harl's life. He had a bow now, would learn to shoot it well, would be allowed on the hunt soon. This was the first and most important step that put him on the path from childhood, the path that would one day lead him into the world of hunters.

Although his arm was sore, his fingertips blistered, he would not stop. It was his bow, his day. He wanted to be alone with it and had slipped away from the other boys and gone to the small copse close to the camp. All day he had crept between the trees, stalked bushes, sunk his arrows into innocent tussocks—that were really deer that only he could see.

When it grew dark he reluctantly put up the bow and turned back towards the tents. He was hungry and looked forward to the meat that would be waiting. One day he would hunt and kill his own meat. Nock arrow, draw, zumm, hit, dead. One day.

There was a rustle in the tree above him and he stopped, silent and unmoving. There was something there, a dark form outlined against the gray of the sky. It moved and its claws rustled again. A large bird.

It was too tempting a target to resist. He might lose the arrow in the darkness, but he had made it himself and could make more. But if he hit the bird it would be his first kill. The first day of the bow, the first kill that same day. The other boys would look at him very differently when he walked between the tents with his trophy.

Slowly and silently he put an arrow to the string, bent the bow, sighted along the arrow at the dark shape above. Then let fly.

There was a squawk of pain—then the bird was tumbling down from the branch. It landed in the bough above Harl's head, hung there, unmoving, caught by the thin branches. He stood on tiptoe and could just reach it with the end of his bow, prodding and pushing until it fell to the ground at his feet. His arrow stuck out from the bird's body and the creature's round, sightless eyes looked up at him. Harl stepped back, gasping with fright.

An owl. He had killed an owl.

Why hadn't he stopped to think? He moaned aloud at the terror within him. He should have known, no other bird would be about in the dark. A forbidden bird and he had killed it. Just the night before old Fraken had unrolled the ball of fur disgorged by an owl, had poked his fingers through the tiny bones inside, had seen the future and the success of the hunting from the manner in which the bones were tangled. And while Fraken had done this he had talked about the owls, the only birds that flew by night, the birds that waited to guide the tharms of dead hunters through the darkness towards the sky.

An owl must never be killed.

And Harl had killed one.

Maybe if he buried it, no one would know. He began to dig wildly at the ground with his hands, then stopped. It was no good. The owl knew, and the other owls would know. They would remember. And one day his own tharm would have no owl for a guide because animals never forgot. Never. There were tears in his eyes when he bent over the dead bird, pulled his arrow free. He bent and looked more closely at it in the gathering darkness.

Armun was sitting by the fire when the boy came running up. He stood waiting for her to notice him, but she was in no hurry to do that and poked a bit at the fire first. She was Kerrick's woman now and she felt the warm contentment suffuse her once again. Kerrick's woman. The boys did not dare to laugh at her or point any more and she did not have to cover her face.

"What is it?" she asked, trying to be stern but smiling in spite of herself, too filled with happiness to pretend otherwise.

"This is the tent of the margalus," Harl said, and his voice trembled when he spoke. "Will he talk to me?"

Kerrick had heard their voices. He climbed slowly to his feet, although his broken leg had set well it was still sore when he rested his weight on it, and emerged from the tent. Harl turned to face him. The boy's face was drawn and pale and there were smears upon his cheeks as though tears had been rubbed away.

"You are the margalus and know all about murgu, that is what I have been told."

"What do you want?"

"Come with me, please, it is important. There is something I must show you."

There were strange beasts of all kinds here, Kerrick knew. The boy must have found something that he didn't recognize. He started to turn him away, then thought better of it. It might be something dangerous; he had better look at it. Kerrick nodded then followed the boy away from the fire. As soon as they were far enough distant so that Armun could not overhear him the boy stopped.

"I have killed an owl," he said, his voice trembling. Kerrick wondered at this, then remembered the stories that Fraken told about the owls and knew why the boy was so frightened. He must find some way to reassure him without violating Fraken's teachings and beliefs.

"It is not good to kill an owl," he said. "But you should not let it bother you too much. . ."

"That is not it. There is something else."

Harl bent and dragged the owl out from under a bush by the end of one long wing, then held it up so that the light of the nearest fires fell upon it.

"This is why I came to you," Harl said, pointing to the black lump on the owl's leg.

Kerrick bent close to look. The light from the fire reflected back a quick spark as the creature's eye opened and closed again.

Kerrick straightened up slowly, then reached out and took the bird from the boy's hands. "You did the right thing," he said. "It is wrong to shoot owls, but this is not an owl that we know. This is a marag owl. You were right to kill it, right to come to me. Now run quickly, find the hunter Herilak, tell him to come to my tent at once. Tell him what we have seen on the owl's leg."

Har-Havola came as well when he heard what the boy had found, and Sorli who now was sammadar in Ulfadan's place. They looked at the dead bird and the live marag with its black claws clamped about the owl's leg. Sorli shuddered when the large eye opened and stared at him, then slowly closed again.

"What is the meaning of this?" Herilak asked.

"It means that the murgu know that we are here," Kerrick said. "They no longer send the raptors to spy us out for too many did not return. The owl can fly at night, can see in the dark." He poked the black creature with his fingertip and its cool skin twitched, then was still. "This marag can see in the darkness too. It has seen us and told the murgu. It may have seen us many times."

"Which could mean that the murgu might be on their way now to attack us," Herilak said, his voice cold as death.

Kerrick shook his head, his face grim. "Not may be—but must be. It is warm enough for them this far south even at this time of year. They have sought for us, and this creature has told them where we camp. They will seek vengeance, there is no doubt of that."

"What do we do?" Har-Havola asked, glancing up at the star-filled sky. "Can we go north? It is not yet spring."

"We may have to go, spring or no spring," Kerrick said. "We

will have to decide about that. In the meantime we must know if we are to be attacked. Hunters will go south along the riverbank, hunters who are the strongest runners. They must go one, even two days' march south of this camp and watch the river. If they see the murgu boats they must warn us at once."

"Sigurnath and Peremandu," Har-Havola said. "They are the fastest of foot in my sammad. They have run after deer in the mountains and they run as fast as the deer."

"They leave at dawn," Herilak said.

"There are some of my hunters who have not returned," Sorli said. "They have traveled far and sleep away. We cannot leave this place until they come back."

Kerrick looked into the fire as though searching for an answer there. "I feel we should not wait any longer than that. We must go north as soon as your hunters return."

"It is frozen still, there is no hunting," Har-Havola protested.

"We have food," Kerrick said. "We have our own meat and the meat in bladders that we took from the murgu. We can eat that and we can live. If we stay here they will fall upon us. I feel that, I know that." He pointed to the dead owl and the living creature tight-clamped to its leg. "They watch. They know where we are. They come to kill us. I know them, know how they feel. If we stay we are dead."

They slept little that night and Kerrick was there at the first light of dawn when Sigurnath and Peremandu set out. Both of them were tall and strong, wearing birchbark leggings as protection against the underbrush.

"Leave your spears so they will not weigh you down," Kerrick said. "Take dried meat and ekkotaz, but only enough for three days. You will not need the spears because you will not hunt. You are there to watch. You will have your bows, and you will take a hèsotsan as well for protection. As you go south always stay within sight of the river, even if it takes you longer that way. Go until it is dark and remain by the river at night. Return on the third day if we have not sent for you, for we will stay here no longer than that. Watch the river all of the time—but leave it at once if you see the murgu. If you see them you must get back here as quickly as you can."

The two hunters ran. An easy and steady, ground-eating pace. The sky was overcast, the day cool, which made the running that much easier. They ran along the bank of the wide river, and splashed through the shallows when they were forced to, or climbed the high banks, never letting the water out of their sight. The river remained empty. When the sun was high they stopped, soaked in sweat, and drank deep from a clear stream that fell in a waterfall over a stone bank, then splashed into the river below. They cooled their faces in the spray, then chewed some of the smoked meat. They did not stop long.

In midafternoon they came to a place where the river cut a great loop into the plain. They were on a rise above it and could see where the course of the river curved out, then back.

"It is shorter to cross the bend here," Sigurnath said. Peremandu looked at it, then rubbed the perspiration from his face with the back of his hand.

"Shorter—but we will not be able to see the water. They could pass by and we would not know. We must stay by the river."

As they looked south they became aware of a cloud on the horizon that billowed upwards. It grew while they watched, puzzled, for they had never seen a cloud like that before.

"What is it?" Sigurnath asked.

"Dust," Peremandu said, for he was known for his keen sight. "A cloud of dust. Maybe the duck-bills, a large herd."

"As long as we have hunted them I have never seen a thing like this. It is too big, too wide—and it grows."

They watched as the cloud of dust came closer, until the animals could be seen running before it. A very large herd indeed. There were some of them out ahead of the pack and Peremandu shaded his eyes with his hand, trying to make them out.

"They are murgu!" he cried in sudden horror. "Death-stick murgu. Run!"

They ran, back along the river bank, clearly visible in the knee-high grass. There were harsh cries behind them, the thunder of heavy feet and sudden sharp snapping sounds.

Sigurnath reared up, fell, and Peremandu had only a quick glimpse of the dart that sprouted suddenly from the back of his neck.

There was no escape on the plain. Sigurnath veered left, dirt crumbled from under his feet. He fell from the high bank, turned as he dropped, then hit the water far below.

The two great beasts slowed and stopped at the edge of the bank and their two Yilanè riders climbed down from their high saddles to look down at the muddy river. There was nothing visible. They stood, motionless, for a long time. Then the first one turned and led the way back to the tarakast.

"Report to Vaintè," she said. "Tell her we have come upon two ustuzou. They are both dead. The rest of them will not know of our presence. We will fall upon them just as she has planned."

CHAPTER FIFTEEN

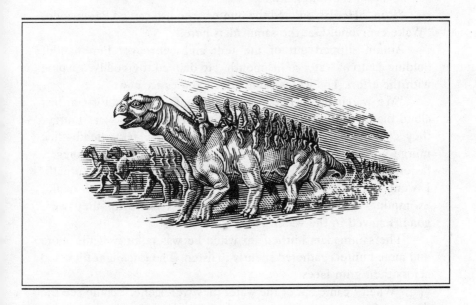

The distant shouts brought Kerrick suddenly awake, staring into the darkness of the tent. Armun was disturbed as well, murmuring something in her sleep as she moved the warm flesh of her body against his. The shouting was louder now: Kerrick pulled away from her, groped for his clothing among the furs.

When he threw back the tentflap he saw the group of hunters running towards him. They were carrying torches and two of them were dragging a dark shape. It was another hunter, limp and unmoving. Herilak ran on ahead of the others.

"They're coming," he called out, and Kerrick felt the hair stir on the back of his neck.

"It is Peremandu," Herilak said. "He ran all day, most of this night as well."

Peremandu was conscious, but completely exhausted. They carried him to Kerrick, his toes trailing in the dust, then sat him gently on the ground. In the flickering light of the torches his skin was pale: sooty patches ringed his eyes.

"Coming . . ." he said hoarsely. "Behind me . . . Sigurnath, dead."

"Are there guards at the river?" Kerrick asked, and Peremandu shook his head weakly when he heard the words.

"Not on the water. Land."

"Run," Herilak ordered the hunters who had carried Peremandu. "Wake everyone. Get the sammadars here."

Armun slipped out of the tent and bent over Peremandu, holding a cup of water to his mouth. He drained it greedily, gasping with the effort. His words came a bit more easily now.

"We watched the river—but they came by land. First a dust cloud bigger than anything we had ever seen. There were murgu, they could not be counted, running fast, heavy feet, death-stick murgu on their backs. The murgu also rode another kind, bigger, faster, scouting ahead. When we ran they saw us. Killed Sigurnath. I went into the river, holding my breath, as long as I could. Swimming deep, with the current. When I came up they were gone. I stayed in the water a long time."

The sammadars hurried up while he was talking, while more and more hunters gathered silently to listen. The torchlight flickered across their grim faces.

"When I came out of the water they were gone. I could see the dust of their passing in the distance. They went very fast. I followed their track, wide as a river through the trampled grass, marked with much dung of the murgu. Followed until the sun was low and I could see that they had halted by the river. Then I stopped too and went no closer. The margalus has said that they do not like the night and do not go about then. Remembering this I waited until the sun had set. As soon as it was dark I circled far to the east so I would not pass near them. I did not see them again. I ran and did not stop, and I ran and I am here. Sigurnath is dead."

He dropped back onto the ground, exhausted again by the effort of speaking. What he had said struck terror into the listeners' hearts for they knew that death was striding close.

"They will attack," Kerrick said. "Soon after dawn. They know exactly where we are. They plan these things carefully. They will have stopped for the night just far enough away not to be observed, yet close enough to strike in the morning."

"We must defend ourselves," Herilak said.

"No! We must not stay here." Kerrick spoke the words quickly, almost without thought; they were driven from him by a strong emotion.

"If we leave they will attack us while we move," Herilak said. "We will be defenseless, slaughtered as we run. It will be better to remain here where we can make a stand."

"Hear me out," Kerrick said. "If we remain here that will be exactly what they want us to do. It is their plan to attack us in this place. You can be sure that the attack has been worked out in all details and is meant to destroy us. Now we must stop and think of the best way to survive. The beasts they ride, I have never seen or heard of them before. That means nothing. They have the resources of an entire world out there. There are strange creatures beyond counting, murgu we cannot even imagine. But now we know about them, now we are forewarned." He looked around. "We chose this place to camp because there was water and we could defend ourselves against attack from the river. Do they come by water as well? Did you see any boats?"

"None," Peremandu said. "The river was empty. They are so many that they need no aid. Their numbers were like the birds when they gather to fly south in the autumn. Like leaves, they could not be counted."

"Our thorn barrier will be trampled down," Kerrick said. "So will we. We must leave at once. Go north. We cannot remain here."

The murmuring died away. No one wanted to speak, for all of this was too unusual, too new. They looked to their leaders. The sammadars looked at Herilak. The decision was his. His face was as grim as theirs, grimmer—for the responsibility now was his alone. He looked around at them, then straightened his back and slammed his spear butt onto the ground.

"We march. The margalus is right. If we stay here it is certain death. If we have to make a stand it will be at the spot of our own choosing. The night is only half gone. We must make the most of the darkness remaining. Strike the tents . . ."

"No," Kerrick broke in. "That would be a mistake—for many reasons. It will take time, and time is one thing we do not have. If we pack the tents the travois will be heavy laden and that will slow us down. We take our weapons, food and clothing—nothing more."

The women were listening as well and one of them wailed at this loss.

"We can make new tents," Kerrick said. "We cannot make new lives. Load the travois with only the things I have said, the babies and small children can ride as well. Leave the tents standing. The murgu will not know that they are empty. They will attack, use up their darts, that will take time. We need all the time that we can get. This is what I tell you to do."

"Do as the margalus orders," Herilak said, pointing his spear. "Go."

The mastodons trumpeted their complaints at being disturbed, but cruel blows in the delicate corners of their mouths moved them out. The fires before the tents were stirred to life and the travois were quickly lashed into position. Kerrick left Armun to load what was needed and hurried out of the encampment, to the head of the forming column where Herilak was waiting.

Herilak pointed north.

"The land rises there, you will remember. The hills are wooded and rough, with the stone of the mountains pushing through the ground in some places. We must get there before they catch up with us. It is there that we will find a position that can be defended."

The moon rose before they were ready and dawn was that much closer. They went out in single file, the mastodons squealing as they were goaded into a shambling run, the hunters trotting alongside. They had hunted this land for a long time now and knew every crease and fold. The sammads took the easiest and fastest track north.

When dawn spread the first gray light over the landscape the column was stretched out, no longer running, but still moving. The mastodons were too weary now to complain and slogged steadily on, putting one great foot ahead of the other. The hunters walked as well, looking behind them although there was nothing there to be seen. Yet. The march continued.

A long, wearying time passed before Herilak called a halt.

"Drink and rest," he ordered, looking back the way that they had come, waiting for the straggling column to close up. He waved Peremandu to him. "You know how far away from our encampment the murgu were. Will they have reached it by now?"

Peremandu looked to the south and his eyes narrowed with thought. He nodded reluctantly. "It took me a longer time, but they are much faster. They will be there by now."

"And will soon be after us," Herilak said grimly. He turned and looked to the east, then pointed to the foothills. "There. We must find a place to make our stand there. Move out."

The land soon began to rise and the tired mastodons slowed and had to be urged on. The path they were following took them up a valley, with a stream winding down the bottom of it. One of the hunters who had been scouting ahead came trotting back to Herilak.

"The valley gets steeper and will soon be hard to climb out of."

They turned up the slope then, and when they had breasted it Herilak pointed to the even steeper, rock-strewn hill above. It rose steadily to forested heights beyond.

"That is what we want. If we lie in wait up there they cannot attack us from behind. They must come up this slope. They will be in the open while we will be hidden among the trees. We will make our stand there."

Kerrick heard this with a feeling of relief as he came stumbling up. His leg throbbed with pain after the tiring walk and each step was agony. But there was no time to think about himself now. "That is a good plan," he said. "The beasts are tired and cannot go much further. They should be taken deeper into the woods, to eat and to rest. The women as well. We must all get some rest because we will go on after dark again. If the numbers of the murgu are as great as Peremandu has told us, then we cannot possibly kill them all. It will be enough to stop them. What do you say to this, Herilak?"

"I say that this thought is hard as stone. But I think that it is also true. We will wait for the attack at the forest edge. The mastodons will go deeper among the trees. Har-Havola, I want strong runners from your sammad to find a way through the forest and beyond while it is still light. We will fight. After dark we will go on."

The stragglers were still working their way up the slope when a hunter shouted a warning and pointed to the west, at the growing cloud rising up beyond the first of the foothills. The sight of it hurried the last of them on their way.

A fresh breeze was blowing, rustling the bare branches above their heads. Kerrick sat next to Herilak on the soft grass, the afternoon sun warm on their faces, carefully feeding darts into his hèsotsan. The cloud was closer still. Herilak rose and waved the hunters to cover.

"Conceal yourselves," he ordered. "Do not squeeze the death-sticks until I order it—no matter how close they come. Then kill them. Slaughter them until they pile high and cannot get by their own dead. Do not retreat until you are ordered to. Then do it, but just a few at a time. Get behind the trees. Let the others pass by you. I want hunters hiding and killing, never stopping. Let them die among the trees just as they will die on the hillside. Remember, we are all that stands between the murgu and the sammads. Do not let them pass."

The murgu were close, the dust cloud now roiling up from the last valley that the sammads had climbed. Kerrick stretched full length behind the trunk of the large tree, the hèsotsan resting on a fallen branch. The grass on the slope swayed as the breeze moved across it. A flock of birds rose up from the grass and winged overhead. The rumble, like distant thunder, grew louder.

A row of dark forms came suddenly into view on top of the ridge, moving slowly but steadily. Kerrick lay motionless, pressed to the ground, aware of the rapid thudding of his heart.

The riding beasts were large, looking a bit like epetruk, striding forward on their thick hind legs, heavy tails swishing through the grass behind. Each of them had a Yilanè rider straddling its forequarters. Now they paused, looking up at the slope and the trees beyond. Waiting there as the rumbling grew louder.

Kerrick gasped as the crest of the ridge darkened with the running figures, low beasts with too many legs. They stopped as well, milled about, armed fargi on their backs. Four legs to a side, eight in all. Tiny heads on thick necks. Raised and bred to carry, to bring the fargi here, more and more of them all of the time. They surged and crowded each other—then started ahead.

The wind blew from them, carrying the cries of the Yilanè, the loud hammer of feet, shrill animal screams, the sour, bestial smell of the creatures.

Closer and closer, looming high, coming forward along the track straight towards the handful of hunters hidden beneath the trees. Every detail of their spotted hides was now clear, the fargi clutching their weapons and blinking out through the dust, the Yilanè on their larger mounts forging ahead.

Herilak's warbling cry was small against the loud thunder of the attackers.

The first death-sticks cracked out.

CHAPTER SIXTEEN

Kerrick fired at the nearest Yilanè, missed, but hit her mount instead. The creature reared up—then fell heavily. The rider dropped to the ground, unhurt, aiming her hèsotsan. Kerrick's next dart caught her in the neck and she crumpled into the grass.

It was a slaughter. The first row of attackers fell before the concentrated fire from the trees. Many of the lumbering, eight-legged beasts were hit, dropped as well, spilling the fargi from their backs to the ground. Those few that kept coming forward were killed well before they reached the line of trees. The survivors fell back, became entangled with the riders who were still coming forward. The darts flew into the jumbled mass and the bodies piled higher. The attack stumbled to a halt, encumbered by the dead, the air filled with the pained cries of wounded fargi crushed beneath the fallen beasts.

Orders were being called out now by mounted Yilanè grouped to the rear of the attackers. Under their direction the fargi struggled to seek cover, to fire back. Kerrick lowered his own weapon to listen, understanding some of what was being said. One of the riders rode free of the attackers, calling for attention, issuing orders. Kerrick raised his hèsotsan but saw that she was carefully staying out of range. Her voice was clearly heard now, making order out of chaos. It was clear to Kerrick as well.

He froze. Eyes wide, hands clenched and muscles locked. That voice. He knew that voice.

But Vaintè was dead, he had killed her himself. Stabbed deep. Killed her. She was dead.

Yet it was undeniably her voice; loud and commanding.

Kerrick leaped to his feet, trying to see her clearly, but she was facing away from him. Then, as she was turning back in his direction, he was hit hard in the back, tumbled to the ground, dragged back into cover. Darts rustled in the leaves around him. Herilak released him, sought cover himself.

"It was her," Kerrick said, his voice tight with the effort. "The one I killed, the sammadar of all the murgu. But I killed her, you saw me."

"I saw you stab a marag. They can be very hard to kill."

Still alive. There was no doubt. Still alive. Kerrick shook his head and lifted the hèsotsan. There was no time to think about that now. Unless he could kill her again. Still alive. He forced his thoughts back to the battle.

So far few darts had been fired by the attackers, so sudden and overwhelming had been the disaster. But now they found shelter behind the bodies of their dead and began to fire back; the leaves rustled and stirred at the impact of the numberless darts.

"Don't expose yourself!" Herilak called out. "Stay down. Wait until they attack."

The Yilanè who had survived the first charge now kept their large tarakast safely behind the mass of uruktop and fargi. There were loud cries as they ordered the attack to be pressed home. Reluctantly, the fargi rose and ran forward, died. The attack was broken even before it began.

"We stopped them," Herilak said with rich satisfaction, looking out at the corpse-strewn slope. "We can hold them."

"Not for too long," Kerrick said, pointing down the hill. "When they attack from the sea they use a formation called the outstretched-arms. They go out to both sides, then come in behind. I think they are doing that now."

"We can stop that."

"For a little while. But I know their strategy. They will attack on a wider and wider front until they turn our flanks. We must be ready."

Kerrick was correct. The fargi climbed down from the eight-legged uruktop and spread across the face of the hill, coming forward slowly. They died—but more were ordered up behind them. The slaughter was great, but the Yilanè commanders did not care. More and still more fargi advanced, sheltering behind the dead, some even reaching the edge of the forest before they fell.

It was midafternoon when the first fargi found protection among the trees. Others joined them and the Tanu defenders had to draw back.

A different, yet equally deadly, battle now began. Few of the fargi had any experience in woodcraft. When they left their cover death usually sought them out. Yet still they advanced. There was no front to the battle any more, hunters and hunted mixed together in the gloom beneath the trees.

Kerrick fell back with the others, the pain in his leg almost gone now, trying to keep the bulk of the trees between himself and the fargi. Yet when he straightened up there was a sharp crack and a dart hit the bark of the tree close to his face. He spun about, his spear ready in his left hand, sinking it into the fargi who had come up behind him, wrenching it free then hurrying deeper into the forest.

The retreat began again. Whispered commands started the mastodons along the escape route, the hunters gathered behind them and guarding their backs. There were other, harsher commands being called through the forest now and Kerrick stopped, cupping his hand to his ear. He listened carefully, then turned and ran back through the trees to find Herilak.

"They are withdrawing," Kerrick said. "Without seeing them I can't be sure of everything that they are saying, but there are bits of it I could make out."

"Are they retreating, beaten?"

"No." Kerrick looked up at the darkening sky above the trees. "It will be night soon. They are regrouping in the open. They will attack again in the morning."

"And we will be long gone. Let us now fall back and join the sammads."

"There is one thing that must be done first. We must search the forest, find as many of the death-sticks as we can. Then we can leave."

"You are right. Death-sticks and more darts. We have fired too many."

Night had fallen by the time they had searched out the weapons and returned with them to the sammads. Kerrick was the last. He stood looking back down the slope until Herilak called after him. He waved the big hunter to him, pointing.

"Let the others return with the weapons. I want both of us to get closer to the murgu camp. They don't like the dark. Perhaps there is something that we can do there."

"An attack during the night?"

"That is what we will have to find out."

They walked slowly, weapons ready, but the enemy were gone from the hillside. Yet they had not gone far: their encampment was clearly visible on the grassy slopes beyond. A vast collection of dark bodies drawn together, silent and motionless.

The two hunters took every precaution. Stooping low in the grass when they drew close, then crawling forward silently, weapons ready. When they were a long arrowshot away from the Yilanè camp Herilak stopped Kerrick with a light touch on the shoulder.

"This is too easy," he whispered into his ear. "Don't they have guards of some kind?"

"I don't know. They all sleep at night. We must find out."

They had crawled forward just a few paces more when Kerrick's fingers touched something, a stick, a length of vine perhaps, hidden by the grass.

It moved sluggishly between his fingers.

"Get back!" he called to Herilak as the glow sprang up from the darkness ahead. A dim light that quickly grew brighter and brighter until they could see clearly. And be seen. There was the crack of weapons and darts rustled quick death into the grass around them. They crawled as fast as they could, stood and ran into the welcoming darkness as soon as they were out of range. Stumbling and falling, gasping for breath, they did not stop until they reached the ridge above.

Behind them the lights faded, died away, and darkness returned. The Yilanè had learned after the massacre on the beaches. They would not be attacked at night again.

When Kerrick and Herilak reached the sammads the darts and hèsotsan that had been retrieved from the battle had been loaded onto the travois; the retreat began once again. Herilak spoke to the sammadars as they walked.

Four hunters had not returned from the battle in the forest.

They went slowly, far too slowly to escape the attack that

would surely come in the morning. They were all weary after two nights of traveling with little sleep. The mastodons screamed in protest when they were goaded on. Yet still the sammads stumbled forward, for they had very little choice. If they stayed, they died.

The ground was rough, rocky, and uphill most of the way. Their progress became slower and slower and well before dawn it ground to a halt. Sorli brought the message to Herilak.

"It is the beasts. They will not go on, even when we push spears into them."

"Then we stop here," Herilak said with great weariness. "Rest and sleep. We will go on again at sunrise to the next position."

A chill wind came up at dawn and they shivered as they rose wearily from their sleeping furs. They were dispirited and still exhausted. Only knowledge of the sure advance of the enemy drove them forward once again. Armun walked at Kerrick's side in silence. There was very little that could be said now. It was enough to put one foot in front of the other, to prod on the protesting mastodons.

A hunter stood beside the trail, leaning on his spear, waiting for Kerrick to come up to him.

"It is the sacripex," he said. "It is his wish that you join him where he leads."

With great effort, ignoring the throbbing pain in his leg, Kerrick broke into a shuffling run that took him up the column, past the travois and marching sammads. The small children were walking now, the babies being carried by the mothers and older children. Even partially relieved of their loads the mastodons still stumbled with fatigue. They would not keep going much longer.

Herilak pointed at the hills ahead when Kerrick came shuffling up to join him.

"They have found a wooded ridge up there," he said. "Very much like the one we stopped them in yesterday."

"Not . . . good enough," Kerrick gasped, fighting to catch his breath. "There are too many of the enemy. They will get around us again, push us back."

"They may have learned their lesson. Even murgu aren't stupid. They will hold back. They know they will be killed if they attack."

Kerrick shook his head in an unhappy no. "Tanu might do that. They might see others die, be afraid for themselves. But not the murgu. I know them, know them too well. The Yilanè who are riding the large beasts, they will stay to the rear all right. They will be safe. But they will order the fargi to attack just as they did before."

"What if they refuse?"

"They can't. It is impossible for them. If they understand a command they must obey it. That is the way it is. They will attack."

"Murgu," Herilak said, and his lips curled back from his teeth with distaste as he said it. "Then what are we to do?"

"What else can we do but keep going?" Kerrick asked helplessly, his mouth gasping open, his skin ashen with fatigue. "If we stop here in the open we will be slaughtered. We must go on. Find some hill that we can defend, perhaps."

"A hill can be surrounded. Then we will surely die."

The track they were following rose sharply. They needed all their breath now to scramble up it. When they reached the ridge above they were forced to stop. Kerrick was bent double, racked with cramps. Behind them the slow procession toiled up the slope. Kerrick straightened up, gasping, and looked ahead, up the rise they must climb to the hills beyond. Then stopped motionless, mouth gaping, eyes wide.

"Herilak," he shouted. "Look there, up ahead, up on those higher hills. Do you see that?"

Herilak shielded his eyes and looked, then shrugged and turned away. "Snow. Winter still holds fast up there."

"Don't you understand? These murgu can't stand cold. Those creatures that they are riding on won't walk in the snow. They can't follow us up there!"

Herilak raised his eyes again—but this time there was the light of hope in them. "The snow is not that far away. We can reach it today—if we keep moving." He called out to the hunters who were leading the way, waved them back, issued new instructions. Then sat down with a satisfied grunt.

"The sammads go on. But some of us must wait behind and slow down those murgu who follow after us."

There was hope now, and a new chance for existence heartened the sammads. Even the mastodons sensed the excitement, raised their trunks, and bellowed. The hunters watched the column turn, start up the rise to the high hills, then they moved out after them.

Now they would hunt the murgu the way they hunted any

deadly animal. The sammads were well out of sight when Herilak stopped the hunters at the top of the valley. Littered about among the scree here were large boulders.

"We will stop them at this place. Let them get in among us. Then shoot, kill. Wipe out the ones that lead. Drive them back. Seize their weapons and darts. What will they do after that happens, margalus?"

"The same as they did yesterday," Kerrick said. "They will keep contact with us along this front, while at the same time they will send fargi out to swing around the the ridge, to take us from the sides and rear."

"That is what we wish them to do. Before the trap is closed we will pull back—"

"And set more traps for them! Do it again and again," Sorli cried out.

"That is correct," Herilak said, and there was no humor in his cold smile.

They sought places to hide behind the boulders, along both sides of the valley. Many of them, including Kerrick, slept as soon as they lay down. But Herilak, the sacripex, lay unsleeping and alert, watching the track from behind two carefully placed slabs of rock that he had struggled into place.

When the first outriders appeared he passed the word back to wake the sleepers. Soon the valley rumbled with the heavy tread of the uruktop. Yilanè on tarakast rode out ahead of the main group, leading the way. They moved up the hill and past the unseen Tanu, and had reached the crest before the slower uruktop had moved well into the trap.

On the command the firing began.

The slaughter was terrible, far worse than that of the day before. The hunters fired and fired and screamed with joy as they did. The Yilanè above them were brought down, the corpses of their towering mounts falling and slithering into the deadly chaos below. The uruktop died. The fargi riding them died. Those that tried to escape were shot down. The front ranks of the attackers were destroyed and the enemy fell back to regroup. The hunters pursued them, sheltering among the fallen, using the weapons of the dead against the living.

Only when the warning was called out by the sentinel on the ridge did they retreat, running up the valley well out of range of the enemy weapons. They followed the ruts made by the travois, going higher, ever higher, into the hills.

Twice more they ambushed the murgu. Twice more trapped them, killed them, disarmed them. And fled. The sun was dropping towards the horizon then as they stumbled up the trail.

"We cannot go on much longer like this," Kerrick said, swaying with exhaustion and pain.

"We must. We have no other choice," Herilak told him grimly, putting one foot steadily in front of the other. Even his great strength was feeling the strain. He could go on, but he knew that soon some of the others might not be able to. The wind was cold against his face. He slipped, steadied himself, and looked down.

Herilak's victorious shout cut through the fatigue that gripped and numbed Kerrick. He looked up, blinking, then his gaze followed the pointing finger towards the ground.

The track was muddy, churned, and there was a massive mound of mastodon dung heaped upon the deep footprints. He could not understand what Herilak was shouting about. But there were white flecks in the mud and more white on the ground around.

Snow.

It stretched up the hillside before them. Cut with the muddy track the sammads had made. Snow. Kerrick ran, stumbled, to a snowbank beside the track, dug out handfuls of cold white snow and threw them into the air while the others laughed and shouted.

On the top of the ridge they paused, knee deep in the drifts. Looking down at the first of the Yilanè outriders. They reined back their mounts when they reached the sloping field of white.

Behind them the horde of attackers stopped as well. They milled about as the mounted Yilanè joined, conferred, separated again.

They moved then. Not forward, but back down the slope. Slowly and steadily until they had vanished from sight.

CHAPTER SEVENTEEN

The ice that had covered the river had broken, had piled up in jams, until these in turn had been carried away in great floes that had been washed down to the sea. Though spring had arrived there was still ice rimed along the shore in shielded places, snow drifted into the hollows of the banks. But in the meadow, where the river made a wide loop, a small herd of deer were already grazing the thin blades of new yellow-green grass They looked up, ears twitching, sniffing the air. Something disturbed them for they made off among the trees in long, graceful bounds.

Herilak stood in the shadow of the tall evergreen, smelling the pungency of its needles, looking out at the campsite that they had left in the autumn. The grip of winter was broken; spring was earlier this year than it had been for a long time. Perhaps the ice-winters were over. Perhaps. There was the creak of leather bindings behind him in the forest, the quick trumpet of a mastodon. The beasts knew the landscape, they could tell where they were; journey's end.

The hunters came silently from the trees, Kerrick among them. They could stop moving now, make camp here at this familiar place, build brushwood shelters. Stay in one place for awhile. With winter just ended, they could put off thinking about the next winter for some time yet. Kerrick looked up at the white bird passing high overhead. Just another bird.

Perhaps. Dark memories pushed in and clouded the sunny day. The Yilanè were out there, would always be out there, a threatening presence like a storm forever ready to break. Whatever the Tanu did now, whatever they wanted to do, their actions were colored by that deadly presence to the south. The loud, triumphant trumpeting of a mastodon cut through his thoughts. Enough. The time for concern would come later. Now was the time to set up camp, build the fires high, and roast fresh meat. Time to stop moving.

They met that night around the fire, Kerrick, Herilak, old Fraken, the sammadars. Their stomachs were full and they were content. Sorli stirred the fire so that sparks rose up, flared, and vanished in the darkness. A full moon was rising from beyond the trees and the night was still. Sorli pulled out a glowing branch, blew on it until it burned brightly, then pushed it into the stone bowl of the pipe. He inhaled deeply, blew out a gray cloud of smoke, then passed the pipe on to Har-Havola who also breathed deep, at peace. They were a sammad of sammads now and no one laughed any more at the way he and the others from beyond the mountains spoke. Not after the last winter together, not after battling the murgu. Three of his young hunters already had women from the other sammads. That was the way to peace.

"Fraken," Herilak called out. "Tell us about the battle. Tell us about the dead murgu."

Fraken shook his head and pretended fatigue, but when they all pleaded with him, and he saw others gathering around the fire, he let himself be persuaded. He hummed a bit to himself nasally, swayed in time to the humming, then began chanting the history of the winter.

Although they had all been there, had been involved in the events he was reciting—it was better when he told about what had occurred. His story improved with each telling. The escape was more tiring, the women stronger, the hunters braver. The fighting unbelievable.

". . . again and again came up the hill, again and again the hunters stood and faced them, killed them and killed them again and again. Until each hunter had bodies about him so high that they could not be seen over. Each hunter killed as many murgu as there are blades of grass on a mountainside. Each hunter speared through and through murgu, as many as five at one time on his spear. Strong were the hunters that day, high were the mountains of the dead."

They listened and nodded and swelled with pride in what they had done. The pipe passed from hand to hand, Fraken chanted the story of their victories, his voice rising and falling with passion as everyone, even the women and small children, grouped around, listening intently. Even when he had done they were silent, remembering. It was something to remember, something very important.

The fire had died down; Kerrick reached out and threw more wood on it, then sat back dizzily. The smoke from the pipe was strong and he was not used to it. Fraken wrapped his furs about him and went wearily to his tent. The sammads drifted away as well until Kerrick saw that only a few hunters remained. Herilak staring into the fire, Har-Havola at his side, nodding and half asleep. Herilak looked up at Kerrick.

"They are happy now," he said. "At peace. It is good that they feel that way for a while. It has been a long and bitter winter. Let them forget this winter before they think of the next one. Forget the death-stick murgu too."

He was silent then for a long time before he looked up at Kerrick and spoke. "We killed many. Perhaps now they will forget about us too. Leave us alone."

Kerrick wanted to answer differently but knew that he could not. He shook his head unhappily and Herilak sighed.

"They will come again," Kerrick said. "I know these murgu. They hate us just as much as we hate them. If you could, would you destroy them all?"

"Instantly. Filled with great pleasure."

"They feel the same as you do."

"Then what must we do? The summer will be a short one. The hunting may be good, we don't know. But then the next winter will be upon us and what will we do then? If we go east to the coast to hunt, the murgu will find us there. South again, well, we know what happened in the south. And the north remains frozen."

"The mountains," Har-Havola said, the voices pulling him awake. "We must go beyond the mountains."

"But your sammad is from beyond the mountains," Herilak said. "You came here because there was no hunting."

Har-Havola shook his head. "That is your name for my sammad,

from beyond the mountains. But what you speak of as mountains
are merely hills. Beyond them are the true mountains. Reaching to
the sky with unmelting snow upon their summits. Those are
mountains.''

"I have heard of them," Herilak said. "I have heard that they
cannot be passed, that it is death to try.''

"It can be. If you do not know the high passes, then winter
will come and trap you and you will die. But Munan, a hunter of
my sammad, has been past the mountains.''

"The murgu do not know of these mountains," Kerrick
said, sudden hope in his voice. "They never spoke of them.
What lies beyond them?''

"A desert, that is what Munan has told us. Very little grass,
very little rain. He says he walked two days into the desert then
had to return because he had no water.''

"We could go there," Kerrick said, thinking out loud. Herilak
sniffed.

"Cross the ice mountains to die in the empty desert. The
murgu are better than that. At least we can kill murgu.''

"Murgu kill us," Kerrick said angrily. "We kill some and more
come because they are as numberless as the drops of water in the
ocean. In the end we will all be dead. But deserts do not go on
forever. We can take water, search for a way across. It is something
worth thinking about.''

"Yes," Herilak agreed. "It is indeed something that we should
know more about. Har-Havola, call your hunter, the one named
Munan. Let him speak to us about the mountains.''

Munan was a tall hunter with long scars scratched onto his
cheeks in the manner of his sammad and the other sammads from
beyond the mountains. He puffed on the pipe when it was passed
to him and listened to their questions.

"There were three of us," he said. "All very young. It was a
thing you do when you are young to prove that you will be a good
hunter. You must do something very strong." He touched the scars
on his cheekbones. "Only when you have been very brave or very
strong can you get these to show that you are a hunter.''

Har-Havola nodded agreement, his own scars white in the firelight.

"Three went, two returned. We left at the beginning of summer and climbed the high passes. There was an old hunter in my
sammad who knew about the passes, knew the ones to take, and he

told us and we found the way. He told us what sign to watch for, which passes to climb. It was not easy and the snow was deep in the highest passes, but in the end we were through. We walked always towards the sunset. Once beyond the mountains there are hills and here the hunting was good. But beyond the hills the desert begins. We went out into it but there was no water. We drank what we had carried in water bags and when this was gone we turned back."

"But there was hunting?" Herilak asked. Munan nodded.

"Yes, there is rain on the mountains, then snow in the winter. The hills close to the mountains stay green. Once beyond them the desert begins."

"Could you find the high passes again?" Kerrick asked. Munan nodded. "Then we could send a small party out. They could find the path, find the hills beyond. Once they had done this they could return to guide the sammads there, if all is as you say."

"The summers are too short now," Herilak said, "and the murgu too close. If one goes—we all go. That is what I think should be done."

They talked about it that night, the next and the next again. No one really wanted to climb the ice mountains in summer; winter would come quickly enough without going to it voluntarily. But they all knew that something had to be done. There was a little hunting here so they had some fresh meat. There were also roots to be dug, plants and seeds to be found, but these would not last the winter. Their tents were gone and many other things that they had prized. The one thing they still had was the meat they had taken from the murgu, unchanged in the bladders. No one liked the taste of it very much and as long as there was something else to eat it had not been touched. But it could sustain life. Most of it remained.

Herilak watched and waited patiently while they hunted and ate all that they desired. The women were curing the few deerskins they had and there would be tents again when they had collected enough. The mastodons grazed well and their wrinkled hides soon filled out again. Herilak saw this and waited. Waited until they had fed well and the children were strong. He looked at the sky each night and watched the dark moon wax bright, then wane again. When it was dark once again he filled the stone pipe with pungent bark and called the hunters together around the fire.

When they had all smoked he rose to his feet before them and told them the thoughts that had been in his head all of the time since they had returned here to the bend in the river.

"Winter will come as it always does. We must not stay here to meet it. We must go where there is good hunting and no murgu. I say that we cross the high mountains to the green hills beyond. If we go now it will still be summer and we will be able to get through the high passes. Munan has told us that is the only time we can cross. If we go now we will travel light as we did when we escaped the murgu. If we go now we will not have to worry for food for we can eat the murgu meat. If we go now we can be in the green hills beyond the mountains before winter. I say that now is the time when we must pack the travois and start towards the west."

No one wanted to leave; no one could find reason to stay. Between the ice and the murgu they had no choice. They talked about it far into the night, but search as they might they could find no other course open to them. It must be the mountains.

In the morning the travois were assembled and old traces repaired with new leather. Small boys searched the woods for the compact balls of fur and bones that the owls regurgitated and Fraken poked them open and read the omens.

"Not today, but tomorrow," he said. "That will be the time we must leave, at first light. Then when the sun is over the hills and shines here it will see nothing. We must be gone."

That night, after they had eaten, Kerrick sat by the fire tying bits of grass to long thorns from a berry bush. The supply of darts for the hèsotsan were running low, and there were none of the special trees here on which the darts grew. They were not needed. Any bit of material of the same size would be expelled by the hèsotsan. The darts that they made worked just as well, even better if they were carefully done. Kerrick bit the knot off with his teeth. Armun passed by him and threw the food scraps into the fire, then began to tie their few possessions into bundles. She was silent all the time that she did this and Kerrick suddenly realized she had reverted to her old habit of holding her hair over her face.

When she came close he took her by the wrist and pulled her down beside him, but she still turned away from him. Only when he took her chin in his hands and turned her face to him did he see the tears that filled her eyes.

"Have you hurt yourself? What is wrong?" he asked, puzzled.

She shook her head and tried to keep silent but he was worried and made her speak. In the end she turned her head away, held her hair before her face, and told him.

"There is a baby coming. In the spring."

In his excitement Kerrick forgot all about her tears and her worries, pulled her down to him and laughed out loud. He knew about babies now, had seen them born, had seen the pride the parents felt. He could think of no reason why Armun should cry instead of being joyful. She did not want to tell him and kept turning away in her old manner. At first he was worried, then grew angry at her silence and shook her until she cried harder. After this he felt ashamed of what he had done, wiped her tears and held her. When she had quieted she knew that she had to tell him. She pulled back and pointed to her face.

"The baby will be a girl and will look like me," she said, touching the cleft in her mouth.

"That will be very good, for you are beautiful."

She smiled a little at that. "Only to you," she said. "When I was little they poked at me and laughed and I could never be happy like the other children."

"No one laughs at you now."

"No. Not with you here. But the children will laugh at our daughter."

"No, they won't. Our daughter could be a son and he could look like me. Did your mother or father have a lip and mouth like yours?"

"No."

"Then why should our baby? You will then be the only one like that and I am lucky to have one with a face like yours. You should not cry."

"I should not." She dried her eyes. "And I should not bother you with my fears. You must be strong when we leave tomorrow when we go to the mountains. Will there really be good hunting on the other side?"

"Of course. Munan has told us so and he has been there."

"Will there be. . . murgu there? Death-stick murgu?"

"No. We are leaving them behind. We go where they have never been."

He did not add the dark thought that he shared with no one. Vaintè was alive. She would never rest, never stop searching, not until he and all the Tanu were dead.

They could flee, but surely as night followed day she would follow them.

CHAPTER EIGHTEEN

On the fifth day the land began to rise; the west wind was cool
and dry. The hunters of sammad Har-Havola sniffed the air
and laughed aloud, for this was the part of the world they
knew best. They talked excitedly among themselves, pointing out
familiar landmarks, hurrying ahead of the sammads and their plodding mastodons. Herilak did not share their pleasure because he
could see from the tracks and signs just how bad the hunting was
here. A few times he saw that other Tanu had come this way, once
even finding the remains of a fire with the ashes still warm. He
never saw the hunters themselves; they were obviously staying well
clear of this large and heavily armed band.

The trail they were following took them further and further
into the hills, each one higher than the one before. The days were
warm, the sun hot, but they were happy to burrow under their furs
at night. Then one morning at dawn Har-Havola called out happily
and pointed ahead at the place where the rising sun was touching
the high white peaks on the horizon. These were the snow-covered
mountains they would have to cross.

Each day the track they were following rose higher and higher,
until the mountains ahead were a barrrier stretching away into the
distance to either side. They looked unbroken, formidable. Only

when the sammads were closer could it be seen that a river valley led gently up into their heart. The water ran quickly, cold and gray. They walked beside it, following its turns, until the foothills were lost from sight. The landscape changed as well; there were fewer trees and most of these were evergreens.

One afternoon there was a stirring on the mountainside above them and they looked up to see white, horned beasts bounding to cover. One stopped on a ledge, looking down, and an arrow from Herilak's bow sought it out, dropped the creature tumbling down the cliff face. Its fur was curled and soft, the flesh, when they cooked it that evening, delicious and fat. Har-Havola licked the last of the grease from his fingers and grunted happily.

"Only once before have I eaten mountain goat. Good. Very hard to stalk. They live only in the high mountains. Now we must think of fodder for the mastodons and wood for our fires."

"Why is this?" Herilak asked.

"We go higher. Soon there will be no trees, then even the grass will be thin and scarce. It will be cold, very cold."

"Then we must take what we will need," Herilak said. "Without the tents the travois are lightly loaded. We will cut wood, load it. Young branches as well with leaves for the beasts. They must not starve. Will there be water?"

"No, but it does not matter since there will be snow to melt. It can be done."

Although the days were still warm they found frost on the ground now when they awoke in the morning, while the mastodons rumbled their discomfort, breaths smoking in the chill of dawn. Although there were complaints about how thin the air was and old Fraken gasped loudly and could not walk so rode instead on one of the travois, Kerrick found himself filled with a happiness that was new to him. The clarity of the air pleased him, as did the silence of the mountains, the stark cleanliness of sky and rock. So different from the damp heat of the south, the sweat and insects. The Yilanè could have their swamps and endless summer. They were suited for it. They would find life here unbearable. This was not their world here—could they not leave it to the Tanu? Although he looked always at the sky Kerrick saw none of the great raptors or other birds that might be marking their passage. Perhaps the Yilanè would not follow. Perhaps they were safe from them at last.

"That is the highest pass, there," Munan announced one afternoon, pointing ahead. "Where those clouds are, where it is snowing. I remember now how the clouds sweep up from the west so that it snows there more often than not."

"We cannot wait for the snow to stop," Herilak said. "There is little wood and fodder left. We must press on."

It took a long day of continuous struggle to reach the summit of the pass. The snow was deep and the mastodons broke through the crust and foundered in the heavy drifts. It was an exhausting struggle for them all, pushing ahead step after slow step. At nightfall the sammads were still on the slope and were forced to spend a sleepless night there, with the beasts squealing in discomfort through the darkness. Unable to light fires they could only wrap themselves in furs and shiver until dawn. At the first light they went on, knowing only that frozen death awaited them if they did not.

Once past the crest the going was even more difficult, working their way down the steep and icy slope. But they could not stop. The feed was gone and the mastodons would not survive another night in the snow. They went on, feeling their way through the banks of cloud that rolled up the slope to them. They reached the broken scree of rocks and boulders in the afternoon and found that it was even harder to walk on than the snow had been. It was almost dusk when they broke through the clouds and felt the setting sun warm on their faces. The valleys opened out below them and, far distant yet, there was a trace of green vegetation.

Darkness fell but they stopped only long enough to build a fire and light torches. In their flickering light the exhausted sammads stumbled onward. It wasn't until they were aware that the ground was softer underfoot that they realized the ordeal was over. They stopped then, on a slope beside a rushing stream of snowmelt where the ground was tufted with clumps of grass. They dropped, exhausted, while the mastodons squealed and tore out great clumps of grass with their trunks. Even the preserved murgu meat tasted good that night.

The worst was past; going down the valleys proved to be far easier than climbing them had been. Very soon they were back among the trees where the mastodons gorged themselves on the green leaves. The hunters were happy. They had seen the fresh droppings of mountain goat that day and in the morning swore that there would be fresh meat. But the goats were too wary and climbed to safety, vanishing well before the hunters were within arrowshot. It was the following day, in a meadow set between the trees, that they stalked a herd of small deer, killing two before the others fled. There were not only deer to eat here, for the pine trees were a kind they had never seen before, with sweet nuts inside the pinecones. The mountains were behind them, the future bright.

It was on the next day that the stream they were following ended in a rocky pool. There were the tracks of many animals in the mud beside it. The pool itself had no outlet. The water must run underground from this place; they had seen this happen before.

"This is where we will stop," Herilak said. "There is water here, grazing for the beasts, good hunting if we have read the signs right. Here is what we will do. The sammads will stay in this place and the hunters will bring in fresh meat. There are berries, roots to be dug. We will not go hungry at once. I will go on with Munan who has been here before to see what lies ahead. Kerrick will come with us."

"We must carry water in skins," Munan said. "There is little water after this, none in the desert."

"That is what we will do," Herilak said.

The change began at once, as soon as the three hunters were lower in the hills. There were few trees now, the grass was dry, and there were more and more of the spiny, dangerous-looking plants. As the foothills grew flatter the grass became sparse and they walked on gravel and drifts of sand. All of the plants now were spiny and dry-looking, each spaced far from the others. The air was dry and motionless. A lizard wriggled out of sight when they approached. Nothing else moved.

"It has been a long hard day," Herilak said. "We will stop here, one place is like any other. Is this the desert you talked of?"

Munan nodded. "It is all very much like this. Some places with more sand, sometimes broken rock. Other than these spine-plants nothing grows. There is no water."

"We will go on in the morning. It must have an end."

The desert was hot and dry and despite what Herilak had said it appeared to be endless. They walked for four days, from sunrise to sunset, resting in the middle of the day when the sun was high and it was too hot to go on. At the end of the fourth day the mountains were only a gray line on the horizon behind them. Ahead the desert was unchanged. At sunset Herilak stood on a small rise, shading his eyes as he looked west.

"The same," he said. "No hills or mountains, nothing green. Just more desert."

Kerrick held up the water skin. "This is the last."

"I know. We return in the morning. We have come as far as we can. Even now we will have no water for the last day's walking. We will drink well that night, when we reach the hills again."

"What will we do then?" Kerrick asked, piling up dry twigs for their fire.

"That must be thought about. If the hunting has been good perhaps we can stay in those hills. We will see."

When it was dark there was a hooting of an owl, close by. Kerrick shook himself, suddenly wide awake, feeling a sudden chill. It was just an owl, nothing more. They lived here in the desert, eating the lizards. Just an owl.

The Yilanè could not know they were here, could not have followed them through the snows of the mountain passes. They were safe.

Yet that night he dreamed of Alpèasak, was once again among the scurrying fargi. There was Inlènu∗ at the other end of the lead. He moaned in his sleep but did not wake, did not know that he lay with his fingers clamped on the iron ring about his neck.

When Kerrick woke at dawn the dream was still with him, pressing down on him like a great weight. It was just a dream, he kept telling himself, but the feeling of disaster stayed with him as they walked.

They made good time on their return journey. With their food and water gone they had less to carry and could move faster across the dry desert, then on to the grassy slopes of the foothills. It was late in the afternoon when they came over the last ridge, their mouths dry, looking forward with pleasure to the water that lay ahead. The track they were following led through thick undergrowth that crackled as they pushed by. Herilak was leading the way, climbing steadily. He saw that he was outdistancing the others and stopped to let them catch up.

As he did the arrow strummed past him and thudded into the ground.

He hurled himself to one side, calling out a warning as he did. Lying behind the bole of a tree he took an arrow of his own from his quiver and nocked it to the bowstring. A voice called from the slope above.

"Herilak, is that you? Did you cry out?"

"Who is that?"

"Sorli. Be on your guard. There is danger in the forest."

Herilak looked carefully about but saw nothing. What danger

was there here? He did not want to call out again. Kerrick appeared among the trees, moving warily. Herilak waved him forward, signaled to keep on up the trail. When Munan had passed as well he followed them, silent and alert.

Sorli was waiting for them, concealed from sight behind the large boulders. Other hunters from his sammad were close by, hidden from below, peering back down the hill. Sorli waved them past, then fell in behind them. Once over the ridge he took the arrow from his bow.

"I heard you moving through the brush, then just saw your outline. I did not know it was you, that is why I let fly the arrow. I thought it was the others. They attacked this morning, just after dawn. The hunters on guard were killed, but gave the warning. They killed one of the mastodons too, perhaps for the meat, but we drove them off before they could do anything to it."

"Who were they?"

"Not Tanu."

"Murgu!" Kerrick heard the terror in his voice as he spoke the word. *Not here, no, not here too.*

"Not murgu. But not Tanu as we know Tanu. There is one we killed, you will see. They had spears but no bows. Once the arrows struck among them they broke and ran."

They walked along the trail and Sorli stopped and pointed to a dead body.

The corpse lay where it had fallen, face down in the brush. There was a bloody hole in its back where the arrow that had made the mortal wound had been cut out. There were furs tied around the waist. The corpse's skin was darker than theirs, the long hair black instead of light. Herilak bent and heaved the corpse over, pushed the furs aside with the butt of his spear.

"A hunter. He could be Tanu except for the skin and that hair."

Kerrick bent and pulled up an eyelid; a misted black eye stared up sightlessly at his blue one. Munan leaned over to look as well, then spat with distaste.

"Harwan," he said. "When I was small I used to be frightened when they told stories about the black men from beyond the high mountains who came in the dark to steal children and eat babies. They were called the Harwan and were ferocious and terrible. Some said that the stories were true. Others laughed."

"Now you know," Sorli said. "They were true. And there is another thing. Look at this."

He led them a short distance up the hill to the dark form stretched under the trees. Herilak looked at it and grunted with amazement. "A longtooth, one of the biggest I have ever seen."

It was immense, half again longer than a man. The creature's mouth gaped in death, the two long teeth that gave it its name projecting, large, deadly, sharp.

"It came with the dark Tanu—and there were others as well. They marched with them like mastodons, attacked when they were told."

Herilak did not like it in the slightest. "This is dangerous. Armed Tanu and these creatures. Where did they come from?"

"From the north—and they went back to the north. It may have been a hunting party."

Herilak looked to the north and shook his head. "Then that way is sealed to us. So is the way west, at least at this place. We do not know how many of these dark Tanu there are, or how many longtooth run at their sides. We do not want to fight them. That leaves us only one direction to go."

"South," Kerrick said. "South through these hills. But there may be murgu there."

"There may be anything there," Herilak said, his face set in hard lines. "It does not matter. We must go. The desert may end there, the hunting may be good. Now let us go drink the sweet water. Keep guards out during the night. We leave at sunrise tomorrow."

CHAPTER NINETEEN

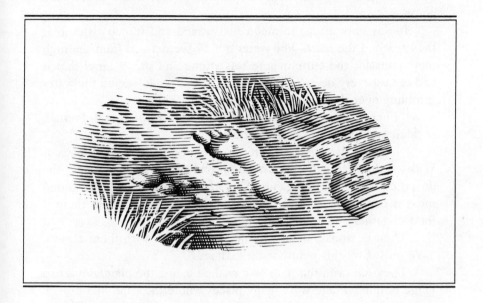

A child could have read the signs of the sammads' passage, so clearly were they marked in the soft turf. The deep ruts cut by the poles of the travois, the large footprints of the mastodons, their high-heaped dung. Herilak made no attempt to obliterate these tracks—but hunters waited in hiding, some of them a two-day march behind the sammads, to make sure they were not being followed. Days passed and there was no evidence that the dark Tanu or their longtooth companions were behind them. Despite this Herilak still made certain that there were guards ready and watching, day and night.

Since all of the valleys and ridges led down from the high mountains, flattening out and vanishing on the arid plain, they went down from the hills to the plain itself. Instead of working their way across the ridges, the march continued along the edge of the desert. Hunters went ahead, scouting the valleys for water. When they camped each evening the mastodons would be led up the valley to drink and browse.

The march continued. The hunting was sparse in the foothills and on the plain. The grasslands at the foot of the hills began to extend further and further into what had been only arid desert, cut now and again by dry watercourses. But there was no water upon the grassy plain, little or no animal life. They could only go on.

It was only after the moon had waxed and waned twice that they reached the river. The water must have drained from the high mountains for the current here was strong and the channel that it had cut was very deep. They stopped at the brink, seeing the water tumbling over the rocks below, sending up white spray.

"There is no way to cross the river here," Kerrick said. Herilak nodded and looked away downstream.

"It might be wisest not to cross it—but to follow it instead. With all this water there must be an end to the desert. Where the desert ends we will find game. This we must do for even the murgu meat is coming to an end. We have to find a place where there is food to gather and animals to hunt."

Then he spoke aloud the thought that was with them always. "We must find this before winter comes."

They followed the river as it snaked across the plain and into a range of hills. There were many places where the bank had broken down, where they could water the mastodons. At some of these sites there were also the track of deer. And something else. It was Munan who spoke of it first. He joined Herilak and Kerrick at their fire and sat down, his back to the hills.

"I have hunted for many years," he said. "Only once was I hunted myself. Let me tell you about that. It was in the high hills that you call mountains where I was tracking greatdeer. The trail was fresh and it was early morning. I walked silently, yet I felt something was wrong. Then I knew what it was. I was being followed as well, watched. I could feel eyes on me. When I knew this to be true I jumped about suddenly—and there it was on the ledge above me. A longtooth. Not close enough to spring, not yet. It must have been tracking me—just as I tracked the greatdeer. It looked into my eyes, then it was gone."

Herilak nodded in agreement. "Animals know when they are being watched. Once I watched some longtooth and they turned because they felt my eyes. A hunter can sometimes know when there are eyes upon him."

"We are being watched now," Munan said quietly, poking at the fire. "Do not turn your heads, but get wood and when you so do look at the hill behind my back. There is something there, watching us, I am sure of that."

"Get wood, Kerrick," Herilak said. "Your eyes are good."

Kerrick rose slowly and walked a few paces, returning with some sticks that he pushed into the fire.

"I cannot be sure," he said. "There is a ridge of rock near the top of the hill, dark shadow below the rock. The animal might be there."

"There will be extra guards out tonight," Herilak said. "This is new country. There could be anything in these hills. Even murgu."

There was no alarm during the night. Before dawn Herilak woke Kerrick and they were joined by Munan. They had agreed on the stratagem the night before. Going different ways, silent as the shadows around them, they approached the rocky ledge from the sides and below. When the sun rose they were in the positions they had chosen.

When Herilak called like a bird they closed in. They met before the ledge, weapons ready, but there was nothing there. But something had been there. Kerrick pointed. "The grass has been flattened, broken in this place. Something was watching us."

"Spread out. Look for tracks," Herilak said.

It was Munan who found the mark. "Over here, in the sand. A footprint."

They bent close and looked. In silence, because there was no possible way of mistaking the creature that had made it.

"Tanu," Herilak said, standing and looking to the north. "Could the dark Tanu have followed us here?"

"That would not have been easy," Kerrick said. "And if they had done it they would have to have circled around us into the hills, to get ahead of us. This print is from different Tanu. I am sure of that."

"Tanu behind, Tanu ahead." Herilak scowled at the thought. "Must we fight then in order to hunt?"

"This Tanu did not fight—but only watched," Kerrick said. "Tanu does not always kill Tanu. Only with the cold winters did that begin. Where we are here, this far to the south, the winters are not as bad."

"What do we do?" Munan asked.

"Watch for them as well, try to talk to them," Kerrick said. "They may be afraid of us."

"I'm afraid of them," Munan said. "Afraid of a spear in the back."

"Then we are each afraid of the other," Kerrick said. "As long as we march together, with many spears and bows, these new Tanu may be too afraid to come close. If I go ahead on my own, taking just my spear, perhaps I will meet them."

"It is dangerous," Herilak said.

"All life is dangerous. There are Tanu out there, you see the print before you. If we do not try to make peaceful contact we have only one other choice. Do we want that?"

"No," Herilak said. "There is enough death without our killing each other. We will stay at this camp today. Give me your arrows and bow. Do not go too far into the hills. If nothing has happened by midday, return then. Is that understood?"

Kerrick nodded, passing over his weapons in silence. Then he watched and waited until the two hunters had returned the way they had come, down the hill towards the tents, before he turned his back on them and started slowly up the slope.

There was rock and hard soil here so that whoever had made the footprint made no others—nor did he leave any trail that could be followed. Kerrick climbed to the next ridge and looked back at the tents that were far below him now. This would be a good place for him to wait. It was open and no one could slip up on him without being seen. And if he had to flee his way was clear. He sat down, facing the valley, cradling his spear, watchful and aware.

The hills were silent, bare and empty of anything that moved, other than the ants in the sand before him. They were struggling with a dead beetle many times their size, trying to carry it to their nest. Kerrick watched the ants—and from the corners of his eyes watched around him as well.

Something itched the back of his neck and he brushed at it, but there was nothing there. He still felt something, not really an itch, but a sensation of some kind. Then he recognized it, remembered Munan's description of what he had felt. He was being watched.

Slowly he stood and turned about, looking up at the grassy slope of the hill and the stand of trees beyond. No one was visible. There were some bushes on the hillside, but they were thin and offered no cover. If he were being watched it had to be from behind the trees. He looked at them and waited, but nothing moved. If the hidden watcher was afraid then he would have to take some initiative himself. Only when he started to put his spear down did he realize that his hand was tight-gripped about the shaft. His only protection. He did not want to discard it. Yet he must if the unseen watcher—or watchers—were to believe that he came in peace. With an effort of will, and a decisiveness that he did not feel, he hurled it aside. There was still no movement under the trees.

Kerrick shuffled one foot forward, then the other. His throat was dry and the sound of his heart beat loudly in his ears as he walked slowly towards the trees. He stopped when he was a long spear throw from their cover, unable to force himself any closer. Enough. It was time for those in hiding to make a move. He raised his hands slowly, palms outward, and called out.

"I have no weapons. I come in peace."

Still no response. But was there a movement in the shadows beneath the trees? He could not be sure. He stepped back a pace and called out again.

A stirring in the darkness. An outline. Someone was standing there. Kerrick took another step backwards and the figure moved towards him, coming into the sunlight.

Kerrick's first reaction was fear. He swayed backwards but managed to control himself before he turned and ran.

The hunter had black hair and a dark skin, was beardless. But his hands were empty like Kerrick's. Nor was he wearing skins like the hunter in the foothills. There was something white bound about his head, white leather also about his loins. Not gray-white, but white as snow.

"We will talk," Kerrick called out, taking a slow step forward.

At this movement the other figure turned, almost ran back into the cover of the trees. Kerrick stopped when he saw this. The other recovered and, even at this distance, Kerrick could see that the man was shivering with fear. As soon as he realized this Kerrick sat slowly down on the grass, his hands still raised peacefully.

"I will not harm you," he called out. "Come, sit, we will talk."

After that Kerrick did not move. When his arms grew tired he lowered them and rested them palms upwards on his thighs. He hummed to himself, looked up at the sky, then around at the empty slopes, making no sudden motions that might startle the stranger.

The other hunter took a single hesitating step forward, then another. Kerrick smiled and nodded and did not move his hands. One single, shaking step at a time the other moved forward until he was less than ten paces away. Then he dropped to the ground, sitting cross-legged like Kerrick, looking at him with wide and terrified eyes. Now Kerrick could see that this was no youngster. His skin was wrinkled and the black of his hair was shot through with gray. Kerrick smiled, made no other motions. The man's jaw moved and Kerrick could see his throat working, but only a harsh sound came out. He swallowed and was finally able to speak. The words came in a rush.

Kerrick could understand nothing. He smiled and nodded to give the other some assurance as the low and sibilant words continued. Then the other stopped speaking suddenly, bent forward and lowered his head.

Kerrick was baffled. He waited until the hunter had looked up again before he spoke.

"I cannot understand you. Do you know what I am saying? Do you want to know my name?" He touched his chest. "Kerrick. Kerrick." There was no response. The other just sat and watched, jaw hanging open, his eyes round and white against his dark skin. Only when Kerrick had stopped did he nod his head again. He spoke some more, then stood and walked back towards the trees. Another hunter stepped out of the shadows and handed him something. There were others moving behind him, Kerrick saw, and he gathered his legs under him, ready to stand and run. When none of them came forward he relaxed a little. But he kept watching the trees as the first one returned. The others stayed where they were.

This time the hunter came closer before he sat. Kerrick saw that he was carrying a dark bowl of some kind filled with water. He raised it in both hands and drank, then leaned far forward and put it on the ground between them.

Hunters who drink together are sharing something, Kerrick thought. It is a peaceful act. He hoped. He watched the other closely as he reached out and picked up the bowl, raised it and drank from it, returned it to the grass.

The other reached down for the bowl, picked it up and poured the remaining water onto the ground beside him. Then he tapped the bowl and said one word.

"Waliskis."

Then handed the bowl back to Kerrick. Kerrick was puzzled by the actions, but he nodded and smiled in an attempt at reassurance. He held the bowl close and saw that it was made of some dark brown substance that he could not identify; he looked at it more closely. Rough and brown, but decorated with a black pattern near the top edge. He turned it in his hands—and discovered that there was a larger design in black on the other side.

It had been well done, a clear, black silhouette. It was not a random blotch or a simple, repeated pattern. It was the figure of an animal. The tusks were obvious, the trunk as well.

It was a mastodon.

"Waliskis," the other said. "Waliskis."

CHAPTER TWENTY

Kerrick turned the bowl over and over in his hands, then touched the representation of the mastodon. The other nodded and smiled, repeating "waliskis" over and over. But what did it mean? Did these Tanu also have mastodons? There was no way to tell, not if they couldn't speak to each other. The other now pulled gently at the bowl until Kerrick released his grip, then turned and went back to the trees with it.

When he returned the bowl was filled with cooked vegetation of some kind, lumpy and white. The hunter scooped out some of the food with his fingers and ate it, then put the bowl on the ground. Kerrick did the same; it tasted quite good. As soon as he did this the stranger turned and hurried back under the trees again. Kerrick waited, but he did not return.

Their meeting seemed to have ended. No one appeared when Kerrick called out, and when he went slowly across the field to look in the grove of trees he found it empty. The encounter was puzzling— but encouraging. The dark hunter had shown no weapons, but had brought water and food. Kerrick picked up the bowl, retrieved his spear, and returned to the tents. The hunters on guard called out when he appeared and Herilak ran up the hill to greet him. He tasted the food, approved of it—but had as little idea of its significance as Kerrick had.

The sammads gathered to listen when he returned, and he had to tell the story over and over again. Everyone wanted to taste the new food and the bowl was quickly empty. The bowl itself was an object of great interest. Herilak turned it over and over and tapped it with his knuckles.

"It is hard as stone—but too light to be stone. And this mastodon is just as hard. I understand none of this."

Even Fraken would not venture an opinion. This was all new to him as well. In the end Kerrick had to decide for himself.

"I'm going to go back tomorrow, in the morning, just like today. I'll bring them some meat in the bowl. Perhaps they meant to share food with us."

"Perhaps they meant for you to feed the mastodons with it?" Sorli said.

"We have no way of knowing anything," said Kerrick. "I'll bring them some of our meat. But not in their bowl. Let me bring them one of the woven trays with the designs."

Before it became dark Armun took the best tray, one that she had woven herself, and washed it clean in the river. "It is dangerous to go back," she said. "Someone else can go."

"No, these hunters know me now. And I feel that the danger is over, the worst part was when I first went up there. These new Tanu hunt these grounds and we must be at peace with them if we are to stay. And we have nowhere else to go. Now we will eat, but save the best pieces of meat to put on the tray for me to take with me."

There was no one in the meadow below the grove when Kerrick arrived there the following morning. But when he threw his spear aside and went across the grass with the tray a familiar figure appeared under the trees. Kerrick sat down and put the tray down before him. This time the other came forward without fear and sat in the grass as well. Kerrick ate a piece of meat, then pushed the tray over and watched while the hunter took a piece and ate it with signs of pleasure. Then he turned and called out loudly. Five more hunters, all black-haired and beardless, dressed in the same manner, appeared from the grove and walked towards them.

Now it was Kerrick's turn to be fearful. He sprang to his feet and backed away. Two of the newcomers were carrying spears. They stopped when he moved and looked at him with open curiosity.

Kerrick pointed at them and made motions of throwing a spear. The first hunter sensed his meaning and called back what must have been a command for they placed the spears on the grass before they started forward again.

Kerrick waited, arms folded and trying not to show concern. It all looked peaceful enough—but they could be concealing blades under their white leather. They wouldn't even need blades, the six of them could overwhelm him and kill him easily enough if they wanted to. He would have to take that chance. Either that or turn and run.

When they came closer Kerrick saw that two of them were carrying short clubs. He pointed to these and made clubbing motions. They stopped and talked among themselves, and it took them awhile to understand his meaning. Apparently the lengths of wood were not clubs at all. One of them went back to the spears and Kerrick stood ready to run again. But he was just demonstrating the use of the wooden tools. He held one in his hand and fitted the butt of his spear into a notch in the other end. Then, with the spear resting on his arm and held in place by his fingers, he leaned far back and sent the spear high into the air. It hurtled up, then fell back to the ground, plunging deep into the earth. Kerrick could not tell how the device worked, but it certainly made the spear go much further. Kerrick did not move again when the hunter dropped the wood beside the spear and came to join the others.

They grouped around him, talking excitedly in high voices, as interested in Kerrick as he was in them. They reached out tentative fingers to touch the two skymetal knives that hung from the ring about his neck, touched the ring itself with murmurs of wonder. Kerrick looked closely at their leather coverings—and realized that they weren't leather at all. When he ran his fingers over the piece that one of them had bound about his head, the hunter took it off and handed it to Kerrick. It was soft as fur, and when he looked closely he saw that it was woven like a basket, though the substance it was made from was as fine as hair. He started to hand it back but the hunter pushed it away and pointed to Kerrick's head. When he pulled it down over his hair all of them smiled and made appreciative noises.

They all seemed satisfied by this first contact and talked among themselves in low murmurs, reaching some decision. The newcomers turned and started back towards the grove. The first hunter pulled at Kerrick's arm and pointed to the others. His meaning was obvious; they wanted him to accompany them. Should he go? Perhaps all of this had only been only a ruse to capture or kill him. But they seemed so natural about it, the two spearmen even picking up their spears as they went and continuing on without looking back.

This convinced Kerrick. If it were a trap of some kind they would not have gone near the spears; other armed hunters could easily have been waiting among the trees. He had to act as if he believed their innocence. He must not show them his fears. But he was not leaving his own spear behind. He pointed back to it and started that way. The first hunter ran ahead of him and picked the spear up. Kerrick had a single pang of fright as he trotted back, spear held ready. But he merely handed it to Kerrick, then turned his back to follow the others. The tension eased a bit; perhaps they really were as peaceful as they acted. He took a deep breath; there was only one way to find out. They stopped at the edge of the grove and turned back to look at him.

Kerrick let the breath out slowly, then followed after them.

Their path took them over the top of the hill and down the other side. There was a gorge here and Kerrick realized that it had been made by the river they had been following, which looped out through the hills and back again. They followed a clearly marked path now down towards the river, until they were walking along its bank.

With each turn the rock walls rose higher, the river beside them rushed faster. They walked along a narrow bank of rock and sand that would surely be covered by the high waters of spring. Parts of the rock wall had broken loose here and the water splashed and broke into spray over giant boulders in the stream. They had to climb up an ever larger slide of tumbled stone that must have filled the deep ravine for the river now roared over and among the rocks, foaming high against the vertical rock face on the other side. The climb was getting more difficult. Kerrick looked up—and stopped suddenly.

Dark-haired, spear-armed hunters were looking down at him from above. He called out to the hunters climbing ahead of him and pointed. They looked up and understood, shouting orders that sent the others back out of sight. Kerrick went on then to the top and stood, panting, looking back the way they had come.

The mounded boulders fell away from him to the dark waters of the river, far below. High cliffs rose from the river on both sides.

This natural barrier could be easily defended by the armed hunters who had drawn aside to let him pass. It was a perfect defensive position—but what was it guarding? Curiosity now replaced fear as he clambered down the inner face of the barrier and hurried after the others.

As they walked the landscape changed. The rock walls receded and sandy mounds appeared beside the river, dotted here and there with vegetation and stunted trees. After a short distance the land became flatter and greener, with low shrubs stretched out in even rows. Kerrick wondered at this regularity until they passed a group of men digging at one of the rows.

He marveled then at two things: the rows had been planted that way on purpose. And there were hunters working among the plants, doing woman's work. It was most unusual. But the Yilanè had planted fields around their city; there was no reason that Tanu could not do the same, that men should labor in them as well as women. His eyes followed the green rows to the rock wall of the valley beyond, up to the dark openings in the stone.

They passed a group of women next, all of them wrapped in the soft white substance, pointing at him and chattering in high-pitched voices. Kerrick knew that he should be feeling fear here in this valley, among these dark strangers, but he did not. If they had wanted to kill him they would certainly have done it long before this. He might still be in danger, but his curiosity was overwhelming any fears he still had. There was smoke from fires ahead, children running, the cliffs were closer—and he stopped with sudden realization.

"A city!" he said aloud. "A Tanu city, not a Yilanè one."

The hunters he had been following stopped and waited while he looked about him. Notched beams of wood, they must have been entire treetrunks, reached up the cliffside to the openings above. The beams could be climbed for he saw faces peering down at him. There was a rush and bustle here, also like a Yilanè city, with many activities he could not understand. Then he noticed that the hunter he had first met was waving him forward, towards a long, dark opening in the base of the cliff. Kerrick followed him inside and looked up at the rock wall that slanted back above. He blinked at it in the gloom, barely able to make out details after leaving the bright sunlight outside. The hunter was pointing at the rockface above.

"Waliskis," he said, the same word he had used when he pointed at the water vessel.

Kerrick looked up at the tracings in the rock and began to understand something of what the hunter was trying to say.

There were beasts there, marked out in color upon the rock, many of them like the deer that he recognized. In pride of place above them all, almost life-size, was a mastodon.

"Waliskis," the hunter said again and bowed his head towards the representation of the great beast. "Waliskis."

Kerrick nodded in agreement without understanding the significance of the painting at all. It was a good likeness, as was the black mastodon on the bowl. All of the paintings were most realistic. He reached up and touched the deer, saying *deer* aloud at the same time. The dark-haired hunter did not seem interested. Instead he stepped back into the sunlight and waved Kerrick after him.

Kerrick wanted to stop and look at all the fascinating activity taking place, but the other hurried him along to one of the notched logs that stretched up the cliff face. He clambered up to the ledge above, then waited for Kerrick. The climb was an easy one. There was a dark opening behind the ledge with a chamber of some kind beyond. They had to stoop to enter. There were pots and other articles on the stone floor, a heaped pile of skins to the rear. The white-clad hunter spoke and a thin voice answered from the skins and furs.

When Kerrick looked more closely he saw that someone was there, a slight figure that lay under the coverings with just the head visible. A seamed and wrinkled face. The lips worked in the toothless mouth and the whispering voice spoke again.

"Where do you come from? What is your name?"

CHAPTER TWENTY-ONE

As his eyes adjusted to the gloom of the chamber, Kerrick saw that the old one's skin, though dark with age, was as fair as his, the eyes blue. The hair that might once have been light was now gray and sparse. When the thin voice spoke again he listened and could understand most of the words. Not Marbak as he knew it, but more like that spoken by Har-Havola's sammad from beyond the mountains.

"Your name, your name," the order came again.

"I am Kerrick. I come from beyond the mountains."

"I knew it, yes I did, your hair so light. Come closer so Huanita can see you. Yes, you are Tanu. See, Sanone, did I not tell you I could still speak as they do?" The weak voice rustled with dry laughter.

Kerrick and Huanita talked then, Sanone, for that was the dark hunter's name, listening and nodding approval though he could not understand a word. Kerrick was not surprised to discover that Huanita was a woman, captured by hunters when she had been a young girl. Everything that she said was not clear and she tended to ramble. Many times she fell asleep while talking. Once when she awoke she talked to him in Sesek, the language of the Sasku, as these dark-haired people called themselves, and grew angry when he did not respond. Then she called for food and Kerrick ate as well. It was late afternoon by the time Kerrick broke off.

"Tell Sanone I must return to my sammad. But I will be back here in the morning. Tell him that."

Huanita fell asleep then, snoring and muttering, and could not be aroused. But Sanone seemed to have understood what Kerrick was going to do because he walked with him back to the rock barrier, then called out orders to the two spearmen on guard there.

Once past the barrier Kerrick ran most of the way back to the encampment by the river, trying to reach the tents before dark. Herilak must have been concerned about his day-long absence for there were hunters in the hills waiting for him, calling out eager questions. He waited until he was back among the tents and had drunk deep of the cool water before he spoke. Herilak, Fraken, and the sammadars sat close, the rest of the sammads in the circle around.

"First you must know this," Kerrick said. "These dark Tanu are called the Sasku. They are not going to fight us or drive us away. They want to be of help, even give us food, and I think that this is because of the mastodons."

There was a murmur of surprise at this and he waited until they were quiet before he went on.

"I feel just as puzzled by this as you do since I do not understand them completely. There is an old woman there who speaks in a way that I can understand, but what she says is not always clear. The Sasku do not have mastodons. But they know of them, you can see the mastodon on the bowl here, and they have a large painting of a mastodon and other animals in a cave. Again the meanings are not that clear, but something about mastodons is very important to them even though they do not have any. They have seen ours, seen that the mastodons obey us, so therefore they will aid us if they can. They do not wish to harm us. And they have many important things like stores of food set aside for the winter, bowls like this, too much to remember all at once. In the morning I return to them with Herilak. We will talk with them, with their sammadars. I do not know exactly what will happen but there is one thing that is certain. We have found a safe place for the winter."

It was more than just a refuge from the winter; it promised to be safe haven from the storms of the world that had engulfed them. The Yilanè had never been here—nor had the Sasku ever heard of them; they could understand little of what had happened to the hunters since the old woman dozed and forgot to translate such complex thoughts. What was important was that they wanted the newcomers to stay close by. This had something to do with the Harwan, the dark hunters to the north, who had always been a constant bother with their raids. The barrier in the river had begun as a natural landslide, but the Sasku had been levering boulders and rocks into it for years to construct the massive barrier that now barred access to the valley from the north. The valley beyond the rockfall widened out between its high walls and contained wooded hills, flat pastureland as well. Further to the south the high rock walls closed in again, constricting the water's flow so that the river became narrow and fierce, filled with rapids, so that no boat could pass that way. Despite these barriers the Harwan still caused trouble, coming into the valley at places where the rim was low so that the Sasku had to stay on guard at all times. None of this would happen if the sammads stayed close by; the Harwan would keep their distance then. The Sasku would be happy to supply them with food. It was an arrangement that suited everyone.

The sammads stayed in their tents by the river, for the grazing was good enough there and in the wooded highlands above. The hunting was not good, and it would have been a hungry winter had it not been for the Sasku. They were free with their food for they seemed to have an abundance of it, all grown in their fields beside the river. They asked nothing in return, though they were grateful for fresh meat after a successful hunt. If they did ask anything, it was only the privilege of seeing the mastodons, for coming close to them, for the ultimate favor of being permitted to reach out and touch their wrinkled, hairy skins.

Kerrick's pleasure was even greater than theirs since he found every aspect of the Sasku's life fascinating in the extreme. The other hunters took no interest at all in the Sasku, even laughing at the males who grubbed in the dirt like women. Kerrick understood the Sasku better, saw the relationship between their work in their fields and the pastured animals of the Yilanè, understanding the security that was guaranteed by a food supply that did not move about with the seasons. Since there were more hunters than game, the hunters of the sammads were pleased to see him spending so much time with the Sasku. He stayed many nights in the rock-carved rooms and in the end brought Armun and all their furs and goods to the rock chambers in the cliff. They were made welcome, the women and children gathering around in admiration of her fair looks, hesitantly touching her shoulder-length hair.

Armun proved to be very quick at picking up the language spoken by the Sasku. Kerrick went often to the old woman, Huanita, and learned some of the Sasku words from her and their way of speaking. Armun was eager to learn these as well and practiced them on the other women when he was away. They laughed and covered their mouths when she spoke, and she smiled because she knew that there was no malice in their laughter. When they finally understood what she was trying to say they would speak the words correctly, over and over for her, as though she were a child, and she would repeat after them. In a short time she was the one who was teaching Kerrick and he no longer had to rely on the old woman and her senile vagaries.

With Armun working hard to learn the new language, Kerrick could devote all of his time to investigating the fascinating activities and skills of the Sasku. He discovered that the hard bowls were really made from soft clay found in a thin layer in one particular hillside. The clay was molded and shaped while still wet, then put in an immensely hot oven to dry, an oven shaped from stones and more of the clay itself. Wood burned beneath it day and night and the heat worked a change that turned clay to stone.

Of even greater interest were the fibers they used for ropes and cord, that they wove into cloth to be made into clothing. These came from a little green plant called charadis. The seeds were not only good to eat, but when hammered and pressed produced an oil with many uses. However it was the stems of the plant that were of most value.

The charadis stalks were put into shallow ponds and heavy rocks were placed on top of them to hold them under water. After a certain time the soggy stalks were removed and dried in the sun, then beaten on stone slabs. Special wooden tools with prongs were used to rake out and separate the fibers, which the women then twisted and spun into strong lengths. Many of these lengths could be wound together to make cords and ropes, which were then knotted into nets for fishing and catching animals. Best of all, the thin lengths were stretched on wooden frames, many of them, close together. Then the women wove other threads back and forth between them to make the white fabric that Armun so greatly admired. She soon discarded her skins and furs and dressed as the other women did in the soft charadis cloth.

Armun was happy among the Sasku, happier than she had ever been in her life before. Her baby would be born soon and she was grateful that she was warm and comfortable here and not spending the winter in a cold tent. She had no desire, big as she was, to climb the barrier of stone to go back to the sammads by the river for the birth. But this was not the important reason. Her sammad was here, Kerrick her sammadar. She dated the beginning of her real life from the moment he had looked into her face and had not laughed. The Sasku did not laugh at her either, taking no notice of her divided lips at all, lost as they were in admiration of her fair skin, her hair as pale as charadis. That is what they called it, for it was almost as white as the cloth itself. She felt at home among them, talking easily now in their language, learning to spin and cook the crops that they grew. The baby would be born here.

Kerrick did not question the decision, was pleased by it if anything. The cleanliness of the stone caves, the soft luxury of the woven cloth, was far superior to the windy tents and vermin-ridden furs. Life with the Sasku was, in many ways, like the bustle of life in a Yilanè city, though he did not often make this observation consciously. He did not like to think of the Yilanè at all, and let his thoughts slip away from them whenever some chance resemblance brought them to mind. The mountains and desert were a barrier: the Yilanè could not find them here. That was the way it should be. He had responsibilities now and they took precedence over everything. The birth was the important thing. Though only to him and Armun. Another birth was of greater importance to the Sasku and it was all that they could talk about.

The mastodon cow, Dooha, was also giving birth. This would be her fourth calf so that she and the sammads accepted it as a natural occurrence.

Not so the Sasku. Kerrick was beginning to understand some of the reverence that they had for the mastodons. They knew many things about the world that the Tanu did not, in particular they knew about the spirits of the beasts and rocks, about what lay beyond the sky, where the world had come from and what the future would be like. They had special persons called manduktos who did nothing except pay attention to such matters. Sanone was first among them and led them, just as the manduktos led the rest of the Sasku. His powers were very much like that of a Yilanè eistaa. Therefore, when he sent for him Kerrick went at once to the cave. Sanone sat before the image of the mastodon and waved Kerrick to sit beside him.

"You have journeyed a great distance to reach this valley," Sanone said. Like the Tanu the Sasku came slowly to the subject at hand. "And you battled with the murgu who walk like men. We have never seen murgu like this so you must tell me of them."

Kerrick had told him often about the Yilanè but he did so once again knowing that this was a step along the way to whatever reason Sanone had for this visit.

"Such killing, such creatures!" Sanone trembled when he thought about the evil the Yilanè had done. "And they killed not only Tanu but mastodon as well?" There was unconcealed horror in his voice when he said this.

"They did."

"You know a little our reverence for the mastodons. You have looked at the painting above me. I will now tell why these great creatures are held in such esteem. In order to know this you must understand how the world came into being. It was the creator, Kadair, who made the world as you see it now. He made the water to run, the rain to fall, the crops to grow. He made it all. When he made the world it was solid rock and barren. Then he took the form of a mastodon. When the mastodon-who-was-Kadair stamped his feet the rock opened and the valley was formed. The mastodon's trunk sprayed water and the river ran. From the mastodon's dung the grass grew and the world was fertile. This was how the world began. When Kadair left, the mastodon stayed behind to remind us always of what he had done. This is why we worship the mastodon. Now you understand."

"I do and am honored to hear of these things."

"The honor is ours to have you here. For you lead the people who tend the mastodon and you have led them here. For this we are grateful. The manduktos gathered last night and talked of this, and then we watched the stars all the rest of the night. There were portents there, burning fire in the sky, trails of fire all pointing this way. There is meaning in these things. We know them to mean that Kadair had guided the sammads here for some hidden reason. Last night that reason became clear. You were guided here so that we could witness the birth of the mastodon calf."

Now Sanone leaned forward and there was great concern in his voice when he spoke. "Can the cow be brought here? It is important that the calf be born here with the manduktos in attendance. I cannot tell you why this is important because that is a mystery we must not speak about. I can assure you there will be great gifts if you will permit this. Will you do it?"

Kerrick respected their beliefs, though he did not understand them, so he spoke with care. "I would say yes at once, but it is not for me to decide. The sammadar who owns the cow named Dooha will decide. I will talk with him and tell them of the importance of this."

"It is of an importance that you cannot understand. Go to this sammadar. I will send manduktos with you, bearing gifts, so our sincerity will be clear."

Armun was sleeping when he returned. Kerrick moved silently so as not to awaken her. He bound on his leggings with the thick soles and left. Sanone was waiting on the ground below. Two of the younger manduktos were with him, bent under the weight of the woven baskets on their backs.

"They will accompany you," Sanone said. "When you have spoken with the sammadar you will tell them if our request has been granted. They will run here with the news."

Kerrick was glad to stretch his legs; it had been a long time since he been to the campsite. At the rock barrier he saw that the river was high; the snow was melting in the distant valleys. Once past the barrier he pushed on at a steady pace, then had to stop and wait for the heavily laden manduktos to catch up with him. The sun was warm and the spring rains had turned the grass green. Blue flowers were springing up on the hillside. He pulled off a long stem of sweet grass and chewed on it while he was waiting for the manduktos.

They went on, through the small stand of trees and out into the meadow where he had first met Sanone. He could see the river from here and the campsite beside it.

It was empty, deserted.

The sammads were gone.

CHAPTER TWENTY-TWO

Kerrick was surprised by the disappearance of the sammads, even a little disturbed, but the effect on the two manduktos was astonishing. They dropped to their knees and wailed pitifully. Their unhappiness was so great that they paid no attention to Kerrick when he spoke, and he had to pull at them to draw their attention.

"We will follow them, find them. They won't have moved very far."

"But they are gone, perhaps destroyed, vanished from this earth, the mastodons dead," the younger one moaned.

"It is nothing like that. The Tanu of the sammads are not bound to one place like the Sasku. They have no fields or rock dwellings to live in. They must move always to find food, to search for better hunting. They have been in their camp all this winter. They will not have gone far or they would have sought me out and told me. Come, we will follow them, find them."

As always, the tracks of a sammad on the move were easy enough to make out. The deep ruts first pointed north, then swung west into the low hills. They had been walking for only a short time when Kerrick saw the thin twists of smoke rising up ahead and pointed this out to the relieved manduktos. The grooves and tracks led back to the river, to a place where the high bank had been broken and trampled, leaving a trail down to the water. The manduktos, their earlier fears now replaced by excitement at the sight of the mastodons, hurried forward. Some children saw their approach and ran shouting with the news. Herilak strode forth to greet them, smiling at Kerrick's white clothing.

"Better than furs in the summer—but you would freeze in a real winter. Come, sit with us and smoke a pipe and you will tell me of the happenings in the valley."

"That I will do. But first you must send for Sorli. These Sasku have gifts for him—and a request."

Sorli was summoned and smiled with pleasure at the baked cakes of ground meal, the sweet, fresh roots, even some of the rare and highly regarded honey. The manduktos looked on anxiously while he poked through the baskets, were relieved at his smiles.

"This will be good eating after the winter. But why do they bring such gifts to my sammad?"

"I will tell you," Kerrick said in a serious voice, pointing to the gifts and the manduktos while he spoke. "But you must not smile or laugh at what I say, for this is a serious matter to these people. Think of all the food they have given us, all the food to come. You know how they have great reverence for the mastodons?"

"I do. I do not understand it, but it must be of some importance or they would not act as they do."

"Of greatest importance. Were it not for the mastodons I do not think they would have helped us at all. Now they have a request. They ask for your permission to bring the cow Dooha into the valley so that her calf will be born there. They promise to feed and tend to her during the birth. Will you agree to that?"

"They wish to keep her? I cannot let them to that."

"They won't keep her. She'll just be there until her calf is born."

"In that case she will go. Where the calf is born is of no importance."

"But you must make it sound important, in the way that you talk. They are listening closely."

Sorli turned slowly to face the two manduktos, raising his hands palm outwards. "It shall be done as you ask. I will take Dooha there myself, today."

Kerrick repeated his words in the language of the Sasku, and the manduktos bent low in honored acceptance.

"You will thank this sammadar," the older mandukto said. "Tell him that our gratitude will never cease. Now we must return with the word."

Sorli looked after their retreating backs and shook his head. "I don't understand it—and I'm not going to try to. But we will eat their food and ask no more questions."

There was a feast then, and all of the sammads shared the fresh food. Kerrick, who had eaten like this all of the winter, did not touch the Sasku food; instead he took great pleasure in chewing on a piece of tough smoked meat. When they were done, the stone pipe was lit and passed and Kerrick drew on it gratefully.

"Is this site better than the old one?" he asked.

"For now," Herilak said. "The grazing is better for the beasts here, but the hunting is just as bad. We have had to go as far as the mountains to find game, and that is dangerous for the dark ones hunt there as well."

"What will you do then? The hunting may be bad—but there is all the food we need from the Sasku."

"That is good for one winter—but not for a lifetime. The Tanu live by hunting, not begging. There may be hunting to the south, but we have found that there are barren and waterless hills on the way and they are hard to pass. Perhaps we should try."

"I have talked to the Sasku about these hills. There are some valleys there where there is good hunting. But the Kargu, that is what they call the dark ones, are already there. That way is closed. Have you looked to the west?"

"Five days once we walked out into the sand, then we had to turn back. It was desert still, nothing growing except the spine plants."

"I have talked to the Sasku about that as well. They say that there are forests if you are able to reach the other side. Most important, I think that they may know the trail across the desert."

"Then you must ask them. If we can cross and find a place that has good hunting, without murgu there, why, then the world will be as it used to be, before the cold, before the murgu came." Herilak's face fell as he spoke and he stared, unseeing, at the dead fire.

"Do not think of them," Kerrick said. "They will not find us here."

"They will not leave my thoughts. In my dreams I march with my sammad. See them, hear them, the hunters, the women and children, the great mastodons pulling the travois. We laugh and eat fresh meat. Then I awake and they are dead, dust blowing on that distant shore, white bones in the sand. When I have these dreams, then all these sammads about me are strangers and I want to leave and go far away. I want to go east back over the mountains, to find the murgu and kill as many as I can, before I die as well. Then perhaps in the stars I will find peace. My tharm will not dream. The pain of memory will end."

The big hunter's fists were clamped tight, but his fingers only closed on empty air, for the enemies he fought were as invisible as his thoughts. Kerrick understood, for his hatred of the Yilanè had been just as strong. But now, with Armun, his child on the way, the life among the Sasku was as full as he had ever wished. He could not forget the Yilanè, but they were in the past and now he wanted only to live in the present.

"Come to the place of the Sasku," he said. "We will talk with the manduktos. They have knowledge of many things, and if there is a way across the desert they will know about it. If the sammads do go there you will have the twin barriers of the desert and the mountains behind you. The murgu will never cross both of them. You can forget them then."

"I would like to. More than I desire anything else I would like to put them from my mind during the day, from my dreams at night. Yes, let us go and talk with the dark ones."

Herilak was not like the other hunters who laughed at the Sasku who worked here in the fields, strong males digging in the dirt like women instead of stalking game as real hunters should. He had eaten the food raised here, had lived well through the winter because of it. When Kerrick showed him how the plants were grown and stored, he listened with close attention.

He saw how the tagaso was dried, with the tasseled, yellow ears still on the stalks, then hung from wooden frames. There were rats here, mice as well, who would have grown fat on this provident food supply had it not been for the donsemnilla who kept their numbers down. These sleek, long-nosed creatures, many of them with their young hanging on their mother's backs, tiny tails wrapped about her larger one, stalked the vermin in the darkness, killed and ate them.

They stopped to watch the women who were scraping the dried kernels from the ears, then grinding them between two stones. This flour was mixed with water and heated before the fire.

Herilak ate some of the cakes, still hot enough to burn his fingers, dipping them in honey and biting on the hot peppers that brought pleasureful tears to his eyes.

"This is good food," he said.

"And always abundant. They plant it, harvest it, and store it as you have seen."

"I have. I have also seen that as they depend on the green fields, so do the fields depend on them. They must stay in this one place forever. That is not for everyone. If I could not roll my tent and move on I do not think I would find life worth living at all."

"They might feel the same way about you. They might miss returning to the same fire in the evening, not seeing the same fields in the morning."

Herilak thought about this and nodded agreement. "Yes, that is possible. You are the one who sees things in a different way, Kerrick, perhaps because of all those years living with the murgu."

He broke off when he heard someone calling Kerrick's name. One of the Sasku women was hurrying towards them, crying out in a shrill voice. Kerrick looked worried. "The baby has been born," he said.

He ran off and Herilak followed at a more leisurely pace. Kerrick was concerned because Armun had been so upset of late. She wept daily and all of her earlier fears had returned. The baby would be a girl and would look like her, then it would be laughed at and scorned just as she had been. Kerrick could do nothing to change her mind; only the birth itself would remove her black doubts. The women here were skilled in these things, he had been told. He sincerely hoped that they were as he clambered up the notched log to their quarters.

One look at her face told him all that he need to know. All was well at last.

"Look," she said, unwrapping the white cloths that swaddled the infant. "Look. A boy to make his father proud. As handsome and as strong."

Kerrick, who had no experience of infants, thought it wrinkled, bald, and red, nothing like him at all, but had the intelligence to keep his opinions to himself.

"What is his name to be?" Armun asked.

"Whatever you like for now. He will be given a hunter's name when he is grown."

"Then we will name him Arnwheet, for I wish him to be as strong as that bird, as handsome and as free."

"A good name," Kerrick agreed. "For the Arnwheet is also a good hunter with the best eyesight. Only an Arnwheet can hang from the wind, then drop and take its prey. Arnwheet will become a great hunter when he begins life with a name like that."

When Kerrick called down to him Herilak climbed easily up the notched log to the rooms above. He went inside and saw that Armun was nursing the baby, surrounded by a circle of admiring women. Kerrick stood proudly to one side. The women brought her food, jugs of water, whatever she needed. Herilak nodded approval.

"Look at the strength in those hands," he said. "How they clutch, the muscles working in those mighty arms. There is a great hunter there."

Herilak admired the luxury of the surroundings as well. The clay pots holding water and food, the woven mats and soft cloth. Kerrick took a finely carved wooden box from a ledge and held it out to him.

"Another secret that the Sasku have is here. Let me show you. With this you no longer need to drill wood or carry fire with you."

Herilak looked on in wonder as Kerrick took a lump of dark rock from the box, then another polished stone with grooves scratched in its surface. He next took up a pinch of powdered wood. With a quick motion he struck one stone with the other—and a spark flew into the wood. He had only then to blow on it and it burst into flame. Herilak took the two lumps of rock in his hand and wondered at them.

"There is fire captured in this rock," he said, "and the other stone releases it. The Sasku do indeed have strange and powerful secrets."

Kerrick carefully put the box away. Herilak went to the ledge outside and marveled at all the activity below, and when Kerrick joined him he pointed and asked Kerrick to tell him about it. Herilak listened closely as he explained the spinning and weaving, then showed him where the smoking oven was, the oven where the pots were fired.

"And there, on those racks, those red spots are the chilies that brought tears to your eyes. They are dried then crushed. Inside the bins are the sweet roots, different kinds of squash as well. They are good when baked, and even the seeds are ground into flour. There is always food here, no one is ever hungry."

Herilak saw his enthusiasm and happiness. "Will you remain here?" he asked.

Kerrick shrugged. "That I do not know yet. It is familiar to me, living in a place like this, for I lived for many years in the city of the Yilanè. There is no hunger and the winters are warm."

"Your son will dig in the ground like a woman instead of following the deer."

"He doesn't have to. The Sasku hunt deer, with their spear-throwers they do it very well."

Herilak said nothing more about this, but his feelings were clear in the way he held his head when he looked about him. This was all very interesting, good enough for those born here, but in no way comparable to the life of a hunter. Kerrick did not want to argue with him. He looked from Herilak to the Sasku digging in the fields and could understand them both—even as he had understood the Yilanè. Not for the first time did he feel suspended in life, neither hunter nor tiller of fields, Ter or marag. They went inside then and his eyes went to Armun holding their son and knew that he had a base now, a sammad of his own no matter how small. Armun saw this look in his face and smiled at him and he smiled back. One of the women came from the cave mouth and whispered to him.

"A mandukto is here and would talk to you."

The mandukto stood on the ledge, wide-eyed and trembling. "It has been as Sanone said. The mastodon is born—as is your son. Sanone asks to talk with you."

"Go to him. Say that I come with Herilak." He turned back to the big hunter. "We will see what Sanone wants. Then we will talk to the manduktos, find out if there really is a way across the desert to the west."

Kerrick knew where to find Sanone at this time of day, for the afternoon sun was slanting across the valley, shining into the cavern at the base of the cliff to illuminate the paintings on the rock wall there. Like Fraken, Sanone knew many things and could recite them from the rise of the sun in the morning to the darkness at night. But Sanone shared his knowledge with the other manduktos, the young ones in particular. He would chant and they would repeat what he said and learn his words. Kerrick was permitted to listen, and recognized the honor in this for only other manduktos were normally permitted to hear what was being said.

When they came close Kerrick saw that Sanone was sitting

cross-legged before the great mastodon painting, looking up at it, while three of the younger manduktos sat before him, listening intently.

"We will wait here until he is done," Kerrick said. "He is telling the others about Kadair."

"What is that?"

"Not what, who. They do not talk of Ermanpadar here, they do not know how he shaped the Tanu from the mud of the river. They speak instead of Kadair, who in the guise of a mastodon walked the earth alone. He was so lonely that he stamped his feet on the black rock so hard that it cracked open and the first Sasku came out."

"They believe this?"

"Yes, very strongly. It is very meaningful to them. They know of many other things, spirits in the rocks and the water, but all of these were made by Kadair. Everything."

"Now I see why they welcomed us here, gave us food. We brought them the mastodons. Do they have any of their own?"

"No. They just know of them from the paintings. They believe we brought them the mastodons for an important reason. Now that the calf has been born they may know the reason. I do not understand everything about it, but it is of great importance. The young ones are leaving, we can talk to Sanone now."

Sanone came forward to greet them, smiling with pleasure. "The mastodon calf is born, did you know that? And I have just been informed that your child has been born as well. This is a matter of great import." He hesitated. "Has your son been named yet?"

"Yes. He is called Arnwheet which means the hawk in our language."

Sanone hesitated, then lowered his head as he spoke.

"There is a reason for these births on the same day, just as there is a reason for everything that happens in this world. You led the mastodon here, and that was for a reason. Your son was born the same day as the calf, and that was for a reason. You have named him Arnwheet and you know well the reason for that. This is our request. We wish that your son's name be given the calf as well. This is of great importance to us. Do you think that the sammadar will permit this to be done?"

Kerrick did not smile at this strange request, for he knew how seriously Sanone and the others took their beliefs. "It will be arranged. I am sure that the sammadar will agree to this."

"We will send more gifts to please the sammadar and to convince him to agree to this request."

"He will agree. Now I have a request in return. This is Herilak who is the leader in battle of the waliskis people."

"Tell him that we welcome him here, for his victories in battle brought the waliskis to us. His arrival has been known to us. The manduktos will gather and we will drink the porro that has been made for this occasion."

Herilak was puzzled when Kerrick told him what was happening. "They knew that I was coming? How can that be?"

"I don't know how they do it, but I do know they can see the future far better than old Fraken can with his owl vomitings. There are many things I still do not understand about them."

The manduktos gathered in silence, bringing the large covered pots with them. They were finely made and each had a black mastodon baked into its surface. The drinking cups were also decorated in the same manner. Sanone himself dipped each cup into the frothy brown liquid, handing the first one he filled to Herilak. Kerrick sipped at his and found the porro bitter but strangely satisfying. He gulped the contents down, just as the others did, and the cup was refilled.

Very quickly a strange dizziness went through his head, which began to feel very light. He could tell by Herilak's expression that he was feeling this as well.

"This is the water of Kadair," Sanone intoned. "Kadair comes to us through this and shows he is watching and listening."

Kerrick was beginning to realize that Kadair was more powerful than he had suspected.

"Kadair guided the waliskis people here, that is known. When the calf was born the child of Kerrick was also born so that Kerrick could give them the name. Now the leader of the waliskis people comes to us for guidance for he seeks a way across the desert to the west."

When Kerrick translated this Herilak's eyes were wide with awe. These people could read the future. He listened intently as Sanone went on, waiting for Kerrick to tell him the meaning of what was being said.

"The waliskis people will leave us for their work is done. The manifestation of Kadair on earth is here. The calf Arnwheet is here and will remain with us. This is what shall be."

Herilak accepted this without question. He believed now that Sanone could see the future, and what he spoke would come to pass. Some of the dizziness was going from Kerrick's head and he hoped that Sorli would feel the same way about the loss of the calf. Yet it was a good bargain for they had been fed for the entire winter by the Sasku.

Sanone pointed to a young mandukto and called him forward.

"This is Meskawino who is strong and will show you the way across the desert. I will tell him the secret of the pools of water in the empty wilderness and he will remember. I will tell him the signs to look for and he will remember. No one alive has crossed the desert but the way is remembered."

The sammads would leave, Kerrick knew. But would he be going with them? Their decision was an easy one—his was not. What was his future going to be? He thought of asking Sanone, but was almost afraid to hear the answer. His cup was refilled with the porro and he seized it up and drank it greedily.

CHAPTER TWENTY-THREE

This was the valley of the Sasku. A wide and rich valley that stretched between the protecting rock walls, high and impassable. In the beginning there had only been solid rock here, but that had been cut through by Kadair on the first day after the world was born. Or so it was taught. Nenne believed this for the evidence was right before his eyes. Who but Kadair could have had the power to slice solid rock as though it were soft mud? Kadair who had torn the earth and rock apart, then scratched the bed of the river into the valley bottom, then filled it with fresh water. All this was obvious. Nenne sat in the shadow of the ledge and thought about these things, for he always listened closely and remembered when Sanone talked of such matters. Thoughts like these filled his mind as he watched and guarded their valley.

Only Kadair could cut through the rock in an instant, but it was true that even the strongest rock wore away in time. The walls of the valley had fallen away in this place, leaving a slope of rock and scree that could be climbed. The Sasku went this way when they left the valley to hunt. That is why Nenne sat and watched the slope now, for where they could go out others could come in. The Kargu hunted in the hills beyond.

Nenne caught a quick movement up among the rocks, but it

was gone in an instant. An animal perhaps, or a bird. Perhaps not. The Sasku did not trouble the Kargu as long as they kept their distance. They were even permitted to come in peace to trade their meat for cloth or pots. But they had to be watched. They preferred to steal, in any case. And they stank. They lived in the open like animals, and were certainly closer to animals than they were to the Sasku, even though they could speak. But they did not speak well and their furs smelled, they smelled. The flash of movement came again and Nenne leaped to his feet, his spear in his hand.

There was something there, something big, moving between the large boulders. Nenne fitted the spear to his spear-thrower, stretched it out along his arm.

The Kargu scrambled into view. He must be tired for he paused often to rest. Nenne watched, unmoving, until he was sure that this one was alone. The place where he stood guard had been chosen because it commanded the trail below. Anyone entering the valley here must pass by him. As soon as he was sure that there were no others following the Kargu, Nenne dropped silently from the ledge.

There was the sound of sliding rocks, then the slow thud of running feet. The hunter passed between the tall pillars of stone that stood like sentries at the top of the cutting. As soon as he had passed Nenne jumped out and slammed the butt of his spear hard into the interloper's back. The Kargu screamed hoarsely and fell. Nenne stepped on his wrist then kicked the other's spear away, pushed the point of his own spear into the filthy furs that covered the Kargu's stomach.

"Your kind are not permitted in the valley."

A twist of the spearpoint made the message clear. The Kargu glared up at him, dark eyes framed by his matted beard and hair.

"I go through . . . to hills after," he said thickly.

"You go back. Or you stay here forever."

"Faster going through. To other sammads."

"You came here to steal, nothing else. Your kind do not pass through our valley, you must know that. Why are you trying to do that now?"

Reluctantly and clumsily the Kargu told him why.

The porro was finished and Kerrick was glad of it. It had done strange things to his head. Whether they were good or bad things, he wasn't sure. He stood and stretched, then went outside the

picture-filled cavern where Herilak joined him. They watched as
Sanone led the manduktos in solemn procession to the newborn
mastodon calf where it rested on a bed of straw. They chanted in
unison and Sanone rubbed red pigment onto the creature's tiny
trunk. Its mother did not appear to be concerned by the attention;
she chewed calmly on a green branch. Kerrick was about to speak
when moving figures at the riverbank drew his attention. One of
them, with dark hair and dressed in furs, had to be a Kargu, and he
wondered at his presence here. He knew that the hunters came
sometimes to trade, but this one was empty-handed; the Sasku
walking behind him carried two spears. He jabbed the Kargu with
one of them and pointed towards Sanone, ordering the hunter in
that direction.

"What is it?" Herilak asked. "What is happening?"

"I don't know. Let me listen."

"This one came into the valley," Nenne said. "I brought him
to you, Sanone, for you to hear what he has to say." He prodded
with the spear again. "Speak. What you told me."

The Kargu looked around, scowling, rubbing the sweat from
his face with a filthy hand, smearing the dirt there even more.

"I was in the hills, hunting alone," he said reluctantly. "All
night by a waterhole. Deer never came. Went back to the tents this
morning. All dead."

A cold premonition seized Kerrick as Sanone spoke. "Dead?
Your sammad? What happened to them?"

"Dead. Arderidh the sammadar, no head." He made a swiping
motion across his throat with his finger. "No spear, no arrow. All
dead. Just these."

He dug inside his furs and took out a folded scrap of leather
and opened it slowly. Kerrick knew as he unwrapped it, knew what
he would see there.

Small, pointed, feathered.

Darts from a hèsotsan.

"They have followed! They are here!"

Herilak bellowed the words aloud, a roar of mighty pain. His
fist lashed out and smote the Kargu's arm so hard that the hunter
screeched in pain. The darts fell to the ground and Herilak ground
them underfoot.

The Sasku looked on in amazement, unable to understand,
and Sanone looked to Kerrick for some explanation. But Kerrick

felt the same mixture of black anger and fear as Herilak did. He drew in a shuddering breath and forced out the words.

"It is them. From the south. The murgu. The murgu who walk like Tanu. They are coming again."

"Are these the murgu you told me of? The ones you have fled from?"

"The same. Murgu of a kind you have never seen nor thought possible. They walk and talk and build cities and kill Tanu. They killed my sammad, they killed Herilak's sammad. Every hunter, every woman, every child. Every mastodon. Dead."

At these last words Sanone nodded with solemn understanding. He had given this matter much thought ever since Kerrick had first told him about the murgu. He had not spoken of it until now; he had not been sure. The surety came now for it had been taught, and he knew the teachings, and he knew that there was only one creature that would dare to kill a mastodon.

"Karognis . . ." he said, in a voice so filled with loathing that those closest to him shivered and stepped back. "The Karognis is loose on the land and is now close to us."

Kerrick was only half-listening for he was not interested in what Sanone was saying. "What do we do, Herilak? Do we flee once again?"

"If we flee again they will only follow again. Now I know the meaning of my dreams. This is the day that I saw coming. I will meet them and I will fight. Then I will die. But it will be a warrior's death for many of the murgu will die with me."

"No," Kerrick said, the word harsh as a slap across the face. "That would be good if you were one man and wanted to die. But you are the sacripex. Do you want the hunters and the sammads to die with you? Have you forgotten that the murgu are as numberless as the sands upon the shore? In open battle we can only lose. So now you must tell me. Are you the sacripex who will lead us in battle—or are you the hunter Herilak who wishes to go alone against the murgu and die?"

The big hunter was a head taller than Kerrick and stood looking down at him, his hands opening and closing now, hands that could reach out and kill. Yet Kerrick was as angry as he, staring back at him in cold silence, waiting for his answer.

"Those are harsh words, Kerrick. No one speaks to Herilak in that manner."

"As margalus I speak to the sacripex. To the hunter Herilak I would speak differently, for his pain is mine." His voice softened now. "It is your choice, great Herilak, and no one can decide for you."

Herilak stared down in silence, his fists now clenched so tightly that his knuckles were white. Then he nodded slowly, and when he spoke there was understanding and respect in his words.

"And so shall the son teach the father. You make me remember that I forced a choice upon you once, and you listened to me and you left the murgu and became a Tanu hunter once again. If you could do that, then I must do my duty as sacripex and forget what I saw in my dreams. But you are margalus. You must tell us what the murgu are doing."

The incident was over, forgotten. Now there were decisions to be made. Kerrick looked at the Kargu hunter, eyes unfocused and looking through him, deep in thought, seeing instead the Yilanè and the fargi who had come here. Trying to see what they were doing and how were they doing it. The Kargu moved uneasily under his unseeing gaze as long moments passed before Kerrick spoke to him.

"You are a hunter. You found your sammad dead. What tracks did you find, what sign?"

"Many tracks, those of beasts I have never seen before. Came from south, go back south."

Kerrick felt a sudden leap of hope. He turned to Herilak, translated the Kargu's words. Groped to divine the meaning of the Yilanè movements.

"If they returned they must have been part of a larger body. A small group of fargi would not come this far, it would be impossible. Their creatures fly, they know where we are before they attack. They knew the Kargu were camped in that place so they attacked swiftly and slaughtered them. That means they know where the sammads are. And they know about the Sasku and this valley."

Sanone's words broke through his thoughts, drawing his attention back to the present.

"What is happening? I understand none of this."

"I spoke of the murgu who walk like men," Kerrick said. "They are coming now from the south, in great numbers I believe. They want only to kill us. They have ways of knowing where we are well before they attack."

"Will they attack us as well? What will they do?" Sanone asked, an echo of Herilak's same question.

"They will know about this valley. They will kill everyone here because you are Tanu."

Would they do that? Kerrick thought. Yes, of course. They would surely attack the sammads at the encampment first, then come here. But when? They would have to swing wide around the valley, might even be doing that now. But would they strike now, this very afternoon? It was a terrible thought that at this very moment the sammads might be under attack, destroyed. No, the Yilanè did not think that way. Find the prey, lie up overnight, attack at dawn. They had done this in the past, it had always succeeded in the past, they would not change it now. He turned swiftly to Herilak.

"The murgu will attack the sammads at the encampment in the morning, I am sure of it. Tomorrow morning or the next one at the latest."

"I go now to warn them. The sammads must leave at once."

He turned and ran and Kerrick called after him.

"Where will you go? Where can you flee that they cannot follow?"

Herilak spun about, faced Kerrick and his distasteful facts.

"Where? North, that might be best, to the snows. They cannot follow us there."

"They are too close. They will catch you in the hills."

"Then where?"

Where? As Herilak cried the words aloud Kerrick could see the answer clearly. He pointed to the ground.

"Here. Behind the rock barrier, in this valley with no exit. Let the murgu come after us. Let them face the death-sticks and the arrows and the spears. Let their darts strike the hard rock instead of us. Let us lie and wait for them. They will not pass. They will think they have trapped us here—but it is we who will have trapped them. We have food and water here, strong spears to aid us.

"Let them attack us and die. I think that the time for running away has come to an end." He turned to face Sanone, for their survival depended upon him now. "The decision is up to you, Sanone. The sammads can go north—or we can come into this valley and wait for the murgu attack. If you let us in you risk the lives of all your people. They may not attack . . ."

"They will," Sanone said with calm assurance. "For now the future has become as clear as the past. We have lived in this valley, gathering our strength, waiting for the mastodon to return. You have done that, brought them to us so that we may defend them. In the mastodon is the power of Kadair. Outside is the Karognis seeking to destroy that power. You do not know about the Karognis but we do. As Kadair is the light and the sun, so is the Karognis the night and the darkness. As Kadair put us on earth, so does the Karognis seek to destroy us. We know of the Karognis's existence, knew that he would come one day, and now we know his guise, know that he has come. These murgu are more than you think they are—and they are less. They are strong—but they are the Karognis on Earth and war against Kadair and his people. That is why you came to us, that is why the mastodon child Arnwheet was born. He is Kadair incarnate. We are here to see that the Karognis is stopped. Call them in, all of them, quickly. The battle is about to begin."

CHAPTER TWENTY-FOUR

"How ugly these creatures are," Vaintè said. "If anything this one is uglier than most."

She put out one foot and turned the severed head over with her claws. There was dust now on the face and hair, caked into the dried blood of the neck.

"Different as well," Stallan said, poking the head with her hèsotsan. "See how dark the fur is. This is a new type of ustuzou. All of the others had white skins and white fur. This one is dark. But these creatures also had sticks with sharp stones attached to them, wore scraps of dirty fur about their bodies."

"Ustuzou," Vaintè said firmly. "In need of killing."

She dismissed Stallan with a movement of her arm and looked about at the organized bustle of the fargi. The sun was still well above the horizon, as it always was now when they stopped for the night, for there were many preparations to be made. While the uruktop were being unloaded and fed, other fargi were spreading the sensitive vines out in circles around the camping place. Nothing could approach now in the dark without being detected. The light-creatures had been bred to be much brighter now, and were slightly sentient so that they pointed at the area that had been disturbed, washing it with eye-burning light. Of greater interest were the bundles of melikkasei that the fargi were carefully unrolling beyond the vines. A new development, plants that were photosensitive and harmless to handle during the daylight hours. But after dark poisonous thorns sprang up from their recesses, the death in their sharp tips ready for any creature that might touch them during the night. They retracted only when the sky was bright again.

A squat Yilanè slowly approached Vaintè. Okotsei, slow and ugly with age—but possessing a brain second to none. It was Okotsei who had developed the creatures that could see and record images by starlight. She had been improving the process ever since, so that now she had her flying beasts in the air night and day—and the pictures they brought back were available almost as soon as they had returned. Okotsei extended a handful of flat sheets as soon as she had caught Vaintè's attention.

"What is this?" Vaintè asked.

"What you requested, Eistaa. These were taken soon after dawn this morning."

Vaintè took the pictures and looked through them carefully. There was no change. Long shadows stretched from the skin cones by the river, reaching out as well from the mastodons in the field nearby. No change. The fears that had possessed her three days ago when the camping place had been discovered empty had proven groundless. The brutes had not fled but had just moved from one site to another. They were not alarmed; the presence of her striking force was still undetected.

"Show me this same place on the larger picture," she said.

The birds flew by night and by day, close to the ground and high in the sky. There was no escape for the ustuzou now. This new picture, taken by a high-soaring raptor, revealed vast stretches of river, the river valley as well, and large parts of the surrounding countryside. Okotsei tapped it with her thumb.

"This is the place where we slept last night. Now this is the ustuzou lair that was destroyed, where that head in the dirt came from." Her thumb moved. "We are at this place now. The ustuzou you are searching for are here, by the river."

"They are the ones I seek, you are certain of that?"

"I am certain only that they are the only group on this side of the snow-mountains that have mastodons with them. There are other ustuzou packs here, here and here. A larger group is in this valley by the river. Further to the north, beyond this picture, there are more of the creatures. But nowhere, except in this one place, are there any mastodons. On the eastern side of the mountains, yes, there are many groups like this. On this side—just the one."

"Good. Take these to Stallan so she may plan the attack in the morning."

The fargi whose duty it was brought Vaintè the evening meat and she was scarcely aware when she seized it and ate it, so great was her concentration on her plans. Her thoughts were all on the multifaceted labors that had brought her and the armed fargi to this place at this time. Once again she went through all the parts to be sure that none were missing, no work incomplete, no detail forgotten. All was as it should be. They would attack in the morning. Before the sun had set Kerrick would be dead—or in her hands. Better in her hands, her thumbs opened and closed with the thought, far better in her hands.

She tried to be unemotional about it, logical, but she was finished with logic now and hatred was seething through her. How many pictures had she looked at? There was no counting. One group of ustuzou looked like any other, the creatures themselves were hard to tell apart. Yet she was sure that the one she sought was in none of the earlier pictures of the packs to the east of the mountains. Only when she had looked at the picture that revealed the mastodons, the only mastodons west of the mountains, had she had the feeling that she had found him at last. Tomorrow she would know for certain.

With the coming of darkness she slept—as did all the Yilanè. Protected by their carefully laid defenses. There were no alarms that night and their sleep was not disturbed. At first light the fargi stirred and preparations for the day's march, the day's battle, began. There was little warmth in the sun yet and Vaintè kept the large sleeping cloak wrapped about her when Stallan joined her as she watched the loading. Everything moved smoothly with true Yilanè organization, groups and group leaders moving efficiently about their appointed tasks. Water, meat, and the other supplies were loaded on the specially bred large-size uruktop. The pleasure of the operation was spoiled for Vaintè when she became aware of Peleinè signaling for attention.

"Vaintè, I would speak with you."

"This evening, when this day's work is done. I am busy now."

"This evening may be too late for the work you desire may not be done."

Vaintè did not move or speak, but one eye looked Peleinè up

and down with cold scrutiny, although Peleinè was too distraught to be aware of her displeasure.

"I wish it were otherwise, but there is much talk among the Daughters and many are worried. They begin to feel that a mistake has been made."

"A mistake? You assured me that you were no longer to be called the Daughters of Death but were now the Daughters of Life in everything. True citizens of Alpèasak, with your errors put behind you, ready to help and aid in all matters. Therefore I saw to it that all rights and honors were restored to those that followed you, raised you up to serve by my side. It is too late now to talk of mistakes."

"Hear me out, mighty Vaintè." Peleinè wound her thumbs together in unconscious misery, her palms showing distressed colors to match. "Speaking of matters and making decisions is one thing. Carrying them out is another. We came with you of our free will, came across the sea, the land and the rivers with you since we agreed that what you are doing is correct. Agreed that the ustuzou are predatory animals that must be slaughtered just as meat animals are slaughtered."

"This you agreed."

"This we agreed before we saw the animals. Two of the Daughters were with the party that found the ustuzou pack yesterday."

"I know of this. It was I who sent them." To blood them, she thought, that was what Stallan said. Blood them. Stallan always did this with fargi who sought to become hunters. There were many who could not easily kill for they had been too long in the cities, too long from the sea, too far from their origins to kill quickly and efficiently. A killer does not think; a killer reacts. These Daughters of Death thought too much, thought all of the time and did very little else. Blooding them would help.

Peleinè was having difficulty in speaking. Vaintè waited with barely controlled patience.

"They should not have gone," Peleinè finally said, her meaning muffled by unnecessary movements of her limbs.

"You presume to question my commands?" Vaintè's crest was erect, quivering with rage.

"They are dead, Vaintè. Both dead."

"They cannot be. The resistance was slight, none were injured."

"These two returned. They spoke of the ustuzou camp and

said that it was not unlike a small city, the ustuzou had many strange artifacts as well, and they cried out in pain as they died. Both of them had used their hèsotsan and they had killed. When they spoke aloud of this someone said that they were Daughters of Death now, not Daughters of Life, and they agreed that they were givers of death. So they died. Died just as though the Eistaa had taken their names away and ordered them from the city. That is how they died. Now that we know this, we know that we were wrong in our beliefs. Killing ustuzou brings death not life. We can no longer aid you, Vaintè. We cannot kill for you."

Peleinè stopped her nervous movements when she said this for her speaking was done now, what she had to say had been said. The decision had been made. No, not made, had been forced upon them. What would happen next was up to Vaintè to decide.

Vaintè was as unmoving in thought as Peleinè was in anticipation. They faced each other in immobility, eyes staring, feet splayed. Silent.

This was rebellion, Vaintè thought, and it must be stopped at once. But with the thought came the realization that it could not be stopped, that these rebellious creatures would surely refuse to take up weapons in the future. Death was now her enemy. These misguided females had seen two of their number die and believed it would happen to them. Well, they were correct. Death would come to them with certainty now. They would not fight but they still could die. There was no room for noncombatants in this war. They would be taken care of.

"You are dismissed," she said. "Go to your Daughters of Death and tell them that they have shamed their city. Their hèsotsan will be taken from them. They will work—but they will not be required to kill."

Peleinè signed grateful acknowledgment as she turned and hurried away. She should have remained to listen for Vaintè had not finished her speaking.

"Not required to kill. But they will be required to die." She called her tarakast to her, made the fargi leading it bend over so she could mount the creature by standing on its shoulders. Turned it and ordered it to run, to pass the fargi and the uruktop to the head of the advancing column where she would lead the march.

Armed Yilanè on fast tarakast spread out ahead of the army, while others rode to each side and guarded the flanks. Stallan had studied the pictures closely as always and she pointed the way. It was an easy ride to the planned halting place by the river and Vaintè signaled the stop just as one of the scouts came hurrying back.

"Gone," the scout said simply, large group and ustuzou in the meaning.

"They will have moved their stopping place again," Vaintè said, hope-of-this in her movements.

"This may be," the scout said. "I followed the track as it returned to the stopping place where they stayed before. The track went on along the river and into the river valley and that is when I returned to tell you."

"They did not turn away or double back or escape in any other way?" Stallan asked, rigid attention in the forward angle of her body.

"Impossible. I followed until the rock walls rose high and there was but one way to go."

"Trapped!" Stallan said with exultation, pulling her beast close to Vaintè's in order to pass over a picture to her. "See this, sarn'enoto, see the trap they have entered. The river valley is wide but the walls are high with this single entrance along the river. The river exits here over rocks and through rapids. There is no way out there."

Sarn'enoto, an ancient title from the half-forgotten past, now revived. A leader in armed conflict—whom all obeyed. Now she must think like such a leader. She held up the picture and touched it with her thumb. "Here, on this side, you yourself showed me a way down into the valley."

"A way that can be blocked. A force can be sent there to seal the exit, the main force can remain here to attack."

"It shall be done that way. Issue the orders. In these other pictures I see more ustuzou in the valley."

"More ustuzou to die in the valley," was Stallan's ready answer as she raked her sharp claws into her tarakast so that it reared and hissed with pain. She controlled it easily, turned it and thundered off.

The sun was just past the zenith when Okotsei handed Vaintè the latest pictures, still warm and damp. She looked at them closely, then passed them on one by one to Stallan who stood at her side.

"Everything is now ready," Stallan said when she had looked at the last one. "There is no escape." Her thumbs snapped shut and the pictures crumpled and broke. "The cliff path is guarded and sealed. We await your orders, sarn'enoto."

CHAPTER TWENTY-FIVE

"A swift attack along the river," Vaintè said. "First a sudden sweep over the rock barrier killing any of the ustuzou that might be concealed there. Then on into the valley. Order the fargi forward, but do not lead them yourself. There is a possibility that the ustuzou are aware of our movements. If they are, then the first attackers will die. Begin."

The massed fargi advanced along the river bank. They became so crowded forcing themselves through the narrow gap that some of them were wading in the water. Vaintè watched them leave, then settled back on her tail and waited with unmoving patience for the outcome. Behind her the rest of the fargi dismounted and began to unload the supplies. They had scarcely finished before Stallan came wearily out of the valley and walked slowly up to the silent Vaintè.

"Lying in concealment," Stallan said. "We fired but there was no way to tell if we had hit any of them. The first attackers died as you said they might. We retrieved the hèsotsan of the dead, as many as we could, before we drew back from the engagement. I prepared a defensive line out of range of their weapons and came here at once."

Vaintè did not appear to be surprised by this unwelcome report.

"They knew that we were coming. That is why they went to the valley. Now I will see for myself."

Stallan pushed her way through the milling fargi, ordering them to move aside for their sarn'enoto. Beyond them the river swung around the rock face and it was here that Stallan had placed the defending position. Fargi crouched behind rocks, weapons ready, while others dug protective trenches in the soft sand. Stallan raised her hèsotsan and pointed it at the bend.

"It is now time for caution. I will go first."

They advanced slowly, then stopped. Stallan waved Vaintè forward to join her. "You can see the barrier from here."

Vaintè moved carefully forward and the first of the bodies came into view. There were many more of them sprawled at the base of the tumbled rocks, while a few had climbed up a few paces before they fell. The river swung around the barrier, burbling swiftly through the narrow passage. There were other fargi corpses there as well, some lying half in and half out of the water. On the summit of the barrier there were quick movements. The enemy lay in wait. Vaintè looked up at the sun, still high in the sky, before she moved back.

"We will attack again. If I remember correctly the hèsotsan can survive under water."

"They can survive. Their nostril flaps close when they are submerged."

"I thought so. Here is what we will do. An attack on the barrier will be launched. I do not want it to stop when a few fargi are killed."

"It will not be easy. It will be certain death for many."

"Nothing is easy, Stallan, or we would all be eistaa without fargi to serve us. You know that the Daughters of Death will not fight?"

"I have taken their weapons from them."

"Good. But they can still serve in their own way. They will lead the attack on the barrier."

As the meaning sank in Stallan's lips pulled slowly back to display rows of sharp teeth, exposed to show the sharpness of the decision as well as her great appreciation of it.

"You are first and wisest in everything, great Vaintè. Their bodies will draw many of the darts of death so the armed fargi can get through. You are the only one who could have found a way to exact such a great service from these burdensome creatures. It will be done just as you have ordered. The ustuzou and the Daughters of Death will die together. What fitting companions they are for this fate!"

"There is more to the attack than that. We might overwhelm them in that manner but the losses would be heavy. While this attack is being pressed forward I want armed fargi in the water, swimming through that gap. They will strike the defenders from behind, kill them, distract them. Then we will sweep over the barrier and destroy the rest."

The flies were already swarming over the tumbled bodies on the rocks below. Nothing moved other than the flies, their buzzing loud in the silence. Kerrick took a handful of darts and began to push them, one by one, into the hèsotsan.

"They have run away," Sanone said, cautiously raising his head to look.

"The fight hasn't started yet," Kerrick said. "They were just probing to test our strength. They'll be back." He turned to look at Sanone and froze. "Don't move! Stay where you are."

He reached out a steady hand and plucked the dart from Sanone's headscarf. "If this had gone through you would be dead."

Sanone looked down calmly at the deadly bit of thorn and leaf. "Our cloth has values I never thought of. It will not stop a spear— but is proof against this murgu poison. Perhaps we should wrap ourselves thickly and survive in that manner."

Kerrick threw the dart away. "That is why we are safe behind these boulders. Only when the darts fly like leaves in the autumn will we be in danger."

He turned to look at the hunters sprawled along the top of the barrier. They were all armed with hèsotsan and had made good use of them, conserving their arrows and spears. The spear-armed Sasku were on the rear of the barrier and on the ground, ready for support if they were needed. Now all that they could do was wait.

Herilak stood on the summit of the rock wall and was the first to see the attackers.

"They come again," he called out, then dropped into concealment himself.

"Do not waste darts," Kerrick ordered. "Let them get closer this time before you fire."

He knew that this was the correct thing to do. When the first attack had come someone had fired his hèsotsan far too early when the murgu were still out of range, and the others had begun firing as well. This was a waste: the supply of darts was adequate, but the hèsotsan tired and did not react quickly when used too much. This time the defenders would wait until the fargi were climbing the rocks.

They were closer now—and Kerrick suddenly realized that those in front were unarmed. What did this mean? Was it a trick of some kind? It did not matter, in fact it was better for it made them easier to kill.

"Now, fire, now!" he cried out, squeezing his hèsotsan and sending death biting into the skin of the nearest attacker. The Tanu were shouting and firing and still the enemy came on. There was an occasional scream, but for the most part they died in silence. It was the defenders who were making the noise so much so that Kerrick did not hear the voice calling out at first. Then he made out the words.

"The river, there, in the water!"

Kerrick turned, stared, recoiled. Dark spots in the rushing water, more and more of them, some being swept towards the bank. Yilanè, swimming with the flow, dark lengths in their hands, hèsotsan, coming ashore . . .

"Spears, arrows, kill them in the water!" Herilak called out, leaping down from the barrier, his great voice rising above all the other sounds. "Kerrick, stay there with the killing-sticks. They will attack now in force. Stop them there."

Kerrick turned away with an effort, saw that Herilak had divined the enemy's intentions well. Behind the unarmed attackers, now heaped in piles of dead, more and more fargi appeared, firing as they came.

"Don't let them through!" Kerrick shouted. "Stay here, keep firing." He fired himself, then fired again, the fargi so close that he saw the dart grow suddenly from her throat, saw her eyes widen as she fell backwards down the slope.

Now the living were climbing over the dead, using them for cover, firing themselves. The battle was no longer one-sided. One hunter was hit, then another. Kerrick's hèsotsan writhed in his hands when he squeezed it and it took him long moments to realize that it was empty of darts. And there was no time to reload. He seized up his spear, stabbed upwards at the fargi who had clambered to the top, sent her falling backwards and shrieking with pain.

She was the last, the attack was broken for the moment. He

dropped with his back to the stone, gasping for breath, forcing his fingers to move smoothly as he fed darts into the hèsotsan. The others had stopped firing as well for want of targets; he permitted himself a quick glimpse at the river.

A good number of fargi had reached the shore, but they were dead. Along with some of the defenders, for it had been a close run thing. In the shallows the dark figure of a Sasku was draped across the corpse of a Yilanè in obscene embrace. Other corpses, bristling with arrows, floated away in the stream. Sanone called out and Kerrick turned to him, saw him standing on top of the barrier and shielding his eyes against the setting sun.

"They've gone back," he cried. "They have stopped the attack. We have won!"

Won, Kerrick thought, looking around at the Tanu dead. What have we won? We have slaughtered some fargi in a world teeming with fargi. Some of us are dead and they will keep attacking until we are all dead. We have held them but we have won nothing. Even if we beat them back this time they will come again. They loathe us just as much as we hate them. They can find us wherever we hide so we cannot hide. They will follow us wherever we run, so we cannot run.

Not us, he realized then. Me. If all they wanted was to kill Tanu there were plenty on the other side of the mountains. The raptors and the night birds could see everything, watch everyone. Yet this great force had come here, striking directly at this valley like a far-flung spear. Why? Because he was here; it was a chilling thought. Vaintè, it had to be her, still alive, still seeking vengeance.

What could be done? Where could he escape to? What possible defense had they?

Anger possessed him, shook his body, sent him leaping to his feet brandishing the hèsotsan over his head, shouting.

"You cannot do this, Vaintè, you cannot kill us all. You will try but you cannot. This is our land to live in and you cannot cross the ocean with your cold creatures and drive us from it. You will not win here and you will go crawling home with your few survivors as soon as that is clear to you. Then you will come again . . ."

Kerrick realized that Sanone was looking at him in amazement, not understanding a word that he was saying. His temper died but the cold anger remained. He smiled wryly at the mandukto and spoke in Sasku.

"You have seen them for the first time today. Do you like it?

Do you enjoy seeing murgu kill your people? We must put an end to them—once and for all."

Kerrick stopped then, breathing hard. Looking out at the high-piled dead, the handful of living. Could the Yilanè be stopped? If so—how?

There could be only one way. They could retreat no more, hide no more.

The battle must be taken to the enemy. That was the answer, a clear and resolute answer and an inescapable one.

Sanone looked at Kerrick in wonder now as he spoke. No, he was not speaking, for the sounds he was emitting were like nothing he had ever heard before. And as he talked he moved his body, threw his head back, and his arms shook as though he had a seizure.

Kerrick saw the expression on Sanone's face and realized that he had spoken in Yilanè for he was thinking about the Yilanè—and thinking like a Yilanè now. Coldly and savagely analyzing what must be done, examining the facts then reaching a solution. When he spoke again it was in Sasku, carefully and clearly.

"We will take the war to the murgu. We will seek them out in their city far to the south. We will find them there and we will kill them there. When this place that they call Alpèasak is gone so will they be. I know that city and I know how to destroy it. That is what we will do." He turned and called down in Marbak to Herilak at the water's edge.

"You will have the wish that was shown to you in your dream, Herilak. We will leave here and go south and you will be sacripex of all the Tanu who march with us. The murgu will die and you will lead us. I now know what must be done and how to do it—and how to destroy them all. What do you say to that, great hunter? Will you lead us?"

Herilak heard the authority in Kerrick's voice, knew that he would not have spoken this way if he did not know how the deed would be done. Hope tore through Herilak and his wordless roar was answer enough.

"They come again," Sanone called out.

The battle began anew and all thought of the future was forgotten in the threat of the moment.

CHAPTER TWENTY-SIX

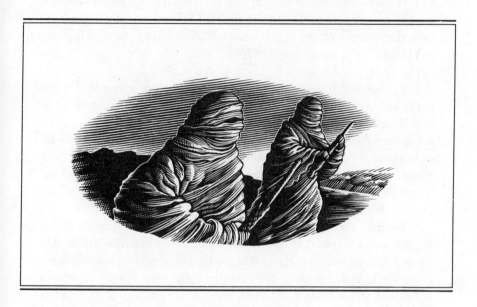

The Yilanè advance broke against the rock wall of the defenders. The fargi died. The spirit seemed to have gone out of them and the attack was not pressed home. It was the last attack of the day because the sun was low in the sky, hidden by a bank of clouds, by the time the few survivors had withdrawn.

Kerrick put all thoughts of future battles from him until the present one was finished. He stood atop the rock barrier, watching the crows and buzzards already starting on the luxurious feast that awaited them below. It would be dark soon. There would be no more attacks now since the Yilanè would be setting up their night camp and preparing its defenses. If he could only see what they were doing. There might be some way to harass them after dark. They could not be allowed to sleep in peace, to prepare themselves for the morning. Their attacks had come too close to succeeding this day: this must not be permitted to happen again. The prey must become the hunter now.

"We must do more than simply lie here and wait for more attacks," he told Herilak when the big hunter had climbed up to join him. Herilak nodded solemn agreement.

"I must follow them," Kerrick said.

"We will follow them."

"Good—but we must not follow them in death. Something happened today. A dart hit Sanone's headband but did not penetrate the twisted cloth. Darts are not like arrows or spears, they are light and do not go in very far."

"They kill just as well. Just a single scratch."

"Their deadliness is clear." His hand swept towards the expanse of corpses and the gathering carrion birds. "I don't want us to join them when we follow after the murgu. But think of this, what if we were to wrap ourselves in lengths of bundled cloth, cloth thick enough so that the darts wouldn't penetrate? If we did that any guards they have placed out there would fire and reveal themselves. They would die, we would not. I do not intend to face all of the enemy. We need approach only close enough to observe them."

Kerrick spoke to Sanone who was quick to appreciate his suggestion and sent two manduktos running for the cloth. He wound the fabric about Kerrick himself, arranging folds and draping it thickly to trap any dart. After folding a narrower length he wound it about Kerrick's head and neck leaving only a slit for him to see through. Herilak took an unfired dart and prodded at the coverings but could not penetrate to Kerrick's skin.

"This is a wonder," he said. "Tell him to wrap me in the same manner. Then we will go out and take a closer look at the murgu."

The wrappings were hot—but bearable now that the sun was low. Kerrick could feel the sweat on his forehead, but the cloths soaked it up so that it did not run into his eyes. He led the way down the outer face of the barricade.

The only way to reach the ground was by climbing over the piled corpses, which moved beneath their weight in a very unattractive manner. Kerrick ignored the sightless eyes and gaping tooth-lined mouths and stepped carefully until they had reached the cleared ground at last. He turned and called back to the watchers on the wall.

"All the murgu here are dead. Wait until we pass the turning ahead. Then you can come down and get all the death-sticks that they left behind. They took what they could, but there are still many we can put to use."

The Yilanè had indeed posted guards. When the white-clad hunters came warily around the bend in the rock wall there were three sharp explosions. They ran forward as more darts were fired, then fired themselves at the fargi among the rocks. Two of them died while the third jumped to her feet and fled; Herilak's dart struck her back and she fell. He reached out then and carefully plucked a dart from the cloth that covered Kerrick's chest and threw it aside. "These coverings are hot—but we are alive."

Kerrick took two darts from the big hunter's coverings before they went on. "I know this Yilanè," Kerrick said, looking down at the third corpse. "She is a hunter, close to Stallan. Stallan will be here, Vaintè as well." His hands clamped hard on the hèsotsan at the thought of aiming it, firing it at those two.

"We will bring their death-sticks with us when we return," Herilak said, scouting forward, weapon ready.

When they had climbed up the riverbank to the plain they could see the Yilanè camp, clearly visible on the open ground ahead. There were great numbers of the riding beasts there, as well as mounds of supplies. And fargi, far more than had attacked that day. Kerrick felt a pang of fear at their numbers and forced himself to remember that the attack had been stopped. If they came again—they would be stopped again. If Vaintè wanted all the fargi dead, then the Tanu would do their best to oblige.

More guards had been posted outside the circle but the sun was below the horizon now and they retreated when the two white-clad figures appeared in the growing darkness, entering the circle of defenses through a gap left by the laboring fargi.

"Alarms and traps," Kerrick said. "See where they have placed them in the grass? Those long-legged creatures behind the barricade must make the light that shone on us that night."

"They are all inside now and sealing the last gap."

"Good. Now let us see how close we can get. They won't come out again, not when it is this dark. I want to see just what defenses they have now."

Herilak was hesitant about going forward against this great murgu army, the fleet-footed riding beasts that could run many times faster than a hunter. But Kerrick strode ahead, knowing the Yilanè well, knowing they would not emerge from the security of their living-defenses during the night. It was still light enough when they reached the outer circle of vines to see the thorns lifting slowly into the air.

"Poisoned, you can be sure of that," Kerrick said. "And at this distance darts fired from inside might reach us here. This is close enough."

"Why don't they shoot at us?" Herilak asked, pointing to the murgu with death-sticks just on the other side of the barrier. They stood silent, looking stolidly at the two hunters. Behind them other fargi were moving about, eating, lying down, taking no notice of the enemy without.

"They have no orders to fire," Kerrick said. "The fargi never think for themselves, so they do nothing without being ordered to. I suppose they have been told to shoot when the lights are alarmed. They will obey." There was a low mound nearby and he pointed towards it. "Now we will discover just what kind of a welcome they have prepared. Even if the darts come this far that mound will give us some protection from them."

Kerrick kicked at the ground until he had torn free a large lump of soil, the long stems of grass still hanging from it. He seized these and spun it about his head. "Get down," he called out as he let fly.

The clod flew high and landed among the defenses. The instant that it hit, the twilight vanished in a blaze of light and there was a continuous crackling sound from the circle, the sound of many hèsotsan being fired at once: the air above them rustled with the passage of countless darts. They remained pressed to the ground as more darts were fired and voices called out loudly. This soon stilled, and after a while the lights dimmed and vanished. Not until then did they dare to stand, looking about and blinking, their eyes still dazed by the glare. There was still enough light to see about them—to see the swathes of large darts stuck into the ground.

"Something new," Kerrick said. "These are bigger than any I have ever seen before—and look how far they have carried. Twice the distance of our death-sticks. They must have bred stronger death-sticks, which have been taught to shoot when the alarm vines are touched. Disturb the vines and the lights shine to the spot and these things fire. Even with the cloths we wear I feel that we would be a good deal safer further away from them."

They moved quickly back, beyond the fall of the last darts, then turned to look back at the dark and silent mass of the enemy camp. Kerrick was dripping with sweat now and he slowly unwound some of the cloth, breathing deeply of the cool evening air. Looking and thinking hard.

"Tell me, Herilak, you are a strong bowman. Could you reach that camp from here?"

Herilak took the cloth from his head and rubbed his streaming face with it, looking to the mound they had left, then beyond it towards the vines and the spindly light-beasts.

"Not easy. A good pull should send an arrow that far, but it would be hard to hit a particular target at this distance."

"Aim doesn't matter, as long as it reaches beyond the defenses. And the Sasku, with their spear-throwers—I believe they could also throw that far."

"You plan well, margalus," Herilak said, laughing aloud. "The murgu are packed in there like seeds in a pod. Impossible not to hit something with a spear or arrow."

"Instead of sleeping soundly I believe that the murgu will have other things to think about this night! Let us mark this place where we stand so we can find it when we return."

"With bows and spears!"

Herilak had been correct. An arrow pulled full length, and pointed high, went well past the lights and found a target within the camp. There was a thin scream of pain and the hunters roared with laughter, slapping one another across the shoulders. They quieted only when Sanone fitted a spear into his thrower, watched him intently as he leaned far back—then sent it whistling through the darkness. An animal screeched and they knew that his point had found its mark as well. Sudden light dazzled their eyes and they recoiled at the cloud of darts that suddenly appeared. They all fell short. The one-sided nighttime battle was joined.

Despite what Kerrick had told them, the others did not really believe that the enemy would lie silent and die without counterattacking their tormentors: they stood ready to run into the darkness when that occurred. The attack never came. There were only flickering lights of some kind, then movement within the camp as the fargi tried to draw back from the probing spears and arrows.

These were not in unlimited supply and Herilak quickly ordered them to stop. The lights died away, the murgu settled down in their sleep—and the arrows started again.

This continued all night, with fresh hunters coming out to take the place of the tired ones. Kerrick and Herilak slept for a bit, then woke and ordered the hunters back to the stone barricade at the first gray light of dawn.

They stood ready all day waiting for the attack, some guarding while others slept. The morning passed and the attack never came. By afternoon, still without a murgu attack, Herilak was beset by volunteers who wanted to scout the enemy positions. He refused them all. Nothing would be gained by losing more lives. When dusk came—still without any sign of an attack—he and Kerrick had themselves wrapped in cloth once again. They went forward carefully, weapons ready, but there were no defenders lying in wait for them this time. Still as cautiously they crept up the river bank and raised their cloth-wrapped heads above the edge, peering through the slitted fabric.

The plain was empty.

As swiftly as they had come the enemy had vanished, their tracks and animal droppings pointing to the horizon.

"They are gone. We have beaten them!" Herilak roared, shaking his fists victoriously at the sky.

"Not beaten," Kerrick said, suddenly dizzy with fatigue. He dropped cross-legged to the ground, tearing the suffocating cloth from his face and looking out at the retreating track. "They have been defeated here, pushed back. But they are like poisonous thorns. We cut them in one place and they only grow stronger in another."

"Then we will root out these thorns once and for all. Destroy them so that they cannot grow and return."

Kerrick nodded solemn agreement. "That is what we must do. And I know just how it can be done. Now we will call together the sammads and the manduktos of the Sasku. The time has come to wipe the Yilanè away just as they have tried to root out and kill us.

"We are going to take the battle to them."

CHAPTER TWENTY-SEVEN

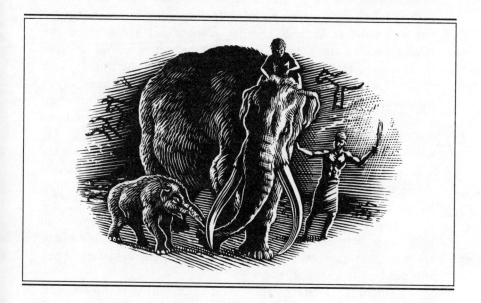

The two boys, dripping with perspiration from their proximity to the flames, added sticks of dry wood to the fire whenever it died down. These blazed up brightly, bathing the cavern interior with a wavering golden light so that the animals painted there appeared to move as the flames flickered. Sanone had not arrived yet, but the other manduktos sat beneath the image of the mastodon as was their right. Kerrick, Herilak, and the sammadars were all seated on the same side of the fire as well.

Beyond the flames were the hunters, with others from the sammads behind them. Sanone had agreed to this with great reluctance since it was the custom of the Sasku for the manduktos to make all the decisions, and he found it difficult to understand that the sammadars did not rule with the same authority. This compromise had finally been reached, with the leaders on one side and the sammads on the other. The Sasku were not sure what to make of this unusual arrangement and only a few came close and listened from the darkness, looking expectantly over the shoulders of those seated before them. They stirred with mixed emotions, pleasure and fear, as a mastodon trumpeted in the darkness. There was a thud of heavy feet, torches coming close, dark forms moving.

Into the circle of light the mastodons came, the great cow

· 405 ·

Dooha being led by Sanone, one of the Tanu boys high on her neck, guiding her. But the Sasku were not looking at her, but at the newborn baby at her side. Sanone reached out and touched the small creature's trunk and a murmur of happiness welled up from the darkness. Only then did he join the others by the fire.

Armun sat just behind the hunters, the baby burbling gently in its sleep, comfortable in the deerskin carrier on her back. Then Kerrick rose to speak and the talking died away. She covered her face with her hands so others would not see her smile of pride. He looked so erect and strong standing there in the firelight, his long hair bound about by a charadis cloth, his beard now fully grown. When there was silence he turned so that they all could hear him as he spoke.

"Yesterday we killed the murgu. Today we buried them, so all here know how many of them died during the attack. We killed them in great numbers and the few that lived have now fled. They will not be coming back, not now."

There were shouts of approval from the hunters at these words, and from the darkness the sound of rapid drumming and the clatter of the Sasku gourd rattles when he had translated his words for them. Kerrick waited until they were silent again before he spoke.

"They will not be back now—but they will be back. They will come back stronger, with better weapons to kill. They always come back. They will return again and again and will not stop until we are all dead. That is the truth and must always be remembered. Remember too those of us who have died."

The silence now was a grim one, Herilak's voice just as grim when he spoke.

"This is indeed the truth," dark bitterness in his voice. "Kerrick knows because his sammad was the first one the murgu destroyed. He alone lived, he alone was taken by the murgu and was held captive by them, learned to speak with them. He knows their ways so you must listen when he talks of murgu. You must listen also when I talk of death for I am here and Ortnar sits there—and all others in our sammad are dead. Every hunter, every woman and child, every mastodon, slain by the murgu."

The listeners moved with the pain of his words and Sanone looked up at the mastodon above him and whispered silent prayers to the memory of those great beasts as he listened to Kerrick's quick translation.

"There is no place to flee to, no hiding place where we cannot be found," Kerrick told them. "The sammads who sit here fought them on the beach of the great ocean, on the plains of the duckbills, and yet again in this valley after crossing the high mountains to escape these murgu. Now the time has come for us to stop running away. We know now that they will always find us. So now I tell you what we must do."

Kerrick paused for breath, looking out at their expectant faces, then he spoke.

"We must bring the battle to them, go to their city—and destroy it."

There were shouts of disbelief at this, mixed with cries of approval. The Sasku called out questioningly and Kerrick translated what he had said into Sesek. Then Har-Havola's voice rose above the others and they grew silent again and listened.

"How can we do this? How can we fight those armies of murgu? How can we destroy an entire city? These are things I do not understand."

"Then listen," Kerrick said. "Here is how it can be done. Herilak knows all the trails that go to the city of Alpèasak because he has led his hunters there and killed murgu there—and returned alive. He will do that again. Only this time it will not be a handful of hunters he will lead but many hunters. He will lead them by stealth through the jungles so the murgu armies will not find them no matter how they search. He will lead the hunters to Alpèasak and I will then show them the way to destroy that city and every murgu in it. I will tell you now how it can be done, I will show you now how it will be done." He turned to the manduktos and repeated what he had said so that they would understand as well.

The silence was absolute. Not a watcher moved. Every eye was upon him as he stepped forward. A baby cried thinly in the distance and was instantly hushed. One stride, then another, brought Kerrick to the fire. He seized up a dry branch and thrust it into the blaze, poked it into the glowing embers until a cloud of sparks rose up. Then he pulled it out, crackling and blazing, and held it high.

"This is what we will do—we will bring fire to their city of trees where there has never been fire before. The murgu do not use fire, do not know of the destruction it can cause. We will now show them. We will set fire to Alpèasak, burn it, raze it, burn every murgu within it and leave nothing but ashes behind!"

His words were lost in their wild howls of agreement.

Herilak strode forward to join him, holding up a burning brand as well, shouting his allegiance, his voice unheard in the tumult. The other sammadars did the same while Kerrick was translating for the manuktos. When he understood Sanone held back, waiting until the noise died away, before striding to the fire. Seizing a burning length of wood and holding it high.

"It is Kadair who made this valley for us and guided us here when there was just darkness. Then he made the stars for us so the sky would not be empty, then put the moon there to light our way. But it was still too dark for the plants to grow so he put the sun in the sky as well, and that is how the world has been ever since. We live in this valley for we are the children of Kadair." He looked slowly around at the silent audience, filled his lungs—then screeched aloud a single word.

"Karognis."

The Sasku women covered their faces and the men moaned aloud as though in pain; the Tanu watched this with great interest, though they understood nothing. Now when Sanone spoke he strode back and forth by the fire, his voice loud and commanding.

"Karognis came disguised as these creatures called murgu and they were defeated. The ones that did not die fled. But that is not enough. While they live Karognis lives and while the threat of his existence lives we cannot be safe. Therefore Kadair came to us in this newborn mastodon to show us the way to defeat Karognis. The mastodon people will attack and kill the murgu." He bent suddenly and seized up another burning branch and swirled it over his head. "We will go with you. Karognis will be destroyed! We will fight beside you. The killers of the holy beasts will be consumed by flames."

His gesture was enough, his listeners did not have to understand his words in order to roar approval. The future had been decided. Everyone wanted to talk then and there was much shouting and confusion that quieted slowly only when Herilak shouted them into silence.

"Enough! We know what we want to do, but I wish to hear from Kerrick how it will be done. I know that he has thought long about this matter. Let him speak."

"I will tell you how it will be done," Kerrick said. "As soon as the snow melts in the mountain passes we will cross the mountains again with all the sammads. We may be seen then by the murgu, we will certainly be seen when we reach the other side. Therefore they must see sammads on the move, women and children, not a

Tanu army on the march. They must be deceived. We will meet
with other sammads as we go west, then we will separate and join
again, confuse our trail. To the murgu we all look alike so they will
surely lose track of us. Only after this has been done will we strike
for the ocean shore. We will hunt and we will fish—just as we did
before when we killed the murgu who came to kill us. They will
see that and they will think about that—and they will believe that it
is another trap."

Kerrick had given this much thought, trying to put himself in
the Yilanè mind, trying to think as they would think. As Vaintè would
think, for he knew that she was still out there, relentless, that she
would keep on leading the fargi against them as long as she was
alive. She would, of course, suspect a trap, would do her best to turn
the trap upon them. There were many ways she could do that—but
he did not care what she did. The sammads would not be there
when she struck.

"It does not matter what the murgu believe," he said. "Because
the sammads will leave the shore before the attackers can reach us.
They will stay just long enough to get food for the winter. This will
be easily done since there will be many hunters—and few to eat the
food. For when we turn back and pass through the hills we will
divide. The sammads will go on to the mountains, to the snow for
safety.

"But the murgu-hunters will go south. Fast. We will carry
some food—but we will hunt for the rest as we go. Herilak knows
the tracks through the hills, for he has been that way twice before.
We will move as only hunters can move through a forest, and
perhaps we will not be seen. But the murgu have many eyes and
we cannot hope to escape them all. It does not matter. They will
not be able to stop us. They have only a few hunters skilled in
woodcraft—and we are many. If they seek us out they will die. If
they send the fargi in armies they will die in armies. We will vanish
into the forests and we will wait until the time is right. When the
dry winds blow, before the winter rains, we will strike them. Burn
them and destroy them. That is what we will do."

It was decided then. If any disagreed they were quiet and did
not speak, for all who spoke wanted to do this thing. They wanted
to fight back.

When the fire had died down and the talking was done they
left the meeting and went to their tents and their rock-walled
rooms. Armun came and walked beside Kerrick.

"Must you do this thing?" she asked, and in her voice was the knowledge that he would do it, so much so that he did not answer. "Do not be too brave, Kerrick. I do not wish to live in a world without you."

"Nor I without you. But this must be done. That creature Vaintè will come after me until one of us is dead. I take the war to Alpèasak to be sure that she is the one who falls. With her dead, the city burned, the Yilanè destroyed, then we will be able to live in peace. But not until then. You must understand. There is nothing else that I can do."

CHAPTER TWENTY-EIGHT

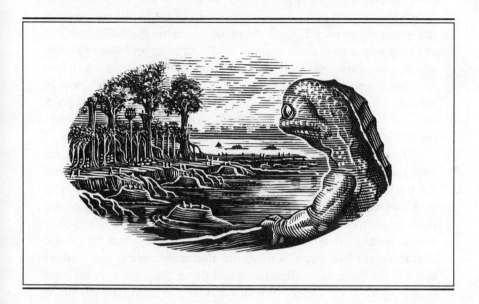

E ver since her return to Alpèasak it had been made clear to
Vaintè that she was out of favor with Malsas<. Nor was the
reason too hard to understand. Vaintè was the first sarn'enoto
the city had ever known, and her power at times had exceeded
even that of the Eistaa herself. Malsas< had approved of this, had
approved of all the preparations Vaintè had made. Vaintè had fallen
from favor only after her return from the west.

Until this had happened the resources of the city had been
hers to command, even the resources of the great continent across
the sea. The fleet of uruketo that had brought the citizens of
Inegban* to Alpèasak had made the voyage many times to the
cities of Entoban* bearing welcome messages, telling them that
there was a whole new world across the western sea, that the city of
Alpèasak was now established there. Alpèasak, growing and expanding in that unknown wilderness, could be of aid to the cities of
Entoban*, could relieve of them of the excess of fargi that clogged
their cities' ways, ate the cities' food. The Eistaa of these cities
were only too happy to rid themselves of the burden of unwanted
fargi, happy as well to grant small favors in the way of beasts and
plants that Alpèasak could make use of.

While this was happening a model of Gendasi was growing

close beside that of Alpèasak. At first only the coast north of Alpèasak was well known and complete in detail, while inland from the ocean there were little or no markings. This gradually changed as the raptors and the newer birds produced more and more pictures of the continent. Skilled Yilanè translated their flat designs into mountains and rivers, valleys, and forests, until the model grew in richest detail. West of Alpèasak there was a warm sea with a verdant coastline. Wide rivers drained into it from a land of plenty, theirs for the taking. Except for the ustuzou, of course.

Their presence in this otherwise perfect landscape was a great annoyance. They were there, almost all of them in the north, and the positions of their packs were carefully noted on the model. The packs were scattered in a thin and broken line from the ocean to the high mountains, just south of the ice and snow. In due time they would be hunted down and slain. When some of them had come south, Vaintè had taken her fargi on the new uruktop and tarakast and sought them out, killed them and drove them back to the land of ice. With each victory like this Vaintè's esteem had grown. It would take a great failure indeed to bring her down from grace.

When more ustuzou had been discovered to the west, prowling comfortably away from the snowy north, Vaintè knew instantly that they must be destroyed. The distance was great, but her urge for revenge was greater. Many uruketo were needed to move the great mass of fargi and mounts to their landing site on the coast. At winter's end Vaintè had led forth an army such as the world had never seen before. They had marched inland, well supplied and equipped with strong defenses. The location of every ustuzou was known and, one by one, each pack was to be overwhelmed and destroyed. This was to be the beginning of the end for the ustuzou.

Then the defeated army had returned.

Word of what had happened had reached the city long before the first fargi had come ashore. When Vaintè had made her report to the council Malsas< had not been present. The Eistaa's absence had been message enough. The council listened coldly to her explanations, tallied up her losses, then had dismissed her. Sent her away like a common fargi.

After this fall from power Vaintè had not gone near the ambesed where the Yilanè gathered each day, where the Eistaa sat, the hub of the city. She stayed away, alone and apparently forgotten, waited for a message that never came. She was out of favor and none came near her lest they share her outcast position as well.

WEST OF EDEN • 413

After many days had passed she did have one visitor, though one that she would rather not have seen. But a meeting with an efenselè could never be avoided.

"It would have to be you," Vaintè said grimly. "The only one who will risk being seen with me, a Daughter of Death."

"I wish to talk, efenselè," Enge said. "I have heard many things said about this last adventure and all of them sadden me."

"I am not that pleased myself, efenselè. When I left here I was sarn'enoto. Now I sit alone and wait for a summons that never comes—and do not even know if I am the sarn'enoto who commands or something lower than a fargi."

"I am not here to add to your misery. Although those who swim to the top of the highest wave . . ."

"Can only sink into the deepest trough. Save your crude philosophies for your comrades. I know all of the stupidities that your founder Farneksei has spoken and reject them in their totality."

"I will make my stay a brief one. I ask you only to tell me the truth behind the whispered stories . . ."

Vaintè cut her off with abrupt silencing slashes of her thumbs. "I care nothing about what the stupid fargi tell one another, nor will I discuss their mindless mouthings."

"Then we will talk only of facts." Enge's movements were grim, implacable and inescapable. "There is a fact known to us both. Peleinè divided the ranks of the Daughters with her doubts and her arguments. She convinced many that your cause was a just one, and these misguided ones swelled the ranks of your army. They went with you on your murderous campaign. They did not return."

"Naturally." Vaintè made only the slightest movements when she spoke, conveying the absolute minimum amount of information, instantly settling into immobility when she was through. "They are dead."

"You killed them."

"The ustuzou killed them."

"You sent them against the ustuzou without weapons, they could only die."

"I sent them against the ustuzou, as I did all of the others. They chose not to carry weapons."

"Why did they do that? You must tell me." Enge leaned forward with anticipation and dread. Vaintè leaned back away from her.

"I choose not to tell you," she said, again with the absolute minimum amount of communication. "Leave me."

"Not until you have answered my question. I have thought long about this and have reached the inescapable conclusion that the reason for their actions is vital to our very existence. Peleinè and I differed in our interpretations of Ugunenapsa's teachings. Peleinè and her followers decided that your cause was a just one so they went with you. Now they are dead. Why?"

"You will get no answer from me, no words to support or aid your destructive philosophy. Go."

There was no crack in Vaintè's wall of grim immobility—yet Enge was equally as steadfast and determined in her assault.

"They bore weapons when they left here. They were empty-handed when they died. You have told me that this was their choice. Your choice was merely that of a murderer, a butcher in the abattoir, sending them to their deaths." Vaintè was not immune to these calculated insults; a shiver trembled her limbs, yet still she did not speak. Enge went on relentlessly.

"Now I ask you—why did they decide to do that? What happened that made them change their thinking about carrying weapons? Something happened. You know what it was. You will tell me."

"Never!"

"You will!"

Enge lurched forward and seized Vaintè's arms tight-clamped between her powerful thumbs, her mouth gaping wide in anger. Then Enge saw the slight movements of joy and she released Vaintè at once, pushing her away and stumbling back.

"You would like me to use violence, wouldn't you?" she said, panting with the effort to control her violent emotions. "You would like to see me forget the truth of my beliefs and sink to your level of desperate violence. But I will not debase myself that much no matter how provoked. I will not join you in your despicable animal corruption."

Rage swept away all of Vaintè's reserve, released all of her anger that had been suppressed since her return and fall from favor.

"You won't join me—you *have* joined me! These marks in my flesh where your thumbs bit deep, where your nails drew blood. Your treasured superiority is as hollow and empty as you are. You grow angry as I do—and you will kill as I do."

"No," Enge said, calm again. "That I will never do, that low I will never sink."

"Never! You will, you all will. Those who followed Peleinè did. They happily aimed their hèsotsan and killed the verminous ustuzou. For one instant they were true Yilanè and not whining and despicable outcasts."

"They killed—and they died," Enge said, speaking softly.

"Yes, they died. Like you they could not face the fact that they are no different, no better than the rest of us . . ."

Then Vaintè stopped, realizing that in her anger she had answered Enge's questions, satisfied her imbecile beliefs.

With the realization of the truth all of Enge's anger had been washed away. "Thank you, efenselè, thank you. You have done me and the Daughters of Life an immense service this day. You have shown us that our feet are on the path and we must walk along it without straying. Only in that way can we reach the truth that Ugunenapsa spoke of. Those who killed, died from that killing. The others saw that and chose not to die in the same manner. That is what happened, is it not?"

Vaintè spoke with cold anger now. "That is what happened—but not for the reasons that you give. They died not because they were better, because they were in some way superior to the rest of the Yilanè—they died because they are exactly the same. They thought they could escape the death of being cast out from the city, nameless and dead. They were wrong. They died in the same manner. You are no better than the rest of us—if anything you are something far less."

In silence, wrapped in thought, Enge turned and left. At the doorway she paused and turned back. "Thank you, efenselè," she said. "Thank you for revealing this immense truth. I sorrow that so many had to die to reveal it, but perhaps that was the only way it could have become known to us. Perhaps even you, in your search for death, will aid in bringing us life. Thank you."

Vaintè hissed with anger and would have torn Enge's throat open had she not gone at this moment. This on top of her indeterminate status was becoming too much for her to bear. Something must be done. Should she go to the ambesed, go before the Eistaa and speak to her? No, that would not do at all for there might be public humiliation from which she could never recover. Then what? Was there no one she could call upon? Yes, one. One who believed as she did that nothing was more important than the killing of ustuzou. She went out and signaled to a passing fargi and issued her instructions.

Most of the day passed and still no one came, until Vaintè gradually went from angry pacing to immobile vacuity, settling into a mindless, thoughtless silence. So dark was this somber mood that she had difficulty in rising from it and stirring herself when she finally realized that another stood before her.

"It is you, Stallan."

"You sent for me."

"Yes. You did not come to see me of your own will."

"No. It would have been seen, Malsas< would have been told. I do not need this kind of attention from the Eistaa."

"It was my belief that you served me. Now you value your own scaled hide more?"

Stallan stood solidly, legs wide-braced, and did not give way. "No, Vaintè, I value my service more. My work is to kill ustuzou. When you lead, I will follow. To the north they crawl like vermin. They need stamping underfoot. When you do not lead, then I wait."

Vaintè's evil humor ameliorated slightly. "Do I detect a hint of admonition there, stout Stallan? The slightest suggestion that my energies would be better disposed of if I had simply acted the butcher and slaughtered the nearest ustuzou? That I should not have mounted my great campaign to track down and kill a single miserable ustuzou?"

"You have said it, Vaintè. I did not. But it should be known that I also share your desire to open the throat of this one particular ustuzou."

"But not enough to pursue him wherever he runs and hides?" Vaintè paced her quarters, back and forth, twisting with anger, her claws ripping into the matting of the floor. "I tell this to you and you alone, Stallan. Perhaps this last attack was a mistake. But none of us knew the outcome when we began, all of us were carried away by the ambition of it. Even she who now will not speak to me." She spun about and jabbed her thumb at Stallan.

"So tell me, loyal Stallan. How is it that you avoided my presence all this time—yet now you are here?"

"The losses are forgotten. After all, most of those killed were just fargi. Now there is talk only of those Yilanè that were murdered in the forest by the ustuzou, the dead males on the beaches. I have seen to it that many of the pictures that the birds bring back are passed about, pictures of the ustuzou for the Yilanè to look at.

The Yilanè look and grow angry. They wonder why the killing has stopped."

Vaintè crowed with pleasure.

"Loyal Stallan, I wronged you. While I hid here in dark anger you were doing the one thing that will bring my exile to an end. Reminding them of the ustuzou. Showing them what the ustuzou have done and will do again. There are ustuzou out there badly in need of killing. Soon they will come to me again, Stallan, because they will remember that killing ustuzou is one thing that I am very good at. We have made our mistakes—and we have learned from them. It will be calm, efficient slaughter from now on. As fruit is plucked from a tree to feed the animals, so will we pluck these ustuzou. Until the tree is bare and they are gone and Gendasi will be Yilanè across all its vast expanse."

"I will join you in that, Vaintè. I have felt since I saw my first ustuzou that it will be ustuzou or Yilanè. One or the other must die."

"That is the truth. That is our destiny and that is what must be done. There will be a day when the skull of the last ustuzou will be hung from the thorns of the Wall of Memory."

Stallan spoke quietly and with great sincerity.

"It will be your hands that hang it there, Vaintè. Yours alone."

CHAPTER TWENTY-NINE

It became Vaintè's custom to visit the Gendasi model every evening just before sunset. By then the builders would have gone, their work for the day completed, and she could have the vast, dim-lit expanse to herself. There she would study any changes of the day, discover if the birds had brought back any pictures of interest. It was summer now and the animals were on the move, the packs of ustuzou stirring as well. She saw the packs come together, then break apart until they could not be told one from the other. Because she had no authority now she could not order flights, so had to accept without question whatever information the pictures revealed.

Stallan came one evening when she was there, bringing newly arrived pictures that she wanted to compare with the physical record. Vaintè seized the pictures eagerly, examining them as well as she could in the failing light. Though there was never any spoken agreement, once Stallan had discovered that Vaintè was there at this time of day, she herself came most days bringing new pictures of the ustuzou movements. In this way Vaintè knew as much as any other in the city about the creatures she had sworn to destroy.

Whenever there were new pictures of the valley ustuzou in the south she examined them closely; she was not surprised when one day the skin shelters and large beasts were gone. Kerrick was not waiting for her return. He was gone. But he would appear again, she was sure of that.

All that long summer she studied the model, kept to herself—and waited. She followed the movements of the various packs, saw that one of the larger packs of ustuzou was moving steadily east. When this ustuzou pack actually left the shelter of the mountains and approached the ocean shore, she waited and said nothing. When they stopped, well within reach of attack from the sea, she still waited. Her patience must be the greater. Stallan reported worried talk among the Yilanè, with the ustuzou this close, anger as well that they were not attacked. Malsas< would hear this talk as well, would see the pictures, would have to do something. The pressure was upon her now, not Vaintè, and this fact enabled Vaintè to control her impatience. It was still a very hard thing to do. But she had everything to gain and little to lose. When the fargi came for her she concealed her elation in unmoving stolidity.

"A message, Vaintè, from the Eistaa."

"Speak."

"Your presence is needed at once in the ambesed."

"Return. I come."

Vaintè had given much thought to this moment, considered how long an interval to leave between the message and her departure. Not long; there was no need to anger Malsas< without reason. She had considered applying formal arm designs, but then had rejected the idea. There must be no obvious display. She simply took a few drops of scented oil on her palms, rubbed some into her crest so that it shone slightly, used the rest on her forearms and the backs of her hands. With that she was done. She left then and did not hurry, but she did take the shortest route to the ambesed. There, in the heart of the city, she had once sat as Eistaa. She returned now—as what? Penitent, supplicant? No, not those, she would die before she asked a favor. She went prepared to accept commands, to serve Alpèasak, nothing more. This decision was in every movement of her body as she walked.

The ambesed was larger now, with all of Inegban* come to swell the ranks of the city's Yilanè. They stood in groups, talking, or milled about slowly from group to group. They were aware of her presence, moved casually to let her pass, but none caught her eye or gave her greetings. She was there—but not there until she had spoken with Malsas<.

The group around the Eistaa opened a path for her as she approached, not appearing to see her, but stepping aside as though by chance. She ignored these half-insults, walking stolidly forward to stand before Malsas<. Stallan was at the Eistaa's side. The hunter looked at Vaintè and her palms colored in recognition. Vaintè returned the greeting, vowing silently to herself to remember the bravery of this simple act of recognition, when all the others had turned away. She stopped before Malsas<, waiting silently until one eye moved in her direction.

"I am here, Eistaa."

"Yes you are, Vaintè." There was a blank neutrality in the statement, neither welcome or rejection. When Vaintè stayed in expectant silence Malsas< went on.

"There are ustuzou to the north, bold enough to approach the shore where they may be found and slain."

"I know of this, Eistaa."

"Do you also know that I have ordered Stallan to go there, to kill them?"

"I did not know that. But I do know that Stallan is the first killer of ustuzou and still the best."

"I am pleased to hear you say that. But Stallan does not agree with you. She feels she is too unskilled to lead and be sarn'enoto in the pursuit of the ustuzou. Do you agree?"

The answer had to be phrased with exactitude. There was great danger here and no latitude for mistakes. When Vaintè began speaking there was sincerity in her movements, followed by firmness of intent.

"Stallan has great skill in the killing of ustuzou and we all learn from her. As to her ability to be sarn'enoto—that is not mine to judge. Only the Eistaa can raise a sarn'enoto up, only the Eistaa can set a sarn'enoto down."

There, it was said. No rebellion, no attempt at argument or flattery, just a simple statement of fact. As always the decisions had to be made by the Eistaa. Others might advise; only she could decide.

Malsas< looked from one to the other while all those present watched in silence. Stallan stood solid as a tree as always, ready to obey the orders she was given. No one who saw her could believe she could ever disagree with the Eistaa. If she said she had not the ability to serve as sarn'enoto it was simply because she believed this to be true.

Nor was Vaintè rebelling against orders. She was here to receive them. Malsas< looked at them both and made her decision.

"The ustuzou must be destroyed. I am the Eistaa and I named Vaintè as sarn'enoto to bring about that destruction. How will you go about accomplishing that, sarn'enoto?"

Vaintè put all thoughts of victory from her, forced herself not to feel the jubilation rising up. Instead she signed simple acceptance of duty, then began to speak.

"All of the ustuzou now avoid the coast where others of their kind have been killed. But once a pack of them came and laid a trap for us. When I see this new pack on the shore I see this same trap again. This means that two things must be done. The trap avoided, the ustuzou trapped instead."

"How will you go about this?"

"We will leave the city in two groups. Stallan will command the first which will proceed north in boats to attack the ustuzou in the same manner that we have done in the past. Her group will spend the night on the shore before the morning of the attack. I will take the second group in fast uruketo out to sea, out of sight of the shore. We will land to the north of the ustuzou and strike suddenly before they are aware of our presence."

Malsas< signed understanding—but puzzlement as well. "That will rid us of the ustuzou pack, but what is to prevent other ustuzou, who may be in hiding, from attacking and killing Stallan and her fargi during the night, while they sleep on the beaches?"

"The Eistaa shows her wisdom in that most important question. When the ustuzou watch Stallan's landing on the shore they will see only meat and water unloaded. Not until after dark will these supplies be opened to reveal our new night weapons. After this has been done, the Yilanè who are proficient in this operation will board the night-trained boats. If the attack comes the boats will leave; only death will remain on the beach."

Malsas< thought about this, then signed her agreement. "Do it that way. It is a well-considered plan. I see that you have given much thought to this, Vaintè."

There was a note of mild admonition in this, that Vaintè while still in doubt about her status, had already been making plans. But it was a very small comment, and a deserved one, and Vaintè did not object. She was sarn'enoto again—that was all that mattered.

Still keeping her elation under control, she spoke as calmly as she could.

"There is something else about the force under Stallan's command that I must tell you about. When we were developing the night weapons we found that there were only a few Yilanè who could operate in the dark, even with lights. It is these specialists who will release the weapons, then follow the light-markers to the boats. The rest of the fargi will have to remain on the shore. If there is an attack there is the strong possibility that all of them will be killed."

"That is not good," Malsas< said. "Too many fargi are already dead."

"I know that, Eistaa, I of all people know that. Therefore it is my strong desire to see no more fargi deaths. So I suggest, since they will not be expected to fight, that we replace the fargi with the Daughters of Death. Surely these parasites on the resources of our city should be good for something."

Malsas< was gracious in her show of appreciation for this suggestion, the color of her palms yellow-hued with pleasure. "You are sarn'enoto, Vaintè, because you produce ideas of this nature. Do it, do it at once."

"The arrangements will be completed this day, the supplies loaded. Both forces will leave at dawn."

The time was short, but Vaintè had been planning this assault for days, not knowing if she would ever be able to order it, but ready still if that opportunity should come. The hurried preparations were accomplished with the efficiency of all Yilanè cooperative ventures, only Enge causing any difficulties at all. She insisted on talking to Vaintè, was fiercely determined to stay until the audience was granted. She was surprised that her request was instantly granted.

"What are these orders you have issued, Vaintè? What do you wish to do with the Daughters of Life?"

"I am sarn'enoto. You will address me that way."

Enge drew herself up—then realized that personal pride was not important now.

"From one lowest to one highest, I spoke in haste, sarn'enoto. Please inform me of the nature of your commands."

"You and your companions will be sent north in boats. You will not be required to use weapons or to kill. We wish only your labors to aid your city."

"There is more to it than that. You have not told me all of your plans."

"No, I have not. Nor will I. You eat the food of Alpèasak, you are protected by those who are ready to die for Alpèasak. When your assistance is needed you will do as you are ordered."

"There is something wrong here and I do not like it. What if we refuse?"

"You will still go. Bound and tied together if necessary, but you will go. Now you will leave my presence. The choice is yours and the decision of no importance to me at all. Leave me. I have much to do."

Vaintè's firmness of mind—and indifference to their decision—must have convinced Enge that the Daughters would be bound and loaded that way if they did not do as they had been ordered. In the first light of dawn the Daughters of Life labored to load the supplies aboard the boats, then boarded themselves without further protest.

Vaintè herself made sure that all the night defenses were there, but she turned away instantly when Stallan hurried up with a file of pictures clamped between her thumbs.

"These are the enlarged pictures you ordered, sarn'enoto."

"Did you see him? Is he with this pack?"

Stallan's movements were ambiguous. "There is one creature that it might be, but they all have fur, they all look the same to me."

Vaintè seized the pictures and went through them quickly, throwing them to the ground one by one—until she found what she wanted. She held the picture up in triumph.

"Here, without a doubt, it is Kerrick! The fur has grown back as you said, but that face, there is no mistake. He is there, on that shore, and he shall not escape. You know what you are to do?"

"I do. It is a good plan."

Having said this, Stallan permitted herself one of her rare demonstrations of good humor. "A very happiness-making plan. It is the first time that I have welcomed an ustuzou attack."

The loading done, Stallan led the boats north. Only at the end of the day did she discover that all of the effort had been wasted. Although they did everything as planned, sailed all day north to reach the appointed beach at dusk, unloaded and prepared the trap, it was not to be sprung. In the last light of day an uruketo appeared beyond the breakers, the accompanying enteesenat sporting about it. A Yilanè waved for attention from the top of the great fin. Stallan commanded one of the night boats to take her out to it. When she was close the Yilanè called down to her.

"I speak for Vaintè. She tells you to return to Alpèasak in the morning. Bring everything back. The attack is not to go ahead as planned."

This was the last thing that Stallan expected. She moved in interrogation and dismay.

"The reason," the Yilanè said, "is that the ustuzou are gone. They have left the beach and returned inland as fast as they can crawl. There are none left for us to destroy."

CHAPTER THIRTY

It was late afternoon before the raptor flew south. The great bird had killed a rabbit earlier in the day, then had flapped up to the top of a tall dead tree with its prey still kicking in its talons. Perching there, it had torn the creature apart and had eaten it. When it was done it remained, sated. The dark lump on its leg was obvious to anyone who might have looked up at it from the huddle of tents below. The raptor wiped its hooked beak clean on the bark, preened its feathers—and finally launched itself into the air. Rising in ever higher circles it turned and flew away to the south.

One of the boys who had been ordered to watch the bird ran at once to tell Kerrick, who shielded his eyes and looked at the sky, saw the white speck vanishing in the distance.

"Herilak, it is gone," he called out.

The big hunter turned from the deer's carcass that he was butchering, arms red to the elbows. "There may be others."

"There may be, we can never be sure. But that flock of seabirds is gone and the boys say that there are no other large birds to be seen."

"What do you think that we should do, margalus?"

"Leave now and not wait for dark. We have all the food we need, there is nothing to be gained by staying here any longer."

"Agreed. We go."

Inside the tents all of their belongings had already been bundled and tied, ready for departure. As the tents came down the travois were lashed to the mastodons and quickly loaded. Everyone was eager to leave the menace of the coast for the security of the mountains. Even as the last loads were being tied into place the first protesting mastodon was trudging heavily away. The hunters looked over their shoulders as they left, but the beach was empty, as was the sky. The fires still smoked on the shore, the half-gutted deer hung from the frame. The sammads were gone.

They walked until dark, stopped and ate cold meat, lit no fires, then went on. The march continued through the night with only brief halts to rest the animals. By dawn they were in the forested hills, distant from the route they had taken on their westward trek to the beaches. The mastodons were freed of the travois so they could graze while the weary sammads slept under the trees.

When Armun opened her eyes the slanting beams of light through the branches showed that it was afternoon. The baby's hungry, fretting crying had woken her. She sat with her back to the bole of the tree and put him to her breast. Kerrick was no longer sleeping at her side; she saw him in the glade talking with the sammadars. His face was set and serious when he trudged back up the hill, but it lit up with a smile when he saw her there. Her smile mirrored his and she took his hand in hers when he sat next to her.

"We are leaving soon," he said, turning away as he saw the loving smile fade from her lips; her hand clenched hard.

"You have to do this?" she said, and it was halfway between a statement and a question.

"You know that I must. It was my plan—I cannot let the others go to the attack without me."

"You'll be leaving me. . ." There was a hoarseness to her voice, all the pain of her lonely life behind her words. "You are all that I have."

"That is not true. You have Arnwheet now and you will keep him safe until I return. I am doing this, all of us are going for the same reason, so that the sammads *will* be safe. There is no security as long as the murgu can hunt and slay us. When they are dead, only then can we live in peace as we once did. Go with the sammads to the meadow at the bend in the river. We will join you there before the winter is out. Stay safe until I return."

"You will come back to me, tell me that."

She had her head down and her rich hair fell across her face just as it had done when he had first seen her. The baby sucked and smacked lustily, looking up at him with round blue eyes. Kerrick reached out and held Armun lightly by the chin, raised her face to his. He brushed the hair aside and ran his fingertips down her face, then lightly across her divided lips.

"Like you, I lived a life alone," he said, quietly so only she could hear. "Like you, I was different from all those around me, hated them all. That is all past now. We are together—and we shall never be apart again after I return. That I promise you."

The loving caress on her lips disarmed her, for she knew that he truthfully meant what he had said, that he could look at her face like this without laughing. The tears welled up and she could only nod agreement as he rose and left. She looked at the baby, holding it and rocking it back to sleep, not raising her eyes again until she knew that the hunters were gone.

Herilak led the way up into the hills, staying in the shadow of the trees all the while. He walked at a fast and steady pace and the others followed. They were all strong and fit, had eaten well before the march began. They were bent now under the weight of the burdens on their back, but most of this was food so their packs would become lighter as they went. It was important at this time not to take the time to hunt, but to put as much distance between themselves and the sammads as they could. When the birds flew, as fly they would, their departure must not be noted. They must vanish into the wilderness.

They went on without stopping until it was too dark to see the track, until they were stumbling with fatigue. Only then did Herilak call a halt. He dropped his burden to the ground and the others did the same, grunting with pleasure. Kerrick came and sat next to him and shared his meat. They ate in silence as the darkness thickened and the stars appeared. Above them in the trees an owl called.

"Are they watching us already? Will that owl tell the other birds that we are here?" Herilak asked, concerned.

"No. That is just an owl. The birds that spy us out talk only to the murgu, not to one another. The raptor that saw us yesterday will not have returned to Alpèasak yet, so they still believe that we are camped on the shore. By the time they discover that we have gone and send others to look for us, we will be far distant. They will find the sammads and track them. They will not think to look for us here. Our danger of being seen will only come again when we are close to their city."

"Then it will be too late."

"Yes, then it will be too late for them."

Brave words, Kerrick thought to himself, and smiled wryly in the darkness. Could this little band of hunters really destroy that mighty city with all its teeming inhabitants? It did not seem possible. How many were there here? Less than the count of three hault, the count of three men. Armed with hèsotsan—but so were the Yilanè. Hèsotsan and arrows and spears to fight a powerful race that had filled the world since the egg of time. The impossibility of this brought a darkness to his thoughts even darker than the night around them. How could it be done?

Yet even as he felt these doubtful thoughts his fingers found the wooden chest he had brought with him from the valley. Inside the chest was the stone with the fire trapped inside it. With fire it might be done, could be done—would be done. With this firm resolve, held to him as tightly as he clenched the chest, he lay on his side and was asleep.

"The first birds that we sent out have returned," Vaintè said. "The pictures have been examined and we think that the ustuzou pack from the shore is close to these mountains now, farther to the north."

"You are sure?" Malsas< asked.

"There is never certainty with the ustuzou since one of the creatures is very much like any other. But we do know that they are on the beach no longer, nor are there any packs of them still to the south."

Stallan stayed behind them, silent, listening. No packs had been found, she agreed with that. But nothing still meant nothing. There was something wrong in all this. She had that feeling, a hunter's feeling, but did not know what was causing it. Malsas<, though not a hunter, all unknowingly shared her sense of unease.

"I don't understand it. Why did the beasts make that long march to the shore—then leave almost at once?"

Vaintè moved with uncertainty. "They hunt for food that they must have for the winter. They fish in the sea."

"They had time for little hunting," Stallan said.

"Exactly," Malsas< said. "Then what was their motive in doing this thing? Do they have motives—or do they simply run about like animals? You kept one for a long time, Vaintè, you must know."

"They think. They reason. They have an animal cunning that can be very dangerous. We must never forget the way they killed the fargi on the beaches."

"Your ustuzou escaped, didn't he?" Malsas< asked. "Was it with that pack on the beach?"

Vaintè spoke as calmly as she could. "I believe so. That one is dangerous for it not only has the animal cunning of an ustuzou but some of the learning of Yilanè as well." So Malsas< was spying on her, knew of her interest in the enlarged pictures. That was only to be expected: she would have done the same herself.

"The creature must be destroyed, its skin hung from the thorns."

"My wish as well, Eistaa."

"Then what do you plan to do?"

"As much as I would like to see that one ustuzou destroyed, I think it is of greater importance to kill all the ustuzou. In the end it will accomplish the same thing. All dead, he is dead."

"That is a wise plan. How will you go about implementing it?"

"With the Eistaa's permission I wish to launch a trumal that will end this menace completely."

Malsas< registered appreciation and doubt in equal parts. She had taken part, as they all had, in trumal in the ocean of their youth—when different efenburu joined together, worked together in harmony against a single object. Many times a school of squid would be too large for one efenburu to handle. When they attacked like this the trumal would always end in complete destruction. There would be no survivors.

"I understand your doubt, Eistaa, but it must be done. More fargi must be obtained from the cities of Entoban∗. More uruketo, more weapons. Then we will go north as spring ends, land, move west. Killing them all. By the end of summer we will have reached the mountains and will turn south then to the warm southern sea. Supplies will be brought to us during the winter. When the next spring comes we shall strike west of the mountains. By the following winter this species of ustuzou will be extinct. Not a single pair will be left to breed in some dark and noisome place. That is what I feel must be done."

Malsas< heard this, accepted it. But she was still concerned about the possibility of such an ambitious plan. Could it be done?

She looked at the model, thought of the vast distances, of the ustuzou teeming there. Could they really all be exterminated?

"They all must be killed," she said, answering her own question aloud. "That is what must be done, this fact cannot be escaped. But can it be done this next summer? Would it not be better to send smaller parties, seek out and destroy these packs that we have found?"

"They will hide, they will go north into the frozen lands where we cannot follow. I wish it could be done in that way. But I am afraid that it cannot. An army of fargi, a sweep across the country. An end to this menace."

"What do you say, Stallan?" Malsas< said, turning to the stolid, silent hunter. "You are our killer of ustuzou. Will this plan do what Vaintè says it will do? Shall we attempt it?"

Stallan looked at the immense model, ordering her thoughts so that she could speak them clearly.

"If there is a trumal the ustuzou will die. I do not know if enough force can be gathered together to do it. I do not rule so I cannot say. What I can say is that if the force is strong enough then the trumal will succeed."

There was silence then as Malsas< weighed everything that had been said while the others waited. When she finally spoke it was a command.

"Trumal, sarn'enoto. Destroy the ustuzou."

CHAPTER THIRTY-ONE

"**E**xcuse the interruption of one so hard-working and important by one of little consequence," Krunat said, hesitating as she approached Vaintè.

Vaintè was standing before the model of Gendasi, concentrating and preoccupied, with the coming attack filling her thoughts. Her greeting was an automatic acknowledgment and it took a moment for her to place the intruder. They had met before, yes, this was Krunat, she had taken over from Sòkain in the design of the expansion of the city. It was her assistants who had built this model of Gendasi, and Krunat had helped in the planning. Now she stood before Vaintè, humble as the lowest fargi. She was an excellent designer although she had too low an opinion of her own worth. With an effort Vaintè drew her thoughts away from the campaign plan and forced warmth into her speaking, despite her annoyance at the interruption.

"It is always an honor to speak with Krunat. How may I help you?"

Krunat shuffled the pictures she had brought, humility in every movement of her body.

"First, gratitude of the greatest order, Vaintè, for your development of the bird-picture technique. It has been of the greatest importance in city planning and expansion. My gratitude is endless."

Vaintè permitted herself only a brief sign of acceptance since she did not wish her growing impatience to show. Krunat went slowly through the pictures as she talked.

"To the north of Alpèasak there are pine forests, but the soil is poor and sandy. I have been considering extension of canals to bring water to the area, perhaps the creation of wallows for some of the larger food-beasts. So there have been many pictures made of this area, all of course of no interest to you. Except, perhaps, this one. It could be of little worth, but we are interested in the native life forms for possible exploitation, so I had this one enlarged . . ."

Vaintè's irritation was so great that she dared not speak, but some of her feelings seeped through when she tore the picture roughly from Krunat's thumbs; the designer cringed back.

A single glance changed Vaintè's manner completely. "Good Krunat," she said warmly, "you were right to bring this to me. Can you point out the place on this model where the picture was made?"

As Krunat turned to the model Vaintè examined the picture again. An ustuzou, there could be no doubt, carrying a stone-pointed stick in one paw. This fool had stumbled upon something of importance.

"Here, Vaintè, it is near here that the site of the picture is located."

So close! It was just an ustuzou, an animal, but its presence so far south was annoying. Even worrying. There might be others with it. Yilanè had been murdered before by these creatures near the city. She signaled a fargi to her.

"Bring the hunter Stallan here at once. And for you, wise Krunat, my thanks and the thanks of Alpèasak. This creature is up to no good and it will be taken care of."

Stallan was as concerned by the picture as Vaintè had been. "Is this the only picture?"

"Yes, I went through them all before Krunat took them away."

"The picture is at least two days old," Stallan said, then pointed to the model. "If the ustuzou is still coming south it—or they—could be at this place by now. What are your orders, sarn'enoto?"

"Double the guards around the city. Be sure the alarms are functioning as they should. Then tell me what the terrain is like here. If these creatures are coming towards Alpèasak can you get in front of them, stop them?"

Stallan pointed her joined thumbs at the model, towards the wooded scrubland beyond the city. "Thorn bushes and thick brush here, almost impossible to get through unless the game trails are followed. I know these tracks well. Let the birds fly, the owls will be best, and find where the ustuzou are. When they have been located I will take my best hunters and lay a trap."

"Do that." Vaintè's crest was erect, vibrating. "I think that Kerrick is out there. Only he would have the temerity to come this close to Alpèasak, to bring other ustuzou with him. Kill him for me, Stallan. Bring back his hide. Pin it with thorns to this wall where we can watch it dry."

"Your wish is my wish, Vaintè. I want this death just as you do."

"This is the last of the smoked meat," Kerrick said, using a twig to clear the maggots from the hard lump. "A few of the hunters have ekkotaz left, not very much though."

Herilak chewed firmly on his leathery fragment of meat, maggots and all. "There is game closer to the city. We'll have fresh meat then."

Even here, in the shade of the pine trees, the air was close and hot. Flies buzzed about their heads, landed in the corners of their eyes. It had been a long march, and a tiring one. Yet weary as the hunters were, there were no complaints. Only a few of them were visible beneath the trees, the rest out of sight. But Kerrick knew they were there in the forest, tough and ready. His only fear was that he was leading them to their certain deaths. He had this morbid thought more often now, the closer they came to the city.

"We march," Herilak said, climbing to his feet and slinging his bow over his shoulder where it rested against the hèsotsan in its carrying bag. The big hunter felt more secure with his spear in his hand when they walked.

Kerrick signaled to the nearest hunter who passed on the order. The march began again with Herilak leading as he always did. They followed him across the rolling, brush-covered plain, then along the edge of a tree-hung swamp where stinging insects rose up in swarms. The swamp had its outlet here, through a gorge between low hills. Herilak slowed, nostrils flaring, then signaled a halt. When the command had been passed he walked over and sat by Kerrick under the shade of a willow at the water's edge.

"Did you see the birds ahead? They circled the trees, then flew away without roosting."

"No, Herilak, I never noticed."

"You must notice everything in the forest if you wish to remain alive. Now smell, breathe in deep. What do you smell?"

"Swamp." Kerrick smiled, but Herilak's face remained grim.

"I smell them ahead. Don't turn to look. Murgu."

Kerrick felt his heart beat wildly and it took an effort of will not to turn his head. "You are sure?"

"There is no doubt."

"What do we do?"

"Kill them before they kill us. Stay here. Wait until I send word, then go slowly into the valley. Keep your death-stick ready."

"Do I go in there alone?"

"No. The Sasku will be with you. The hunters will be with me. They know how to stalk."

Herilak slipped silently back along the trail, spoke quickly to the hunter sitting there. They both vanished among the trees. Soon after that Sanone appeared leading his spear-armed Sasku.

"What is happening?" he asked. "Herilak signaled us forward speaking your name. Where have he and the hunters gone?"

"Keep spread out along the trail," Kerrick called out. "Don't bunch up." Then in a lower voice he told Sanone what was happening. The mandukto was not happy.

"Are we bait for a trap then? When we have been killed will their deaths be our vengeance?"

"I think that we can trust Herilak to stalk them among the trees. He has done it before."

They waited in silence, looking around at the dark wall of the jungle that concealed unknown dangers. Something moved and Kerrick raised his weapon before he realized that it was one of Herilak's hunters. The hunter waved them forward before vanishing among the trees again.

Kerrick led the way, trying to ignore the fear that gripped them all. The dark gorge looked menacing; an army of Yilanè might be concealed there. Weapons ready, aimed, about to fire . . . He took step after slow step, clutching the hèsotsan so hard that he felt it stir in his grip.

There was a sudden scream of pain from among the trees, then another, followed instantly by the sharp crackling fire of hèsotsan. Kerrick hesitated, should they go forward? What was happening in the gorge? He waved the Sasku down, ordered them to seek cover and keep their weapons ready.

There was the sound of breaking brush, running footsteps coming towards them. Kerrick raised his weapon as a dark figure came into view under the trees ahead, burst out into the sunlight.

A Yilanè! He aimed, fired, missed when the dart was deflected by a bush. The Yilanè turned and looked at him.

Time stopped. He was close enough to see the rapid rise and fall of her chest as she fought for breath, the wide-gaping mouth and rows of teeth. To look into her face and recognize her. There was recognition in her eyes as well, a change in posture that revealed naked hatred.

The moment ended as one of the Sasku spears slammed into a tree at her side. She dived sideways and vanished between the trees before Kerrick could aim his weapon and shoot again.

"Stallan!" he cried, "It is Stallan!"

He crashed wildly after her, heard the Sasku following him, but stopped again when he saw how thick the undergrowth was. He would never find her in there—though she might find him. He went back to the game trail just as Herilak came trotting up. Soaking in sweat, but smiling and shaking his spear victoriously.

"We hit them from behind, stupid murgu. They lay in hiding and never stirred until we reached them. All are dead."

"All but one. The leader, Stallan. I shot and missed."

"That happens. It does not matter. They know we are here but there is little that they can do about it. But we are warned now and they won't get that close a second time."

"What do we do?"

"Take their death-sticks. Go forward. I think that the battle for this city has begun."

CHAPTER THIRTY-TWO

Vaintè was conferring with Malsas< over details of the planned trumal when they heard the rising sounds of alarm from across the ambesed. Yilanè, turning to look, were brusquely pushed aside by Stallan as she made her way towards the Eistaa. As she came close the reason for the disturbance was obvious. Her skin was scratched and filthy with mud; some of the cuts still ran with blood. She came on until she stood before Malsas<—then slumped in defeat. This in itself was shocking for no one had ever seen her other than erect and proud. They listened in silence as she spoke.

"Disaster, Eistaa. All dead. I alone have returned."

"I do not understand. Dead, how?"

Stallan raised her head and her back straightened with anger. "I set a trap. We were to kill the ustuzou when they came close. But they are animals, I should have known better. They came behind us and we were not even aware that they were there. Every hunter and fargi, killed. I fled. If I had stayed to fight I would be dead. You would not know what happened. I have told you. Now I die for I am shamed. You have only to speak the words, Eistaa . . ."

"*No!*" Vaintè called out as loudly as she could, angry and demanding, the negation rude in its intensity. Stallan gaped, alarmed, her death request forgotten for the moment. Even Malsas< reacted only with shock at this interruption. Vaintè spoke quickly then, before surprise turned to anger.

"I mean no insult, Eistaa. I spoke as I did only to save the life of Stallan. Do not command her to die. She is too loyal to the city, the city must be loyal to her. I ordered her to take her hunters and trap the ustuzou. If there is blame then the blame is mine. We need this brave fighter. The deaths were not her fault. We war with the ustuzou. Do not let her die for taking that war to them. I know I spoke in haste. I now await your judgement."

Vaintè stood with lowered head. She had taken a terrible risk speaking out like this and might very well die herself for her temerity. But Stallan was too valuable to lose now. Stallan, the only Yilanè who had greeted her when she was the outcast within this city.

Malsas< looked at the two figures bent before her and considered what they both had said. In the silence the only sound was the shuffling rasp of feet as every Yilanè in the ambesed pressed forward to listen. A decision must be made.

"You spoke with crude haste, Vaintè. At any other time that would have been unforgivable and your death would have followed. But I smell too many other deaths in the wind and I would have you live to defend Alpèasak, just as you would have Stallan do the same. There is need for you both. Now tell me the meaning of this cruel event."

"First my thanks, Eistaa. Like Stallan I live only to serve Alpèasak. The meaning is clear, and the meaning of past events are clear as well. An armed and dangerous force of ustuzou marches on Alpèasak. They must be stopped. The meaning of the visit by the creatures to the coast is now known as well. It was a ruse to distract us. When they returned to the mountains they separated and this pack of savage animals came south, secretly, determined. As soon as I found out about their presence hunters were sent to attack them. We were defeated. It must be our last defeat or I fear for our city."

Malsas< was shocked by her words. "What harm can these beasts cause to Alpèasak?"

"I do not know—but I fear. The determination of their advance, the strength of their attack causes that fear. Would they dare risk so much if they did not plan damage of some kind? We must see to our defenses."

"That we must do." Malsas< turned to Stallan. "I understand

even more why Vaintè risked her own life to save yours. You were the one who designed the defenses of this city, Stallan, is that not true?"

"It is, Eistaa."

"Then strengthen them, reinforce them. You speak for the Eistaa. Demand anything you need. The safety of our city is between your thumbs."

"I shall not let it slip, Eistaa. With your permission I shall see to it now."

Malsas< looked after her retreating back with confusion and disbelief. "It is hard to understand affairs in this new land of Gendasi. Nothing is as it was in Entoban*. The natural order has been violated with ustuzou killing Yilanè. Where will this end, Vaintè? Do you know?"

"I know only that we will fight these creatures. And we must win."

Yet try as hard as she could, Vaintè still could not keep the movements of doubt from what she said. All there could see the fear clearly in what she said.

Herilak held up his arm when he heard the shrill scream from the forest ahead. The hunters stopped as well—then looked around in fear as the scream echoed again: a heavy thudding shook the ground beneath their feet.

"Do you know what that is?" Herilak asked.

"I think that I do," Kerrick said. "Go forward slowly now because the first fields should be just ahead."

The trees were close together here and the game trail that they were following wound between them. Herilak led the way with Kerrick close behind him. The thudding sounded again and more screams—then Kerrick called out.

"Stop here! See those vines ahead, across the trail? They stick to the skin and can't be pulled off. I was caught by them once. Warn the others. We are at the outermost fringes of the city now."

They went forward cautiously, though any sounds they might have made would surely have been drowned out by the tumult in the meadow ahead. At the forest edge they stopped and looked with awe at the open field beyond.

Two immense creatures, each larger than the largest mastodon, were circling each other in the high grass, while a third looked on. Their wrinkled hide was yellowish-brown, their wide heads were heavily armored, while blood-red, bony plates covered their backs. One of them lunged at the other, snapping a horny, toothless beak, screaming loudly. The other turned sideways, swinging its tail around so that the great bony club at its tip lashed out. It hit the earth with a ground-shaking thud as the first creature moved aside to avoid it.

"Ruutsa," Kerrick said. "They do that when they are fighting over a mate. That's the female, there, eating grass. I know this field—I know where we are!"

He stamped a flat spot into black soil, then bent and scratched lines on it with the tip of his stone knife.

"Herilak, look—this is what the city is like. They have a model there that I have studied so long that I know it by heart, even now. This is what it looks like. The sea is here, these are the beaches, then the wall. Here is the ambesed, a big empty space where they all meet."

Herilak watched intently as Kerrick sketched the city, then the fields about it.

"The fields surround the city in circles, wider and wider, and the ruutsa are right here."

Herilak looked closely at the scratched lines, tugging at his beard in thought. "Are you sure that is where we are? It has been a long time since you left this place, they might have changed the fields, moved the beasts around."

"Never, not the Yilanè. What is, is, and never changes. Little things may be different from day to day, but once a thing is set it is that way forever."

"Then I believe you, since you are the only one who knows the murgu so well. . ."

A cry of pain cut him off and they turned to see one of the Sasku hunters rear up, then fall heavily to the ground. They ran to his aid and Herilak reached to tear the thorn-tipped vine from his arm: Kerrick stopped him.

"Don't touch that—or you are dead too. It is too late to help him. The poison is in his body."

The Sasku's back arched with pain and there was foam on his lips, pink with blood where he had bitten his tongue. He was paralyzed and unconscious—but it took him a long time to die.

"Unless you want this kind of death, don't let anything touch you until we are well inside the fields," Kerrick said. "Watch where you walk, don't brush against any kind of plant. Some of the vines will stick to you, or as you have just seen—others will kill."

"Is all of the city like this?" Herilak asked.

"No, just the outer edge. To keep marauding animals—and Tanu—away. Once we get past this barrier the only danger will be from armed guards. They are protected and hidden behind walls and may be hard to see."

"But they must sleep at night," Herilak said.

"They must, but there may be night alarms here now. We will find their positions and stay well clear of them."

"What is the plan then?"

Kerrick went back to the diagram on the ground and pointed to the outer circle. "We must get past these fields. Most of these creatures, grass-eating ones like the ruutsa in this field, won't attack unless they are disturbed."

He lifted his head and sniffed the air. "The wind is from the west, so we must circle around to this spot, to have the wind behind our backs. Once past the fields the trees of the city begin. They are close together there. Once the fire starts and spreads there will be nothing to stop it."

"Is there any dry wood to be found there?" Herilak asked.

"No, I don't think so."

"Then we will search for it now, take it with us."

"Wait until we have reached the fields to the west of the city. The wood can be collected then, everything made ready. We want to get through the outer barrier around sunset. All of the Yilanè, other than the guards in their outposts, will have returned to the city by then so we will not be seen. We will avoid the guards and reach the place where the trees begin by dark. Then we will start our fires."

All three ruutsa were grazing quietly when they left, their battle forgotten.

It was late afternoon before they had worked their way around the outermost fields. None of the game trails seemed to go in the right direction, so they had to force their way through the groves of trees and thick, tangled undergrowth. When they came to a sluggish stream Kerrick called a halt, then passed the word for them to gather together. The water ran clear towards the center of the stream so they waded out there to drink. When they had drunk their fill Kerrick told them what was to be done, stopping often to translate his orders to the Sasku. They all listened with grim attention for this was journey's end. Victory or certain death.

They listened intently, not noticing while he was talking that the sky was clouding over. Kerrick broke off as a few drops of rain struck his skin.

Herilak looked up at the sky and scowled. "If it rains then we cannot attack—for the city will not burn."

"It is still the dry season," Kerrick said, with more assurance than he felt. "This won't last." He did not dare consider what they would do if it did rain.

They spread out to find dry wood, glancing apprehensively at the sky as they went. It stayed dark and the wind increased; thunder rumbled on the horizon.

"We cannot wait until evening," Herilak said. "We must start the fires before it rains."

"There will be murgu about, we may be seen."

"A risk we will have to take. Help me prepare a way through the thorn barrier while the others find wood."

They tore thick branches from the trees and pressed them down over the tangled and poisonous vines. In the open field beyond great duck-billed creatures looked at them with widened eyes, before they bounded away. Herilak trampled down the branches and crossed first, waving the others after him as they came back with the dry wood.

They gathered inside this barrier and waited until all had returned. Only then did they start forward warily with Kerrick leading the way. After all this time he had returned to Alpèasak. Overhead the thunder rumbled closer and he broke into a run as the first drops of the coming storm spattered on his shoulders.

CHAPTER THIRTY-THREE

The baby slung on Armun's back was awake and crying unhappily, soaked and chilled by the driving rain. Kneeling on the ground she was wet through herself, cold, black with mud on her arms and legs where she had been digging up the bulbs with her sharp stick. Lightning flared briefly in the sky and the crack of thunder that came immediately after it hurt her ears. Ermanpadar was displeased with something. It was time to return to the tents. The baby wailed even louder as she picked up the basket of bulbs and rose to her feet.

Something moved through the rain above and she looked up to see the bird silently floating by on widespread wings. It put out its legs and landed heavily on the high branch, then sat looking down at her with cold eyes set above its cruel, hooked bill. Armun could see the black bulge on its leg and she turned and ran with terror through the trees. Thunder, lightning, and the bird that told the murgu where they were. Fear choked her as she fled to the safety of the tents.

Vaintè was looking at the model of Alpèasak when the fargi brought her the word that an uruketo was coming into the harbor. She dismissed the messenger with a sharp movement of her arms, but her concentration had been broken. Looking at the model of the city did not help. The defenses were strong and Stallan was strengthening them. There were no weak spots that she could see, no places where the ustuzou could do any harm, other than killing some of the meat animals. She was only irritating herself standing here.

She would go greet the uruketo and see what cargo it held. More fargi were on their way from Entoban* as well as hèsotsan of increased power. Many of the cities of that great continent were responding with aid. Her army would be strong, the ustuzou would die.

When she reached the open way she was aware for the first time of the banked-up clouds and the distant rumble of thunder. There was the sudden patter of large raindrops around her. It looked as though a storm was on the way. It was no concern of hers; she had far more important matters to think about.

Krunat followed the group of fargi down the dusty path, her assistant hurrying behind with a bundle of wooden stakes. Each one of the fargi carried a young fruit tree from the nursery, roots balled and ready for planting. This time Krunat was going along with the working party to make absolutely sure that the trees were planted where they belonged. Some of the Yilanè in this city were as stupid as fargi, forgetting instructions and botching the simplest jobs. She had found a number of fields and plantations that did not match the model at all and had had to make corrections. Not this time. She would put in the markers herself and make absolutely sure that the trees were planted where they belonged. She rolled one eye up towards the darkening sky. It looked as though it might rain. Good, fine for the new trees.

A turning in the track took them to the edge of a green field. A line of fargi were coming across the grass towards them. That was Krunat's first thought—but there was something wrong about them. They were too tall, too thin. Fur on them.

She halted, frozen with shock. Ustuzou here, in the city? It was not possible. Her assistant passed her just as the sharp crack of hèsotsan sounded across the field.

Fargi curled, fell, her assistant dropped the stakes with a clatter as a dart caught her in the side. Krunat turned in panic, ran back into the safety of the trees. She knew the city well, there were guards near by, they must be warned.

* * *

"One of them is getting away, there!" Herilak called out, starting forward.

"No time!" Kerrick called out. "We don't have much farther to go—and we must start the fire before the rain comes."

He ran now, gasping for breath, with the tired hunters running behind him. That row of trees ahead, that would be the place. He heard hèsotsan being fired behind him but he dared not look, ran on.

He stumbled and dropped beneath the tall oak tree, threw down his weapons, and dragged the carved box from the bag at his waist. There was more firing and loud shouting as Herilak ran up.

"They know we are here. Killed some, so did they. They are back in the trees now and we're holding them."

"Get me the branches," Kerrick called out, forcing himself to move slowly as he knelt and took the fire stones from the box. When he took out a pinch of dried wood as well a sudden gust of wind blew it from his hand; raindrops spattered on the leaves above. A length of branch was dropped beside him, then another.

Slowly, go slowly! It must be done right the first time because there would be no second chance. With trembling hands he placed the wooden box on the ground, spilled all of the dried wood dust inside it. Stone against stone now, struck sharply together, just as he had done it countless times before. The long sparks shot out, again and again.

A thin curl of blue smoke drifted up from the box.

He bent over, blew on it gently, added the flakes of dried leaves to the tiny glow, blew again. A thin red flame flared brightly. Bit by bit he added all of the leaves, then dug the bits of bark and twig from his bag. Only when all of these were burning brightly did he risk looking up.

There were bodies behind him in the field, Tanu and Yilanè both. Not as many as he had feared. Herilak had driven the attackers away and had placed hunters as guards. They were crouching behind trees, weapons ready, preventing the murgu from coming back. Herilak hurried towards Kerrick now, his face running with sweat, smiling widely at the sight of the blaze.

The wooden box itself was burning when Kerrick pushed it into the stacked wood, then piled thicker branches on top. Heat flared out and drops of rain sizzled as they fell into the fire. He dared not look up at the approaching storm as he built the fire higher and higher. Only when the lengths of wood were burning brightly, the heat of them forcing him to keep his arm before his face, did he cry out as loudly as he could.

"Now! Everyone—to the fire! The city burns!"

His shout brought excited cheers, running feet. Branches were pulled out, carried away, crackling sparks falling in their wake. Kerrick seized up a branch himself and ran into the thicket, pushing it before him among the dry leaves. They smoldered and smoked—then burst into bright flame. He moved on, lighting other bushes, until the heat drove him back and the smoking branch burnt his hand. He threw it through the flames into the trees beyond.

All along the edge of the grove shouting hunters were setting more and more trees alight. Flames were already shooting up through the branches of the oak before him, jumping to the next tree. A single branch remained in the fire that he had lit and Kerrick grabbed it up and ran with it, past the others. Past Sanone at the far end who was in among the trees, firing them. Kerrick went on a good distance before he jabbed the torch into the undergrowth. The wind whipped the sparks away and in an instant the brush was alight.

Flame and smoke were shooting high into the air now, roiling darkly against the already darkened sky. The trees crackled and blazed, thunder rumbled. The storm had still not broken.

The fargi were having difficulty in rounding up the beasts for the daily slaughter. Something was disturbing them, they kept rushing from one side of the pen to the other, even knocking down one of the fargi, their eyes rolling so that they shone whitely. The Yilanè in charge was shouting loud orders to no avail. She was suddenly aware of a crackling noise and a strange, pungent smell. She turned about to see the sheets of sunlight climbing skywards, black stormclouds behind them. The smell came again, and a wave of warm and delightful air. What was happening, what could this mean? She could only stand and stare as the flames came close, licking at the nearby trees. Wonderfully warm. The animals were screaming behind her as she walked over and held her hand to the warmth and light. Then she screamed as well.

Ikemend opened the hanalè door a crack and looked out. Akotolp made a peremptory gesture of command, ordering her to open it wide.

"First you send for me—then you block my way," the fat scientist said, her jowls waggling at the affront. "Admit me at once."

"I abase myself," Ikemend said, ushering Akotolp in, then sealing the entrance behind her. "The males have been quarreling again, it is the weather perhaps. There is an injury. . ."

"Bring the creature here at once."

The firmness in her voice and the abrupt movements of her body sent Ikemend scurrying away. She returned almost at once pulling a truculent Esetta∗ after her.

"This is the one," she said, pushing the male forward. "Starts fights, causes trouble, got what he deserves."

Akotolp ignored this as she seized Esetta∗'s arm and turned it over to examine it. Her thumbs gave an extra squeeze when she did this and Esetta∗, his back turned to the guardian, half-closed one eye in a sultry gesture. Akotolp always enjoyed these visits to the hanalè.

"Scratches, nothing more, antiseptic will take care of this. Males will be males. . ." She broke off suddenly and raised her head, her nostril flaps opening wide as she sniffed the air.

"That smell—I know that smell," she said, agitation and worry in the movements of her limbs. She hurried to the outer door and opened it despite Ikemend's protests. The smell was stronger now, the air filled with it.

"Smoke," Akotolp called out, worry and concern strongly present. "Smoke comes from one chemical reaction only—fire."

Esetta∗ drew back trembling at the strength of Akotolp's feelings, while Ikemend could only signal stupidity and lack of understanding. The smoke thickened suddenly and a distant crackling could be heard. There was now urgency and the necessity for speed in Akotolp's command.

"There is a reaction called fire and we could be in danger. Assemble the males at once, quickly, they must be taken from here."

"I have no orders!" Ikemend wailed.

"I am ordering it. A matter of urgent health-need, threat of death. Bring them all, follow me, to the shore, to the ocean."

Ikemend did not hesitate, but hurried away at once. Akotolp paced back and forth, worried and concerned, unaware that she still held Esetta∗'s trembling arm and dragged the frightened male after

her. A gust of wind sent smoke roiling through the open door that
started them both coughing.

"We cannot wait," Akotolp said. "Follow!" she called out
loudly, hoping the sound could be understood, then hauled the
wailing Esetta* after her.

When Ikemend came back into the corridor, the reluctant
males trailing after her, she experienced great satisfaction when she
saw that it was empty. She hurried to close and seal the outer
door, ordering the males back to their quarters, relieved that there
was no longer a conflict of orders. What place could be safer than
the hanalè?

A warmth began to penetrate the walls which was most sooth-
ing and satisfying. She only felt a pang of fear when the first flames
burnt through the entrance.

It was late by then to do anything to save her charges. She died
with their pained cries in her ears.

Alpèasak burned. The wind-whipped fire sprang from tree to
tree, the leaves of one igniting the leaves of the other. The shrub-
bery below blazed up, the walls, the floor matting, everything
caught fire, everything burned.

For the Yilanè it was an inconceivable disaster, a physical fact
that they could not understand. There is no natural fire in a tropical
rain forest so they had no knowledge at all of fire. Some of their
scientists did, but only as an interesting laboratory phenomenon.
But not like this, nothing like this. For here was smoke and flame,
burning on all sides. Attractive at first, an enjoyable source of heat,
then an inescapable pain. So they died. Burnt, consumed, blackened.
The fire swept on.

Confused, fearful, the Yilanè and fargi converged on the
ambesed, seeking guidance. They filled it to bursting yet still more
came, pressing forward until the great open area was jammed solid.
They sought advice from Malsas<, pressed close to her, were pushed
against her until she ordered them back. Those closest tried to
obey, but to no avail against the panic-stricken hordes behind.

There was even greater panic when the flames reached the
ambesed. The crowded Yilanè could not escape; they crushed back
in fear. Malsas<, like many others, was trampled and dead long
before the flames swept over her.

In the sky above the storm still rumbled distant thunder; the
clouds built up in darkened mountains. There was salvation there,

though the Yilanè were not aware of it. Never having seen fire they had no knowledge that water could stop it.

Alpèasak died, the Yilanè died. From the fields to the ocean the flames raced, burning everything before them. The clouds of smoke rose up to the black clouds in the sky and the roar and crackle of the flames drowned the cries of the dying.

The hunters sprawled on the ground, blackened by the fire, exhausted. The armed Yilanè they had been battling had either been killed or driven back into the flames. The fighting was over—the war was over, but they were too tired to understand this yet. Only Kerrick and Herilak stood, swaying with fatigue but still standing.

"Will there be survivors?" Herilak asked, leaning heavily on his spear.

"I don't know, possibly."

"They must be killed as well."

"Yes, I suppose so."

Kerrick was suddenly sickened by the destruction of Alpèasak. In his need for revenge he had not only killed the Yilanè—but this wonderful city as well. He remembered the pleasure he had taken in exploring it, in discovering its secrets. Talking with the males in the hanalè, watching the myriad animals that filled its pastures. No more, gone. If there had been a way to kill the Yilanè and save the city he would have taken it. There had been no way. The Yilanè were dead and so was Alpèasak.

"Where will they be?" Herilak asked and Kerrick could only gape, too tired to make out his meaning. "The survivors. You said there might be some."

"Yes. But not in the city—that is gone. Some in the fields with the animals perhaps. On the shore, the beaches, they might have survived there. When the flames die down we can go see."

"That will take too long. I have seen forest fires before. The big trees will smolder and burn for days. Can we get to the beaches along the shore?"

"Yes, there are sandbanks most of the way, all of them exposed at low tide."

Herilak looked at the sprawled hunters, then grunted and sat down himself. "A short rest first, then we go on." Above him lightning flashed and thunder rumbled distantly. "Ermanpadar likes the murgu as much as we do. He holds back the rain."

When they finally went on they skirted the blackened, smoking trees, then made their way beyond them through the unburnt fields and pastures. Though the smoke had disturbed them at first, the animals in the fields here now grazed quietly. Deer bounded away at their approach and gigantic horned and plated creatures watched them pass with little curiosity. When they came to a stream of fresh water they found it covered with floating ash; the hunters had to push it aside to drink. The stream led down to the sea.

The tide was out and they could walk along firm, cool sand, the ocean to one side, the blackened, smoking ruins of Alpèasak on the other. They went with weapons ready, but there was none to oppose them. When they rounded a headland they stopped. There was a river ahead and something large and black just barely visible through the drifting smoke, coming in from the sea.

"An uruketo!" Kerrick called out. "It is going towards the harbor. There may still be some of them alive there, near the river." He broke into a run and the others hurried after him.

Stallan looked at the bodies of the Yilanè, sprawled on the river bank or floating in the water. She pushed one that lay nearby with her foot; the fargi rolled over, eyes closed and mouth gaping, barely breathing.

"Look at them," Stallan said, disgust and repugnance in every movement. "I brought them here, forced them to safety in the water—and still they die. They close their stupid eyes, roll back their heads, and die."

"Their city is dead," Vaintè said wearily. "So they are dead. They have been cast out. There are your deathless ones if you wish to see who lives." Her movements were rich with disgust when she indicated the group of Yilanè standing knee-deep in the river.

"The Daughters of Death," Stallan said, her disgust just as clear. "That is all that remains of Alpèasak? Just those?"

"You forget us, Stallan."

"I remember that you and I are here—but I do not understand why we are not dead with the rest."

"We live because we hate too much. Hate the ustuzou who did this. Now we know why they came here. They brought their fire and they have burned our city. . ."

"There, look, a uruketo! Coming towards the beach."

Vaintè looked at the dark form slipping through the waves. "I ordered them away when the fire came close, told them to return when it was gone."

Enge saw the uruketo as well and left the other survivors and waded ashore. Vaintè saw her coming and chose to ignore her attitude of inquiry. When Enge saw this she stood before Vaintè and spoke.

"What of us, Vaintè? The uruketo comes close yet you choose not to speak to us."

"That is my choice. Alpèasak is dead and I wish you all dead as well. You will remain here."

"A harsh judgement, Vaintè, to those who have never harmed you. Harshly spoken to one's efenselè."

"I disown you, want no part of you. It was you who sowed weakness among the Yilanè when we needed all of our strength. Die here."

Enge looked at her efenselè, at Vaintè who had been the strongest and best, and rejection and distaste were in every line of her body.

"You whose hatred has destroyed Alpèasak, you disown me? I accept that and say that everything that has been between us will be no more. Now it is I who disown you and will obey you no longer."

She turned her back on Vaintè and saw the uruketo close offshore, called out to the Daughters.

"We leave here. Swim to the uruketo."

"Kill them, Stallan!" Vaintè screeched. "Shoot them down."

Stallan turned and raise her hèsotsan, ignoring Enge's cries of pain, aimed, and fired dart after dart at the swimming Yilanè. Her aim was good and one after another was hit and sank beneath the water. Then the hèsotsan was empty and she lowered it and looked about for more darts.

The survivors had reached the uruketo, the scientist, Akotolp, and a male among them, when Enge turned away. "You bring only death, Vaintè," she said. "You have become a creature of death. If it were possible I would abandon all of my beliefs just to end your life."

"Do it then," Vaintè said mockingly, turning and raising her head so the skin was taut on her neck. "Bite. You have teeth. Do it."

Enge swayed forward, then back, for she could not kill, not even one so deserving of death as Vaintè.

Vaintè lowered her head, began to speak—but was stopped by Stallan's harsh cry.

"Ustuzou!"

Vaintè spun about, saw them running towards her waving hèsotsan and pointed sticks. With instant decision she closed her thumbs and clubbed Enge to the ground with her fist. "Stallan," she called out as she dove towards the water, "to the uruketo."

This was what Kerrick saw as he ran up the river bank. The dead Yilanè on all sides, the living in the water. A single one standing, looking towards them, a Yilanè he would never forget.

"Don't shoot!" he called out loudly, then again in Sasku. "That marag is mine." Then he spoke in Yilanè as he went on, his meaning blurred by his running but still clear.

"It is I, Stallan, the ustuzou who hates you and means to kill you. Do you flee, great coward, or do you wait for me?"

Stallan did not need these taunts, barely heard them. For her the sight of Kerrick's running figure was enough. This was the creature she hated more than anything else in the world, the ustuzou that had destroyed Alpèasak. She dropped the empty hèsotsan and roaring with rage she charged at him.

Kerrick raised his spear, his hèsotsan forgotten, pushed it hard at Stallan's body. But Stallan knew wild animals well and moved aside so it slipped past her harmlessly, hurled herself on Kerrick and bore him to the ground. Her thumbs clutched into his hair and pulled his head back. Her solid muscles were rock-hard, he struggled but could not move. Straight at his neck she lunged, jaws gaped wide, rows of pointed teeth plunging down to tear his life out.

Herilak's spear hummed past, caught Stallan full in the mouth, in between her jaws and into her brain. She was dead even before she slumped to the ground. Kerrick pushed her gross weight from him and climbed shakily to his feet.

"Well thrown, Herilak," he said.

"Get down, move aside!" Herilak shouted in return, tearing his bow from his shoulder. Kerrick turned about and saw Enge climbing to her feet.

"Put your bow up," Kerrick ordered. "All of you, lower your weapons. This one will not hurt me."

There was a heavy splatter of raindrops, then more and more, then a downpour of rain. The threatening storm had finally broken. Too late to save the city of Alpèasak. Now it thundered down, a heavy tropical rain, hissing into clouds of steam when it struck into the smoldering ruins.

"You have brought us death, Kerrick," Enge said, her voice loud enough to be heard above the hammering rain, sorrow in her every movement.

"No, Enge, you are wrong about that. I have brought life to my ustuzou, because without me creatures like this dead meat before me would have killed us all. Now she is dead and Alpèasak is dead. That uruketo will leave and the last of you will be gone. I will bring my ustuzou here and it will be our city. You will go back to Entoban* and you will stay there. They will remember with fear what happened here and will never come back. You will remind them about the death here. See that they never forget it. Tell them how they all burned and died. The Eistaa, her advisors, Vaintè . . ."

"Vaintè is there," Enge said, indicating the ship. Kerrick looked but could not tell her from the others who were climbing onto the creature's broad and wet back. She had not died after all. The one he hated the most, still alive. Yes, he hated her—then why this sudden feeling of pleasure that she had not died?

"Go to her," he shouted, the loud words drowning out his mixed feelings. "Tell her what I have told you. Any Yilanè that comes here again shall die here. Tell her that."

"Can I not tell her that the killing is over? That there is life now, not death? That would be best."

He signed a simple negative. "I had forgotten that you were a Daughter of Life. Go tell her, tell them all that if they had listened to you all the dead in Alpèasak would now be alive. But it is too late for peace now, Enge, even you must realize that. There is hatred and death between us, nothing more."

"Between ustuzou and Yilanè, yes, but not between us, Kerrick."

He started to protest. There could only be hatred. This cold creature could mean nothing to him. He should raise his spear and kill it right now. But he could not. He smiled crookedly.

"That is true, teacher. I will remember that there is at least one marag I have no desire to kill. Now go with that uruketo and do not return. I will remember you when I have forgotten all of them. Go in peace."

"Peace to you as well, Kerrick. And peace between ustuzou and Yilanè as well."

"No. Simple hatred and a wide ocean. As long as you stay on your side you will have your peace. Go."

Enge slipped into the water and he leaned on his spear, drained of all emotion, and watched as she swam to the uruketo and climbed aboard. Then, as the uruketo moved out to sea he felt a great weariness pass over him.

It was over, ended, through. Alpèasak was gone and all with her.

His thoughts went to the mountains to the north, to the circle of hide tents in a bend of the river. Armun was there waiting for him. Herilak came slowly to his side and he turned to the big hunter and took him by the arms.

"It is done, Herilak. You have had your vengeance, we have all had ours. Let us take our spears and go north before winter comes.

"Let us go home."

THE WORLD
WEST OF EDEN

YILANÈ

Translator's Note: The following section has been translated from Yilanè, an exercise that poses formidable problems. Of necessity the translation must be a "free" one and the translator apologizes in advance for any errors or discrepancies that may have crept into the text.

HISTORY OF THE WORLD

It must be pointed out at the very beginning of this particular history that it differs from many 'histories' currently popular. It differs in *kind*, a fact that the judicious reader must always take into consideration. For far too long Yilanè history has been the province of the fabulist and the dreamer. Whereas the intelligent Yilanè would be offended at any guesswork or wild speculation in a physics or a biological text, the same reader will allow any sort of imaginary excess in a work of history. A perfect example of fiction purporting to be fact is the currently popular *history* of this world that describes how a giant meteor struck the Earth 75* million years ago and wiped out 85 percent of the species then alive. It goes on to explain in great detail the manner in which warm-blooded creatures developed and became the dominant life forms on this planet. This sort of thing is what the present authors deplore; wild speculation instead of accurate historical research. No meteor of that size ever struck the Earth. The world as we see it is the world as it always has been, always will be, world without end. It is necessary therefore, in the light of other works of this nature, that we define the term *history* before we can proceed.

History, as it is known today, is far too often a very inexact science, so inexact that it is more fiction than fact, more speculation than presentation. This is due to intrinsic aspects of the Yilanè nature. We care little where we have been—but we know exactly where we are going. We are happy with changes of a short duration while, at the same time, we demand that the future shall be as the present, changeless and

---

*For those readers not acquainted with large mathematical terms, see page 466 for a complete description.

unchangeable. Since this need for long-term continuity is essential to our very nature we tend to feel unhappy about the past because it might have contained long-term changes that we would find offensive. Therefore we refer vaguely to 'the egg of time' and assume in doing so that this was when the world was born, whole and new—and changeless ever since.

Which is, of course, nonsense. The moment has now arrived in Yilanè history to declare that history as we have known it is worthless. We could have referred to this present work as new-history, but refrain since this gives an element of credence to the 'old-history'. We therefore reject all other works of history to this date and declare that there is now only one history. This one.

In creating this history we are grateful for the very few Yilanè with an interest in the sciences of geology and paleontology. We wish to honor these sciences and declare them true ones, just as true as physics or chemistry, and not the subjects of sly laughter as they have been up to now. The past existed, no matter how much we might like to ignore this unpleasant fact. We feel that it is intellectually more courageous to admit it and accept this fact, to admit that the Yilanè did not appear suddenly when the egg of time cracked open. This is the true history and a far more exciting and fulfilling one.

Permit us one more slight divergence before this history begins. We do not intend to go back to the absolute beginning and the birth of prokaryote life. That story has been unfolded in far greater detail in other works. Our history begins about 270 million years BP (before the present) when the reptiles were already well established in their dominant role on Earth.

At that time there were four main groups of socket-toothed reptiles that are referred to as thecodonts. These primitive creatures were equipped for a life of hunting for their prey in the water. They swam easily by moving their sizable tails. Some of these thecodonts left the sea and went to the land where their manner of walking proved superior to many other creatures like the proterosuchians, the ancestors of the present day crocodiles. You have seen the clumsy way that crocodiles walk, with their feet widespread, waddling along with their body actually hanging between their legs. Not so the superior thecodonts who thrust their entire limbs down and back with an upright stride.

Since the history of those days is written only in rocks, in the fossils preserved there, we find many gaps. While the details to fill these gaps may not be present, the overall record is still amazingly clear. Our remote ancestors were creatures called mososaurs, marine lizards of a very successful nature. They were specialized for their life in the sea with a tail fin, while their limbs had modified into flippers. One particular form of mososaur was *Tylosaurus*, a large and handsome creature. Large, in that the *Tylosaurus* were greater in length than six Yilanè. Handsome in that they resembled the Yilanè in many ways. The reason for this is that they were our direct ancestors.

If we place a representation of the skeleton of a modern Yilanè beside the skeleton of a *Tylosaurus* the relationship is immediately obvious. The digits of the limbs, hidden by the superficial flesh of the fins, reveal four fingers and four toes. So now we have two fingers on each hand and two opposed thumbs. The tail is our tail, suitably shortened. The resemblance is also clear in the rib cage, a flowing wave of ribs from clavicle to pelvic girdle. Look at these two similar skeletons and you see past and present, side by side. There we are, developed and modified to dwell on land. There is our true history, not some vague statement about appearing from the egg of time. We are the descendants of these noble creatures who some 40 million years ago became the Yilanè.

THE EARLY YEARS

Much of what follows is of necessity guesswork. But it is *appropriate* guesswork that fits the facts of the fossil records, not flights of fancy such as imaginary giant meteors. The record in the rocks is there to be read. We simply assemble the parts and fit them together, just as you might reassemble the broken pieces of an eggshell.

If you wish to assemble all of the pieces yourself, then consult the relevant geological and paleontological texts. In them you will discover the origin of species, how earlier species are modified to become later ones, and you will find revealed the history of the various ice ages, the phenomenon of continental drift, even the record sealed in rock that the magnetic pole was not always to the south, the way it is now, but has varied between north and south through the geological ages. You could do all of this for yourself—or you can be satisfied with our description in abbreviated form.

See then the world as it must have been 40 million years BP when the first simple and happy Yilanè roamed the Earth. It was a wetter and warmer world, with all the food they needed there for the taking. Then, as now, the Yilanè were carnivores, feasting on the flesh of the creatures that filled the land and the sea. The young, then as now, gathered in efenburu in the sea and worked together and ate well. What happened when they emerged on land is not clear in the geological record and we can only guess.

Having learned cooperation in the sea, the Yilanè certainly would not lose it when they emerged from the ocean and walked on solid ground. Then, as now, the males were surely the same simple, kindly creatures and would have needed protection. Then, as now, the beaches would have been guarded while the males were torpid, the eggs growing. Food was plentiful, life was good. Surely this was the true egg of time, not the imaginary one, when life was simple and serene.

In that early existence can be found the seeds of Yilanè science as we know it today. It can be seen in the Wall of Thorns here in this city. To defend the males, large crustacea were seized and brandished at predators, their claws a powerful defense. The bigger the claws, the more powerful the defense, so the largest would have been selected. At the same time the strongest and most offensive corals would have been chosen to defend the beaches from the seaward side. The first crude steps along the road to the advanced biological science we now know would have been mastered.

But this simple existence was doomed to end. As successful Yilanè grew strong and filled the Earth they would have outgrown that first city on the edge of that ancient sea. Another city would have grown, another and another. When food shortages threatened, the logical thing would have been to wall in fields and raise food animals and guard them from predators.

In doing this the Yilanè proved their superiority to the inferior life forms. Look at Tyrannosaurus, a carnivore just as we are carnivores. Yet these giant, stupid creatures can only pursue with violence, tear down their prey, waste most of the good meat on its carcass. They never think of tomorrow, they neither tend herds nor do they cull. They are witless destroyers. The superior Yilanè are intelligent preservers. To a scientist all life forms are equal. To destroy a species is to destroy our own species. Our respect for life can be seen in the manifold beasts in our fields, species that would have vanished millennia ago had it not been for our efforts. We are builders, not destroyers; preservers, not consumers. It is obvious when these facts are considered why we are the dominant species on this planet. It is no accident; it is only the logical end product of circumstance.

PHYSIOLOGY

In order to understand our own physiology we must first consider the physiology of other animals. Simple creatures, like most insects, are poikilothermic. That is, they are at one with their environment; their body temperatures are the same as the ambient air temperature.

While this suffices on a small scale, more complex organisms require regularization of body temperature. These animals are homeothermic, that is, they have a body temperature that is relatively constant and mostly independent of the temperature of the environment. The Yilanè belong to the kind of animals that are warm-blooded and exothermic. All of the important animals in the world are exothermic since this way of controlling body temperature is far superior to that used by the ustuzou who must expend energy continually in order to maintain the same body temperature at all times.

We are one with our environment, utilizing the natural temperature differences to maintain the consistency of our own body temperatures. After a cool night we seek the sun; if we grow too warm we face into the breeze, expose less of our bodies to the sun, erect our crests or even seek the shade. We do this so automatically that we are no more aware of regulating our internal temperature than we are of breathing.

There are many other ways that our physiology is superior to that of the endothermic ustuzou. Not for us their endless search for food to feed the ravening cells. Our metabolism changes to suit the circumstance. As an example, on long voyages by uruketo we can simply slow down our bodily processes. Subjective time then passes quickly, while each individual will require less food.

An even more striking example of physiological superiority, unique to the Yilanè, is the inseparable relationship of our metabolism to our culture; we are our city, our city is us. One cannot live without the other. This is proven by the irreversible physiological change that takes place, in the very rare instances, when an individual transgresses the rule of law, does that which is inadmissible by Yilanè propriety. No external physical violence is needed to penalize the errant individual. Justice is there within her body. The Eistaa, the embodiment of the city, our culture and our rule of law, has only to order the errant individual to leave the city while also depriving this same individual of her name. Thus rightly rejected, the errant individual suffers the irreversible physiological change that ends only with her death.

The mechanism is hormonal, using prolactin which normally regulates our metabolism and our sexual behavior. However, when an errant individual is forcefully reminded of trangression her hypothalamus overloads and she enters a continuous but unbalanced physiological state. In our ancestors this was a survival factor that caused hibernation. However, in our present evolved state, the reaction is inevitably fatal.

DIET

It has been said that if you look into a creature's mouth you will know what she eats. Dentition denotes diet. A nenitesk has flat-topped, square teeth for grinding up the immense amounts of vegetable matter it must eat, with sharper-edged teeth in the front for cutting and tearing its food loose. The neat, attractive rows of cone-shaped teeth in our jaws denote our healthy and carnivorous fish-eating diet. The thickness and strength of our jaws indicate that mollusks once played a large part in our ancestors' diet for we did—and still can—crush the shells of these tasty creatures with our teeth.

REPRODUCTION

There are certain things that Yilanè do not talk about, and this is right and proper in a well-ordered society. When we are young and in the sea, life is endless pleasure. This pleasure continues when we are fargi; our simple thoughts should not be burdened with subjects too complex to understand.

As Yilanè we not only can consider and discuss any matter, but we must do this if we are to understand the world we live in. The life cycle of the Yilanè is perfect in its symmetry and we begin our observation of this circle of life at the time it begins, when the young emerge from father's protection and enter the sea.

This is the beginning of conscious life. Though all of the earliest activities are inborn reflexes—breathing, swimming, gathering in groups—intelligence is already developing. Communication begins, observation, cogitation and conclusion are initiated. Members of the young efenburu learn by observing the older ones.

This is where language begins. There are two main schools of thought about the origin of language among those who make a study of languages. Leaving out the detailed arguments, and phrasing them in a popular way, they might be called the swim-swim and the ping-ping theories. The swim-swim theory postulates that our first attempts at communication are brought about by imitations of other creatures in the sea: that is, a movement of the hand and arm in imitation of the swimming movement of a fish would indicate the idea of a fish. On the other hand the ping-ping supporters say that sound came first, the sounds that fish make being imitated. We cannot know, we may never know, which of these theories is true. But we can and have watched the young learning to communicate in the open sea.

The elements they use are all of the ones that they will use later, but simplified to a great degree. Basic movements of the limbs, colored indications with the palms, simple sound groupings. These suffice to join the members of each efenburu together, to build the strong bonds that will last through life, to teach the importance of mutual aid and cooperation.

Only when they emerge from the sea do the fargi discover that the world can be a difficult place. We may speculate that in distant times, when our race was young, the competition was not as severe. Only when communication in an advanced society became of utmost importance did the individual begin to suffer.

It is a law of nature that the weak fall by the way. The slow fish is eaten by the fast fish and does not breed. The faster fish survive to pass on their genes for swift-swimming. So it is with the Yilanè, for many of the fargi never learn to speak well enough to join the happy intercourse of the city. They are fed, for no Yilanè refuses food to another. But they feel insecure, unwanted, unsure of themselves as they watch others of their efenburu succeed in speaking to join in the busy life of the city. Dispirited, they fish for their own food in the sea, wander away, are seen no more. We can feel for them, but we cannot help them. It is a law of nature that the weak shall fall by the way.

It goes without saying that, of course, these self-chosen rejects are all female. As we know, all of the males are sought out and cherished the moment that they emerge from the ocean. Doomed would be the culture that allowed these simple, sweet, unthinking creatures to perish! Wet from the ocean they are brought to the hanalè to lead the life of comfort and ease which is their due. Fed and protected they live happy lives, looking forward only to the day when they can perform the ultimate service of preserving their race.

WARNING. What follows may be too explicit for some to absorb. Details may offend those of too delicate sensibilities. Since the authors of this study wish only to inform, anyone who feels they would not be happy with material of this sort should read only the following paragraph, then skip ahead to the section labeled "Science."

There is a process within *reproduction* whereby a small portion of male tissue, called a sperm, is united with a small portion of female tissue, called an ovum. This ovum becomes an egg, and the male carries the egg in a special sac. When carrying the egg, and keeping it warm and comfortable, the male gets very fat and happy and sleepy. One day the egg hatches and a lovely youngster goes into the sea, and that is all there is to it.

The union of the sperm and the ovum takes place during a process with the technical term *intercourse*. There follows a description of this event, the details of which are of a possibly offensive nature.

A male is brought to a state of excitement by the stimulations of a female. When this happens one or both of the male reproductive organs becomes engorged and emerges from the penis sac at the base of the tail. As soon as this occurs the female mounts the male and receives the penis into her cloaca. At this point mutual stimulation, which need not be described, causes the male to expel a large number of sperm. These specialized organisms find and unite with ova inside the female body to produce fertilized eggs.

With the sperm is also released a prostaglandin that produces a reaction within the female body that causes rigidity in the limbs, among other things, that prolongs the sexual union for a lengthy time, a good portion of the day. (Intercourse without production of the hormone is technically named a *perversion* and will not be discussed here.) During this period, the fertilized eggs quickly develop and grow, until they are extruded into the male's pouch.

The female's part is now finished, her vital role fulfilled, and responsibility for the continuation of the Yilanè race now becomes that of the male. The fertilized egg now contains the genes of both male and female. The implanted eggs now grow placentas and increase in size as they draw sustenance; for this to occur major changes happen in the male body. There is first the urge to return to the sea, the warm sea, and this is done within two days, since a stable temperature is needed for the maturing eggs. Once on the beach and in the sea the male enjoys a physiological change, growing torpid and slow, sleeping most of the time. This state remains until the eggs hatch and the young are born and enter the sea.

It should be mentioned, though it has no bearing upon the continuation of our species, that a few males die on the beaches each year as their bodies resist the metabolic change back to their normal condition. But since this only affects males it is of no importance.

Thus the life-cycle of the Yilanè begins anew.

SCIENCE

There are many sciences, each a specialized system of study, too detailed to go into in this brief history. Those interested can consult specialized works that deal with chromosome surgery, chemistry, geology, physics, astronomy, and so on. Note will only be taken here of genetic engineering and mathematics.

Like all else in Yilanè history the true history of our biological development is lost in the mists of time. We can, however, make some logical assumptions that explain the facts as we know them now. With patience enough—and time enough—any biological problem can be solved. In the beginning it can be assumed that crude breeding was the only technique that was used. As time passed, and greater interest evolved in how reproduction actually took place, research into gene structure would have begun. The first real breakthrough would have been when the researchers succeeded in crystallizing the genome, that is bringing about evolutionary stasis. Only when we can stop evolution can we begin to understand it.

At this point the uninformed reader may be puzzled and might be inclined to ask—how does one stop evolution and make genetic changes? The answer is not a simple one and in order to answer it we must begin at the beginning.

In order to understand genetic engineering some knowledge of the biological makeup of life on this planet must be considered. Organisms exist as two grades. The simplest are the prokaryotes, ordinary bacteria, blue-green bacteria, blue-green algae, viruses and so on. The other larger and more complex life forms, the eukaryotes, will be considered in a moment. First let us look at the prokaryotes.

All of these have their genetic material as rings of DNA, or RNA in some viruses. These tiny organisms seem to be economizing on their genetic material because many of these coding regions overlap. They possess special DNA sequences between genes for at least two purposes. Firstly, the control of gene function, such as the turning off of gene transcription by the products of the coded enzyme in operons, and for providing sequences recognized by transcription or replication enzymes; secondly, there are DNA sequences that incorporate the DNA between them into other strands of DNA. (Examples would be into a host bacterium, for a plasmid or a bacteriophage, or a host eukaryote cell for a virus.) There are bacteria that produce a few enzymes which actually snip or join DNA by recognizing specific sequences for snipping or joining between two nucleotides. By using these enzymes it is possible to determine the sequence of DNA lengths. This is done by digesting them sequentially with enzymes which recognize the different sequences. Then each mixture of shorter resultant sequences is analyzed with other enzymes.

This is a lengthy process requiring millions of tries. But then Yilanè patience is infinite and we have had millions of years to develop the process. In order to recognize particular sequences, radioactive DNA or RNA messengers are attached specifically with base complementation along their length. Afterwards, special enzymes are used to remove a specific length and insert it into another organism's DNA ring.

This is the way that bacterial DNA rings are modified: Firstly by the use of plasmids, natural bacterial 'sex' sequences; secondly, by phages, viruses that naturally attack bacteria; thirdly by using cosmids, artificial DNA circles with special joining sequences, any of which can be tailored to include new or modified genes, so that the modified bacteria can make new proteins.

So it can be seen that it is relatively easy to change the protein chemistry of bacteria, simple eukaryotes such as yeast, and to reprogram other eukaryotic cells in a similar simple manner.

It is much more complicated to produce desired changes in the larger eukaryotic animals. In these creatures the egg itself is programmed in the mother's ovary, where it builds upon itself in the foundation of the embryo's development. Only after completion of this embryonic structure does each cell produce proteins that change the cell itself, as well as other nearby cells, in a process that finally results in the juvenile organism. How this process has been mastered and altered is too complex to go into in this curtailed discussion. There are other facets of Yilanè science that have to be considered.

Mathematics must be discussed since many Yilanè have heard of this, and since all of the sciences employ it, though they will not have run across it at other times. The following explanation, although brief, is accurate.

The science of mathematics is based upon numbers. If you wish to understand numbers, spread your hands out before you, palms down, and inner thumbs touching. Wriggle your outside thumb on the right. That is called number *one*. Now moving one finger at a time from right to left, the adjacent finger is *two*, the next finger *three*, the inner thumb *four*. Left inside thumb *five*, fingers *six* and *seven*, and finally the outside thumb on the left is *ten*. Ten is also called *base*, a technical term that we will not go into here. It is enough to know that numbering starts over again after the *base* is reached, ten-and-one, ten-and-two, right up to two-times-ten. There is no limit to the number of multiples of ten that you can have. That is why numbers are so important in the sciences where things are weighed, measured, recorded, counted, and so on. Mathematics itself is very simple, just a recording of things that are bigger than things, smaller than other things, equal or not equal to other things.

The origin of mathematics is lost in time. Although mathematicians themselves believe that the base ten was chosen because we have ten fingers. They say that any number may be chosen as a base, though this seems highly unlikely. If we took two for a base then 2 would be 10, 3 would be 11, then on with $4 = 100$, $5 = 101$, $6 = 111$ and so on. Very clumsy and impractical and of no real use. It has even been suggested that if ustuzou could count, a singularly wild idea in any case, that their base 10 would be our 12. All our numbers would change as well; the 40 million years of Yilanè existence would shrink to a mere 30 million years. You can see where such unwise speculation might lead so it is best we abandon such unhealthy theorizing.

CULTURE

We have had to introduce a number of new terms in this history, and *culture* is another one. It might be defined as the sum total of the way we live as it is transmitted down through the ages. We can assume that our culture had historical beginnings, though we cannot possibly imagine what they might have been. All we can do is describe our existence now.

Every Yilanè has her city, for Yilanè life revolves around the city. When we emerge from the sea we can only look on in speechless awe at the beauty and symmetry of our city. We go there as fargi and are taken in and fed. We listen and learn from others. We watch and learn. When we can speak we offer our services and are treated kindly. We see all the manifold life of the city and are drawn to one part or another. Some of us serve humbly and well with the herds and in the slaughterhouses.

As a city is built in rings, with fields and animals outermost, the living city next, the birth beaches and the ambesed at the heart of it, so also is our culture built. The large circle of fargi outermost. Within that circle are the assistants and the trained laborers in the various specialities. They in turn circle about the scientists, the supervisors, the builders—all those at the peak of their learned skills. They in turn look to the city leaders, and all look to the Eistaa who rules. It is logical, simple, complete, the only possible culture to have.

This is the world of the Yilanè. It has been this way since the egg of time, and will go on forever. Where there are Yilanè there is Yilanè rule and law and all are happy.

At the two poles of our globe there is great cold and discomfort and Yilanè are too wise to penetrate these places. But only recently it has been discovered that there are comfortable places in this world where there are no Yilanè. We owe it to ourselves and to the world to fill these empty spaces. Some of these places contain ustuzou, unpleasant ustuzou. In the interests of science we must examine these creatures. Most readers will close this volume now since they have no interest in such matters. Therefore what follows in the section beginning on page 476 is for those with specialized interests.

Translator's Note: Here the translation from the Yilanè ends. For some understanding of the complex—and fascinating—problems that face the translator working with this unusual language, please see the following section.

LANGUAGE

Slow development, for millions of years, has created a rich and complex language. So complex, in fact, that many never manage to master it and never become Yilanè. This cultural handicap separates the race into two subgroups, one of which, barred from the life in the cities, remains in a feral state, living off the life in the sea for the most part. They do not breed because of their inability to protect the torpid males from predators. Their loss means that the gene pool of the species is slowly being altered, but the process is a glacially slow one.

The Yilanè speak in a linked chain of gestalts, with each gestalt containing one to four concepts. Each gestalt also has a control sign which is indicated by a stylized body posture or movement that has some relationship to the overall meaning. These gestalts are rarely the same because they have so many possible combinations, approximately 125,000,000,000.

Any attempts to transcribe Yilanè in English presents formidable problems. Firstly, the control signs, the stylized body positions, have to be considered. An incomplete listing, with stylized transcription symbols, follows:

Hunch	↑	Star	✳	Whirl	✝
Cower	⟩	Climb	⊓	Sway	↓
Stoop	⊓	Fall	⊤⊤	Shake	⋆
Stretch	Y	Lift	Ч	Reach	⊣

Diamond	⃟	Leap	⊣	Reach	⊣
Squat	⋔	Rise	∟	Sit	⋏
Lie	⊟	Push	⋋	Neutral	I
Embrace	⅄	Swim	∿	Tailsweep (clockwise)	⌀
Bask	✕	Plunge	⌁	Tailsweep (anticlock)	⌁

The sounds of Yilanè approximate those of humans, but for a basic understanding it is not necessary to consider all the differences. However, in English transcriptions zh is the sound in rouge, x the ch in loch. Th and dh are rarely used. There are four extra symbols denoting sounds particular to Yilanè. They are ' (glottal stop), < (tock), ! (click) and * (smack of lips).

The richness of the language and the difficulty of accurate transcription can be seen in the translation of the following expression:

To leave father's love and enter the embrace
of the sea is the first pain of life—the first
joy is the comrades who join you there.

First the kernel string of gestalts, each one with a separate controller, numbered C1 to C12 for ease of reference:

C1 (✕) *enge*
C2 (⊟) *han.natè. ihei*
C3 (⋋) *aga.ptè*
C4 (⌁) *embo.[1] *kè.[2] ka<*
C5 (⌁) *igi. rubu. shei[3]*
C6 (∿) *kakh.shei. sèsè*
C7 (⅄) *hè. awa. ihei*
        //[4]

---

[1]At this point circumambience is also suggested by rotation of the tail tip.
[2]Warmth also suggested by movement of jaw muscles as if to gape.
[3]Note that units 4 and 5 are linked by controllers, 3 and 5 by paired opposite concepts at the start.
[4]The Yilanè pauses here and repeats gestalts in reverse order to form a deliberate balance or chiasmus.

C8 (✻) hè. vai<. ihei
C9 (∿) kakh. shei. intè
C10 (Y) end. pelei. uu
C11 (∿) asak. hen
C12 (⊣) enge

A literal translation of this, with the definition of the control signs in brackets, reads as follows;

C1 (Bask)   Love
C2 (Lie)   Maleness. Friend. Senses of Touch/Smell/Feel
C3 (Push)   Departure. Self
C4 (Fall)   Pressure. Stickiness. Cessation
C5 (Fall)   Entry. Weightlessness. Cold
C6 (Swim)   Salt. Cold. Motion
C7 (Cower)   Numeral 1. Pain. Senses of Touch/Smell/Feel
C8 (Star)   Numeral 1. Joy. Senses of Touch/Smell/Feel
C9 (Swim)   Salt. Cold. Hunt
C10 (Stretch) Vision. Discovery. Increase
C11 (Swim)   Beach. Male/Female
C12 (Reach)   Love.

A broad transcription of this would be:

> *Enge hantèhei, agatè embokèka iirubushei kaksheisè, hèawahei;*
> *hèvai'ihei, kaksheintè, enpeleiuu asahen enge.*

The most accurate translation into English would be in verse, but barring that, this is an approximate translation:

> *The love of your father, to be expelled from it and go into*
> *the cold unloving sea, that is the first pain of life : the first*
> *joy of life (in that cold hunting ground) is to come upon your*
> *friends and feel their love close round you.*

The basic differences between human language and Yilanè are so great as to be almost insurmountable for someone attempting to learn Yilanè. Human beings, talking to each other in different languages, start by picking things up and naming them. Rock. . .wood. . .leaf. After some understanding, they go on to actions: "Throw the rock, pick up the leaf."

This just cannot happen with the Yilanè. They do not name things but describe them. Instead of the noun 'chair' they would say "Small wood to sit on." Where we would use a single noun, 'door', the Yilanè would have different constructions. "Entry to warm place." From the other side it might be "Exit to a cold place."

These are concepts that Ysel never understood. (See page 97.) She did memorize a few words and had some slight idea of the use of controllers. When Vaintè attempts to talk to her the exchange goes like this:

Vaintè says; (✳) esekapen (↑) yidshepen (Y) yilei-besat (Y) efenduuruu (↑) yilsatuu (✳) yilsatefen.

This can be translated as: (Star) top-demand (Hunch) this-one-speaking-demand (Stretch) speech-difficulty equality (Stretch) life-continuation-increase (Hunch) speech-equality-increase (Star) speech-equality-life; in translation, "I personally demand it most urgently! Speak, please, as well as one of the Yileibe. This way you will keep on living and growing. Speech means growth—please! Speech means life—understand!"

The best that Ysel can do is say, "has leibe ènè uu"; she thinks that she is saying "I find it hard to talk, please." What comes out, however, fatally for her, is more like "female—age/entropy—suppleness —increase." The mistakes she has made are:

1. *has* does not mean 'I,' but 'female.' The confusion was caused by Enge pointing to herself when she said it.
2. *leibe* does indeed signify 'difficult'—if it is said with a controller that implies some degree of constraint, for instance "Hunch," "Stoop," or "Squat." Without this, the meaning edges towards '*age*,' that is the process of something running down, not only Yilanè.
3. *ènè* does not mean '*talk*' at all, but indicates suppleness since the Yilanè associate these ideas very often.
4. *uu* is a common termination used by Enge in her lessons for encouragement. But it signifies concepts like "growth, go on, try." It does not mean '*please*.'

Since Ysel has no tail she cannot make the cower gesture correctly. In addition she makes the fatal mistake of imitating Vaintè's last posture, the Star, that of threatening dominance. So Vaintè thinks that Ysel was saying something like "The old female grows adroit," or possibly even "Growing supple puts years on females." This is nonsense and Vaintè rightly loses her temper, her anger fed by the fact that she was polite to this animal; she may not have cowered but she did hunch as well as star. Ysel's fate is sealed.

By contrast Kerrick comes out with: (**>**) esekakurud (**ч**) esekyilshan (**I**) elel (**I**) leibeleibe.

That is he communicates (Cower) top-disgust-cessation (Lift) top-speech-volition (Neutral) longlong (Neutral) hardhard; Vaintè understands this as "I very much don't want to die. I want very much to talk. (Giving up). Very long, very hard." At first Vaintè doesn't notice the 'lift' for he has no tail. But she does recognize the 'cower' and slowly realizes what he is trying to say.

YILANE`-ENGLISH VOCABULARY

(Note: this list includes both single elements and some commonly repeated gestalts.)

aa	in
aǵa	departure
aǵlè	passage
aka	disgust
akas	growing land
akel	goodness
akse	stone
alak	succession
Alakas-aksehent	Florida keys
alè	cage
alpè	beauty
ambei	height
ambesed	central meeting place
anat	bodily extremity
ankanaal	land-surrounded ocean
ankè	presence
apen	demand
asak	beach
ast	tooth
asto	movement
awa	pain
ban*	home
buru	circumambiance
dee	this
ee	out
eede	that
eesen	flatness

efen	life
efenburu	group formed in childhood
efenselè	member of an efenburu
eisek	mud
eisekol	dredging animal
eiset	responsibility
eistaa	city leader
eksei	caution
elin	small
embo	pressure
empè	commendation
end	vision
enet	lake
ènè	suppleness
enge	love
enteesenat	plesiosaur
ento	each single
Entoban*	Africa
erek	speed
esek	top
esekasak	birth-beach guardian
esik	south
espei	posture
eto<	shoot
fafn	catch
far<	inquiry
fargi	one learning to speak
gen	new
Gendasi	North America
gul	hearing
han	maleness
hais	mind
hanalè	male residence
has	female
has	yellowness

NB. These two concepts are always distinguished by choice of controller.

hè	numeral 1
hen	male/female
hent	revolution
hèsotsan	dart-firing weapon
hornsopa	genetic shape
huruksast	monoclonius

igi	entry
ihei	sense of smell/touch/feel
ineg	old
Inegban*	home city
inlè	large size
intè	hunt
ipol	rub, buff
Isegnet	Mediterranean
isek	north
ka<	cessation
kain	line of sight
kakh	salt
kal	poison
kalkasi	thornbush
kasei	thorn
kem	light
khets	convexity
kiyis	east
kru	short
lan<	copulation
leibe	difficulty
lek	badness
mal	absence of worry
man<	last
Maninlè	Cuba
melik	dark
natè	friend
nefmakel	bandage-creature
neni	skull
nenitesk	triceratops
nin	absence
ninsè	the unresponsive
nu*	adequacy
okol	gut
onetsensast	stegosaurus
pelei	discovery
rubu	weightlessness
ruud	cessation

sas<	speed
sat	equality
selè	bondage
sèsè	motion
sete	purpose-oriented group
shak	change
shan	volition
shei	cold
sokèi	cleared land
son*	element
stal	prey
takh	clean
tarakast	mount for riding
tesk	concavity
top	run
tsan	animal
tso	excrement
tuup	fat, torpid
unut	crawl
unutakh	hair-eating slug
uruketo	mutated icthyosaur
uruktop	eight-legged beast of burden
urukub	brontosaurus
ustu	blood
uu	increase
ustuzou	mammalia
yil	speech

TANU

The history of the Earth is written in its stones. While there are still unanswered questions, the overall history of our planet from the Palaeozoic Era up to today is recorded in fossil remains. This was the age of ancient life, 605 million years ago, when the only creatures in the warm and shallow seas were worms, jellyfish, and other backboneless animals. The continents then were still joined together in a single large land mass that has been named Pangea.

Even then some of the sea creatures were using lime to build shells for protection and support. The development of internal skeletons came later, with the first fish. Later fish had lungs and lobe-like fins that could be used to support them when they emerged from the sea and ventured onto the land. From these the amphibians developed the ancestors, about 290 million years ago, of the first reptiles.

The first dinosaurs appeared on Earth just over 205 million years ago. By the time the first sea-filled cracks were appearing in Pangea 200 million years ago, the dinosaurs had spread all over the world, to every part of the first giant continent that would later separate into the smaller continents we know today. This was their world, where they filled every ecological niche, and their rule was absolute for 135 million years.

It took a worldwide disaster to disturb their dominance—a ten-kilometer-wide meteor that struck the ocean and hurled millions of tons of dust and water high into the atmosphere. The dinosaurs died. Seventy percent of all species then living died. The way was open for the tiny, shrew-like mammals—the ancestors of all mammalian life today—to develop and populate the globe.

It was galactic chance, the dice-game of eternity, that this great piece of rock hit at that time, in that manner, and caused the the global disturbance that it did.

But what if it had missed? What if the laws of chance had ruled otherwise and this bomb from space had not hit the Earth? What would the world be like today?

The first and most obvious difference would be the absence of Iceland, for these volcanic islands mark the place where the meteor struck and penetrated to the mantle below.

The second greatest difference would be in the history of global climate, still not completely understood. We know that different ice ages came and went—but we do not know why. We know that the polarity of the Earth has changed in the past, with the north magnetic pole where the south is now—but we do not know why. It seems a certainty that if the meteor had not hit and the incredible atmospheric change had not occurred, that the same progression of ice ages and accompanying continent building would not have occurred in precisely the same manner.

Look at our world as it might have been.

The rule of the dinosaurs is unbroken. The world is theirs and they are dominant on every continent—and the Yilanè rise above them all.

Except in the western hemisphere. Although South America is dominated by reptiles this is not completely true to the north. The land bridge of Central America that connects North and South America has been sunk beneath the ocean at different geological times. At one crucial time the break coincided with the spread of the vast sea that covered most of North America. An ice sheet stretched south almost to the edge of this inland sea so that for millions of years the climate was northern, barely temperate in midsummer. The cold-blooded species died out and the warm-blooded species expanded, developed, and became the dominant life forms of this land mass.

In time, as the ice sheets withdrew, the mammals expanded north. By the time the land bridge of Central America rose from the sea again the warm-blooded creatures ruled the continent between the oceans. Yet they could not stand against the slow return of the reptiles. There is no defense, other than retreat, from armored creatures weighing 80 tons or more.

Only in the north, in the foothills and the mountains, could the mammals survive. Among them were the New World primates, from whom the Tanu are descended.

There are no Old World mammals here because the Old World is saurian. There are no bears or canines. But the New World deer abound, from small species to immense ones as large as a moose. The mastodon are here as are many marsupials including saber-tooth tigers. Mammalia in rich diversity live in the fertile band south of the ice and north of the cold-blooded saurians.

Most of the Tanu, imprisoned by a harsh environment, have never developed beyond the hunter-gatherer stage. But at this they are immensely successful. There are some exceptions, like the Sasku, who have moved on to a stable existence of neolithic farming. They have developed the settled skills of pottery and weaving, as well as a more complex and stratified society. But this does not mean that they are superior in any way to the hunting Tanu who have a rich language, simple art forms, many survival skills, and a basic family group relationship.

THE MARBAK LANGUAGE

Marbak, like the other languages spoken by the Tanu, is a modern dialect of the lost parent language that has been named Eastern Coastal. In Marbak 'man' is *hannas*, the plural *hannasan*. Variations are *hennas* in Wedaman, *hnas* in Levrewasan, *neses* in Lebnaroi, and so on.

All of the names of these small tribal groups are descriptive, for example, Wedaman means 'the island ones,' Levrewasan 'tent-black-ones,' that is the people of the black tents. Like man, *hannas*, woman *linga*, plural *lingai*, has widespread similarity. A person, sex not specified, is *ter*, while the plural *tanu* is generally accepted as referring to all other people.

The most common masculine noun declension is:

	SINGULAR	PLURAL
Nominative	hannas	hannasan
Accusative	hannas	hannasan
Genitive	hannasa	hannasanna
Dative	hannasi	hannasanni
Locative	hannasi	hannasanni
Instrumental	hannasom	hannasom

MARBAK-ENGLISH VOCABULARY

alladjex	shaman
amaratan	immortal ones (divine creatures)
arnwheet	hawk
atta	father (dim.)
bana	son (dim.)
beka	to knot
benseel	sphagnum moss
dalas	soup
eghoman	the vowed ones
ekkotaz	nuts and berries
elsk	mastodon
erman	sky
ermanpadar	sky-father, a spirit

hans	war party
hannas	man
hannasan	men
hardalt	squid
hault	twenty
(count of a man)	
himin	mountain
istak	path
kurmar	river
kurro	boss
levrelag	camping ground
levrewasan	the black tent people
ley	(burnt) clearing
linga	woman
lingai	women
madrap	moccasin
margalus	murgu counsellor
mar	hair
marag	cold-blooded animal
marin	star
marsk	icthyosaur
murgu	plural of marag
nat	killer
naudinz	hunter
parad	ford
sammad	mixed male/female band
sammadar	elected head of the sammad
stessi	beach
tais	corn
tanu	people
ter	person
terred	group of people on a mission
terredar	head of same
tharm	spirit
torsk	ichthyosaur
torskan	ichthyosaurs
torskanat	ichthyosaur's bane
ulfadan	long-beard
wedam	island

ZOOLOGY

BANSEMNILLA *(Metatheria: Didelphys dimidiata)*: A reddish-gray marsupial with three deep black bands down its back. It has a prehensile tail and opposable toes on its hind feet. It is carnivorous, favoring rats and mice, and is bred by the Sasku to eliminate these vermin from their corncribs.

BOAT *(Cephalopoda: Archeololigo olcostephanus mutatus)*: Yilanè surface water transport. Propulsion is obtained by a strong jet of water expelled to the stern. The creatures have only rudimentary intelligence like their ancestral squids, but can be trained to follow certain simple commands.

CLOAK *(Selachii: Elasmobranchus kappe mutatus)*: Used by the Yilanè for warmth during the night or inclement weather. These creatures have absolutely no intelligence, but if they are well-fed they will maintain a body temperature of approximately 102° F.

DEER *(Eutheria: Cervus mazama mazama)*: A small deer with antlers as unbranched spikes. It is found in great numbers in the North Temperate Zone. The Tanu value these creatures both for their meat and their skins. The hides are tanned to make clothing and small leather articles. (e.g. moccasins [madrap] and bags).

ENTEESENAT *(Sauropterygia: Elasmosaurus plesiosaurus)*: A predacious marine reptile well adapted to pelagic life and relatively unchanged since the Cretaceous period. They have small short heads and long snake-like necks. The paddle-like flippers are similar to those of the marine turtle. Newer varieties have been developed with greater cranial capacity that enable them to be trained to supply food for the larger uruketo *(Icthyosaurus monstrosus mutatus)*.

EISEKOL *(Eutheria: Trichechus latirostris mutatus)*: An herbivorous aquatic mammal which dredges for underwater plants in its original unaltered state. Gene manipulation has greatly increased the animal's size so that it can be utilized for underwater channel clearing, as well as dredging.

ELINOU *(Saurischia: Coelurosaurus compsognathus)*: A small and agile dinosaur, much appreciated by the Yilanè for its pursuit and destruction of small mammalian vermin. Because of its colorful markings and complaisant nature it is often given the status of a pet.

EPETRUK *(Saurischia: Tyrannosaurus rex)*: The largest and most powerfully armed of the great carnosaurs. Over 40 feet long, the males weigh up to 7 tons. The forearms are small but strong. Because of its great weight it is quite slow, therefore attacks only the largest animals. A large amount of its diet is obtained by driving smaller carnivores from their kill.

GREATDEER *(Eutheria: Alces machlis gigas)*: The largest of all the deer. It is distinguished from other members of the *Cervidae* by the spread of the impressive antlers of the males. Hunted by the Tanu, not only for its meat, but for its hide which is preferred for use in covering their tents.

HÈSOTSAN *(Squamiata: Paravaranus comensualis mutatus)*: This species of monitor lizard has been so modified that it now bears little resemblance to the original. Steam-generating glands from *Brachinus* beetles violently project a dart which is poisoned when it passes over the sex organs of a commensal *Tetradontid* fish. This poison, the most deadly known, produces paralysis and death when as little as 500 molecules are present.

LONGTOOTH *(Metatheria: Machaerodus neogeus)*: Long-tusked member of the marsupial tiger family. A large and ferocious carnivore that uses its greatly extended upper canine teeth to bring down its prey. Some Kargu hunters have a commensal relationship with these beasts to aid them in hunting.

MASTODON *(Eutheria: Mastodon americanus)*: A large mammal noted for its long upper tusks. It has a prehensile trunk reaching to the ground. Its domestication by the Tanu permits them to cover great distances when hunting and foraging, using the mastodons to pull large travois.

NENITESK *(Ornithischia: Triceratops elatus)*: Herbivorous quadruped characterized by the possession of three horns set in a bony protective shield, unchanged since the Cretaceous period. They reproduce by laying eggs. Their brain capacity is small and their intelligence even smaller. Since they are slow growing they are of little use for meat supply, but are extremely decorative.

ONETSENSAST *(Ornithischia: Stegosaurus variatus)*: The largest of the plated dinosaurs. These immense herbivorous creatures are protected from attack by two rows of plates down the neck and back, as well as heavy spikes on the tail. They first developed in the late Jurassic and only careful preservation by the Yilanè has prevented the destruction of this living fossil.

SANDUU *(Anura: Rana catesbiana mutatus)*: Extensive gene manipulation has altered this animal in almost every way; only its outer skin reveals its origins. Magnification of up to 200 power is available by proper use of sunlight directed through the different organic lenses of its head.

TARAKAST *(Ornithischia: Segnosaurus shiungisaurus mutatus)*: A sharp-beaked carnivorous dinosaur, the largest examples being over 13 feet in length. They are difficult to train and require great strength to manage, but when properly broken make a desirable Yilanè mount.

UGUNKSHAA *(Squamata: Phrynosoma fjernsyna mutatus)*: Since the Yilanè language is dependent upon skin color and body movements, as well as sound, keeping written records is impossible; therefore writing has never developed. Historically, knowledge was passed on verbally, and the recording of this information only became possible when an organic liquid crystal display was developed for visual accompaniment of the auditory memory records.

UNUTAKH *(Cephalopoda: Deroceras agreste mutatus)*: One of the highly modified animals used in Yilanè technology. This cephalopod digests protein matter, especially hair and modified epidermal plates with ease.

URUKETO *(Ichthyopterygia: Ichthyosaurus monstrosus mutatus)*: This is the largest of the "fish-lizards," a family of immense aquatic dinosaurs. Millennia of gene surgery and breeding have developed a strain of icthyosaurs very different from the parent stock. There is a large chamber situated above the spine and centered on the dorsal fin that is used for both crew and cargo.

URUKTOP *(Chelonia: Psittacosaurus montanoceratops mutatus)*: One of the most extensively modified of the Yilanè animals. Used for land transportation, it can carry heavy loads for great distances since after gene-doubling it has eight legs.

ACKNOWLEDGMENTS

In writing this novel I have sought the advice of experts in various fields. The biology of the Yilanè is the work of Dr. Jack Cohen. The Yilanè and the Marbak languages are the work of Prof. T. A. Shippey. This would have been a far different and lesser book without their help and advice. My gratitude to them is infinite.

5 4 19